DANGEROUS CHARMER

"I think you scant different from any other woman, no matter Curran's regard for you. The man has slight experience of women," he mocked, as the ball of his thumb traced the line of her jaw and brushed her full lips lightly. One corner of his mouth tipped up as she tried to jerk her head away. "Where there is temper, there is passion—and haven't you a temper? And wouldn't it be a great loss to myself should I be denied a taste of such passion?"

Cian's gaze became a warm amber over Bronwynn's every feature. His tone was soft, gently caressing.

"Did you know that he spins a fine tale—of ourselves falling in love, and wedding? Doesn't he even have us with a troop of sons strong of thew and daughters fair of face? Think on it. Wouldn't it be a fine thing to be free of this place, one day, with the wind in our faces, the rain on our tongues? The very least to be said on it," he chuckled, "is that sure. I must be preferable to that weak willed, slack-muscled popinjay your King Edward would have you marry."

The warmth of his body, the caress of his voice, the soft stroking of his thumb across her lips, along her jaw, had quieted Bronwynn's struggle to be free of him. His soft words had sketched a picture that filled her with a yearning so strong she ached with it. But his chuckle brought her chin up.

"Aye," she spat out, "and wouldn't it be a fine thing to seduce the ward of *my* King Edward and then send her back to him with the babe of an Irish lordling in her belly?"

"Aye, and wouldn't I find pleasure in it, so," he whispered, and his mouth lowered to hers . . .

DANGEROUS GAMES   (0-7860-0270-0, $4.99)
by Amanda Scott

When Nicholas Barrington, eldest son of the Earl of Ul-
combe, first met Melissa Seacort, the desperation he
sensed beneath her well-bred beauty haunted him. He
didn't realize how desperate Melissa really was . . . until
he found her again at a Newmarket gambling club—being auctioned off by her father to the highest bidder. So,
Nick bought himself a wife. With a villain hot on their
heels, and a fortune and their lives at stake, they would
gamble everything on the most dangerous game of all:
love.

A TOUCH OF PARADISE   (0-7860-0271-9, $4.99)
by Alexa Smart

As a confidence man and scam runner in 1880s America,
Malcolm Northrup has amassed a fortune. Now, posing
as the eminent Sir John Abbot—scholar, and possible
discoverer of the lost continent of Atlantis—he's taking
his act on the road with a lecture tour, seeking funds for
a scientific experiment he has no intention of making.
But scholar Halia Davenport is determined to accompany
Malcolm on his "expedition" . . . even if she must kidnap
him!

AN IRISH WIND

Kate O'Donnell

Zebra Books
Kensington Publishing Corp.

http://www.zebrabooks.com

ZEBRA BOOKS are published by

Kensington Publishing Corp.
850 Third Avenue
New York, NY 10022

Zebra and the Z logo Reg. U.S. Pat. & TM Off.

First Printing: February, 1998
10 9 8 7 6 5 4 3 2 1

Printed in the United States of America

Again, to my sons, Gregory and Gary.
and to Alice, Reah, and
Gracie—three muses.

(1)

Rudulf came up behind her, fingers curling to scarcely cup her shoulders—that Bronwynn had expected. Like a cat, she had sensed his approach in the lifting of the tiny hairs at the back of her neck, had heard a faint scruff of a shoe on the rough planks of the wall walk. She refused, though, to turn as he neared, or to flinch at his touch. Still, the stir of his breath, the light tracing of his lips down from under her ear to the neck of her mantle caught her by surprise. A slight shudder ran through her and she wondered if it was of pleasure or revulsion. Nor did Rudulf, she realized, repressing a second tremor, care which it was. Yet she hoped that it was of pleasure. So much scheming, plotting and measuring had gone into her very presence in Ireland, so many of the plans and hopes of others. Even the wishes of Edward of England, himself, rested on the shoulders cupped by Rudulf's spidery fingers and plushy palms. Why Ireland, she had asked Edward while still in England, why Rudulf de Broc?

"He is Piers de Bermingham's stepson and a favorite of

his mother—and de Bermingham is a warrior proven loyal to me."

"All cause to recommend de Broc to you, my Lord, and not to me. Nor is it de Bermingham you wish me to wed."

"De Broc's handsome, so 'tis reported by some, and young, with a strong arm. He'll serve you and your lands well."

But Bronwynn had learned to beware her monarch's beguiling smile.

"Aye, *my* lands. You would have me wed de Broc and gift him with my lands—because de Bermingham is a proven warrior, loyal to you, no more?"

Edward's good humor turned into a scowl that could daunt most men.

"I also think of you—'tis past time you've wed," he rapped out. "De Broc would also give you brats enough to keep your mind on female matters and off those best left to men and to the clergy."

Bronwynn lifted a dark eyebrow at Edward and Marguarite, his wife, smiled down into her embroidery. Edward had a fiery temper and could be a bit pompous and condescending, but he was also indulgent with the young female wards of his court, those hostages or fosterings from Scotland, Wales, Ireland, or England, itself. Silently, Marguarite thanked the saints that there were always such women and girls about and always there seemed to be one with wit and tongue enough to challenge her monarch. Then the queen frowned, concerned for the peace of her household and her lord's wishes. Bronwynn Fitzhugh, she knew, would not obey as easily as Edward would have it, nor could she be readily coerced. Her mother had passed her lands on to her under the Welsh law allowing women to inherit, yet she had not necessarily done her daughter a service. This could become a battle—and one only Bronwynn would lose, however strong and stubborn the girl. Yet, Marguarite, who could always get her way with her doting husband through sweetness and charm, did not know what strength was required of Bronwynn to stand up to her lord or how truly alien her brashness was to her true nature.

"You say I think too much," Bronwynn mocked, "and on subjects best left to men. Would you have it both ways, my Lord? If women are not educated, aye, and better than our fathers, brothers and husbands, how can we be trusted to manage their properties when you would summon those worthies to crusade or war or to preying on their neighbors? Would you have us then, on the return of the glorious, certainly victorious males, smile sweetly at their strutting and retreat gracefully back into our kitchens, our solars, our nunneries?" She shook her head at the folly of such a notion. "You cannot coax a hen back into its egg, my Lord. And Rudulf de Broc's youth does not necessarily recommend him to me. Better an old man, I think, a Methuselah with a limp pizzle and no heirs and myself soon widowed, with no man ever after to try to rule me."

"Good luck to any man foolish enough to think he might," Edward snorted, "but de Broc is willing to try the task."

"Aye," she continued, as though not hearing him, "a wealthy old man to leave me his estates. With my own besides, I could then take a husband of my own choosing, a young man with well turned thighs—but landless, of course, so he will be properly grateful and deferent to me in all matters. But you would have de Broc for me," she stated, lifting her chin, her whimsical mood banished by the rage she felt at being such a pawn. "And you would even have me go to him in Ireland. You say he cannot be spared from there the while, the Irish being an unruly race. I think, though, that you, being set on the match, wish me gone to the ends of the earth—so Ireland is named—so I will, then, do anything to return, including marrying your Rudulf de Broc."

"I am but asking that you consider him," Edward placated. "I would not force you into a match you find repugnant. You know that."

"Do I?" Bronwynn asked, fighting a sense of defeat. Edward would, she knew, despite the tolerant smiles, his mollifying manner now, attempt to do just that. He was a strong king, and one of his strengths was a willingness to bend everything and everyone to what he perceived as best for England. So he saw the match he proposed for her. Nor was de Bermingham fully trusted, no matter what Edward said. The king would not so press the match if he was. But de Bermingham was henpecked, so it was gossiped, and what his wife wished was a well-dowered bride with estates in Wales for her son. Such would pleased her and a well pleased wife would go far in guaranteeing her husband's loyalty. Yet, it was Bronwynn who was to pay the price.

The king had laughed, then, had teased, and she had bantered back, and Marguarite had worked her embroidery, a smile about her lips. And she was now in Ireland. There had also been Cecily to consider. Her sister was as much a pawn as Bronwynn. There was something so helpless about Cecily, a frailty and childishness which only called upon Bronwynn to show herself strong, no matter how false a strength it was. Perhaps, she sometimes thought, so was everyone's no more than a sham. But, whatever strength she had shown, she was here, a guest at Carrick Castle, and Rudulf still stood too near to her. His presence, too, was as real as the stone walls beneath her, hidden by a combing sea of mist.

"Did I startle you?" Rudulf murmured into her hair, and Bronwynn wondered if she hadn't caught just a hint of hope in his voice. Stepping out from under his grasp, she turned to face him as he asked, voice round with insinuation, "and does my touch disturb you?"

Bronwynn studied the pale yellow eyes staring back at her down a long Norman nose. They protruded slightly from beneath heavy, fleshy lids—like those of a toad, she thought. Her shudder, she decided then, had indeed been of revulsion. Still, she shrugged one shoulder and drew her mantle closer about herself as she turned to rest her elbows on the parapet and look out over the fog lapping at the rough edges of the walls. Moving once again to stand too close, Rudulf lifted a strand of her dark hair, examining it, winding it about his finger. The tips of his small, crimson lipped mouth were pouted as he waited for her answer and Bronwynn wondered how he had become so dissolute in so few years. He hardly yet needed to shave.

"I scarcely know you," she equivocated, refusing to retreat again from his faint odor of mildew, his hot breath on her neck. Silently, she cursed Edward Plantagenent. "Would you have me," she countered, "such a woman as welcomes caresses from a stranger?"

"I would have you such a woman as welcomes the loving attention and touch of her betrothed, a woman who awaits as eagerly as I the pleasures of our marriage bed."

Bronwynn's gaze slid sideways and fell again. His chin, she noted in that swift glance, was a just a shade undercast. That was the trouble. Everything about him was a bit too little or too much, too soft or too hard. Yet Edward had said he was thought to be handsome—and so he might be—by women attracted to a jack-a-dandy, or to a cold youth ruled more by motive than emotion, sensuality than passion. He certainly thought well of himself—and dressed as such. An extravagant fashion had recently been adopted by the crown prince and, consequently, the young bloods at court. It was the cote-hardie, a hip-length waistcoat type garment to be worn over a full-sleeved blouse and skin tight hose—all in violent color schemes. But a provincial tailor had given the fashion his own bend, creating for Rudulf an absurd costume from one already ridiculous. Or perhaps Rudulf's garments were the deliberate result of a tailor's perverted sense of humor, a sly revenge. The Irish were said to have such, and Rudulf took himself too seriously to ever suspect himself the goat of such a joke. That would be the beauty of it.

Rudulf's cote-hardie—just a trifle too short—was scarlet on one side, daffodil yellow on the other. The colors were reversed in his hose and the sleeves of his blouse, which was slashed to display the contrasting color yet again. Even the tassel of his cap was scarlet and daffodil. Surely, too, he had stuffed his codpiece; no man could be that large naturally. And what he truly wanted, more than a woman in bed, was her lands, Bronwynn knew, and to be gone, to be in England, as were so many of the Norman overlords of Ireland. And he seemed to think it his due. That she resented most of all.

Bronwynn smiled, hating herself for the cloying sweetness of her voice, for her simpering flattery—and for the jerking of her nerves.

"But we are not betrothed nor do I wish to be seduced into such a choosing," she dimpled. "The decision to wed should be made with a clear head, and your presence, Sir, addles mine. Nor is it in your character, gentle knight that you are, to seek to do so. Marriage is not a sacrament I wish to make for politics or property or for the benefit of others—even Edward Plantagenant—and to my own loss and sorrow. 'Twas not the kind of marriage my mother had nor is it the kind she wished for me—and she arranged it that it need not be so." But what she would do if the king insisted, Bronwynn did not know. While he could not place repugnant marriage vows in her mouth, he could force her—and Cicely—into a nunnery. She could not afford to insult or alienate de Broc or his stepfather, not yet, not until she found a way out of the situation. In the meantime, Rudulf's need and greed—and his vanity—could be used against him, if only to hold him at bay. Her smile arch, Bronwynn touched the hand resting near hers on the parapet wall with one languid fingertip. "I wish but for more time, my Lord, time to come to know you better. Surely you—and your stepfather—will grant me that."

Rudulf lifted her gloved hand and pressed a kiss to her palm as he gazed beguiling up at her from under his fringed bangs. Yet he wondered if he was being played with—and his eyes held a thwarted fury.

"Ah, Lady Fitzhugh, isn't your slightest wish but my heartfelt dream? Your happiness my only quest? Time is as aught compared to such. And in Ireland," he added, his voice assuming an edge of bitter humor, "isn't time the one thing we all have aplenty?"

Bronwynn's eyelashes fluttered down, then up, revealing a glimpse of guileless grey eyes.

"Didn't my Lord Edward speak of you as noble, as ever courteous and gentle? Does he not ever hold you in honor and trust? Nor would he have placed me in your stepfather's care if he did not know Piers de Bermingham to be a man of respect and honor, not only as your stepfather, your guardian, but as a brave, proud knight, also. I had not expected aught, nor received aught, but courtesy of you. Still, I thank you for your pledge that you will not press me."

But he could not recall any such a promise—and she had put him and the subject of marriage off so adroitly. Furious and unable to display it, Rudalf saw Brownynn lift her chin, pointing with it out beyond the castle walls in a gesture all too familiar to him. The Irish, too, used that mannerism. It was but another annoying habit, he told himself, he would rid her of when they were married, such as her way of looking too directly at a man. And she was asking him a question.

"Tell me, my Lord, what lies out there. I've seen only Dublin and the road here—and both all shrouded in fog and rain. What I did see seemed little different from much of Wales and England—all small towns and bad roads—and castles, always castles. I've often wondered what their true accomplishment is. Don't they but keep their inhabitants locked in, as much as they keep your neighbors shut out—and both prisoners?"

Yes, Rudulf thought, there would be changes made. Bronwynn would ask fewer cunning questions. A brat or two would rid her mind of that strange thinking suitable only for priests and philosophers, and his fists would drive out whatever mistaken Welsh notion she had of the privileges of women. It was said, too, that she pampered her people. That, also, would change—when he had her properties in hand. Still, he smiled into her wide eyes, his lips curled in indulgent humor.

"Without castles," he explained, as though to a child, "we would not be able to hold our lands, our subjects in hand, especially those newly taken. Look at the Welsh, the Irish. Don't they outnumber us? Yet, we hold the Welsh within a ring of castles and the Irish are kept out of the Pale the same way. This one serves that purpose, not only for my stepfather, but for Edward. After all, Piers hold his lands at the king's sufferance."

Bronwynn's dark eyebrows quirked in innocent bewilderment.

"But don't the Irish, then, hold you, too, in confinement?" She looked at him brightly, as though expecting his participation in her absurd conjecturing. Then she shrugged. "But you haven't told me of Ireland, what it looks like, its entertainments, its people. Are there indeed men with the tails of asses, as Giraldus Cambrensis would have it, and are the Irish as melodious on the harp as he also stated?"

Rudulf waved a languid hand out over the field of mist, then gave an exaggerated shudder. He did not want to be standing there discussing the marriage of Lady Bronwynn's mother or landscapes or the purpose of castles. He wanted to be gone from out of the rain and wet, from off the castle wall—and most especially, gone from Ireland. And the method of his leaving stood next to him. Yet, she had neatly blocked his purpose in having her alone—and the seduction his stepfather had hoped would come out of it. He peevishly swiped a droplet of water from off the tip of his nose with the back of a soggy glove.

"It rains," he stated petulantly, gaze narrowed on the fog. "It always rains. That—and Ireland—has not changed in the hundred and more years we've been here and it will not change in the next hundred and more. I cannot be gone soon enough."

"But this is scarcely a mist," Browynn stated, biting her tongue against the accusation that that was, in truth, why he wanted her. Such a confrontation would only put him on guard, would drive him to other, less gentle means of persuasion. Let him think her coy and naive. It could only buy her time until he realized otherwise. She lifted her face to the soft damp, seemingly oblivious to his discomfort and anger, yet unable to suppress a certain satisfaction in his distress.

"Surely, you do not think it never rains in Wales?" she giggled, her glance sliding coquettishly over him. "Indeed, 'tis said the climate of Ireland is the more temerate, all told. And aren't there hearts which will break should you leave? I've seen one or two Irish maids and they're comely—fine complexioned and straight of build. Giraldus Cambrensis called them so, and he was a priest! Surely, they would find you handsome, with your fine Norman features and dressed as brightly as any peacock.''

Her gaze dropped admiringly over him. His long nose, she noted, was blue with the damp and cold. He had been too vain in his new cloths to don a cloak and the scarlet of the one half of his cote-hardie was bleeding into the daffodil of the other. The tailor had not only had a sense of humor, but had also used shoddy merchandise, and Bronwynn hoped he had the intelligence, too, to be long since gone. Nor had Rudulf's codpiece diminished. Surely, it would in the cold, she thought. Grown men could not be so very different from the baby boys she had observed— not that Rudulf de Broc could be called a grown man. Unaware her appraisal was scarcely flattering, Rudulf preened, then scowled.

''Whatever Giralddus Cambrensis's opinion, I don't find the women attractive.'' He snuffled a droplet of mucus back into a wide nostril and wondered just who this Cambrensis man was. ''They wear the hems of their kirtles up above their knees and go about without shoes, perhaps the better to trot their infernal bogs. It but displays their thick ankles and draws the eye of many a man but new over from England—and to no purpose but to tempt and taunt. They are all as cold as this hell-damned climate and as unfriendly. They think themselves too good for us and call us the invader, the Sassenach. They look a man full in the face and laugh. They talk as freely as any man, with no thought for modesty and restraint. They are bitches, every one, aye, and witches, too, some priests will tell you. Hasn't many a Norman soldier been seen keeping one or another of them company, only to disappear, the woman with him, never to be seen again? Lured away they are, by magic into the hills and mountains, into the bogs.'' He made the sign to ward off evil, middle fingers tucked under, little and fore finger extended. "Aye, the women are all witches—if not fairies."

More likely, Bronwynn thought, the soldiers had run away. Women such as Rudulf described had to have a certain allure, as did the native way of life. Wasn't it something Edward, too, deplored—that so many of the men sent to Ireland went native? If they didn't just disappear, they married Irish women and adopted the native way of dress and the native way of riding without stirrups, if only to prove they could. And Rudulf was, Bronwynn, realized, one of those men teased and taunted—and thwarted. She could also easily see him employing force or coercion—and pain—to get what he wanted—and women avoiding him as a result. There was something in him that frightened her. He reminded her of a spoiled child who, if denied, would willfully destroy what he most wanted out of spite. Still, she had not yet, Bronwynn realized, decided not to accept him. To refuse him would create so many other decisions and situations. She would have to ask about him, especially among the servants. His mother or her ladies would not give her honest answers, and she needed to know how best to deal with him, to play him, for play him she must. But a sly look was crossing his eyes and Rudulf stepped closer to her still, pressing her back against the parapet.

"Myself, I like Norman women," he whispered, "deep bosomed, blond women with wit enough to hold down both their eyes and their voices. Women who know their proper place—beneath a man—in bed or out of it."

His voice held a lickerish insinuation that sent a chill down Bronwynn's spine—it was so at odds with his youth. Yet she refused to give way under his nearness. Placing the palm of her hand on his narrow chest, she swayed even closer for just an instant.

"Ah, my Lord Rudulf," she simpered, "if you think to

flatter me, remember that I'm not Norman. Even my father was but half. Nor am I blond." She glanced sideways up at him from slanting eyes which widened at a sudden thought. Pushing Rudulf away, she stepped back, the better to look at him.

"And the priests do aught about the witchcraft?" she demanded, her quavering tone convincing Rudulf of her fear, her outrage. "Or your stepfather? Or yourself? Surely," she simpered, managing to sway toward him yet hold him at bay, her hand firm against his chest, *"you* can do something, as strong as you are, with such prowess of arms. Surely, they threaten us all. We have had witches in Wales and they are burned at the stake there!"

"We cannot do such, not in Ireland," Rudulf told her, flushing at the admission of such a weakness as though it was his own, a pimple on his chin a white glare against the crimson. "If we tried, half the country would be tied to the stake and the other half rising in rebellion. Our priests are forever preaching against witchcraft, but 'tis said half the native clergy still secretly follow the old ways, the pagan ways, and how do we fight that? Aye, such heretics should be burned, but it is not political to do so—not yet—but we'll get to it, and mostlike with help from the Irish, themselves. After all, wasn't it complaints of such by some few of the Irish clergy that gave Rome cause to sanction our invasion of Ireland in the first place?"

"Was it?" Bronwynn asked, her eyebrow's puckered dubiously. "I had thought 'twas the greed of some few Irish bishops who saw the wealth of the people going to the monasteries instead of into their own pockets, and thus into Rome's. Didn't the bishops go crying to Pope Adrian of it, the first English pope ever, by the by, saying that nowhere else in Europe did the monasteries have such influence? Wasn't it the Church's first deed in Ireland to divide the land into bishoprics, taking the people, the power—and the wealth—from the monasteries?'' Her eyes were artless as she shrugged and smiled. "Still, would any of it have happened had not Dervorgilla eloped with MacMurrough, King of Leinster, and if her husband, Tighernan O'Rourke, had not avenged the insult? And weren't they all of an age to know better, too, Dervorgilla being forty if a day, and her seducer sixty? If Diarmuid MacMurrough had not been banished to England, where he convinced Henry II to aid him in reclaiming his lands, would we be standing here, at all, and wouldn't Ireland be a different place for our absence—and certainly less civilized?"

Rudulf shrugged his disdain of history—and her knowledge of it. But she was still leaning against him. Feeling a swelling against the padding in his codpiece, he attempted to draw Brownynn closer still.

"Ireland can scarcely be called civilized yet," he murmured, "and I only wish to be away from it—with you."

But Bronwynn had deftly slipped from his embrace to clasp his hands, holding them between them.

"You, my Lord, move much too swiftly for me," she scolded playfully, her dark eyelashes fluttering shadows on her pale skin. "Haven't I asked for more time? Do you seek to overwhelm me with your charms, your persuasions—when but a few moments ago you gave me your oath you would not do so?"

Rudulf scowled, reluctant to retreat and uncertain how to do so. But this was not a woman he could take by rape, not yet. And Bronwynn only smiled more brightly at him.

"And your talk of witches and fairies only whets my curiosity. I've but arrived in Ireland and you would have me leave it, when there is so much I've not yet seen. They say the monastery at Clonmacnois is magnificent and I would like to know if the people of the West truly have tails. Oh, and I would dearly love to witness fairies emerging

from out of their secret places beneath an enchanted hill—
they say the Tuatha De Danann can be seen so if the night
is right, and if you are patient enough! No," she said,
shaking her head, "I don't think I will wish to leave Ireland
for yet a while."

Thwarted, frustrated, Rudulf could only stare with rage
into her beguiling features. He was, after all, he lied to
himself, a warrior, a man of action. He had little experience
in a war where the weapons were words. Perhaps his stepfather would know how best to handle her. Didn't he, too,
have an interest in this? Then he laughed scornfully to
himself. Piers de Bermingham was even more a man of
war than himself, yet look how his wife twisted him around
her finger. Still, the man was cunning, even perfidous,
some said. It would not hurt to seek his advice.

And there was always force. He could force her, now,
here, and even perhaps put a brat in her belly. That would
settle the issue fast enough. Kidnapping and rape of a
reluctant woman had been done before, often enough,
with the courts and the church ruling after that, since the
deed was done, the damage beyond repair, it might as well
be given the sanction of marriage, with the pair wedding.
How else claim a recalcitrant woman? How else could a
man of scant land and strong purpose better himself, winning not only a wife, but her properties? But they said this
one was a pet of the Lord Edward, himself. She might find
a means to complain to him, and hadn't he heard that
the king was a man walked over by his wife, that he
espoused the gentle ways of chivalry and decried the old
means of advancement? It would not pay to anger his
monarch. But what if Edward had sent her here because
he secretly wished him to take her in hand, to force her
in the way Edward wanted her to go? Yet, he could not
take that chance, not yet. But Bronwynn's gaze had
dropped over him, dismay crossing her features.

"Ah, but my Lord," she gasped, releasing his hands and stepping away from him, "surely you are cold! You are scarcely garbed for this weather, and look you—the fog has destroyed your fine garments!"

Rudulf stared down at himself to find the canary of his tights splotched with crimson, and the crimson streaked to pink. His teeth gritted against an oath, he scrubbed at the splotches and silently vowed to hang the tailor who had dared to so humiliate him. And if the bitch dared laugh at him . . . But there was only concern on Bronwynn's features as he squinted suspiciously up at her, the sodden, swinging tassel of his cap dripping water down his cote-hardie.

"Perhaps," she gently suggested, "you had best go change. 'Tis a pity about your garments, but red can be such an unstable color. I only hope the dye has not stained your skin. Red will do that, too."

His gaze jerked up again, but the laughter he had thought he heard was not reflected in her concerned eyes. Still, his jaw clenched. He had been defeated at every turn and there was little he could do but retire gracefully. There would be other opportunities, he promised himself, and with better success. Bowing, he offered her his arm.

"Ah, no, my Lord," she demurred, eyelashes aflutter. "I think I'll stay up here a while more. I've not had a moment alone since leaving court, not on the road nor on the ship, and I'm one to crave solitude occasionally. Nor will I find it at your stepfather's table or with your mother. Isn't there always much company about her, loved woman that she is? You will forgive me, will you not?"

He bowed once again, his face a parody of adoration. His eyes, though, upturned as he kissed her hand, were malignant with impotant rage.

"Your servant, my Lady," he muttered. Turning, the long, curled toes of his shoes almost tripping him, Rudulf stalked away in all his dignity, disappearing down the stairs. Bronwynn stared after him, a worried frown between her eyebrows. She had alienated him, that she knew. She had also injured his vanity—poor popinjay that he was—and that was doubly dangerous. Still, she had gained time, whatever the cost to her own pride. And, no, she could not marry him, no matter how much Edward wanted the match. A way would be found out of it somehow.

Drawing the hood of her mantle over her head, she turned to gaze out into the fog. It looked, she decided, almost thick enough to step out upon, and she wished she could do that, could simply step over the wall and walk away from Carrick Castle on top of the fog. But she would only plummet to her death, a fate, perhaps, preferable to marriage to Rudulf de Broc, she thought wryly. Now, too, courtesy demanded she wait upon Melusine de Bermingham—and there was supper to suffer though, all the while playing the simpering, flattering fool to a man she feared and scorned. Nor could she delay going down much longer. Still, Bronwynn tarried until the discomfort of her hands, clenched with fear and the damp, at last drove her to turn away from the wall and walk toward the stairs descending into the keep.

But a man was there, blocking her way. He knelt, a long, sinewy hand twisted into the shaggy hair of a huge, loose-limbed wolfhound, and Bronwynn wondered, flushing with a strange sense of shame, how much of her conversation with Rudulf he had overheard. His dark hair glistened with mist and he was gazing up at her with narrowed eyes. A mantle of wolf skins was tossed over his shoulders, but his broad chest was naked beneath the leather jerkin he wore. A kilt of saffron hued wool was wrapped about his waist, held up by a sword belt, its scabbard empty. His rawhide shoes were wrapped up to his knees with leather thews crisscrossed around his calves. Tossed over his back and wrapped in the plushest green velvet embroidered in gold thread with curious beasts of convoluted shapes and mystical origins was a large triangular object—a harp, Bronwynn guessed. A belt of the softest leather illuminated in red, yellow, blue and green, with a continuous band of elliptical curves and divergent spirals, of stylized leaves and flowers, held it in a position to be readily drawn to the owner's fingertips. Around one thick bicep he worn a gold torque belying the roughness of his clothing. He must be Irish, Bronwynn thought, to be dressed so, and a bard, to be carrying a harp of such value.

Then he stood, a tall, slim, broad shouldered man. Bowing slightly, his gaze never leaving her face, he motioned her on to the stairs, the mocking gesture telling her he had, indeed, overheard her playing of Rudulf de Broc and that he scorned it. Drawing her mantle closer still, Bronwynn walked past, then glanced back. His gaze was still on her and never before had she seen such disgust, such abhorrence, such malignant dislike on a human visage.

Cian O'Connor stared after Bronwynn Fitzhugh, his line of dark eyebrow knit into a glowering scowl. She was just as he would have expected her to be. Like the rest of her sex, she was coy and conniving, flattering and fickle. Unobserved, silent as Ireland's mists, he had watched her play that poor callow Rudulf de Broc like the fish he was. She had but flashed the right bait and he had risen to it, eager and snapping as a trout. Then, once caught, she had tossed him back, only to play him once again, drawing him in, releasing him, tossing him yet another, different fillip, until the unhappy fool fairly reeled with confusion.

He had to feel almost sorry for the poor, bewildered dupe—or he would had de Broc not been a Norman, a foreigner, a Sassenach. In truth, though, they were well matched and didn't they deserve each other so, coming as they both did from such a perfidious, unconscientious race. And she was here to take the pimpled youth from Ireland—one Sassenach the fewer—so perhaps he should be grateful to her—but he was not.

He knew women such as she too well to grant her the least advantage, the least benefit of the doubt. Such women could only be trusted in one position, Cian told himself, and that was beneath a man with their thighs parted to him, their throats purling passion. Even then, no man could be certain the passion was not feigned. And of course there were diseases. What woman would not lie of such things, if it would profit her? And no few men would do the same, his mind niggled at him, to lie between those white thighs, no matter that even the ancient laws of Ireland, themselves, derided such deceit. And if the laws did not, they should. But he shoved the thought away with his memories, his pain, with the reminder of Bronwynn Fitzhugh's coquettish playing of Rudulf de Broc.

She bore keeping an eye on. Who knew what game of her own she played, regardless of Edward of England's wishes for her. And she might prove to be the key required to slip the walls of Carrick when the need arose—and it would. The saints knew he would need a way out, then, and desperately. If Bronwynn Fitzhugh was the only one at hand, he would not hesitate to use her so.

But it was her half lifted hand, her tentative smile on first catching sight of him, that deepened Cian's black scowl further still. That smile had frozen into the stunned bewilderment of a child wrongly punished and he had never been able to bear to see a child hurt. Nor could he easily put such a smile from his mind.

(2)

Bronwynn sat on a low stool, watching Melusine de Bermingham prepare for supper. She was the ideal Norman beauty, with her pink complexion and pale blond hair, her tall, voluptuous body and tiny mouth. She shaved her eyebrows in the Norman fashion and plucked her hair far back from her forehead, giving her features the blinking blandness of an infant's. Many men found her attractive. Banal poems were composed to her beauty, her graciousness. Songs lauded her virtue, her grace. But there were lines of discontent at the corners of the round blue eyes she was skillfully outlining with kohl and the small mouth she colored with a red cloth drooped in sulky petulance. There was a harshness, too, to the hair falling past her waist in brittle waves, as though she lightened it with cow urine—many women did, to fit the ideal. Yet, she was not so old, Bronwynn thought, calculating. Melusine had been but fourteen, a child bride to a man three times her age with half a dozen sons already, when she gave birth to Rudulf, and he was sixteen, a year younger than Bronwynn.

Melusine had been widowed while younger than Bronwynn was now, but she was a woman used to getting her own way, pampered as she had been all of her life. Bronwynn could see that in the arrogant set of her chin, in the hair brush she snatched and threw across the bower when her maid tugged too hard at a tangle.

And how many women had solars in a country where most castles were crude affairs of one tower? There were many such single towers in England, too, where the lord of the manor and his wife retired to a curtained bed in a recess in the great hall, the knights and ladies, men and maid servants sleeping in the rushes on the floor near them. Even Marguarite, accompanying Edward on his constant touring of his realm, graciously accepted the bed of the lord of the manor and his wife when there was nothing else to be offered. Never had Bronwynn heard her complain of the snores, of the fleas or the lack of privacy. But Melusine had her solar above the great hall, with its curtained bed, only sharing it with her ladies and maids and her husband. Here, too, Bronwynn and Cecily would sleep. Melusine even had a mirror of Venetian glass, warped and mottled, true, but a real mirror. Bronwynn had only seen one other—and that had been Marguarite's. It was no wonder Piers de Bermingham so wanted Bronwynn wed to his stepson, supporting as he was the expensive whims of his wife.

But Cecily was gazing at Melusine in wide eyed adulation. Why wouldn't she, Bronwynn wondered. It would be almost like looking into a mirror. She and Melusine certainly appeared more like sisters than did Cecily and Bronwynn. They were both blond, pink complexioned, with round blue eyes. It was Bronwynn who had inherited the dark hair—so undesired by fashion—of their Welsh mother, and her sister who had taken after their half Norman father. Cecily preened often enough over it. Yet, Marguarite was dark and her Edward loved and humored her well enough—too much, some said.

Now Cecily sprang up to follow the flight of the hair-brush, then returned with it and appropriated the task of grooming Melusine's hair.

Watching her sister's careful hands, seeing Melusine's image peer and pout from the mirror, Bronwynn wished that it had been Cecily who was first born. She would have been happy enough to marry whomever Edward chose for her, as long as her husband did not trouble her with the management of the estates which would have gone with her, as long as she had silk to wear and maids to serve her. As it was, should Bronwynn defy Edward, angering him enough to subject her lands to forfeiture, they would both be out on the road.

Then they could always join the gypsies. Bronwynn smiled to herself at the whimsy. Cecily could dance and she could tell fortunes. Her father had called her his fey little witch often enough. But such a life would hardly suit her sister.

Cecily would be forever carping at her, her whine nagging with each turn of the caravan's painted wheels. Nor could they join a nunnery—not if they had been dispossessed by the king. They would be lucky to receive alms at the kitchen door. Even if the abbess did not fear Edward's ire, she would never accept them without a dowry. Nor would Cecily be happy in a nunnery, even if there had been dowry enough to keep her in silks and maid servants all of her life. There would be none of the male adoration her sister so thrived upon. Bronwynn could not even have Cecily married before herself. For all her beauty, any man who could keep her in the manner she had been reared would demand a dowry, and Bronwynn, no matter that she was an heiress, had no money. It was held for her— and her future husband and lord—by Edward, just as her father had held it in his king's name—and what the king gave away, he could take back. Her lower lip caught between her teeth, her brow furrowed, Bronwynn sat on her stool and watched her sister.

Cecily, too, scowled, but in concentration as she plaited Melusine's hair, as she coiled it into rolls and secured it with pins beside the lady's ears. Almost reverently, she bound both the chignons in fine pouches of gold netting, then placed a veil of gossamer linen over Melusine's head. Over it all went a circlet of gold.

Mouth drooping, eyes haughty, Melusine observed Cecily's handiwork, and Bronwynn was suddenly put in mind of the Irish warrior she had seen on the parapet. He and Melusine were a world apart, yet each world had its predators; at least in his they were not disguised in fine linens and silks, in nets and circlets of gold. Yet, she wondered at the animosity the man bore her. Melusine could tell her, and Bronwynn opened her mouth to ask, then closed it again. What the other woman would make of her question, she did not know, but there was a rapaciousness in her eyes, a calculation she did not trust. Melusine had an agenda of her own and she was designing enough to employ anything and anyone who came within her grasp to accomplish it, including an Irishman dressed in aught but pelts and leather.

Briefly, Bronwynn wondered if she did the woman a disservice. After all, she had but met her the night before, when she had been tired to stumbling from the long journey, with Cecily still to look after. There had been but a few short words exchanged the next morning over breakfast— words and a smile of welcome—along with an assessing, measuring glance from thoughtful blue eyes. Then she had been dismissed with such a quick flick of a disdainful eyelash and complacent lift of a nonexistent eyebrow that Bronwynn had thought she had surely imagined it. But

Melusine's gaze had gone on to Cecily and her eyes had
widened, then narrowed, reminding Bronwynn of a cat's
on seeing a bird. Her features had momentarily turned
to flint. Yet, she had gone to Cecily and smiled sweetly,
rearranging a lock of her pale blond hair, and had linked
her elbow with the young girl's to lead her to the head
table. She had even insisted that Cecily share her trencher,
displacing her husband, all the while smiling honey at him.
Thus, adroitly, she had aligned with herself a girl who
could have become her greatest rival and had inspired in
her husband a resentment and jealousy toward that same
threat.

No, Bronwynn decided, Melusine was not someone in
whom to confide even a curiosity toward a stranger chance
met on a wall walk. She, also, had more important things
to worry about, for Cecily was fast falling under Melusine's
spell. Her sister, Bronwynn knew, was an easy victim of
flattery and small attentions.

Melusine stood and lifted her arms as a maid secured a
gilt and jeweled girdle above her slim hips. That done,
and uncaring of the interrupted preparations of the other
women, she picked up her purse and swept from the chamber. The other ladies scrambled about to pick up last min-
ute items, to secure hair still unbound and hastily don
shoes and girdles and veils, then hastened out after her.

Loitering behind, Bronwynn looked about at the chaos
of the chamber, at the maid servants, tardy to their own
tables, who tidied up after Melusine and her ladies. It was
strange, she thought, remembering those slim hips, that
Melusine had never had another child, after giving birth
to Rudulf so young—and her lord so desperately seeking
proof of her affections. With several sons by his first wife,
he was not infertile. Perhaps Melusine deliberately, secretly
denied him. There were ways, Bronwynn had heard, and
potions, nor did she think Melusine was one to balk at a

foul taste if being denied her way was the alternative. It was something to keep in mind, she told herself. Against Melusine who knew what weapons would be needed or when—and a sword could be drawn from the most unlikely scabbard.

(3)

"That," Cormac McAuley whispered into his young chieftain's ear, "is a wee, winsome piece, that is."

"I am not particularly attracted to blonds," Cian O'Connor murmured back, casting an indifferent eye at the dais at the far end of the great hall, then attending himself once more to the spiced venison in his trencher. "They tend to be insipid."

"I did not know you to be particularly attracted to any one type," Cormac. " 'Twould seem to me you've a rare antipathy for all of them. So much so that I worry and toss and turn when you share a pallet with me, to always have my arse to the earth. Have you not noticed 'tis so?"

"I've noticed aught but yourself snoring the whole night through—and half the morning with it, in dreams, perhaps, of woman—there's little else on your brain."

"And what else," Cormac demanded, his bantering tone turning bitter, "is there to think on in this hell hole? But the women are pretty. That bitch Melusine would have nothing else but winsome maids around her, if politics did not demand that the wives of her husband's retainers serve her, also. I'm thinking she feels a picture as lovely as herself deserves a pretty frame. It bends her wee nose out of shape that they're not all of her choosing, but those who are suit me well. Although you might notice, none are ever quite as lovely as herself—from a distance and ourselves not dwelling on the wrinkles coming on her—and the sag beneath the chin.''

His raillery sounded hollow even to his own ears and Cormac's jesting wound down to a halt. If Cian was bitter toward women—and the Normans—he had cause, more even than most Irishmen. Fenella McKenna, too, had been sweet and round, beautiful and pliant, a woman built for sighs and cuddles. And she had been blond. But Curran McAuley, on the other side of Cian, was leaning forward to address his brother.

"Thinking of quiff again, are you?" he asked crudely of Cormac, and his brother grinned to himself. Curran was the largest, the gruffest, the most rudely spoken of them all. Yet it was all a sham. Women somehow sensed it and flocked to him like wrens to a furse bush, much to the chagrin and feigned displeasure of his wife, Sine. She, in her plump equanimity, knew her man. She knew he listened and nodded and patched the wounds of those same women as gently and with as much concern as he tended the skinned knees of each and all of his children. He gave those women, each and every one, the same undivided attention, his warm brown eyes intent and caring. Then he came home to her to roll about on their marriage bed like a large, clumsy puppy, two or three children with them, until he would send the children away and draw the curtains closed. Then he was truly hers. But it was somehow important to him that he be treated by his brothers, blood and foster, and by the warriors of his sept as rough, brutal and quick tempered—when he wasn't playing the poet or

the clown. And so they did, out of their intense love and
respect for him.

"So, now, and yourself," Cormac demanded, "are you
telling me you think of aught else but quiff, unless it be
battle and blood and bashing bone and brain? Are you a
bard, now, and that a harp and not an empty scabbard
hanging from your belt?"

"You'll not see me without a sword," Curran explained,
his ill temper feigned, "be it of one kind or another. And
haven't I a nether sword, so, for an empty scabbard—that
one up there?" His chin jerked toward the dais in the
mannerism so despised by Rudulf de Broc. "Though I
cannot say I dislike any one type—blond or other, they all
bed as sweetly."

"Aren't you both thinking yourselves the valiant swords-
men, whether your foe women or the Sassenach?" Cian
asked into his ale. Yet his narrowed gaze held on the dais.
"And if 'tis so, then what are we doing here and ourselves
prisoners, whether they name us hostages or no?"

But he may as well have spoken to the wind, for Cormac
again leaned past him to address his brother.

" 'Twas not the blond I was remarking on. That one
seems too much of our Lady Melusine's humor for my
comfort. 'Twas the other lass who caught my gaze."

The line of Curran's foxy brown eyes followed his brother's pointing chin. Settling his elbows on the table, he
stroked his russet hued mustache from beneath his nose
to the long ends curling below his mouth in an unconscious
parody of an evil minded lecher.

"Why do we call such a girl dark?" he mused. "Haven't
I seen people much more dark-complected than that one
in the Holy Land?"

"Ah, Holy Mother," Cormac groaned to Cian, " 'tis
another of his tales of the Holy Land. Wouldn't you think,
then, that he was the only man ever gone crusading? Why

couldn't Da have sent another one of ourselves instead, and simply put a gag on the man for a year or two, if his dinning was so sore on his ears?''

"Why," Curran continued, ignoring his brother's taunting and Cian's glowering perusal of the table top, "there were such in the Holy Land with skins the hue of a peat stained pool and beautiful they were, all vivid and alive with color. Couldn't a man know just by looking at them they'd be as hot to hold and as lively to bed as the heat of their eyes?''

"Now," Cormac said as an aside to Cian, "he'll be telling us he's seen a green woman—or a yellow.''

"Didn't I see a woman, once," Curran reminiscenced, ignoring Cormac, while a corner of his mouth twitched in amusement. "Now, she was almost blue, so black she was, with the velvet shine on her of the darkest berry. Her skin was the very shade of the night sky and her mouth was a wide pink rose—so soft, so sweet it appeared—a pillow it was against which a man could rest his weary brow. And eyes like a doe's she had, all brown and startled.''

Cormac snorted his disgust and reached around a ducking Cian to thump his brother on the shoulder with a blow that would have fallen a lesser man. But Curran, grabbing at a mug his elbow had struck, ignored him. His eyes were misty as he continued his rhapsody.

"And hips on her! I'm telling you, my boyos, she had hips on her a man could bury his very fists into, and herself riding him into an early death—and him all the while thanking the saints for the great pleasure of it. Aye, she was almost blue, and didn't I see her with my very own eyes? But I've only heard tell of the yellow women—from far to the east, they say—with eyes the shape of almonds.'' He demonstrated the shape with thumb and forefinger. "But you'd not know of almonds, having never been to the Holy Land. A nut it is, and sweet, and the Saracens make a dish of them all ground up with chicken and honey. To taste it is to think you are being fed by the angels!"

For a moment, Curran paused, lost in his memories, while Cormac grinned at Cian, only to receive an indifferent shrug. Then Curran shook himself, like a dog emerging from water.

"But we were speaking of that one there and, no, I'd not call her dark, though the Normans would prefer her fairer. Why, I would not know. Hasn't her skin the very sheen of new poured mare's milk? Isn't it as white as the forth of blossoms on the hawthorn in the spring, so, and her mouth as crimson as its berries? And her hair— couldn't a man sit her on his lap and himself buried to the hilt in her, and that hair all falling down about them both like a curtain of raven wings? She has a little nose, too, nor is she horse-faced as are so many English women. And when she blushes, won't her cheeks go as crimson as her mouth, then?"

"She is haughty now, yet didn't I see her coquettish and deceitful but a while ago?" Cian commented, his gaze brooding on the dais.

"More like she's frightened," Curran insisted, one russet eyebrow cocked speculatively on his chieftain. "Look at the family she's to wed into and with no choice in the matter, herself, at all. Isn't that enough to scare the very soul out of anyone with a smidgen of sense? Nor would I judge that one lackwitted. And amn't I willing to wager she'd not be given to female wiles like her sister, had she the choice? Nor would I try to tell you the hawthorn has no thorns, and sharp they are, but isn't it honest in its display of them and isn't it, like the rose, all the more sweet for being not so easy, then, to claim?"

"That one would play a man like a puppet on a string and no purpose to it but the gratification of watching him squirm, yet you would see her as aught more than a hawthorn brier and as innocent," Cian stated, his features knitted into a scowl of scorn and enmity. "Didn't I watch her play so up on the wall-walk with that poor, piddling excuse for a man she cuddles up to now. At least her sister would expect a trinket, if aught else, or a compliment for playing the trifler. That one would not know the truth of her own word or purpose if it blew back over her own teeth at her!"

Both Curran and Cormac turned to peer at him, astonished at his vehemence, and Cormac wondered if Cian had seen her ride in the night before. Had he noticed how tired she had been, he wanted to ask, yet she had supported her whining sister, had held her chin up in pride, her smile remaining graciously intact. But Cian did not acknowledge their quizzical stares, and Curran had learned, too, the occasional value of silence. Eyes narrowed, features brooding, Cian stared at an acrobat juggling an apple, a lighted torch and an unsheathed knife.

"Haven't I a wager for the pair of you," he mentioned casually. But there was no humor in the set of his jaw. His long fingers absently rubbed the hard skull of the huge wolfhound whose chin rested on his thigh. "The pick of Booka's next litter to the man who first lays that one on her back. That bitch of Egan O'Ryan's he covered a few months past should have whelped by now. Aye, and a pair of them to the man who gets her with child. Would that not put the Lady Melusine's nose—and all her plans, out of joint?" Cian laughed, eyes cold, his mouth set, as though he had sunk his teeth into bad meat. "And while you are at it, why don't you try thinking of a way to escape this hellhole—yourselves being both so quick to whine of it. Myself, I'm thinking that one—or her sister—might be the key. The English are not the only ones with a hand at hostaging."

" 'Tis our honor—and our oath—that keeps us here,

and no key," Curran said softly, wondering at Cian's anger, his acrimony. Nor was he a man to disrespect a woman, no matter Fenella McKenna's perfidy. "All our thinking and scheming will not change that."

"Won't they break their own oaths first, so—and their honor with them—when it is expediant to do so?" Cian demanded. "Isn't that always their way? And we had best be ready to move then, or we might die here for our lack of fore-sight. Study on it. None of us, I'm thinking, are ready to dance at the end of a hempen rope for Piers de Bermingham."

Curran scowled into his ale, aware Cian was correct. The Sassenach had proven themselves a perfidious breed in Ireland—and Piers de Bermingham no better than the worst of them. He would have no compunction in violating either an oath or a treaty. Still, Curran thought, chewing at an end of his mustache and squinting up at the dais, he had to argue with Cian on one thing. The lass was a wee, winsome thing.

Applying herself to the trencher she shared with Rudulf seemed the safest thing Bronwynn could do. To look to her right, beyond Piers de Bermingham, was to see her sister, features enhanced and glowing at each word from Melusine. It was to watch her emulate each gesture the older woman made, from the affected manner in which she picked at a leg of swan to the way she sucked grease from each fingertip. To look at the acrobats was to know that each frown of scorn on Melusine's face at an imagined clumsiness, each smile of approval at some slight feat was repeated on Cecily's. Closer, there was Piers himself, in a pout over his wife's favoring of Cecily. He glowered into the trencher he shared with no one, responding only in grunts to each of Bronwynn's efforts at conversation. And she needed his conviviality, if only as a buffer between herself and Rudulf's attentions.

Rudulf was drunk. His breath was sour with it. He had at first leered and pawed at her, his words slurred as he attempted a disjointed conversation. Draping a flaccid arm over her shoulders, he leaned over her as she, jaw tight with anger and frustration, surreptitiously fought off his advances and tried to clean a smear of grease his pawing had left on the thick silk of her surcoat. Drawing back, he would stare owlishly at her, then belch and giggle an apology. Yet, there had been a viciousness beneath his sodden joviality that had him snarling at a servant, and kicking at a hound under the table. It could, Bronwynn sensed, as quickly turn against her.

Always, too, she was under the gaze of the man from the wallwalk, and no matter how hard she tried to divert her own glance, it always returned to meet his. He sat and stared at her, eyes implacable, seemingly undisturbed by the conversation shouted over and around him by his companions. Yet, they had discussed her for a few moments, the three of them. That she had seen in the slant of their shoulders toward each other, in their furtive glances, in the faintly abashed grins of men in lewd conversation. Uncomfortable, Bronwynn tried to look anywhere but at them. Who they were, she still did not know, and there was only one way to find out.

She looked at Rudulf with distaste. Forearms pressed against the table for balance, hands splayed on it to keep the forearms from sliding out from under his elbows, elbows far out to the side to form a tripod with his spine, Rudulf seemed to fight to stay conscious. He was too drunk to realize he denied Bronwynn access to the trencher they shared, nor did she care. Just looking at him, she told herself, would be enough to ruin her appetite. His small, red mouth slack and wet, he held his sparse eyebrows as high on his brow as they would go, perhaps to keep his eyelids ajar. His breathing stentorious and moist, he stared at the base of his goblet, forcing his eyes wide each time the gems encrusted there blurred to his vision. When Bronwynn touched his damp fingers, he slowly, carefully turned to look at her, as though afraid of injuring himself. Leaning cautiously back, then forward, then slightly back again, he at last brought her into focus.

"My lady?" he asked, enunciating carefully.

"I was wondering who those three men might be," she told him.

Squinting, Rudulf attempted to follow her gaze. Then, blinking, he looked back at her.

"They're Irishmen," he stated, as though to an idiot or a child.

"I know they are Irishmen," Bronwynn answered. "I but wondered which."

"They are O'Connor's men," Rudulf stated. At the inquiring lift of Bronwynn's eyebrow, he nodded sagaciously, head wobbling. "Calvach O'Connor, that would be, a chieftain still holding land hereabouts—if an Irishman will admit to holding land at all. 'Tis the clan's, they'll tell you. Except the clan holds it for the King of Leinster, who holds it for the King of Ireland—the Ard-Righ. Except there isn't an Ard-Righ anymore. But if there was a King of Ireland—or of Leinster—and they didn't like him, they would elect another. Who ever heard of such a thing? Isn't kingship a God-given right and not to be disputed by mere man?" He shook his head, almost unbalancing himself, was struck with a random thought and giggled. "They even call us 'Sassenach', thinking we are Saxons, or the sons of Saxons. But my stepfather intends to rid himself of Calvach O'Connor soon enough," he added boastfully, returning at last to the original subject.

"Is he such a threat to your stepfather, then," Bronwynn wondered, "a mere chieftain?"

"A mere chieftain—the King of Offaly? Or so the Irish call him." Rudulf giggled. "A tuath king he is—the king of more than one tuath—a tuath being a smaller holding yet. But my stepfather cares aught for that. He's a covetous man, is my beloved stepfather, and O'Connor holds most of Offaly."

"And what do they here?" Bronwynn asked, lifting her chin toward the Irishmen. Rudulf peered at her, wondering at all of her questions and at her naivete.

"They're hostages. We hold them, and the O'Connor holds a son of my stepfather—a bastard son—and they, valuing their bastards as much as their legitimate offspring, think we are unnatural enough to do the same." Then he chuckled and wagged his finger at her. "And they could hardly be guests, now, could they, dressed as barbarously they are?" He peered into her face, a bleary eye cocked. At her encouraging smile, he sneered, "The dark one, that young lordling, the one ever glooming and yet thinking himself so much better than anyone else, is Calvach's son. Although blood means little to them. I've told my stepfather that that one is useless to our purpose, and the men with him. 'Tis the fosterings who count with the Irish, above all natural kinship or kinship by marriage." Rudulf took a long gulp of wine, the adolescent bulb of his Adam's apple, with three long blond hairs on it, bobbing obscenely. Carefully placing the cup on the table, he studied it morosely for a long moment. There was something he wanted to tell her, something he should not speak of, Bronwynn sensed, and she scarcely dared to breathe. At last, his glance slid sideways to her—and beyond to his stepfather. Piers was tossing his knife into the table top with a haphazard flick of his wrist and no regard to the damage he was doing. He certainly was paying no attention to his stepson and Bronwynn wondered if he ever did. Looking back at Bronwynn, Rudulf beckoned her closer, his eyes sly and gleeful with his secret. "Now, if we but held a foster son of Calvach's, we could take the Place of the Weir and scant harm to anyone."

"No harm to anyone?" Bronwynn repeated stupidly.

Ruduf shrugged, almost losing his balance. He sighed, her ignorance trying his patience.

"If we were to take the Place of the Weir, Laracorra, the Irish call it, and if Calvach chose to go to war over it, then he would lose a beloved foster son, would he not? My stepfather would have him strung from the battlements, meat for the crows, before Calvach could call the clans. No, he'll not fight—not and lose a foster son, however little care he gives the get of his own loins. He would fuss and fume, stomp and threaten and send angry letters to Edward, and all the while my stepfather would be building a castle there. By the time Edward chose to investigate, the deed would be done, nor would the king want a Norman castle in Irish hands, especially an O'Connor's."

Leaning back to see her more clearly, Rudulf beamed his satisfaction, his pride in such subterfuge. Smiling admiration at his cleverness, she asked, "What is the Place of the Weir?"

Her gaze sought the son of Calvach O'Connor, then flinched away at the animosity in his eyes. Yet, her questions concerned him. But Rudulf was staring at her, eyes gloating at her ignorance. He seemed almost sober in his triumph.

" 'Tis a hospital built on a bridge right over the river. The Irish build all their pest houses so." He shrugged, disdaining the native ignorance. "But 'tis by the river Boyne, and the river Boyne runs through land held by the O'Connor, but only a nod from ours. Fat grazing there is around it, though, and my dear stepfather feels much cheated to have it in another man's hand. After all, so

much of his own land is bog, and my dear stepfather is
not a man free of envy or one to easily allow another
something better than his own and it so near to his grasp.
You can almost see it from the battlements and many is
the time you can find him up there, gritting his teeth in
anguish and lust."

Small, pointed teeth gleaming, Rudulf smiled his pleasure at the thought of his stepfather's rage. Smiling with
him, Bronwynn then wondered, "But Lord Piers doesn't
hold a foster son of O'Connor's, you said. So, how can he
intend to gain it?"

Holding her breath at his sour odor, she obeyed his
beckoning finger and leaned closer.

"He'll take it anyway. Why not? There's no one there
but a few of the ill and infirm, a physician-priest and wise
woman or two—maybe a druid. All told, they'll be no
match for armed men, but O'Connor will mostlike go to
war to take it back. So Piers will have to hang his son, and
O'Connor will then hang Piers's bastard. Whatever they
do, the outcome will be the same—the Irish will lose. They
always do—and will until they learn to wear armor. All
told, 'twill be but a few men dead and a small price to pay
for Laracorra."

Forgetting Rudulf's reeking breath, Bronwynn leaned
closer still to him.

"When?" she whispered.

But a huge, meatlike hand snaked its way around her
to grasp the back of Rudulf's neck. Its hair-studded knuckles were white with the strength of the grip as Rudulf was
lifted half off the bench and shaken. Ducking down
under the thick forearm, Bronwynn peered up at Piers de
Bermingham. His heavy face was florid with rage and drink
and he shook his stepson once more.

"Are you so besotted that you dare whisper my business
to your queen?" he demanded. But Rudulf hung from his

huge fist, choking and flailing about like a gaffed fish, and
Bronwynn answered for him.

"He was but telling me of the Irish custom of building
houses for the ill and infirm over rivers," she explained,
her features innocuous. "Didn't we do the same in Wales,
thinking fresh air and sunshine, the sound of the wind
and the water healing? Then the English came and taught
us 'tis better to keep the ill altogether in dark, closed
rooms, to bundle them up in warm blankets and incense.
The English taught us much, all said."

Piers stared at her, his tiny eyes squinting to see if the
sarcasm he thought he had heard in her voice was evident
in her face. But Bronwynn gazed back at him, eyes innocent.

" 'Tis said of you, girl, that you've too wise a mouth on
you and not the sense to keep it closed, that you are strong
minded and stubborn, and do not know a woman's proper
place."

"It is also said," she stated sweetly, "that I've a few
redeeming qualities—such as lands in Wales."

Piers's features reddened further, until Bronwynn wondered if he would go into apoplexy. His nostrils flared and
his blue-stubbled jaw clenched.

"You do not play with me, girl," he warned.

"No, I do not play with you," Bronwynn answered, her
cool tone telling him it was no game. Then she asked, "Do
the gossips not also have it that I am such a one as to cut
my nose to spite my face?"

There was a threat implicit in her soft voice and Piers
heard it. She was one, he suddenly realized, who, if pushed
too far, would simply walk away, leaving Carrick, her lands,
her king, his stepson, even her sister behind. Where she
might go, he did not care, but her lands would not stay
with him, and Rudulf, certainly, would never see them.
They would revert to Edward and his king, Piers knew,

would hardly be pleased with him either, no matter the royal rage at the girl. And, more important, neither would Melusine. He stared at Bronwynn a moment longer, measuring her, wondering how far he could push her. When he found that point, he promised himself, then he would move. Until such a time, he would watch and wait. Then he released Rudulf, letting him drop face first into the trencher he shared with Bronwynn, before he turned back to his wife.

Rudulf coughed and sucked for breath through his misused throat. Taking pity on him, Bronwynn rubbed his back until he could breathe once more, until he lifted his face from the trencher and looked at her.

Grease was smeared across his forehead and cheek, and beaded on his eyelashes. A shred of swan's meat clung to an eyebrow, but his gaze was steady. And in his eyes was such enmity and resentment that Bronwynn flinched from it. Wondering at his hatred, she realized it was not so strange. She, a woman, had placed herself between him and his stepfather's wrath, had lied to protect him—and had succeeded. She had stood up to Piers de Bermingham, had defied him—something Rudulf had never dared to do—and, worse, she had, for the moment, won. She had publicly humiliated a weak man, had made him feel weaker yet—and had gained his implacable hatred.

Across the room, thicket-thick russet eyebrows twisted into a knot of interest and curiosity, Curran McAuley studied the tableau on the dais. When he turned to speak, however, Cian O'Connor had stood to leave the hall, snapping his fingers for the hound padding at his heels.

(4)

A late morning sun had burned off the mists of the day
before when Bronwynn climbed the steps to the wallwalk.
But she was not to be alone, she realized, seeing the son
of Calvach O'Connor and one of his men already there.
For a moment, she considered retreating back to the solar,
then decided not to give them the gratification. It was too
beautiful a day to be closed up within a stifling chamber
filled with the scattered garments, cluttered accouter-
ments, and the smell of women. Seldom did she have the
opportunity to satisfy her need for solitude, and rarely in
a setting of her choice. Even a maid to help her with her
hair would have been too much company that day. Nor,
from the closed expression on the face of O'Connor, from
the resentful manner in which he had turned at her intrusion to look her up and down, his sinewy fingers halting
with a jar the singing of his harp, did she need to worry
that he might accost her. Yet, suddenly, she wished she
had worn something more attractive than her most ancient
gown with its narrow, old fashioned sleeves and a worn

out, stained surcoat. Her hair, too, hung below her hips,
freshly washed, snarled and damp. She looked like a tatter-
demalion. Then she smiled to herself at the perversity.
What should she care what they thought? Ignoring them,
Bronwynn sat in a crenature in the wall and twisted about
to look out over the bailey far below.

Early that morning it had been a colorful melee of eager
men and hounds, of ladies with hunting hawks, of plunging
horses and scurrying footmen. The only things, now, to
disturb its quiet were a few thin pigs and scratching chickens and a couple of stable boys kneeling in the dirt and
dung, tossing dice in a game of hazard. The second red
haired Irishmen, brother, she guessed, to the one with
O'Connor, was down there, also, practicing at the butts,
and Bronwynn could occasionally hear the thrum as he
released the string of the longbow and the thwack of an
arrow entering the target. A flutter of pigeons rose from
the walls only to settle again. A flock of blackbirds wheeled
up and into the sun, while high over head a solitary eagle
hovered against a blue, cloudless sky. Beyond the walls of
the bailey the bogs and fields of Ireland stretched far and
away, their green calling her to follow into the fading
distance of blue haze. Eyes wistful, Bronwynn gazed out
for a long moment. At last, sighing, she turned to attend
to her hair, her lower lip caught between her teeth.

Soon she was absorbed in her work and scarcely aware
that strong fingers once again drew forth a desultory melody from an ancient harp. The sun shone warm on her
head and shoulders as, tress by tress, her slender fingers
picked apart snarled knots, separating them, then smoothing them with a wide toothed comb into silken skeins.
Long strands of hair floated about her, lifted by the soft
breeze climbing the castle walls. They hovered about her
face, held aloft, it almost seemed, by a few light notes of
random song. Then a large shadow fell across the sun and,

blowing a wisp of hair from out of her eyes, Bronwynn looked up, startled. A block of a man stood gazing down at her.

" 'Twas in my mind that you might have need of a hand with the comb, my Lady, and myself experienced as a maid," Curran said in a heavy brogue, while the harp commenced a tune that mocked his chivalry, that cast an insinuating doubt on the suitability of its object. He blushed and scowled at the intrusion, then blundered on. "I had not thought to frighten you—and yourself with your back to such a great fall."

Bronwynn blinked at the offer, then thought about what could have been a threat. But there was no menace in the man's warm brown eyes, in the gentle, long-lipped mouth beneath a thick, drooping mustache. His hedge of russet hued eyebrow quirked in concern and she smiled.

"You didn't frighten me. All told, what would you or Ireland profit from my death? Am I not here, not to stay myself, but to take an Englishman away?" Her eyes laughed at him, then she asked, "Can you truly comb out my hair?"

"I've done so for my wife often enough, my Lady. I'm Curran McAuley," he added. He nodded toward his companion, ignoring the snickering notes sounded on heavy brass strings by his lordling. "That one ever gloaming is Cian O'Connor."

"And does the man himself speak in his sullenness," she taunted, disturbed, suddenly, by the harp's insulting innuendos "or does he but let wood and metal offer affront and tell of his discontent for him? And isn't it safer than speaking of it? Who would dare appear foolish enough to challenge a man for what offense they but think they might hear in a random note, a wayward melody?" For a moment so brief she was not certain she had heard it, the notes rose in a lilting laugh to acknowledge a point well made. Bronwynn ignored them. "And what," she wondered, not quite trusting Curran, "is your true purpose in approaching me?"

"Well, in truth," Curran blurted, suddenly, inexplicably angry at Cian and discovering he liked the woman before him, "haven't we—myself, my brother, Cormac, and himself, that one there—a wager, so, that one of the three of us will bed you?"

"Do you?" Bronwynn asked. Her voice had gone flat and her gaze lowered to conceal her hurt. But the harp saw it and dared laugh. She swallowed hard, willing back sudden tears, and when her eyes lifted once more her features were steady and undisurbed. A small smile played about the corners of her full mouth. "And what," she wondered, "would the stakes be?"

Curran turned redder still and his chin lifted to indicate the great hound sitting next to Cian O'Connor. The dog gazed back at Bronwynn and smiled, his long tongue lolling, his wise eyes regarding her from beneath shaggy grey brows.

"A puppy—one of that one's get," Curran mumbled.

"I would guess," she commented lightly, "that his whelps have some value."

Bronwynn looked back at Curran, eyes solemn as she waited for his response. He ignored the snorting comment of the harp. He had been long aware of his young chieftain's ability to speak with long fingers on brass strings. There had been many a time he had silently cursed him for it, but now it was Bronwynn's nonchalant reply that disconcerted him. He wasn't certain what he had expected, shock, perhaps, or anger or tears, a sobbing protest of virtue questioned or a denunciation of the spurious ways of all men, but certainly something more feminine, more ladylike than this cool humor. It embarrassed him and his features went a deep crimson, his gaze settling everywhere but on her, while the harp mocked his discomfort. Fidgeting, shifting from foot to foot, he wiped at his brow with a huge, freckled hand and at last looked back at her. And beneath the mild, smiling interest in her eyes he saw her hurt, her anger—and the strength of will it took to hold her features so calm, so contained against the emotions within her—and against the harp's insolent insinuation of a woman with scant honor and guileful ways. He bowed his head briefly before her strength and courage and said, his wry humor honoring her own, "They have, indeed, great value, my Lady."

Her eyes darkened in gratitude, then he saw a twinkle grow in her eyes, a twitch at the corner of her mouth that became a teasing laughter transforming her features into an enchanting beauty. He had, in truth, seen her as a wee, winsome lass before, and a woman he would have turned to look after when she walked past, but now . . . He stared at her, stunned, wondering how he had missed her beauty and wondering, suddenly, irrelevantly, if Cian had noticed it. He refused to look at him; the man as stubborn as the devil himself. To but mention it would be to have him running the other way with no glance backward to see what he had left behind. And he had seen, for wasn't the harp whispering that beauty was, in truth, only skin deep? Still, this was a woman for the man—one who could tease him from his glooming, one with warmth and joy and strength enough to draw him from his pain and anger, a woman who could make him forget another. As though to answer his unspoken thought, the harp sang of a wistful yearning, a painful need, then was abruptly silenced, as though it had spoken out of place and been reprimanded.

His gaze took in the flare of dark eyebrows, the wide eyes set in a heart shaped face. Her cheekbones were high, her nose small and straight. But there was also a line to her small, square chin that spoke of a bullheadedness to match his lord's. Nor did she pluck away the slight widow's peak on her wide brow. That, too, showed either stubbornness or a disdain of fashion—and Curran would opt for stubbornness. It was her jaw that took her features from dull perfection into the distinctiveness that created true beauty. It was just the slightest bit askew, one side curving out, the other in, and when she smiled, he saw that her teeth did not quite align. But her eyes were the color of smoke rimmed by indigo—and weren't grey eyed women supposed to bring good luck?

Those eyes, too, saw him as he was—the soft, gentle man beneath a crude and blunt speech and aspect, a man easily wounded by a word or an insignificant slight—yet they were still warm on him. Curran grinned back, then risked a glance at Cian, Bronwynn's gaze following his.

Ignoring them, the harp silent beside him, Cian lounged on the wide planking of the parapet, back against the battlement, seemingly oblivious to all but the sun on his face and the shape of his hound's skull under his caressing fingertips. A straw was tucked into a corner of his mobile mouth and occasionally he tweedled it between his teeth. His features were smooth, free of anger, but one dark eyebrow was tucked into a frown, whether of annoyance or against the sunlight, Bronwynn could not guess. Turning back, she held out the comb.

"I'll trust you, Curran McAuley," she stated. "I know my own virtue well enough not to fear a man bent on seduction, especially one who states his intent. Somehow, though, I doubt you see your wife very often to comb her hair—not if you follow that one."

Accepting the comb, Curran drew up a long strand of hair and, starting at the ends, gently separated the tangles. Eyebrows tucked in concentration, he put it aside and picked up another.

"I see my Sine often enough," Curran told her. "Hasn't she been brought to childbed seven times, so?"

"That is more than a few," Bronwynn agreed, almost asleep from the soothing hands in her hair, from the warmth of the sun. "She might even be glad, ofttimes, to see the back of you."

"She is," Curran stated, his features bland, concealing his laughing pride, "and three times of those seven, she gave me twins."

Bronwynn's gaze jerked up to his and he could see her do a rapid calculation in her mind.

"Ten," she stated.

"Four sons, six daughters, and all of them redheads, like me," Curran smiled proudly, then a shadow of yearning crossed his brown eyes. He scowled, applying himself more diligently to his task.

"You miss her," Bronwynn stated.

"I do, and the children. My Sine keeps a warm hearth— all comfort and ease, it is." He frowned at a particularly tough snarl. "She has hair like yours—long, so, but not so black. It shines more russet in the sun, like Cian O'Connor's there—and why not so—herself being his half sister."

Leaning forward, Bronwynn ran splayed fingers through her hair, lifting it away from the back of her neck. Through its fall, she looked again at Cian O'Connor. Eyes closed, he still lounged against the wall, long form sprawled. Only the movement of the straw and his fingers on the hound's head indicated that he did not sleep. Straightening, Bronwynn allowed Curran to return to his task.

"He has lovely hair," she commented—while a part of her mind whispered that it was to Cian O'Connor she spoke. " 'Tis the color of a seal's back."

"It is, or of the deep of a bog pond stained with the peat, where the sun strikes into it. Yours, though," he told her, lifting long strands to let the light filter through, "is so black, 'tis almost blue. It is almost the color of a woman

I saw, once, and wasn't she the hue of the darkest grape?
On crusade, it was, in Egypt . . ."

His garrulity was interrupted by a snort of laughter
quickly suppressed. Peering up through her hair at Curran,
Bronwynn saw he was scowling at Cian. The other man
had not moved and his eyes were still closed, but a corner
of his mouth twitched. She stared at him, eyebrows meshed
at what she decided was a private joke, and not one necessarily to Curran's liking. But she had learned one thing;
the man spoke English.

"Do you grow grapes in Ireland?" she asked in an effort
to clear away Curran's frown, and he looked back at her.

"We do, but each year the frost claims more of them—
or so it feels to me. A soothsayer once told me that the
world is getting colder, that in a few hundred years we'll
have no grapes at all in Ireland. My Sine tells me 'tis myself
growing older and feeling the chill the harder in the scars
and the bones broken in the following of that one about."

"Why do you follow him—if your Sine is so warm and
his company so dangerous?"

Curran shrugged. It was something he had wondered
about often, himself.

"He is the son of my tuath king. Who else would I
follow?" he asked. Then his heavy eyebrows met in a scowl
and he shifted where he stood. "But 'tis more than that—
loyalty always is in Ireland. We need the bond and the
blood, too. I've been with him since he was old enough
to follow us about, all the larger boys, and, somehow, at
some time, the habit reversed itself, with myself on his
heels. I've always been with him—but for the crusades—
and he was still too much the puppy to go with me there.
And the danger? Mayhap that is part of the bond we share.
Nor is the danger so often on my mind, but in plights such
as this. Isn't there too much time to brood, here, and
myself not normally given to the habit? Isn't it the feeling

of being caught like a rat in a trap and knowing your
fate is not your own, but is in the hands of others—and
themselves uncaring whether you live or die, as long as
their purpose is served? If we are to die, 'twould be done
to us with no regret or hatred—with no passion or
regard—not for us. And the true grief of it all is that there
is some poor idiot and his men with him in the hands of
that one's sire thinking the same thoughts as myself, feeling
the same need to be out and about, with the wind in his
face, with a horse—or a woman—beneath him."

"Couldn't you have gone on the hunt?" Bronwynn
asked. "Isn't it your oath that holds you here? Hostages
in England are rarely confined by aught but their word."

"We could have done, but somehow, for me, for us, 'tis
worse, yet, than these walls. It is all there—the wind playing
like a harp about your ears, the mists on your skin, the
green smell of the earth, the horse between your knees—
but you still are not free. At least, in here, there is no
pretense of being aught but a prisoner—no matter the
name put on it. Nor do we forget, in here, that we can so
easily be put to death. Isn't it a thing of import, that, not
so much for ourselves, but for them," and his chin lifted
toward the faint belling of distant hounds on the hunt,
"that there is no misunderstanding of our purpose here,
that they never think we are here in friendship or in aught
but resentment and disdain—or that they think we think
we are?"

"They would kill you and your brother? I thought 'twas
the custom to take revenge only upon the family member
of the offending person, not on the retinue of the hostage,
also," Bronwynn stated, wondering at the ease with which
they spoke of such a gruesome subject.

"In Ireland, with the Sassenach, 'tis a matter of expediency, and it isn't expedient to leave a witness to speak of
an atrocity, to arouse grief and rage over it, no matter that

we might have done the same to their own—and that one knows it.'' His chin jerked toward the belling on the hounds once more, but it was Piers de Berminghan he indicated this time. ''But at least 'twould not be ourselves to have done such, and no honor to the man, no compassion—that the people know of us. But to leave witnesses alive to create a martyr with their words? Ah, no, for won't we Irish follow a dead martyr long before we'll let a living man lead us? And doesn't de Bermingham well know it?''

''You follow that one,'' Bronwynn mentioned, but there was only wry affection and a compassionate understanding in her tone.

Curran shrugged again.

''His mother died when he was but a babe. 'Twas my Sine who took him under her wing, and herself scarcely more than an infant. She taught him his manners and kept him with his tutor when he would run wild after us. She kissed his scrapes and patched his wounds, wiped his nose and calmed his grievings—and all the while myself loving her. How could a part of him not rub off on me and herself loving him? She wiped his arse, too, though he would have you thinking, if he could, that he hasn't a need to squat like normal men. Immortal, he thinks he is—invincible.''

''And he needs someone like you about to remind him that he is no less human than the rest of us,'' Bronwynn asked, ''that he, too, can make mistakes, if only in keeping the company of men like yourself?''

Curran smiled at her gentle teasing. Nor was she aware, he thought, that it was not aimed at him. Cian, too, had heard it. Not opening his eyes, not moving but to remove the straw from between his teeth, he addressed Curran.

''Find out what she knows of de Bermingham's plans,'' he ordered in Irish. ''Such a man would connive in a cloister and I know he plots something. Soft enough toward you she is to tell you anything, if you but ask her rightly. Wouldn't she betray him easily enough, I'm thinking, and her Lord Edward, too, if 'twas but put to her properly?'' Then he reinserted the straw.

Bronwynn had turned toward him when Cian began to speak. Not lifting her gaze from him when he was done, she asked Curran, "Doesn't that one speak English? I would think he would—to but be informed of what we say and find nothing lost in the translation. I would think he would speak French, too, for the same purpose—and Latin, that he could eavesdrop on the intrigues of the clergy.''

Curran could only grin; she was correct in her conjecture. But Bronwynn had risen from her seat in the battlement to shake her hair back and gather its gleaming lengths in one long twisting strand and tie it in a knot at the back of her neck. Then she walked toward Cian O'Connor, seeming almost to stalk him like a cat. Her shadow fell across his face and she knew he was aware she stood there. Yet, only when she nudged his calf with the toe of her yellow leather shoe did his fingers slip under the collar of his softly growling hound and he opened one eye to peer up at her, a dark eyebrow tucked into a feigned scowl of bewilderment.

"I am of Wales. *My* lord died,'' she told him, the Welsh she spoke close enough to the Irish that he could not mistake her words, "at a bridge over the River Yrfon in 1282 at the hands of an English lieutenant of infantry.''

But Cian only stared up at her, his gaze derisive. Then he looked at Curran, dismissing her with his slight shrug.

"Was it not Llewelyn ap Gruffydd who died at the Orewin Bridge?'' he asked Curran conversationally. "Twenty three years ago, it would be—and myself thinking 'twas the Irish and not the Welsh with the long memories for men who fought against impossible odds, who died for foolhardy causes. Nor was that one even born when the Prince of Wales was slain by the hand of Edward of England's man.'' Then his voice grew contemptuous. ''Yet, if I'm not mistaken, 'twas at Edward's table she was nurtured and 'tis at Edward's bidding she now graces us—and the callow Rudulf de Broc—with her company. And is it not Edward's purpose she is here to fulfill?''

Turning to stare up at her, Cian juggled the straw from one corner of his mouth to the other with a quick flick of his tongue. He smiled up at her, but his eyes were cold and mocking and well satisfied, the cruel golden eyes of a bird of prey, and Bronwynn wanted to nudge him again with her yellow leather shoe, but harder, so much harder— and where she had heard it would hurt so much more than on his leg. She wanted to slap away that smile of scorn, she who held in contempt those who felt force was an option in each and every disagreement. Nor was there, she realized, silently damning sudden, shaming tears of rage and hurt and blinking them back, any use in trying to explain why she was in Ireland or in telling him she, too, was, in her way, a hostage. That, she sensed, he already knew and did not care about. He continued to study her, the straw twitching jauntily up and down between his teeth, his smile a confrontation.

''I doubt,'' she said at last, turning back to address Curran, ''that my future father-in-law would hang this one,'' and she nudged Cian once more with her toe, ''with no hatred or passion. I am certain 'twould be with the greatest of pleasure and satisfaction—if this one,'' and she nudged him again, harder, ''dared treat with de Bermingham as demeaningly and rudely as he treated with me. But he would not so dare, would he? Not and himself in de Bermingham's power. Tell me, Curran McAuley, is it only women and those powerless to fight back that he treats so?''

But Curran, she knew, would not answer her and she glanced once more at Cian. He stared back, smile and straw still in place, but his eyes had narrowed, had gathered back his rage and scorn. He studied her a long moment, his disparaging gaze dropping over her only to rise again, seemingly to touch every inch of her—and find each of those completely wanting. Then he picked up his harp once again. He looked down at it, scowling, before his long fingers called forth a derisive, demeaning melody.

Turning angrily on her heel, Bronwynn started for the stairs, then paused at the sound of Cian's voice.

"So, my Lady, will you not tell me of our jailer's plans for us?"

For a long moment, Cian thought she would not answer. Her back a rigid, silent repudiation, she stood waiting to see, to hear what he—or the harp—would do next. It was the harp which spoke at last.

Wouldn't he and his men understand it if she did walk away and let them die with no warning, it whispered. Didn't he, they, realize that she was of the Sassenach and reared to their dubious sense of honor, of mercy, and that she was a woman and thus weak and her fear of de Bermingham understandable? And wasn't he the son of an Irish king? Hadn't his people learned long since the futility of begging succor of the foreigner? Wasn't it better so, then, the harp queried, to be dead with his pride unsullied—and his clan's—than to crawl on his knees seeking pity from a Sassenach woman? Yet wasn't such, the harp laughed wryly—the pleading of a man for one favor or another of a beautiful woman—often and always the role of a male? And she *was* beautiful, it hastened to assure her, wheedling then, no matter the rude manner toward her earlier.

Then the harp's singing became contrite as it sought to apologize. It became wistful as it sighed of the yearning to once again ride long, golden beaches, the wind in the

face, the taste of salt on the tongue. It sorrowed, weeping
for high hills where tall standing stones and soft grasses
were warmed by the sun and for other, more secret places
where sacred wells trickled from beneath lichen-green
stones, their waters, whether blessed by saint or fairie, so
sweet, so pure in the mouth.

But these were not places for a man alone, whether he,
himself, would ever see them again, the harp lamented.
For what value was there in the taste of salt if there were
no other lips to lick it from, the tongue's tip seeking its
brininess in the corners of a soft mouth, in the sweetness
of the hollow of a collar bone? And the tall standing stones,
were they not meant as sanctuary for lovers, the warmth
of the grasses beneath them gentle against love heated
flesh, their crushed fragrance to be remembered through
many a long winter? What better way, too, the harp wondered, to sip that sweet holy water than to dribble it drop
by drop from fingers calloused by brass strings into the
honeyed cup of a naval and to then lap it up from the soft
skin of a belly with a needful tongue, with gently nipping
lips that followed that sweet liquid down to a sweeter moisture still?

The harp's notes trickled like that tender fall of water
over Bronwynn as the harp attempted to seduce. They
trailed languid fingers of music over the line of a jaw
the harp admired as lovely and down a collar bone to be
touched with sweet kisses of melody. It pressed a soft mouth
against the blue vein in the crook of her elbow, drawing
to that tender spot a heat that but grew with each pulse
of her heart and of the song to completely envelope Bronwynn. It held her mesmerized as it lightly grazed down
each knuckle of her spine, lifting the fine hairs there, and
curved into the inward turnings of her waist, the outward
line of her hips. It settled, finally, to throb within the
deepest, most intimate part of her, bringing a warmth, a

need such as Bronwynn had never felt before—and the gravest insult.

Still, for the briefest of moments, she felt her back soften in response, her knees weakening beneath her, her very soul drawn by the spell of music Cian O'Connor had woven around her. Then her spine stiffened to become a rigid statement of rage and pain. The lift of her chin became a repudiation of the harp's plea for word of its master's fate—and of the insult dealt her by its attempted seduction. Her fists were clenched at her sides so hard Curran could see her knuckles gleaming white.

Her chin rose higher still with her fury and her eyes were narrowed with contempt when she turned to look at him once more. Meeting her gaze, Cian but cocked one languid eyebrow, as though wondering in just what way he had offended her, then he set aside his harp to pull, once more, at his wolfhound's small ears. The straw between his teeth twitched once, his lips curving into a slight smile that acknowledged at last her fury, her scorn—and its justification—while still mocking it. Bronwynn held his gaze, hating him for the insult he had given her, for the strange, threatening feelings he had aroused in her. But it was Curran she spoke to, as though Cian, himself, was too far beneath her regard to address.

"De Bermingham covets something called the Place of the Weir," she stated, "and he feels a bastard son scant a price to pay for it. Nor will he hesitate to go to battle, should The O'Connor try to hold it—or to slay a hostage. And he is prepared to go to battle. He thinks Calvach O'Connor holds that one," and her chin jerked at Cian, "in little regard, as he might very well do, and the man so very unloveable. I would suggest you find yourself another place to be—and soon—even if you have to violate your oath to do so. But I would miss you, Curran McAuley."

Bronwynn's smile flashed once more at him, transforming her features in that manner that had so transfixed Curran before, then she was gone down the stairs.

Cian straightened, leaning forward to stare after her. His smile was gone and his eyebrows were meshed into a frown.

"You know, sure," Curran assured him, "that your father would never put you in such jeopardy, that he would let de Bermingham take Laracorra first. Isn't it yourself who is the apple of his eye, no matter the delusions of the Sassenach?"

"I know," Cian nodded, his mouth a stark line, "and 'tis what angers me. I'll not have my father held helpless so. Nor will I allow de Bermingham to take aught else of ours. Hasn't the man taken far too much already—and our pride the least of it?" Then he looked up at Curran. "If he thinks my father places no value on me and if he, himself, places no value on his own son, bastard or no, then won't we but have to find a hostage he will value— and more than he covets the Place of the Weir?"

Cian held Curran's gaze a long moment, his face suddenly grim with purpose, although the straw still twinkled. Then he wrapped his arms about his knees and stared down the stairs Bronwynn had descended, his scowl thoughtful.

(5)

"Bronwynn?"

Blinking, Bronwynn looked up to see her sister's concerned features.

"Did I startle you?" Cecily wondered, her smile tentative. She reached out hesitantly to touch her sister's hand. "Were you daydreaming?"

Shaking her head, trying to gather her thoughts, Bronwynn glanced around the hall. Pages and maid servants were bustling about, cleaning up the remnants of the morning meal. Knights and ladies were clustered together, planning that day's entertainments or chores. To go hawking or hunting, she guessed, to summon a bard or a juggler, to spin, to weave or embroider, to tend to armor or to practice at the butts or at the quintain. Wishing her problems were so simple, she turned back to her sister. And why, she wondered, did Cecily approach her, when she had been Melusine's very shadow since they had come to Carrick, deserting her for the flattering attentions of the Lady de Birmingham. No matter that Bronwynn told

herself her sister was young, that she would soon tire of
Melusine's shallowness, it hurt. She even slept in Melusine's bed, when Piers de Bermingham did not demand
his marital rights. And seldom did Melusine grant them,
if the one late night Cecily crept into bed with her was
any indication. The manner in which her sister dimpled
and wiggled and giggled at the grim Cian O'Connor disturbed her, too, and why, Bronwynn did not understand.
Didn't Cecily, she scolded herself, behave like that toward
most creatures sporting a cod-piece?

"I guess I was wool gathering," Bronwynn admitted.

"You must have been, you jumped so," Cecily laughed,
displaying tiny white teeth. "You do too much of it. Melusine says you are much too aloof, much too unaffable.
Why, you haven't gone hunting or hawking with us for
days. Here you sit, now, by yourself, when everyone else is
making plans to go hawking. Nor, I wager, will you join
us."

"I won't. Nor do I think you've missed me, not with
Melusine to demand your every moment."

Cecily glanced away, biting her lip. But when she looked
back, her small jaw was jutted in a parody of her sister's
at her most stubborn.

"Melusine is good to me! She doesn't treat me as though
I am a witless child. She lets me try on her newest clothes.
She lets me wear her cosmetics."

"So I see," Bronwynn commented, eyeing her sister's
brow, from which all hair had been plucked, her round
blue eyes outlined in kohl, her small mouth stained a deep
red. She looked, she thought, like a childish caricature of
her idol, a brightly painted marionette. Then she
shrugged, knowing any criticism would only drive Cecily
closer to the Lady de Bermingham. "I was not invited to
go hawking," she stated instead, hearing a petulant note
in her voice and hating it.

"But you are so difficult to approach, Melusine says."

"Is that why you are talking to me, now?" Bronwynn asked, regretting her waspish words even as she spoke, "To list the faults Melusine finds in me?"

"Oh, no! I've missed you!" Cecily insisted, her flush of guilt belying the rush of words, the fingers she slipped into Bronwynn's hand. "But you avoid us, Melusine and myself, and your betrothed, too. She worries about that—your rudeness to Rudulf."

"He is not my betrothed. I have not yet agreed—and I may not!"

"Bronwynn, you have to. 'Tis Melusine's fondest wish."

"You would see me married to a spiteful, insolent, cruel youth still sprouting pimples because Melusine wishes it?"

"Not only Melusine," Cecily objected, her flush deepening. "Lord Edward wants it—you know that! And everyone is depending so upon it. Me, too. If you don't wed him, we may never be allowed to leave Ireland. And Rudulf is not so bad. If you were not so rude to him, if you did not always avoid him, you might come to like him."

"*I* am rude to *him?*" Bronwynn demanded. "He hates me because I dared stand up for him to that boorish step-father of his, something he hasn't the courage to do. He'll not even look at me when we pass on the stairs, and you know how narrow they are. 'Tis difficult to avoid anyone's gaze or greeting. We share the same trencher, but he sits with his back to me, his shoulder lifted, as though to ward me even off my meal. He even ignored me that one morning when I did join you for the hunt. He left a page to offer his hand to my boot, to lift me into the saddle! Nor do I truly care what opinion your Melusine or her fluttery, tittle-tattling, trifling sycophants have of me. I only wish you had wit enough not to be one yourself."

Instantly regretting her harsh words, Bronwynn reached

out to touch her sister, but Cecily jerked back, her features angry and hurt.

"Well, I like them!" she stated, jaw hard. "And at least they are more exciting to be with than you. You never want to do anything fun. All you ever do is worry and brood. And you are selfish. You don't care for anyone—even me. You would wed Rudulf if you did. You treat me like a child, like you think yourself so much smarter than I am. 'Tis no wonder I like Melusine better than I do you—and her lords and ladies, too. Nor will she, I think, be happy with your opinion of her son."

Turning on her heel, Cecily stalked away. Bronwynn gazed after her, then looked back at the scraps remaining on her trencher. Idly, she picked at a piece of meat, and decided that perhaps it was best that Melusine knew she disliked her son—and his rudeness. Perhaps he would at least treat her with courtesy, if Melusine spoke to him— and she would. The woman had too much at stake for her not to. Then Bronwynn returned to her brooding.

"Would you like to go for a ride, Lady?" a voice asked, and Bronwynn looked up again from her reverie to see Curran McAuley standing before her. She had been lost in thought for quite some while, she realized. A maid was scouring the last table but her own with water and sand, while a manservant was folding up the ones already cleaned and propping them in their place against the wall. The lords and ladies, their maids and retainers, had scattered to their various duties or pleasures. Even Cian O'Connor was gone, to where Bronwynn could not guess—he seemed to find so little interest or value in anything.

Nor had Bronwynn had the opportunity to speak to Curran in the last several days and, strange as she found it, she had missed him. Somehow, he seemed to have become her only friend at Carrick, the only person she felt at ease with, the only one she could confide in. But he was always in attendance on the dour Cian O'Connor and could only nod to her and shrug, his eyes rolling to demonstrate his helplessness, his own frustration. Then he would wrinkle a nose flattened and askew from many a blow and scowl behind Cian's back, eyebrow twisted—a parody of his chieftain's black moods—to bring a smile to Bronwynn's grey eyes. Nor could Cian's silent, watchful brooding be any easier for Curran to bear, she told herself, than Rudulf's sullenness was for her. Yet, she had, once, also, caught a bewildered pondering on Cian O'Connor's features as he stared at her that had confused her, too.

But here was Curran with an offer of a few hours escape from the thick walls and heavy atmosphere, from the cloying smiles of Melusine and her ladies and the thick browed glowering of Cian O'Connor and Piers de Birmingham. Still, she had to ask, if only to see the crimson climb Curran's thick-thewed neck once again.

"And to what purpose, Curran McAuley," she wondered, "perhaps to that intended seduction you once told me of?"

A bright flush rewarded her and Curran looked away, shrugging his shoulders and twisting his head, as though his shirt was, suddenly, too tight and binding him. Yet, when his gaze returned to hers, its twinkle acknowledged the riposte.

"Ah, my Lady," he answered, "and to what other purpose? Surely, 'twould not be to admire the landscape and ourselves dwelling within the most featureless district of all Ireland."

Curran was wrong, Bronwynn decided, gazing up at a deep blue sky streaked by long feathers of cloud. The

landscape around Carrick was hardly featureless and the
Irishman had done his best to acquaint her with each and
every one within an easy riding distance. Riding with her
out of the massive gateway of Carrick, he had led her to
the north end of Carrick Hill. There, perched above a
limestone quarry, was a huge rock—the Witch's Stone. It
had been cast there, he told her earnestly, from Croghan
Hill, rising west of them from the Bogs of Allen, by a witch
at a saint. No one knew which saint, although some said
it had been Patrick, himself, and others, St. Beagan. Not
far from the Witch's Stone, at the summit of Carrick Hill
Curran showed her the Mule's Leap—eight holes in the
earth said to be the footprints of a mule which had run
off with yet another saint. But what had happened after
to the holy man, he could not tell her.

At the south foot of the hill, in a grove of alders, was
Tober Crogh Neeve, the Well of the Holy Cross. Narrow
twines of rags, a few still bright and new, more faded and
tattered with age, each a supplication, hung from the
thorns of the rowen trees as they bent to touch their red
berries to the sacred water. Gleams of gold, silver, brass,
of bits of pottery and valued stones glimmered in the
depths of the peat brown pool. Both Bronwynn and Curran
knelt to whisper a brief prayer, to dip reverent fingers into
the tiny glimmer of brass and blue and cross themselves.
Yet, there had been a feeling of something ancient there,
and Bronwynn wondered what it was that might have heard
her plea for a way free of the plots and plans and the
ambitions of others. Looking back as they rode away, she
unexpectedly shuddered.

"Do you feel it, too, then? I had wondered if you would,"
Curran had asked and Bronwynn reluctantly nodded.
" 'Tis one of the old gods, I'm thinking, one honored long
before our beloved Patrick ever brought the Holy Cross

to Ireland. 'Tis certain, too, 'twas more than scraps of cloth and wee bits of treasure they sacrificed to the well, then."

Bronwynn had turned to him, eyes round, and Curran chuckled, shaking his head.

"Not people," he assured her, "and surely not there. How would they be drowned in that scarcely wet glimmer of an excuse for a holy well? And 'tis probably not a god or goddess, either, but a fairie, so small the pool is. Wouldn't it be but the proper size for a fairie, so, and with the alder trees there, the rowan, and both of them sacred to the old ones, the wee ones?"

"Isn't it heresy to even speak of them—the old people?" Bronwynn asked, smiling at his reassurances in spite of her words.

Curran shrugged.

"And if the old people yet exist? If they still have a wee bit of their ancient powers about themselves, powers not all usurped by our Blessed Holy Church? What if they but sulk, jealous of the propitiations and prayers offered another, newer god strong in his youth—and at a well, a wee, insignificant scant of water—and isn't all water sacred—that was once theirs? What harm can it do to but placate them a wee bit, to but acknowledge them? Mightn't they be, too, a small bit lonely and what harm can it do to but ease their solitude? Surely our Holy Lord Jesus would not begrudge any creature, elf or human, such. And if they haven't gone all weak, but merely hoard their powers, what harm can it do to but nod the head in acknowledgement? The very least said of the little people is that they are spiteful."

"You hedge your bets, Curran McAuley," Bronwynn teased, lifting a mocking chin at him. "You say you are a Christian, why, you even fought in a crusade against the infidel, yet you believe in the faeries!"

Curran leveled a measuring glance at her.

"If you think such ones do not exist," he challenged, "that they warrant no respect, I challenge you to ride with me one night into the Bogs of Allen and chase the will-o-wisp or to loiter near a fairie rath awaiting the Tuatha-de-Danann. And didn't I note your grimace when I spoke of sacrifices in that wee bit of a well back there? Yet, can't I show you a man taken as whole as though he lived yesterday from those same bogs, and himself with a rope about his neck and a hide on him the color of peat, so long has it been since he was given alive to the Druid gods? Long before the birth of our Christ he died, poor misbegotten thing, nor would I like to think he died for aught and himself still looking as though he'll open his eyes on his next breath. The O'Connor has him. I can show you, too, massive stones erected by the ancients. Places to worship the old gods, some say, or to bury their kings. There is one near here—not one of the better ones—but close, on Carbury Hill. Would you go see it and ourselves not having aught else to do this day?"

Now, Bronwynn lay on the top of Carbury Hill, the sky a blue bowl above her. Not, she thought, that it or any of the others about were scarcely tall enough to warrant the label of 'hill', yet it did command a wide view of the central plain of Ireland stretching away into the distance. To the south, she could see the haze of green and brown and lavender that was the tufted reeds and star flowered mosses, the sedges and rushes and ferns of the Bogs of Allen. Northeast, Curran had told her, on a truly clear day, if she squinted, she could see the blue ribbon that was the Boyne. But closer, surrounding her was a wide circle of large, mismatched rocks erected long before by ancient, unknown hands. Nor was it the only such site on Carbury Hill. Some such had been used as burial places, others as a site of defense. The one she lay within, he thought, marked a tomb. There were those foolish enough, once, to dig up such sites out of curiosity, only to be cursed with ill luck ever after, so he, for one man, would leave this place and others like it well enough alone. Nor, Bronwynn thought, had he expected her to dismount to lie in the middle of such a pagan erected, devil-cursed enchantment.

Yet, she felt nothing evil there. There was only a feeling of peace, of serenity. She could hear the call of a lark high above and the gentle soughing of the wind as it dipped the heavy heads of grass before it. The earth smelled of the warmth of the sun and of green, growing things. Sprawled out behind her, flat on his back, arms outflung and the top of his head almost touching hers, his feet, too, pointing toward the outer ring of rocks, was Curran, and Bronwynn wished they never had to leave. But Curran's thoughts had been elsewhere and he mistook the source of her sigh. Scowling to the sky, he folded his arms under his head.

" 'Tis not yourself, truly, that he finds such fault with," he assured Bronwynn and for an instant her breath caught in her throat, then she managed a chuckle.

"Who could ever," she asked idly, stripping a stalk of grass of its head to chew on it, "possibly find fault with a woman so perfect as myself—verily a saint?"

Curran grinned, then shook his head.

"Scarcely a saint. 'Tis Cian O'Connor on my mind and his rudeness to you."

Turning to her side, Bronwynn propped herself up on her elbow and looked at the top of Curran's head. Such a gentle man, she thought, and in such a rough exterior. But why would he think Cian's rudeness disturbed her— she hardly knew the man. Yet it did, more than she cared to admit, and certainly more than it should. Still, she had always been too easily wounded, that she knew.

"Ah, Curran McAuley," she smiled, "I hope your Sine appreciates you. Surely, she has the finest man in all of

Ireland. Your only flaw, as far as I can see, is your misplaced loyalty to that same Cian O'Connor. His rudeness to me seems to be the least of his faults and one I scarcely notice.''

"I notice, and it disturbs me." He craned his head around to look at her, a huge eyebrow crunched against the sun. " 'Tis an insult to you and not worthy of him, or true to his character. 'Tis not from true dislike, I'm thinking, nor do I want you to misjudge the man.''

Bronwynn rolled back to study the sky.

"Curran, I scarcely think of the man at all, much less long enough to judge him rightly or wrongly. He means aught to me. Nor do I wish to spoil a beautiful day discussing Cian O'Connor."

She lied, Bronwynn knew. She hated the man. The slightest lift of a mocking eyebrow and she wanted to claw those knowing eyes out. Nor did it help that she realized he could, really, know nothing about her—or very little. And what did she have to be ashamed of, in truth? Yet, that eyebrow had the power to make her doubt her own worth, question her own integrity—and find them both lacking. And that disdainful, denigrating glance down the length of her and up again—it reminded her of all her faults, her flaws, and many she had not known she had before. Then his gaze would dismiss her, move from her, as though she was insignificant to its perusal, his interest. He had dared, too, to offer a puppy to the man who effected her seduction! Curran might try to shrug it off as a poor attempt at humor, but it was an insult. Yes, she hated him and here was Curran, gnawing the subject like a mastiff with an old bone, unwilling to give it up.

" 'Tis not only you he detests, 'tis all women.''

" 'Twas 'dislike' a moment before. Now, you say he 'detests'." Bronwynn turned to her elbow once more, to scowl at the thick russet thatch of Curran's hair. But she saw a tiny patch of scalp, right at the crown, and she smiled to herself, wondering if he knew it was there and how, in his male vanity, he would greet this first sign of impending baldness. "And 'all women', is it?"

Curran inhaled deeply, then trapped the air in his billowed cheeks, to blow it out in a gust.

"All women," he announced to the sky. "All things bearing a cleft instead of a cod. All but his daughter, and the eyes in his head not setting on her in three years."

"He has a daughter?" Bronwynn snorted. "And how did he set aside his loathing of women long enough to hitch up a skirt and plant a child? I'm only surprised he did not drown her at birth, hating women as he does."

"He did not always hate women. Once, he loved Fenella McKenna."

"Then the saints help Fenella McKenna—to be loved by such a man as Cian O'Connor," Bronwynn mocked, even as a shadow passed over her features at the thought of the Irish lord loving another woman. "And a poor sort of a father he is, not to see his child in three years."

"He is not welcome where she is."

Bronwynn shrugged away the excuse. "I think I would be inclined to sic a dog or two on him myself, but he hardly seems a man to be deterred by a couple of hounds or a door closed in his face, not if he truly wanted something."

Curran rolled over to face Bronwynn, propping himself on his elbows as his narrowed gaze held hers.

"The child is in England, in a Norman castle."

Bronwynn blinked. Suddenly, there was nothing to say. Certainly no derisive gibe was suitable, not in the face of the anger on Curran's features. But it was not directed at her, that she knew, nor did she ever want such rage to be. She could only wonder how Cian O'Connor inspired such fierce loyalty, such appropriation of his grief and fury. If, she thought, Cian felt such emotion at all, and they were not simply spawn of the imagination of Curran McAuley.

After a long moment, he spoke, his gaze still skewering hers.

"Would you care to know why an Irish child, the legitimate daughter of an O'Connor, is lost to a strange land?"

Biting her lip, Bronwynn looked down at a blade of grass she was twisting in nervous fingers and nodded.

"Fenella was the daughter of one of the O'Connor's men, and surely she was one of the most lovely things in all of Ireland. All gilded fair hair she was and eyes as blue as the sea, with skin like the froth on fresh milk. As beautiful as Naisi's Deirdre, and look you how many men died over *that* one, no fault to her, but still they died. Yet Deirdre was loyal, honest, steadfast, while Fenella is simply ambitious and covetous. But Cian could not see it, blinded as he was by that pouting, scarlet mouth, that hair she would twist about her finger while summoning a blush and lowering those eyes in feigned confusion before the onslaught of his manly vigor—that one was born contriving. And wasn't Cian the son of the chieftain and likely to be chieftain, himself, one day?"

"So, they were married, with the child to be born six months later and no shame on it, not in Ireland. It is a part of the Brehon laws, too, that a man must obtain whatever morsel of food his pregnant wife craves should he be able, or he can be fined, and didn't the poor, besotted fool try, too, and himself the laughing stock of all who saw him and those who merely heard the gossip? Led him about by his pizzle, she did, and so sweet she was, butter not melting in her mouth, as her eye inventoried everything in the houses of Calvach O'Connor from the gold torques around the necks of his chieftains and the crimson carbuncles in the silver brooches on the cloaks of his wife and concubines, to the furs on the beds and the fleas within them. It weighed the pots and pans in the cook house, the knives at the belts of O'Connor's men, and the very ashes in the fireplaces. But they were Irish houses, round houses of wood and withe set within wide round walls of stone or timber, and Fenella was not content to live within a rath. She wanted a castle in the Norman manner, with thick walls and narrow windows, steep stairs and drafty halls. Cian would have gotten it for her, too, I'm thinking, had she given him time enough. But Fenella's eye not only weighed the household goods of her father-in-law and the jewels of his women, it noted the furs on the backs of visiting chieftains and the heft of the rings on their thumbs. It dropped lower, to calculate the breadth of more personal jewels, while that mouth stayed all prim and perfect, for our Fenella was inclined toward licentiousness, though Cian saw no evil in her at all. Her eye also saw the gold and rubies in the handle of the sword of Robert de Grenville when he came to treat with Calvach O'Connor in the name of Edward of England. She held it lowered as he spoke of his lands, his castles, and I never saw it meet his, but it must have, for what was to come later. Then he was gone and forgotten—by the most of us.''

Curran paused and cleared his throat, his gaze remote as he stared into the distance. Bronwynn, too, swallowed against a thickness in her chest, wondering at the grief she felt in a story not yet done, for a man she did not like. Shaking his head, Curran roused himself.

''She was like a fat spider in her web through that time, waiting for the birthing, for what Cian brought her, for all else that was to come to her. She went through the confinement as easily as a cat, the midwife said—with no pain—and no pleasure. Unnatural, the midwife called it. It was Cian who greeted the baby with joy, with tears and laughter, holding the wee thing in his two hands like a prayer and himself not knowing if to chortle or to weep, so he did both. It mattered not to him that it was a girl, but we Irish don't place the value others do on sons. Daugh-

ters are a joy to their fathers all their lives in a way sons
outgrow. He doted on her, made a blathering idiot of
himself over her. He loved her more than he had loved her
mother before the baby's birth and he loved the mother,
it seemed to me, twice as much after, in gratitude and
astonishment at the gift of the daughter. Yet the mother
did not share his fascination. She did not suckle her or
cuddle her or sing to her. The only notice she took was
to scowl when the child cried. But Cian could find no fault
with that, saying only that some women are slow to become
mothers. And through it all, the woman smiled that wee
smile she had and she watched and she planned, it seems
now. Then, one day when Cian had gone with his father
to settled a dispute with a neighbor, one day when she
knew he would be away at least a fortnight, Fenella packed
and was gone. Ah, and pack she did, taking anything and
everything that in any way could be argued to be hers, all
that she had brought into the marriage—scant dowry *that*
was—and all which was given her while she was there, for
in Ireland when a man and woman marry, everything they
bring into it remains theirs. Even her dowry returns with
the woman, should they divorce, the man keeping only
the profit of it.''

Curran had been pulling at the grass he lay on, twisting
his fingers into and yanking it out by the roots. Now, tossing
a clump of weeds and soil away, he looked up at Bronwynn.

"She left, eloping with Robert de Grenville, and she was
in her right, for in Ireland a couple have until the end of
the first year of marriage, if unhappy, to leave it. Ah, didn't
she do it by the letter of the law, so, and leave on February
first, the day on which any husband or wife may decide to
walk away from their marriage. She was not one to take a
chance, not our Fenella. And she took the child—and
Cian's heart out of his very chest with her—out of spite,

I'm thinking, though why she hated Cian so, I do not know, for all he ever did was love her.''

Curran shrugged, trying to puzzle it out, and Bronwynn touched his hand, asking, "What did he do then?"

Curran sighed and shook his head.

"We thought he would go mad with rage and grief and nothing would do but that he go after her. At first, I think it was his intention to try to coax Fenella back, but the further he followed after her, to Dublin, to London, to de Grenville's estates in Cumberland, the more clearly he saw her ways. By the time we caught up with her, he wanted only his daughter back. He tried to talk to Fenella, but de Grenville would have none of it, and she but laughed— with the child in her arms. 'Twas the first time she had ever held her, I'm thinking. Cian went mad, then, and tried to take the child by force. They beat him, de Grenvile and his men, until he was senseless, until he bled from his ears, his eyes, his mouth, his nose, until there was but bruised flesh over the whole of him—and shattered bones. They broke his arms, his leg, his ribs. And took such pleasure in the doing of it. We thought he would surely die of it. 'Twas nothing we could do—Cormac and myself and three men, out numbered as we were—though the saints know we tried—and almost dying ourselves. And didn't they kill the spirit of him for a long time after. He was like a kicked puppy for months after we brought him home and even after the flesh of him had long since healed. Nor is he, I'm thinking, healed yet the while."

"Cumberland," Bronwynn mentioned, past the knot of sorrow in her throat, "has intemperate weather. 'Tis wild and remote, far from London and so near the Scots. De Grenville, too, seldom goes to court—and 'tis said he is tight-fisted. Fenella will have little of the comforts she expected and few of the luxuries. Cian can at least take comfort in that."

" 'Tis beautiful there, though, and a pity that Fenella is not one to take pleasure in scenery,'' Curran answered, his smile wry. Then he gnawed his lip, gazing blindly into the distance. At last he spoke. "Nor has he any recourse under Irish law, for when two people divorce, the son stays with the father's clan the daughter goes to the mother's. So he takes comfort in his hatred of the English—and of beautiful women.''

"But I am not beautiful,'' Bronwynn shot back, angry. "Nor am I English.''

"You are the one beautiful thing the English have sent us. But you don't see it, and that but makes you the more threatening to Cian.''

Her jaw only jutted farther and Curran said, "To the Irish, all who come over the Irish Sea are Sassenach, as we, whether we come from the Vikings or the Celts or the Old People, are Irish. 'Tis strange, that, and something I noticed on Crusade,'' he dissembled. "Other peoples place their loyalty in their king or lord. We place ours in Ireland, first, and our kings and chieftains after. If a king or a chieftain is not strong, if he does not rule his clan, his province, or Ireland wisely and well, we but change him for another, a better—if the saints are with us.''

"It must lead to many a battle,'' Bronwynn commented.

"It does,'' Curran grinned, "but in Ireland, if a man cares not for the fighting, he can always become a poet or a bard. Perhaps, 'tis why we have so many of them and some passing bad. But this thinking of ourselves as a whole people might have proved our undoing—or so Cian thinks. He thinks 'tis why we did not unite and resist more strenuously when MacMurrough brought in Norman mercenaries to regain the throne of Leinster from Tighernan O'Rourke. We thought 'twas but another shoving match between kings and, if we did not like the winner, we could but remove him. And we, with our pride in fighting face to face, man to man, with spear and knife, wearing aught but kilts and linen shirts, did not understand the advantage held by men in armor who fight on mailed horses. No more than they can ken the chieftain who sits down at table with his warriors, as I sat with The O'Connor on crusade. Now, our overlords are the Sassenach, but Cian and others hope to change that." His voice gained in fervency. "Haven't we brought in gallowglass from the Scottish Isles to aid us and aren't we stemming the tide of Sassenach castles in some places? Haven't we even turned them back in others? Aren't they held, now, behind stone walls and in dark holes like that one," he demanded, shrugging a massive shoulder in the direction of Carrick, "on the edge of the Pale, and themselves only daring to venture out clad for war with their men-at-arms about them?"

"And your lord has his hatred, his need for vengeance, while de Birmingham has you and your lord."

" 'Tis a strong thing, that hatred," Curran replied. "Don't go mistaking it. And himself half in love with you. Didn't the harp tell me so? Still, 'tis a fine nest of eels we are in and no man fool enough to gamble on the outcome, but for myself. I'll wager we'll slip the noose easily enough. Would you like to go with us, then, little one? Aren't you, too, a pawn, if not in this game, another? 'Twould make for a fine fling, that, with de Birmingham's nose bent all the way back to his ear."

He looked at her from under beetled brows, his gaze a study in exaggerated beguilement. But he was only half joking, Bronwynn realized, and she was tempted. To be free of her duties, of Edward, of Rudulf de Broc! Then she came down with a hard bounce. Her jaw set and she looked away from his hopeful gaze. What if Curran, she wondered, but played her like a trout on a line? What if he was but Cian's man in this, his seduction of her, too?

But Curran was not capable of such dissembling and she met his earnest eyes again.

"Ah, Curran McAuley, you tempt me, even in play, but there is Edward, my sister, my duty. You deceive yourself when you think Cian O'Connor feels aught but distaste for me," she whispered, her laugh catching in her throat. "If he has interest in me at all, 'tis for vengeance."

But Curran's gaze was fervent.

"I am a man in love, for there is my Sine," he insisted, "and who better than a man in love to recognize another? And don't I know the man, so?"

"And don't I know 'tis time we were gone back to Carrick?" she asked, shaking her head at his foolishness. "Won't they be sending after us soon?"

Still, she wondered why Cian would try to so deceive the gullible warrior and she could not repress anger at the thought that he was so successful. And it was rage that clenched her fists about her horse's rein, as she looked up and recognized Cian's dark head and her sister's blond peering over the battlement, as she and Curran entered the castle's courtyard. That, then, she realized, was his game. If one sister would not be seduced, then the other would suffice, if only to revenge himself on the first—and on all Normans.

Jaw set, she stared up at Cian's taunting features, at her sister's set in a strangely smug, triumphant smile. She would, she vowed, put paid to Cian's little plan. Cecily may be a fool, and herself nearly so, but de Bermingham would stop the romance soon enough.

Yet, she rather not approach him. He had not said anything, not yet, about his wish that she marry his stepson. In truth, he spoke to her not at all. Nor did she desire a confrontation with him on the subject. She could, though, have a word with Melusine. Surely she would not want her young ward slipping around corners and ducking into nooks with a half savage Irish lordling. Or she could speak to Cecily directly, Bronwynn thought, regretting the quarrel with her that morning, but she doubted that would have any effect. Cecily often pouted and flounced about for weeks, her perfect nose in the air, after the smallest harsh word addressed to her. If nothing else halted the fledgling affair, then she would have a word with Cian O'Connor—and it would not be one pleasing to him.

(6)

But, in the days that followed, there was no opportunity to speak to Cecily. Her sister arduously clung to Melusine, as Bronwynn had thought she might. As though well aware Bronwynn wished to talk to her—and on what subject— Cecily would smile slyly at her over the Lady de Bermingham's shoulder, gaze knowing. Or she would study Cian O'Connor from under slanted eyes, then look at her sister, her features defiant and smug, one naked eyebrow lifted derisively. Only when Bronwynn was gone and unable to corner her away from Melusine's shadow, would she slip off and disappear, where to, no one would admit to knowing. When she returned, her mouth would be swollen, as though from ardent kisses, and curved up into a plush, well satisfied smile. At last, realizing that Cecily could and had always been able to outwait her at such a cat and mouse game, Bronwynn gave up. As little as she respected her, as little as she wanted to, Bronwynn forced herself to approach the Lady de Bermingham.

But Melusine had merely wrinkled her plucked brow,

the corners of her mouth turning up in a smile mocking Bronwynn's lack of sophistication and concern for her sister.

"Ah, but isn't Cecily of an age when she should practice playing at love? Wasn't I wed at her age and with Rudulf in swaddling clothes? Who better, too, than a half wild Irish lordling? There is not a lady amongst us who does not find Cian O'Connor intriguing, myself included. I wager beneath that glowering, there is a fiery temper, and *that* choler, I have found, goes hand in gauntlet with passion for other things. And are not the Irish said to be fervent in all they pursue?"

Melusine's smile only grew more pointed as she observed Bronwynn's head shake in repudiation and she lifted a pampered hand to halt the younger woman's attempted interruption. Shrugging, she leaned back in her chair.

"Truly," she mocked, "there are times I grow weary of fostering virgins." Yet her eyes were expressionless, cold. Only when one of her ladies giggled, the titter poorly stifled behind bejeweled fingers, did they lighten—and only with acknowledgement of the woman's toadying, of her appreciation of her wit. But, Bronwynn suddenly realized, meeting those empty eyes, the Lady de Bermingham had no sense of wit, of humor. She had merely learned to recognize what others found amusing, and to emulute it, gaining a reputation as witty.

But was she ever bewildered, Bronwynn wondered, by why others laughed? Did she ever feel a lack within herself, a hollow echoing nothing? Or was she empty of all imagination? An invisible hand lifted the fine hairs on Bronwynn's arms at the thought. As though sensing the shudder her ward suppressed, Melusine leaned forward once again, her glance from woman to woman drawing her ladies closer, as though drawn by invisible cords, although it was Bronwynn she addressed.

"And don't we often wonder," she stated, her soft voice hinting at conspiracy, "why it is Cian O'Connor does glower so? Was it by a woman he was wounded? If so, who was she—the one so desirable, so skillful at the Game of Love as to bring the sullen Cian O'Connor to the leash—and to his knees? And, if 'twas a woman who so grieved the handsome Celt, cannot another heal him? Have you not noticed that many women have a penchant for wounded creatures, a bird with a broken wing, a crippled fawn? *I* think it a weakness, yet there is no woman attending me who would not wish to be the one to so succor the man—but for yourself. But you do not, truly attend me, do you," she stated, her cool voice turning opaque with the offense dealt her. "No matter that such is the express desire of our king and your guardian."

Then the corners of Melusine's mouth turned up, but the smile did not reach her eyes. She leaned forward once again, until her gaze was level with Bronwynn's.

"Cecily, however, attends me well. Perhaps the foolish little giddypate will even whisper Cian Connor's secrets to me in the night, should he tell them to her. Such knowledge would make the sharing of my pillow almost worth the while—that and the fact that, when she is there, my lord is not."

Bronwynn stared back into the malignant glee that was Melusine's eyes, yet she had to try again.

"He will seduce her. Would you have it said that a mere child became pregnant while under your charge?"

Melusine chuckled, shaking her head at Bronwynn's ignorance.

"Aren't Irish men said to be most chivalrous, most respectful toward women? And you must know the seduction of virgins is forbidden by the rules of the Court of Love. Only wedded women and widows are allowed such

pleasures. Surely Marguarite did not so neglect your educa-
tion as to leave you uninstructed in that.''

Bronwynn had to look away from Melusine's amused
eyes, her jaw set as she fought her rage. To give into it, to
lose her temper with the Lady de Birmingham would only
alienate the woman farther and forever.

"My Lady," she answered, trying to hold her voice calm,
reasonable, "we are not in Aquitaine, nor even in England.
This is Ireland, at the very edges of the Irish Pale. There
is no Court of Love here. Nor is Cian O'Connor a knight
of chivalry. He is a man of hatred and rage toward
women—and toward the Normans—a justified hatred. My
Lady," she pleaded, leaning forward to place an imploring
hand on Melusine's knee, "I have cause to fear for my
sister and she would listen to you. I only ask that you speak
to her.''

Melusine looked down at Bronwynn's hand with distaste
and Bronwynn withdrew it. She sat back again, chin jutted,
yet a sardonic smile tilted the corners of her full mouth,
while she regarded Melusine with pity. Piers de Birmingham was a fool, she realized, if he truly believed a
marriage between Melusine's son and herself would make
his wife happy, for nothing would, nothing could. The
woman hadn't soul enough or imagination enough for
happiness or grief or love or hatred. She was capable of
shallow pleasures only, seeking them in the manipulation
of others, in watching them feel and enact the emotions
of which she was empty. What constant effort it must take
to keep the very gut of her from collapsing into itself from
such a void, she thought, and Bronwynn resisted the urge
to cross herself as though against a thing dead of soul.

There was a scowl on Melusine's vapid features—as
though she fought to comprehend the curious expression
in Bronwynn's gaze. Then she shrugged uneasily, her laugh
tickling.

"My Lady Bronwynn, your sister is scarcely the child you think she is—nor as foolish. I hardly think her stupid enough to be seduced by a mere savage. So, what harm if she finds the man attractive? Isn't she of the age to do so?"

Knowing she had lost, that if she stayed, she would surely lose the fragile grip on her temper, Bronwynn stood up from her stool. Yet she could not resist one parting shot.

"Cecily," she stated, "is of the age to find anything in a codpiece attractive." Bronwynn watched Melusine's bald eyebrows flare and she shook her head in disbelief. This woman, she marveled, would set a young girl to discover the secrets of such a man as Cian O'Connor for her own titillation, yet she was shameless enough to mime offense at a mere crudity. "Even," Bronwynn added, her temper suddenly flaring beyond control, "a crude, bepimpled, vain coxcomb of a youth without spine enough to stand up to his stepfather and with so little pride that, for his own advancement and a rocky estate in Wales, he permits his mother to play the whore to her own husband."

Melusine's features contorted into a twisted mask of fury as she stood, incoherent with outrage. She pointed at the door with a shaking finger, ordering Bronwynn out, and, calmly brushing down her skirts, Bronwynn turned to go. But she had alienated Melusine de Bermingham completely and nothing would be lost with one more shot. Turning back, she said, "Nor has your son even wit enough to choose a tailor who doesn't make of him the jestingstock of the castle. Perhaps, my Lady, you should dress him, too, while doing his courtship for him."

Swinging on her heel, Bronwynn strolled out the door, leaving an appalled hush behind her. Her own jaw was set in fury and her head pounded with it, blinding her to a tall, slim form on the top of the stairs until she ran into it. She staggered from the impact and strong hands steadied her, setting her back.

"The tailor," Cian O'Connor told her, "would be Tiomoid O'Leary, and he's long since taken himself and his unfortunate sense of humor elsewhere."

"To stitch for other Normans?" Bronwynn asked derisively. Then her fury returned. "You were spying!" she accused. "You stood behind the door and you eavesdropped, like some old woman with aught better to do. How dare you?"

Cian leaned back against the stone wall, arms folded casually across his chest. He was grinning down at her, but his eyes were guarded, intent. He shrugged.

"Like that old woman, I've aught better to do. Cormac and Curran and I slipped out well before breakfast to snare waterfowl, but isn't it cold, chilly work and in a cold, chilly bog? Unlike the heat emanating from my Lady Melusine's solar." And, indeed, Bronwynn caught the faint smell of damp wool, of crushed moss and damp peat. It was the scent of warm, growing things.

"So you eavesdrop, when you aren't attempting to seduce my sister. And where is she?"

All humor gone, Cian straightened away from the wall. Suddenly seizing her wrists, he drew her close to him to stare down at her with tawny eyes gone the color of a winter pond. How, Bronwynn wondered, trying to break free, could gold and green look so cold? But he held her easily.

"Your sister?" he mocked. "Think you I would seduce your sister and herself an insipid, brainless little chit with aught on her mind but testing her charms on every man—youth or greybeard—and herself all in a pout when he does not succumb? She even asked me for a puppy, one of Booka's whelps. I told her what it would cost her. Didn't she then balk at the price, so? And myself thinking even the least of my dogs is worth one night in my bed. Aren't there women who would come to it for the pleasure only?"

Wordlessly, her jaw clenched in anger, Bronwynn tried again to twist against his grip on her wrists.

"I'll scream," she threatened, and he laughed.

"Do so, and bring those harpies in there to your rescue," he suggested, taunting her. "Ah, and wouldn't that complete your humiliation? Or you could stay a moment more with me, now that we've found ourselves with a wee while alone together."

She jerked once more in yet another futile attempt to free herself and he twisted her arms about, entwining them with his, drawing her closer still. He held her easily against his strength and warmth and Bronwynn hated him, hated her own helplessness. She wondered how she had ever felt drawn to the dark pensiveness of his features in repose, to the bitter wrath in his eyes as he observed the foreigners who held his land—and him by his word of honor. She glared up at him and his smile in return was derisive.

"You think I would seduce your sister?" he asked again, shaking his head at the absurdity of the thought, while one finger lightly stroked across the knuckles of a hand he held captive, distracting her. "Haven't I had enough of such women, women who desire a man for the gold he can put about their fair white necks, for the furs he spreads over their bed, for the power of his name reflecting on theirs, women who look into a man's eyes with the sole purpose of preening before their own artful image as it gazes back at them? And don't they think, such women, a smile and the parting of their smooth thighs payment enough for all a man gives them?" His laugh was curt and jeering, but there was a note of deep hurt beneath as he added, "Believe me, my Lady, no smile, no bedding be worth the cost of seducing such a one—and such a one is your sister."

"But she did serve a purpose, did she not?" he stated, his grip only tightening as Bronwynn tried to twist her hands free from his. "Was she not the right bait, so, the little fish luring the bigger fish to me? And like a pretty fish you are, all sleek and smooth and speckled, here," his fore-finger touched one high cheekbone where faint freckles gleamed gold, "like a wee trout, and your eyes glowing silver when you are angry, your cheeks flaming pink. Perhaps my Curran has the right of it, when he sings your steadfastness, your virtue—to Cormac, of course, and not to myself. Doesn't the man know well enough that, when pushed one way, I will go the other? But he thinks himself subtle—and myself more stubborn than, in truth, I am."

"I doubt Curran is far wrong in any assessment of you," Bronwynn spat into Cian's mocking eyes. "Hasn't he named you to me as deadly in your intent, murderous in your rage, a man not to be denied when he sets his mind to something, no matter the wisdom of the advice given him otherwise?"

"Ah, doesn't the man flatter me, so?" Cian grinned, "but 'tis not my attributes we be discussing here, but yours, and I think himself wrong."

Suddenly, the feigned joviality was gone, replaced by an anger springing from an unhealed wound, an old grief, a dream long since destroyed by betrayal. Swinging Bronwynn about, he forced her into a recess in the thick stone wall. A faint shout came from the yard below through the arrow slit at her back, while his broad shoulders and ruthless features blocked all view of the narrow, twisting stairs behind him.

"I think you scant different from any other woman," he rapped out, "no matter Curran's regard for you. The man has had slight experience of women beyond his Sine—and a poor example that one is of the perfidy of

woman. Still, aren't I a man despising bigotry in others?"
he mocked, as the ball of his thumb traced the line of her
jaw and brushed lightly over her full lips. One corner of
his long mouth tipped up as she tried to jerk her head
away and he chuckled. "Mayhap, too, the Lady Melusine
is right, if only in the one thing, when she avers that,
where there is temper, there is passion—and haven't you
a temper? Wouldn't it be a great loss to myself should I
be denied by my own prejudice a taste of such passion? If
'tis there—and if Curran has the right in his opinion of
you—who knows what might come of that one taste?"

Cian's gaze became a warm amber over Bronwynn's
every feature. His tone was soft, wheedling, gently
caressing.

"Did you know that he spins a fine tale—to Cormac—
of ourselves, falling in love, and wedding? Doesn't he even
have us with a troop of sons strong of thew and daughters
fair of face? Think on it, a stór. Wouldn't it be a fine thing
to be free of this place, one day, with the wind in our faces,
the rain on our tongues? The very least to be said on it,"
he added, a complacent note of male vanity entering his
voice, "is that, sure, I must be preferable to that weak
willed, slack muscled popinjay your King Edward would
have you marry. And wouldn't Piers de Bermingham's nose
be bent out of shape over such a thing?"

The warmth of his body, the caress of his voice, the soft
stroking of his thumb across her lips, along her jaw had
quieted Bronwynn's struggle to be free of him. His soft words
had sketched a picture that filled her with a yearning so
strong she ached with it. But his chuckle at the thought of
so discomfiting the Lord of Carrick brought her chin up.
Her jaw tightened in rage at herself for being so easily
beguiled—and by a man turning so facilely from rage and
sullenness to silver-tongued seducer. Surely, the harp ever
slung over his back should have reminded her he was a poet.

"Aye," she spat out, "and wouldn't it be a fine thing to so seduce the ward of *my* King Edward and then send her back to him with the babe of an Irish lordling in her belly? And wouldn't you find great pleasure in so humiliating me—and the Sassanach?"

A muscle leaped in his jaw, then a smile lightened the eyes regarding her as lazily as a cat's. His gaze held hers as she stared defiantly back at him, then dropped to touch her lips.

"Ah, and wouldn't I find pleasure in it, so," he whispered, and his mouth lowered to hers.

His long, hard length pressed her back against the stone wall, rendering her struggles futile. One hand still held her hands clasped between them. The other cupped her head, to tilt it to fit her mouth more closely with his, to hold her immobile. Yet his kiss was soft, his lips touching hers as gently as his breath for a long moment. Then his tongue lightly traced the outline of her mouth and teased its corners, as his thumb pressed against the hinge of her jaw, forcing it to relax, her lips to part, and his tongue moved deeper. It brushed the insides of her lips, then sought her own, to plead, to coax a response—and receiving none but an angry moan of protest. At last, as though impatient with such subtle courtship, his mouth took hers more fully, demanding an answer—and receiving it in Bronwynn's renewed struggles.

Never had Bronwynn been so kissed and she found she hated it. It drew all strength from her flesh and dissolved her bones. It fed a butterfly of ache deep within her until it became a demanding need to be fought, to be accepted, to be gratified. And it was the naked yearning, the aching desire brought to reluctant life by the skillful touch of tongue and lips that, at last, lifted her to her toes to take his mouth more fully still, that stirred the moan of a responding need. Cian felt the flutter of her throat beneath his fingers and the grip of his hand on hers loosened to caress her fingers, her wrist. He drew her closer still, to cradle her, to cherish her down the length of his body, no longer fearful of her escape, and she clung to him, her only support. Only a fluting, beguiling voice brought to a halt her further descent into desire.

"Cian! At last, I've found you. I've looked all over for you. I've been so bored."

Cian's mouth released Bronwynn's and, for a long moment, his amber eyes held hers, before dropping to touch her red, swollen mouth regretfully. Turning at last, he shielded her from sight, his broad shoulders tense as though with indecision. Then they relaxed and he deliberately stepped aside to reveal her to her sister's view.

Cecily stared at her, her mouth open as she blinked. Then her eyes narrowed as her thoughts chased themselves across her features.

Never would Cecily have thought to find Cian displaying interest in another woman, not while courting her, and she blinked again, disbelieving, hurt. Only she had had the charm and innocence to bring him out of his sullenness, his wariness. So the Lady Melusine told her, but here he was in earnest conversation—or worse—with her own sister. Had Melusine lied to her, using her for her own purposes? Cecily gulped back a sob at the idea of such betrayal and realized that, no, Melusine loved her. Hadn't she told her so often enough? And she, herself, was indeed beautiful and charming. She saw it in the eyes of every man who looked at her, all of them denying her nothing on which she set her whims or her heart.

True, Cian O'Connor had not promised her the puppy she so wanted. He had teased her instead, while twisting a strand of her hair about his finger and standing closer to her than she liked. But the hair was blond and her eyes were the blue, her face the perfect oval so praised by the troubadours, so pursued by fashion. Did not every gaze always leave Bronwynn's dark hair and grey eyes to return to her? And something close to contempt flickered in Cecily's eyes as she regarded her sister, chin lifted.

And Bronwynn was betrothed—or almost—and she was not one to dishonor such a pledge, thinking herself too good, even, to indulge in the harmless flirting demanded by the Court of Love. She even thought herself too virtuous, so Melusine said, to associate with those who did. And she would certainly consider herself too noble to trifle with the attentions of another's admirer.

"You were searching for me?" Cian asked, his voice gentle with a strange pity.

Her gaze dismissing her sister, Cecily lowered her lashes to smile beguilingly up at Cian through them.

"I was. I was so bored, with aught to do, with no one to talk to."

"Melusine is in her solar," Bronwynn stated, unable to completely disguise the sarcasm. "I'm certain she would welcome any entertainment you might offer."

Cecily glanced at her sister, this time not bothering to conceal her scorn. But it was Cian she addressed.

"Even I need a change, sometimes," she explained, her eyelashes fluttering, "from needlework, from my spindle, from the company of women, even a woman as charming and pure as the Lady Melusine. I thought we might go hawking. I've a goshawk gifted me by Sir Mortimer I wished to try. He told me the bird is yet not well trained, but I wish your opinion."

"Surely, there are other men you could ask," Cian answered, an amused smile curving his long lips, and she shrugged prettily in reply.

"But there are no other men. They've all gone. I looked everywhere and then the stableboy told me you had just returned."

Bronwynn felt Cian stiffen and heard her own soft intake of breath. Hearing it, too, he grasped her wrist, his hard fingers squeezing an order for silence.

"The men are gone? All of them?" Cian asked, voice steady, concealing his fear. "The men-at-arms, all the knights, too?" And Cecily shrugged again.

"I've not seen any about," she told him. "Just the stable and the kitchen boys—the spit boy and such—the servants, the natives." Then she blushed, remembering Cian was Irish, but he brushed her confusion aside.

"Do you know where they went—and when?"

She shook her head, bewildered by his curiosity, but still eager to please.

" 'Twas early, before light. I went down with the Lady Melusine to see them off. 'Twas almost as though they thought themselves off to war, the way Piers demanded that she offer him a stirrup cup." She smiled with wry amusement at such whimsy, then her eyes widened in alarm. "There isn't, is there—a war about?"

"There is not," Cian assured her, and she lifted one round shoulder and dropped it, disappointed. A sudden, exciting vision of tourneys, of men in gleaming armor and of herself easing the dying of a handsome, faceless knight had captured her imagination. Then another thought struck her. "But Piers did ask after you, wanting to know where you were. The stable boy told him you had gone netting water fowl and he seemed to find comfort in the news—worried as he was of insulting you, I think."

A corner of Cian's mouth turned up in reluctant amusement at Cecily's ingenuousness, but when his gaze met Bronwynn's his eyes were worried, fearful. Then he turned back to Cecily.

"And where," he repeated. "Did anyone say aught of where?"

Standing on the step below him, Cecily tried to remem-

ber, a finger tip brushing the swell of a red lower lip. She
shook her head, then her face brightened.

"I think, mayhap, 'twas his intention to join you. Someone said something about a weir. Isn't that a net?"

"It is, so," Cian told her tenderly. "Or a dam."

He looked back at Bronwynn, his features grim. Realizing he still held the wrist he had taken to keep her silent,
he released it and examined the weals his grip had left.
He scowled and bit his lip, tenderly rubbing at the bright
marks on her white skin. Then he looked at her once
more, meeting grey eyes seeming to wish to heal every
wound they touched.

"Where are Curran and Cormac?" she asked, fear shaking her voice.

"There." His chin jerked up, indicating the wall walk
high up at the top of the narrow, spiraling stairway, and
he smiled ruefully. "They like it up there at the tower's top.
It gives them the illusion of freedom." Then he squared
his shoulders and his features grew hard with purpose.
"They—we—need to be gone from here. Will you tell
them? I daren't leave this one."

Bronwynn nodded and turning, picked up her skirts to
go and bring back Cian's men. But his voice, its edge
burnished steel on her name, halted her. When she looked
back, he was standing with one arm around her sister. His
other hand pressed the tip of his dirk to Cecily's throat.
His eyes, dark with regret, held Bronwynn's.

"I cannot trust you," he said.

A wry smile tipped the corners of Bronwynn's mouth.
Her gaze dropped to the sinewy hand gripping the dagger,
then returned to his.

"Can I trust you?" she asked, and read the answer in
his steady gaze. Turning once again, she picked up her
skirts to climb the steep stone steps to Curran and Cormac.

(7)

It was almost as though Curran and Cormac were expecting her and her news, Bronwynn thought. The soft glow of sunshine through mist seemed bright after the dark of the castle's twisting stair and, for a moment, the men were but two broad shadows against the glare behind them. They turned to face her, straightening away from the wall they leaned against, and she blinked, bringing their concerned features into focus. The hound at their feet growled, then, recognizing her, wagged his tail. Calling him to her, Bronwynn rubbed his jowls.

" 'Tis come," she stated, and a gratified smile curled Cormac's lip, while a worried scowl tucked Curran's.

"De Bermingham and his men?" Curran asked, stepping toward her. "Where are they?"

"At the Place of the Weir, at Laracorra."

"All of them?"

"All but the stable boys and the scullery lads."

"And himself? Where is he?"

"Below, in the stables, having horses saddled," Bronwynn answered, tilting her head back toward the stairs she had come up by. "My sister is with him," she added, nor was there anything else she needed to say.

Her gaze held Curran's, allowing him to read the fear in her eyes—and her trust. He nodded, answering her unspoken question, and drew her close for a quick, reassuring hug. When he released her, his huge freckled fist remained wrapped about the back of her neck, buried in her dark hair. With Cormac and the hound at his heels, Curran guided her before him down the stairs. They passed through Melusine's solar to be greeted by the angry glares and hissings of, "How dare she show her face after so insulting our lady!" But Melusine, remembering the strained look on Cecily's features as Cian O'Connor had guided her through scant moments before, waved them to silence.

She stood, her spindle falling to the rushes of the floor by the pointed toe of her slipper. Ignoring it, she took three steps, then halted, her ladies pressing close behind her, as her confounded gaze followed the curious foursome as they hurriedly descended the spiraling stairs to disappear from her view. Her browless forehead was creased as she attempted to puzzle out the meaning of such behavior. Whatever the Irish kerne's purpose, she decided, Bronwynn did not go with them willingly—the man's huge hand wrapped about the girl's neck told her that—nor had Cecily. Kicking aside the trailing hem of her surcoat, Melusine followed, her ladies behind her.

Bronwynn paused for a moment, framed in the entrance to the keep, Curran and Cormac with her. Gasping for breath from the wild dash down the steep, perilous stairs, she studied the scene before her. It appeared so normal, so peaceful.

Several scrawny chickens were pecking at a pile of horse droppings in the stable yard, vying with some pigeons for

whatever bits of strays oats it might contain. Their nervous
fluttering, the tossing of heads, shaking of wattles and
fluffing of feathers reminded Bronwynn of the ladies of
the castle and, for a brief second, a corner of her mouth
twitched in a smile. A sow was rooting through a heap of
offal, her piglets squealing at her side. Her sister sat on a
mounting block, hands in her lap, her flower face turned
up to the sun just breaking through the morning mists.
Cian stood behind her, one leg propped on the block,
one hand resting on her shoulder, as he watched two stable
boys saddling four horses. From the forge came the clang
of metal against metal and from the midden the stench
of rotting refuse, soon to worsen as the day drew warmer.
A girl walked from the dairy toting a wooden, iron banded
bucket, her back lopsided as she balanced against the
weight. Ignoring the milk slopping over her naked feet,
she shouted a greeting in Irish to two other maids entering
the laundry, their arms heaped full of dirty clothes. They
all seemed oblivious to the jerky, agitated motions of the
stable boys, to the fear on Cecily's face and the dirk held
to her throat. Yet, more than the entreaty in Cecily's eyes
or the urging of Curran and Cormac, it was the squawking
of Melusine's women behind her that drove Bronwynn on
down the stairs to the bawn and to Cian to exchange herself
for her sister.

Thrusting Cecily under Curran's knife point, Cian swung
Bronwynn up on his saddled horse, then mounted behind
her, the grasp he slipped about her waist curiously diffi-
dent, the touch of the dirk's point at the juncture of her
jaw and throat strangely gentle. Still, in a vain attempt to
reassure, Bronwynn's gaze never left the terrified visage of
her sister as Curran backed off with her to a horse of his
own. Jerking his chin toward the stable boys, he ordered
Cormac to help them. Sensing the alarm of their handlers,
the horses fought to break free, nostrils flaring, eyes ringed

with white. And time was growing short for, over the cooing
and flying feathers of startled pigeons rising from the walls
and above the chirping and clucking of Melusine's women
clustered in the vaulted entrance to the keep, could be
heard the grating lift of the outer porcullis.

Hooves thudded hollow on the bridge over the dry moat.
A fragment of crude laughter recalling the frantic, futile
scrabbling of an unarmed monk, a course bray recounting
the useless antics of a pregnant woman echoed from the
deep passageway through the thick outer wall.

"Druids, all of them, and better dead," someone
snorted. "Aye, all said, 'twas good work, God's work, we
did this day," another agreed, "with not a one of them
yet living." And Bronwynn felt Cian's tremor, felt his arm
tighten as he pressed his face into the joining of her neck
and shoulder.

Swinging chain mail whispered against the creaking
leather of scabbard and sword belt, of saddles and clinking
bridles as Cian grieved for the dead at Laracorra. Then,
his deep sigh warm on Bronwynn's cheek, he lifted his
head again, leaving behind a tear to cool her skin. His
eyes, dry suddenly and burning with hatred and fury, stared
at the arched entrance into the bawn of Carrick. Then de
Birmingham and his men spilled out into the yard in a
chaos of color—the greens and yellows and blues of cloaks
and tunics and pennants. And red—the red of blood dry-
ing to the hue of rust on horses and leather and armor.

His knights and men-at-arms pressing behind him, de
Birmingham drew his horse to a halt as his porcine eyes
blinked in disbelief and he waved his stepson to silence.
Rudulf turned then, to see what had captured Piers's attention and rage swept over him. For the first time that he
could remember, his stepfather had acknowledged him,
had praised him, had welcomed him at his side, all due
to his work at the Place of the Weir. Now, a petty Irish

chieftain and that slut, his own betrothed, threatened to take that away from him. Refusing to see the dirk at Bronwynn's throat, he wanted to weep his despair, to charge forward, sword swinging. But de Birmingham's upheld hand—and the silence—held him reined in. It seemed as though no one even breathed. Yet, from somewhere came the mewing of a scared kitten. Cecily, Bronwynn realized. Rudulf looked back at his stepfather to see the small eyes squinted in deliberation as he studied his Irish hostages and the women they held at knife point. At last, the huge man shifted and sat straighter in a creaking of saddle leather and those about him released their breaths in a collective sigh.

"And to what purpose, Cian O'Connor," de Birmingham wondered, "do you sit there with a knife at the throat of my ward—and the king's?"

"I find your hospitality lacking, Sassenach, and wish to leave." Cian's voice was calm in Bronwynn's ear, but his arm had tightened around her, crushing her ribs.

One of de Birmingham's scanty eyebrows quirked in feigned bewilderment, as he tried to remember what had been said as they rode into the ward, what had been said that morning of their plans for the day. He shifted his bulk once more, reaching down to adjust his balls before settling back into the saddle. The O'Connor whelp, he decided, did not necessarily know what had occurred that morning. Or so he would play it.

"You find our hospitality lacking?" he repeated. "Are you perhaps insulted because we failed to invite you to the hunt this morning? If 'tis so, let me assure you that we did ask after you, to be told by the stable boys that you had gone netting waterfowl."

"I do not think," Cian answered, and Bronwynn noted how white the knuckles were that gripped the bridle in front of her, and how the horse shifted, fighting the tight bit, "that either myself or my men would have found your quarry this day a suitable or challenging prey—not for an Irishman. Women and invalids and unarmed monks seldom are."

De Birmingham flushed with rage at the insult—and at Rudulf. How else could O'Connor have known of his intentions, if not through the drunken babbling of his stepson? The Place of the Weir, so long coveted, so recently, so newly his, seemed already to be slipping from his grasp. He gritted his teeth against the urge to level the O'Connor pup to the ground with a huge, mailed fist. But he could not, not while he held a knife at the throat of the king's ward. Nor would his wife be happy, either, if such a marriage prospect for her son was destroyed. Still, the O'Connor brat was not one he wished running free— and with a grudge. God knows, the Irish could hold a grudge! Things were too unsettled in the Irish Pale, the grip of England not quite as secure as it had once been. Not that they were being pushed back, he hastily assured himself, although he sometimes wished, as did King Edward, that the Norman holdings, while dense around Dublin, were not scattered haphazardly all across Ireland, with many surrounded by Irish clans. It just seemed as though it now required more men, more arms to hold what they had taken. And anything gained always seemed to be paid for with an English loss elsewhere. If he could put a finger on just when the tides of fortune had shifted that slight bit, it would have to have been with the coming of the mail-clad, heavily armed, battle-axe-bearing gallow-glass from the isles of Scotland to fight with the clans. The gallowglass were said to be descendents of the clans of Ulster who had emigrated there and married among the Norse—and the saints knew the Irish held to their clans.

No, he did not want this particular whelp running free, although he did not really think he would kill the Fitz

Hugh girl, now, or on the run. A dead hostage, after all, was useless. Still, although the Irish gleefully stabbed each other in the back regardless of clan affiliation, they adopted a strange umbrage when it was done by others. Then the Irish grew fiercely partisan toward their sept—and the O'Connor sept was a large one. Nor were the Irish, as sentimental as they were, likely to view the incident at Laracorra as the military expediency he, himself, saw it. And martyrs, ah, didn't the Irish love their martyrs? While he, himself, had wantonly, stupidly created enough of them at Laracorra to raise the whole treacherous race. And here, his dirk to the throat of one of Edward's favorites, was Cian of the Cursed Harp to put the whole intrigue to poetry and song.

"And what of your father's pledging of yourself to me as a hostage," Piers stalled, "and of your own oath on it? Do you not bring dishonor to not only yourself, but your sire, your sept?"

A rare smile lighted Cian's features, but it did not warm Piers's heart. There was too much rage and grief and contempt in it. Cian shook his head in disbelief and leaned around Bronwynn to stare at Piers, as though hoping his eyes would put a lie to what his ears had heard. But there was nothing in the Norman lord's face but a righteous earnestness and Cian sat back, his breath warm on Bronwynn's neck, his scent in her nose.

His features grim he asked, "You, who put through the deed at Laracorra—and your name to mean perfidy forever—dare accuse me of dishonor?"

"What else would you have it?" de Bermingham chuckled uneasily, his small eyes shifting around, seeking the support of his troops, vainly hoping some one of them had devised a plan to disarm the O'Connor lordling. Some had felt shame at their part in that dawn's deed when Cian had mentioned it. Others had shifted in guilty anger. But they were all held, now, in helpless enthrallment at the drama being played before them. There was, Piers saw, no help there. And he was ever aware of his wife standing amid her ladies observing his impotence, his humiliation. Scowling his frustration, unable yet to concede, he added, "After all, you sit with your knife at the throat of a helpless woman. 'Tis scarcely the act of a chivalrous man."

"Ah," Cian laughed grimly, "and when have you named the Irish chivalrous? Brutal, we are, so the Sassenach have always had it, base, uncivilized, ill mannered and vulgar. The only good said of us is that we can be uncommonly adept at the harp." He leaned forward again, this time to give emphasis to his words. "But there are scant few of us," he stated, the harsh whisper carrying to all corners of the ward, "whose gut would not be turned inside out to the very bowels of him at the thought of perpetrating the deed done this dawn at Laracorra." Straightening, he jerked his chin toward a man-at-arms creeping along the wallwalk high above them. "And have that one throw down his bow."

After a moment's hesitation, after Cian had tilted Bronwynn's head back to better display the long, white column of her neck, de Bermingham shouted the order. A slight smile at the corner of his mouth, Cian watched the spinning fall of the bow, then turned back to Piers.

" 'Tis time, I'm thinking, that I thank you for your hospitality and decline any further presumption upon it." His voice lost its easy brogue and hardened. "So, my Lords, if you will but make way for my men?"

De Bermingham's wide, short hands tightened on his bridle reins. His shifting weight caused his horse to dance, but he still did not move aside. His gaze jerked from Cian to Cian's men to the women standing on the stairs of the keep to the weaponless man-at-arms on the wallwalk, then back to settle somewhere over Cian's left shoulder.

"A dead hostage, true, my Lord de Bermingham," Cian addressed him, seeming to read his mind, "be no hostage at all, but I had not the thought, ever, of departing your hospitality with your blessing. If you are thinking that, mayhap, I've not the heart to slit this one's pretty white throat, let me assure you she is but another Sassenach to me, and what have I to lose? If you are considering gambling on this one's life and then facing your king's wrath with the tale that you had not truly believed I would take it, I will end that thought for you. To prove to you and all witnesses here, I will but have my man slit the throat of your lady wife's latest favorite first. Then, will you tell the Lord Edward you had not thought my threat earnest?"

A gasp of horror came from the women around the Lady of Carrick, but Piers did not unlock his gaze from Cian's to glance at them. He knew his wife and it had not come from her. She had but straightened taller yet in rapt attention. Cecily's mewing had ascended to a gasping squeal and Bronwynn fought down the urge to tell her to shut up, to tell Curran to slap her into silence. Then the Lord of Carrick looked away from Cian, his gaze settling nowhere as he flushed with rage. His tiny, thin-lipped mouth pursed tighter as he backed his horse up and waved his men away.

"They will drop their weapons," Cian ordered.

There was a discordant clanging as knives, swords and pikes fell to strike the earth and each other. "And he goes with us," Cian stated, his chin indicating Rudulf. "Won't I be needing someone to tell your men at Laracorra that they are more needed here attending to you? I doubt they'd believe me, myself having a wee bit of an interest in the place, so."

De Bermingham stared at Cian, his gaze malevolent. He had heard his wife's gasping "No, my Lord!", but still, at last, he nodded his stepson over to join Cian's men. There was little else he could do, not then, but, one day, he

silently vowed, the whole O'Connor clan would pay for
the disaffection his wife would surely show him.

Satisfied, Cian nodded to Cormac and Curran and
watched them pass cautiously through the narrow aisle of
thwarted men, Rudulf and Cecily with them. Only when
he heard their horses's thud on the moat bridge did he
follow with Bronwynn. His gaze, alert to treachery, never
left de Bermingham's as he backed his horse into the
dark passage through Carrick's walls. Then he whirled his
mount, heels slamming into its sides as it bolted out from
the darkness. Its hooves's pounding over the draw bridge
and down the curving road from the castle echoed in
Bronwynn's ears. A shout came from somewhere, then a
thud and a clashing of brass strings she felt through her
bones, through Cian's. She heard his grunt and he slowed
his horse, releasing her to reach one hand back behind
him. Then he grinned down into Bronwynn's horror-struck
features, his mouth quirking at the corners.

"My harp. Didn't the arrow hit the soundbox, so, and
scant damage done, I'm thinking. Fine archery, that,
though," he conceded graciously, cocking an eye at a small
figure high on the castle's parapet. He waved and the
archer lifted a hand in reply, then he heeled his horse
into a trot on down the hill to where Curran and Cormac
waited for them.

"Fine shooting, that," Curran repeated, nodding at the
shaft protruding from the harp slung across Cian's back.

"Wasn't I telling the Lady Fitzhugh so but a moment
past," Cian replied, then his grin turned to a scowl as he
surveyed Cecily. She sat in front of Cormac, her breath
coming in whimpers of fear as she struggled feebly to
escape the circle of his arms. Her tiny hands tugged ineffec-
tually at Cormac's thick wrist even as she leaned beseech-
ingly toward her sister. Tears flowed down cheeks the hue
of apple blossoms, but her eyes were clear and blue as she

slid a quick, appraising glance at Cian from under long, sweeping eyelashes. Heaving a sigh that trembled her high, round breasts, she forced herself under control. Her sobs became gulps, then diminishing hiccups. Biting her swollen lip, she pressed her hand to her mouth and gazed wide eyed at Cian from over tiny fingers. Her lashes dropped once, only to flutter up again beguilingly.

"My Lord," she whispered, voice shaking, "where are you taking me—us?"

Cian's glance dropped over her, and his smile was almost pitying.

"You, we are leaving here."

Cecily blinked, then her plucked brow furrowed in dismay. Her terror had been genuine when Curran had held a knife to her throat and, no matter how she displayed her charms, Cian O'Connor had always seemed more amused than seduced, making his company uncomfortable. But, now, she was to be left behind, with her sister to go. It did not matter to what. Cecily resented it. She slid a glance at Bronwynn, then looked at Cian once more.

"But my sister needs me," she whispered pitifully, "and I her. We've scarcely been ever parted afore and you surely, as a chivalrous gentleman, will not force us so now, and under such perilous circumstances."

Bronwynn turned to Cian, her eyes beseeching, but he shook his head before she could even speak.

"Isn't she safer here, so?" he asked, his gaze hard on Cecily's pleading features. "And scant time it's been that she's spent with you these last days, no matter her protests. 'Tis better to leave her with Melusine—and herself preferring her company, I'm thinking." Cecily opened her mouth to protest the accusation's injustice, but closed it again at Cian's single shake of his head. "She stays here," he repeated. " 'Tis safer so for her, for surely I'll kill the artful, weepy bitch myself should she go with us."

With that, he urged his horse into a trot, Cormac and
Rudulf following, leaving Curran to grin his pleasure from
beneath the thick thatch of his mustache. Ignoring Cecily's
pleas, her sobs and her imploring glances at her sister, he
peeled her fingers from around his wrist and straightened
them, one by one, from the leather of his jerkin. Then,
holding her out from him by her armpits, he dropped her
without ceremony into the middle of the roadway and
rode after Cian. Struggling to turn in the steel grip of her
captor's forearm, Bronwynn peered around him to see
Cecily sitting indignantly in the dust, features outraged.
The furious words she flung at the retreating party caused
Cian to shake his head in amazement.

"Indeed," he stated into the fragrance of Bronwynn's
dark hair, "and aren't I amazed that one has lived as long
as she has. Sure, and haven't you wanted to kill her yourself
from time to time?"

Bronwynn stared up into Cian's amused features. It had
been for something such as this she had yearned but a few
days before, she reminded herself. Hadn't she wanted to
be gone from Carrick, away from the plots and plans and
ambitions of others—and even the responsibility of her
sister? Hadn't she wanted the wind on her skin, the mist
on her tongue? She was to have it, now, and, perversely,
it was being presented to her as a hostage to the brooding
man who had so haunted her with his grieving eyes, his
mocking smile. Almost as though he read her mind, Cian
grinned down at her, but his smile slowly faded as his eyes
held hers, capturing her, claiming her, commanding her,
yet his gaze, too, was held against his will. She saw a promise
within his eyes of passion, of a raging, cleaving, giving and
taking, and she knew he read the same in hers. Lightly,
his gaze touched each feature of her face, to be followed
by his fingertips tracing the line of her jaw from the corner
of her eye to the fullness of her lower lip and down to the

blue vein beating in her throat, and it leaped to a quicker pace. A tendril of her hair was blown across Cian's lips, rousing him, and he brushed it away to fling his laugh of triumph like a gauntlet to the sky. His face, turning to the west, contained all the joy and exaltation of a hawk set free into the wind and he urged his horse forward, the huge hound settling into a easy lope next to them.

(8)

Always, Bronwynn knew, she would remember that look of exaltation on Cian's features as they rode away from Carrick. It had been the expression of a man released from as much a prison of the soul as of the body. And never, she vowed to herself, would she forgive Piers de Bermingham for engraving, with the deed done at Laracorra, the stark lines of hatred and contempt, desolation and cold rage upon his face once more. She had sensed his elation, his passion ebb slowly away from him as they drew closer to the Place of the Weir, to be replaced with apprehension and sorrow as he contemplated what they would find there. She felt him draw away from her, as surely as if he had drawn an impermeable wall of hatred between them, each stone the thought of another woman, a memory of another crime of her people against his.

It seemed, by the time they rode down the river valley to Laracorra, that only a man of no feelings, no soul rode behind her, that the arm encircling her felt nothing. Nor was it with emotion that Cian drew his horse in to survey

the place that had been Laracorra. He studied the twelve
men-at-arms, the two sergeants, and the single knight who
held the place, then nodded Rudulf de Broc on to them.
Dispassionately, he watched as the Norman lordling rode
across the meadow to greet his stepfather's men, to speak
with them, gesturing toward Bronwynn. At last they
mounted and rode off, Rudulf with them and casting an
impotent, vengeful glare over his shoulder. Cian had
waited a long moment then, his mouth grim as he gazed
seemingly at nothing, and his men silent with him. Only
the huge hound whined at the smell of death, while the
horses chomped the grass at their feet. Finally, rousing
himself, seemingly remembering something needing to be
done, Cian lifted her from in front of him, his hands
curiously gentle as he lowered her to stand on the thick
sod of the hill above Laracorra.

"Stay," he ordered, his gaze never leaving the despair
before him, then he rode on toward the Place of the Weir,
his horse belly deep in the grass of the meadow.

And she stayed, knowing he would come to her in time.
Arms clutched about herself, skirts heavy with the damp
of the tall grasses, leather slippers soaked from the wet
sod, Bronwynn looked around—and tried not to see.

The gentle hills of the Boyne valley were veiled green
and lavender with a late afternoon haze. The river itself
was scarcely more than a stream here where a brook joined
it in a trilling ripple, where willow trees dipped their leaves
into its gently swirling waters and trout rose to bubble at
a surface reflecting the hues of the sky. But, further up
the smaller stream, the weir of woven reeds and rushes
had been smashed to fragments by swords and battle-axes,
the fish it had enclosed dead in mud where a pond had
once been. Nearer, the hospital had been set afire with
the other buildings supporting it, the dairy, the chapel, the
laundry, the kitchens. The fires smoldered still in hidden

corners despite the earlier rains which had refused to let it
run full havoc. Furs and blankets were strewn with random,
wanton mindlessness across the lush meadows, their reds
and blues and greens undistinguishable at that distance
from the bodies scattered among them.

Shoulders hunched, hugging herself, rocking herself for
the poor comfort of it, Bronwynn watched. She was cold
and dusk had fallen, yet still the men worked, Cian among
them, by torchlight, now, gathering the dead, wrapping
them in blankets, in cloaks, in rags, to place them, one by
one, in a long line in the tiny cemetery. Then they took
up shovels to begin the digging of the graves. And the
people came to identify their dead, to keen them, as
though word of the misdeed had been sighed to them by
something unseen in the sloughing wind, the slanting
mists. From where, Bronwynn could not guess. The coun-
tryside was so desolate. It was as though they had emerged
from beneath the earth itself, as the Daoin Sidhe were said
to do. And she shuddered. Lifting her eyes, she watched
the stars emerge with the falling of night, and the clouds
as they floated dark over the moon. It was better than
watching the men.

She could go, she knew, so easily. She had but to snare
one of the horses grazing the damp grass of the meadow,
to mount and be gone back to Carrick. But that would
mean back to the man who had done this deed and that
she hadn't the stomach for. Nor did she have, she thought,
the will to do anything but wait for what Cian O'Connor
would bring her.

Curran had come up to her once, bringing her a hunk
of bread which had survived the burning kitchens and a
roasted trout dead in the mud of the weir pond. He had
spoken little, his gaze distracted and grieving, but seventeen had died there, he told her, five monks, three nuns,
two servants and seven patients. That was not so very many,

Bronwynn told herself when he left to return to his grim task, not compared to the thousands and thousands who had been slaughtered during the Crusades, the thousands who had died in Wales—her own people—at the hand of Edward, and among the Albigenses in France, killed by the troops of Simon de Montfort. The last, though, had been heretics, Bronwynn remembered. Still, she crossed herself and breathed a prayer for the souls of the those hundreds and hundreds of people burned to death at the stake, and knew that even one death at Laracorra would have been too many. De Bermingham had defiled a place of healing in the name of petty avarice and never would he be forgiven it.

At last, with the moon behind him, Cian came to her, leading two horses. The weight of his mantle seemed to pull him down, adding but another burden to his broad shoulders. Following his dragging steps was a glistening path through the dew on the tall, damp grasses. Over his shoulder, Bronwynn could see the torches flicker like fire-flies and his features were in shadow. He halted before her, seemed to loom over her and, whatever his intentions, she knew, they were as inevitable as fate.

He stared down at her while the moon seemed to circle on above them, his features expressionless and stark. Unaware she, was weeping herself, Bronwynn lifted a hand to touch the tears that cast a sheen down the lean slopes of his cheeks. Closing his eyes, Cian turned to press his mouth into her palm, his breath hot on her cold flesh with his sob. They stood that way a long moment, swaying in a silent mourning, until he took her face between his hands, cradling it like a chalice offering the mead of forget-fulness. He traced her face with his fingertips, with the hard-calloused palms of his hands, soothing away the tears she had not known she cried. He held her gaze with his for an eternity, before lowering his mouth to hers, his lips so soft she wondered where his breath ended and the kiss began, where the sway of her surcoat against the length of her legs became the heat of his thighs scarcely touching hers. It felt, as he drew her breath from her mouth into his own, as though he sought to taste her very soul in the sigh she released with all of her resistance. Then his mouth contorted into a grimace of rage and pain, bruising hers. He sobbed his fury at de Bermingham's inhumanity, his grief for the people of Laracorra, as his fingers wove painfully into her hair, as he jerked her toward him, twisting her lips to meet more fully with his.

His mouth consumed hers, his teeth pressing her lips against her own, cutting them. His tongue sought hers, twining with it, pleading for solace, for surcease, for oblivion, if for this moment only. And Bronwynn sought to give it in her need to ease his pain, his grief. Her mouth opened under his, to his, her fingers weaving with those cradling her face, clutching at her hair. She sank with him as his knee pressed between hers, as his hand cupped her rounded bottom, tipping her from her feet, easing her to her back into a hollow in the tall, damp grass of the hillside.

She knew he yanked at her skirts, drawing them up, exposing her legs, her thighs, her belly to the cold of the night air, yet she could only stifle a sob of fear, of desire. His fingers sought her, found her damp with heat and need, as his mouth traced a path of bruises under her jaw and down her throat, only to be thwarted in its quest by the neckline of her undertunic. Undaunted, his lips returned to take hers once more, demanding, begging.

She twisted one hand into the hair at the nape of his neck, as the other found the smooth skin at the small of his back, pressing him down as he shifted to settle onto her, into her. All fear gone, she tilted to accept him, to take him, felt the length of him press against her, into her.

Then she gasped from the pain of it, stifling her sob into the heat at the juncture of his neck and shoulder.

But Cian had heard and he grew still and rigid above her, fighting for control. He remained so, his jaw clenched, his gaze holding hers in a silent question. Bronwynn looked away for a long moment, staring over his shoulder at a gibbous moon veiled by shifting clouds, at the twinkling of torches in the meadow not so very far from them. Then she met his eyes again, her answer a smile that but quirked the corners of her mouth, a fingertip that lightly traced the line of his long upper lip. Shaking his head once, he gave up the struggle.

"Ah, forgive me, a stór—my darling," he moaned, his mouth seeking the softness of her throat beneath her jaw. Then he took her more fully, and Bronwynn lifted her body to meet him, absorb him. She closed her eyes, shutting away the moon and the flickering torches, to lose herself and the memory of the deed done at Laracorra in a consummation of lust and heat, death and rebirth.

Bronwynn roused to the feel of Cian's hand gently brushing a tendril of hair from her cheek. At the slough of her sigh, as though it was a signal he had awaited, he lifted himself to lie next to her. His battle scarred hands awkward, he smoothed the skirts of her surcoat back down over her legs and tugged his kilt to once more cover himself. Nor did he speak as he wrapped his cloak about them to protect her from the light misting. Instead, he drew her to him, cradling her head in the joining of chest and shoulder, the beat of his heart in her ear. He held her so, listening to the horses chomp the grass near them, hearing the suppressed murmur of conversation from the meadow of Laracorra—and the wail of a woman's voice lifted in keening. The fragrance of Bronwynn's hair was in his nose, a fragrance of lavender and lilies. And he felt the faint shudder of her body in silent weeping.

"Whisht," he whispered. "Ah, whisht, a stór," but she shook her head. Raising herself to her elbows over him, she stared down at Cian. "Why?" she demanded, a small fist slamming into his chest. "Why?"

Unflinching from the blow, taking her fist in his long, slim hand, he shook his head in impotent apology. There was nothing he could say to excuse the taking of her maidenhead and, if what he had done was not rape, it was too close to it for his liking, no matter the joy he had felt in the taking of her or the surcease from grief and rage she had given him, if only for a short while. Her features, now, were but a dark silhouette against the sky, but still he reached up to touch her jaw, her high cheek-bones, to take her tumbling hair in his hands, to feel the silken weight of it, his hands drawn by the remembered feel of them, of her.

" 'Tis sorry I am," he whispered at last to the night beyond her. "I owe you recompense. The Brehons can tell us what—how much—but 'tis for you to say what shame price you would have of me, nor will I deny it."

Confused, Bronwynn stared down at him as she wiped at her wet cheeks with the back of each hand. Then she realized he was speaking of her lost maidenhood and she shook her head, denying his apology and wondering at the innocence of it. But was it any wonder, a part of her mind mocked, even as her throat ached at the thought of Cian O'Connor so hurt, that Fenella McKenna had found the man such an easy mark? Were all men so conceited as to think that a woman would weep over her lost virginity while the dead lay strewn across the meadow of Laracorra? Or did he think her so shallow? Then she remembered the lessons taught him by Fenella McKenna. Still, she was not Fenella, and anger tightened her jaw and drove her words from her.

"Do you think yourself so great a lover," she demanded, "that I give your taking of me any more concern than the grass stains now on my surcoat? And if that poor, piddling bit of naught below your belly that you gave me is what lovemaking is about, I can well do without it the rest of my life." Then her voice broke on a sob. "And if never knowing such joy again would bring back the people who died here, I would gladly vow it so."

Cian drew her back down to him, holding her struggling form until she quieted against him. He could not help but cringe at the barbed words she had aimed at the most vulnerable part of his anatomy. Then he grinned, wondering how a woman so innocent could know to level such a low blow. He remembered, too, her imploring fingers on his back, her whispered pleas for fulfillment—and the shuddering of her body as she achieved it. Nor had it been the feigned moaning of Fenella. If ever, he thought, there was a woman built for lovemaking, it was the one he now held. If ever a passionate response denied a waspish tongue, it had been the tilting of her hips beneath his thrusts. Somehow, in her own fulfillment, she had seemed to draw his very soul from him, had given, in her own need, even in her innocence, more to him than had any woman before her—and had freely taken what he had offered her. And Cian felt an inexplicable pang at the knowledge that he would never truly have her.

"Ah, Sassenach" he chuckled, "aren't men the great lackwits, so, all of us, and ever thinking of their foolish pride and rampant pizzles?"

It was almost as though he had read her mind, Bronwynn thought. She drew back, trying to see him in the dim light, but there was only the faint glint of white teeth, of his gold earring. And he had laughed at himself, at his own strutting male pompousness.

"All but Curran," she stated, her voice teasingly solemn.

"Ah, all but Curran," he agreed, equally as grave and falling easily into the game. "Isn't he the example all women toss up to their husbands and lovers, so, and the very epitome of all they wish us to be?" Then, growing serious, he captured her fingers to twine his own with hers, as he studied her dim features over their clasped hands. "And didn't I," he said, "do you wrong, then—and a greater one it was than bedding you—in thinking yourself more concerned with the harm I did you than in the deed done here this day by de Bermingham? For that, I ask your forgiveness."

Touching the roughness of his beard-stubbled jaw, the softness of his lower lip with a gentle forefinger, she nodded her absolution. Then she shook her head and her voice grew rough with grief once more, as she asked, again, "But why? Why? How could such great harm be done from aught more than petty avarice? How?"

Sighing, Cian drew her back into his arms and shook his own head in turn.

"Ah, a stór, haven't you the right of it when calling the deed but one of avarice? Did you not warn me of his lust for this place that day on the parapet—and myself helpless to do aught but wait until he sought to take it? And how he intended to use it, how he would have held it, itself being so far from Carrick, I do not know. I can only tell you the how of the deed, and that is that men will sometimes be overwhelmed by a fury. Somehow, too, the less justified the deed, the weaker their prey, the greater their bloodlust. 'Tis as though they punish the victim for the blood on their own hands, for the guilt on their own souls, and must strike them down, and down again, as though 'twas the victim who brought the perpetrator to the deed. But 'twas avarice," he sighed into her hair, "and well they know it, and so needs must strike the harder."

But she was weeping softly and, knowing there were no true words of comfort he could offer, Cian held her, soothing her, while he gazed with blank eyes across the meadow. The torches still floating there offered no answers to the questions troubling his own mind. A stone pressed into his hip, but the nest of cloaks in the thick sod was comfortable enough. As comfortable, he told himself, as many a bed he had made on one campaign or another or on a raid or a rising—and few enough of those had offered him a woman to keep from the fog and dew. But it was the woman, among other things, who troubled his mind, and his mouth quirked into a wry smile before he joined Bronwynn in an uneasy sleep. Wasn't that always the way of it, he thought—that no good came without the bad close before it?

(9)

It was a snuffling, a whiffling and a wet tongue slathering over his ear that woke Cian. He tried to shrug it off and it came, this time, with an anxious whine. Reluctantly opening one eye, he stared up into Booka's grinning snout and scowled his own delight. Then memories of the day before flooded over him. He lay motionless for a long moment, absorbing the pain, the senseless guilt he felt. Yet, he told himself, there was aught he could do. It was done and over, the dead buried. Nothing could bring them back and, now, there was, too, the woman to consider. Still, he delayed facing her.

"Ah, think yourself clever, do you?" Cian asked the dog, raising himself to his elbow and shoving the animal away. "So, and you're not by half when here you are and could you not be, instead, off after a fat hare for the breakfast of myself and this fine lady, then?"

His grin disappearing, the dog wrinkled his shaggy brows and ducked his head contritely. It was Bronwynn who reached up to rub behind Booka's small ears and tug at the wiry beard of his lower jaw. His tongue lolled out again in pleasure and his tail began to thump.

"You cannot be kind to this great, galumphing galoot or you will have him in bed with us—such a bed as it is," Cian warned and, as though to confirm the threat, Booka pressed forward, only to be pushed away by his master. Yielding, the dog sat on his haunches to observe them with wise eyes, and Cian looked at last at Bronwynn. No smile of greeting curved his mouth as he regarded her, his gaze touching each feature of her face. His eyes were intent, as though searching for an answer to a question she did not know, a could not guess at. She gazed back at him, her own visage guarded, as she wondered what to say, what to do. There was so much, she suddenly knew, to be won or lost by the smallest word, the slightest action, and so much of it she had not even known, until the night before, that she wanted. How, she wondered, and when, had a man so morose, so distrustful of women, so rude and arrogant become so important to her? When had she learned to value that rare smile and rarer laugh and to want to elicit them herself?

Or was it the freedom he, himself, and his people, sought that enchanted her, that lured her to follow after him in the hopes of gaining it, herself, through him? And what did that make of her? Or was the mere act of bedding a man—and act, truly, of absurd grapplings and even more ridiculous positioning, of undignified gasps and moanings—was it so seductive? Was it that act, alone, that created the need to touch him, to feel the smoothness of his flesh beneath her palm, and more, to bear his weight again upon her breast, to take him within her, to lose herself beneath him? Was it so strong that she now wished to follow him forever to but gaze at the breadth of his shoulders, the narrowness of his hips, and the vulnerable sweetness at the back of his neck? If so, it was no wonder the clergy named it evil, forbidden. Why was there so much she wanted to know about him, to ask him? And there was that dark grieving in the depths of his eyes, that she had always wanted to heal. She found herself babbling beneath his gaze and hated herself for it, but could not stop.

"I do not know what to do, what to say in a situation such as this one," she burbled, "waking up here, like this. There must be rules, some point of etiquette dealing with just such a circumstance, surely, but, if so, I do not know what 'twould be." She bit her lip, then added on a note of humor, "But Melusine would, I'm certain."

Cian covered her mouth with the palm, shook his head then gently smoothed back her sleep tumbled hair.

"Wouldn't she so, but I'm doubting she's woman enough—or warm enough—to find herself in such a plight. Cold as a witch's heart, is that one. Nor would I be the man to take her, so. Haven't I a higher regard for my balls?" Then the laughter fled his eyes and he regarded her intently once more. " 'Twas on my mind, last night," he said at last, his words seeming to be dragged from him by a will not his own, "to take you to a convent near An Uaimh. You would be safe there and 'twould be less hardship on you than following my heels. Wouldn't we be on the run from booley house to the monks and from one O'Connor to the next, sleeping on the ground, ofttimes, wrapped in aught but my mantle and kilt, and no place safe for us, so? Won't de Bermingham be searching for you, for us, throughout all Leinster? And in the North there are the O'Reillys, the O'Neills, the MacCartans, and O'Donnells, in the West the O' Farrells, the O'Roarkes and the O'Briens, and none of them, mosttimes, a friend of the O'Connors, nor of each other, truth told. Haven't we fought against them in the feudings and on the raidings as oft as next to them and ourselves, mosttimes, glorious?" His grin was boyish in its enthusiasm and pride, then it became rueful. "Now," he added, "I'm wishing we hadn't alienated them, so, and scant shelter they might offer us and that not always to be trusted. 'Twould depend on the length of their memories, the size of the reward offered for you, the price on my own head, and who is friend or foe this season." He shrugged wryly. "So, I'm thinking, yet the while, that 'twould be best for you in the convent. Still, isn't the final decision yours?"

His gaze held hers, giving nothing, asking nothing. But there had been a choice offered her, no matter his grim warning. Nor would he tell her what he truly wanted. To do so would be too close to entreaty, and to be refused too close to rejection. Reaching up, she rubbed her palm over the stubble of beard on his cheek.

"What," she asked idly, "is a booley house?"

He took her hand to enfold it in his, his lips grazing the knuckles as he studied her over it.

" 'Tis but a hut, a shelter at the summer pasturings in the mountains mosttimes. It can be but a lean to, or built of stone or mud and wattle."

"Has it heavy doors and bars on the windows?"

Eyebrows crooked at the strange question, Cian shook his head, and Bronwynn smiled.

"I've scant love of small windows and thick walls and I will find myself within a convent soon enough, should I refuse to wed Rudulf and Edward has his way with me." She bit her lip, eyes lowered as she considered the consequences when she went back to her own people—and she would one day have to go back. But everything had a price—that she had learned young—and freedom seemed the costliest of all. And she could but say she had been a hostage, with no word of where she went and with whom. Who could refute that? She looked up to meet Cian's shuttered gaze.

"Would you have me go with you, Cian O'Connor?",
she asked, and his gaze fell away.

" 'Twill be difficult, ofttimes," he repeated, needing her
to be certain, but she only nodded.

"I know," she told him. "We will be on the run from
booley house to the monks. We will sleep on the ground,
wrapped in your kilt and mantle. Still, won't it be better
than a convent," she teased, "if you are not always glooming about."

One corner of Cian's mouth quirked down into a frown,
but his eyes glowed amber at her over their locked hands,
as he demanded, "Was it Curran told you I am always
glooming? A great lie it is. Don't I remember a day three
years ago when I was almost jovial?" Then his eyes grew
intent on her features as he gently grazed her full lower
lip with the ball of his thumb. The touch was followed by
the warmth of his breath, the velvet of his mouth over
hers. The soft kiss brought a sudden twist of need deep
within Bronwynn's belly and she gave a faint gasp of surprise, then Cian was but gazing down at her again.

"Hadn't we best be off, then?" he asked, but his hazel
eyes gleamed, as though he was well aware of the sensation
he had provoked in her. Clambering up, Cian lifted Bronwynn to her feet, then he paused and looked about.

The sky seemed more to weep than rain, its face so close
to the earth Cian thought he could but reach up to touch
it. It fell in veils, wisping through the reeds along the river
and obscuring all about them but the devastation that was
Laracorra. The horses he had brought with him the night
before, grazing a short distance away, were dark with the
damp. The people stirring about the fires were misted with
it. Even as he stood there, hands on hips, Bronwynn could
see Cian's mood lower to match the day, could feel him
once again to close himself away. Nor was there, she knew,
a way to draw him back. A weight settled in the pit of her

belly as she watched him shake out his mantle, then collect
the horses, leaving her to brush herself down and run her
fingers through her tumbled hair. But when he returned
there was an attempt at a grin about his mouth as he
looked her up and down.

"Good wool, that," he commented, lifting his chin at
her surcoat, " 'tis scarcely wrinkled at all. Those few that
there are will fall out soon enough and who is to know,
then, that you spent the night acuddling on the grass, so?"
His grin grew sad at the sight of her flush and he turned
away. "If you go with me on the hiding," he told her, voice
suddenly harsh, "there will be none who will not think—
and say—that you share my bed, even if you don't, from
your Lord Edward himself to the rudest shepherd we
should chance upon. You can face them with pride or you
can bob and truckle in embarrassment, but 'twas your
square chin and direct gaze, Sassenach, that drew *my* eye
to you the first, then back again, no matter that I did not
choose it so."

Lifting her gaze, she met his, and raised her chin. His
mouth lifted into a wry grin of acknowledgement and he
took her hand to study its palm a brief moment. Then,
turning, he led her down the meadow to his men. Each
step brought them closer to the desecrated sanctuary that
had been Laracorra, to the seventeen graves lined like raw
cicatrix in the cemetery. Somewhere, too, on the short
walk toward the odor of damp, burned wood, of the dank
mud of the drained fish pond he had released her hand.

They stared at her, the people, from underneath sodden
hoods of cowhide or buckskin, a resentment in the eyes
that dully studied the foreign cut to her clothing, the fine
linen of her undertunic, the heavy cloth of her mantle.
She stood in leather shoes cut up about the ankle, while
the mud curled between the naked toes of many of them.
They shivered from hostility and from the damp despite

their shaggy bratts of striped wool or sheepskins. She was the stranger, the Sassenach, and it had been her people who had done this deed. She was the hostage and that role they understood, yet, no matter that the wool of her surcoat had not held its wrinkles, there were still grass stains down its length and the dark-rust marks of her lost maidenhood spotted on the skirt. In lying in the grass with Cian, she had but taken one more thing from them. Even the stout priest, his features more given to merriment than grief of censure, but dipped his tonsured head to her, his gaze sidling away in discomfort.

A woman, her features, grief-smeared, offered her a baked trout on a makeshift platter, but would not lift her gaze. A man stood and offered her the stool he sat upon, its seat half charred, but he turned his back to her when he squatted down to finish his own scant meal.

Only Curran had paused to look her in the face, his eyes searching hers. Finding, at last, what it was he sought, he only nodded and turned away, seemingly satisfied. Then, he looked at his lordling's grim features and a sense of humor he could not suppress even in the most grievous of times laid claim to his tongue before his mind could halt it.

"You'll be keeping the puppy, then?" he asked innocently enough.

"The puppy?" Cian wondered, but Bronwynn's chin had lifted and her eyes widened in shocked surprise as she remembered that Cian had promised a puppy to the first man to put her on her back. Glancing at Cormac, she saw him blink, then bite his lip to contain a chuckle. "What puppy?" Cian asked.

"The pick of Booka's next litter that you wagered the one or the other of us one night at Carrick while at our trenchers. Have you forgotten and are you thinking, then, too, that you might keep a pair of them?"

And Cormac could no longer restrain a howl of glee that drew the disapproving frowns of the people around them. His eyebrows meshed, Cian scowled and turned narrowed eyes to Bronwynn, his tongue forming an apology. But she was gazing back at him with calm features and eyes dancing with laughter, and he felt his own mouth quirk in response. Then his gaze grew serious.

" 'Twould be a sorrow in me," he told Bronwynn, "should I not be allowed to keep all of them."

Then he returned to his own meal, leaving her with a throat closing over her own grief, for never, she knew, would she be allowed to stay, not in Ireland, not with Cian O'Connor.

It was Curran, too, who, when their horses were saddled, when she and Cian were mounted, reached to grasp Cian's bridle. Protecting his thick hedge of eyebrows from the drizzle with a wide, freckled hand, he looked up at his chieftain and asked him the question Bronwynn would not.

"Do you go to your father, then?"

As though resenting the query, Cian scowled down at Curran, while Bronwynn looked from one to the other, a puzzled line between her brows.

"For a day or two," he answered, voice cold.

"You're thinking 'twill be safe, so," Curran wondered, "and de Bermingham with his nose bent and araging all about?"

"De Bermingham dulled his men full well on this venture, here, and he'll not sharpen them soon for another, certainly not to go calling on Calvach O'Connor." He paused and, briefly, a shadow of anger and grief crossed Cian's features, then he shrugged it off with a bitter grimace. "I've not seen my father for a year and more and won't the man want word of this deed, so, brought to him by the son he's not set eyes on so long? Won't he prepare

the fatted calf, then, and himself so happy to see me—
and the invisible dead of Laracorra at my back? And what
harm can the Sassenach do me and herself being with
me?"

Not looking at her, Cian jerked his chin toward Bronwynn and Curran nodded, stepping back.

"Tell my Sine, then, that I'll be there in a day or two—
when all is done here."

He slapped Cian's horse on its haunch and stood back
to watch them gallop away from the Place of the Weir. Nor
did he rouse himself from his dark reverie for a long while
to return to his grim task.

The drizzle of the day led them west out of the valley
of Laracorra. It beaded on the eyelashes and whiskers of
their horses, tickling them until they shook their heads,
scattering a fine spray over their riders. It soaked through
leather and wool to pucker fingertips and numb toes, to
bedraggle down to the ends of hair and to drip from the
tip of the nose. There was little to see but sheets of mist
and if there was a road beneath them, Bronwynn would
not guess it. In front was the back of Cian's sagging mantle
and the shifting haunches of his horse. Once, an errant
breeze caught the translucent curtains of rain, drawing
them back to reveal their own silver reflection in a peat
stained lake. Amid tall, dark reeds stood a single snow
white egret. Bronwynn heard, for a short while, the calling
of shepherds and the bleating of their sheep, then the
sound was muffled by the wet, but they were never seen.
A partridge flew up from under her horse's hooves, startling it, then the animal sunk back into its dispirited plod-
ding.

Glancing up, seeking the sun, Bronwynn tried to put a
time to the day, but there was only more grey overhead,

and she stretched, easing a kink in her back. Wiping the mist from her eyes, she drew her hood closer and thought to ask Cian where they were, how long they had to ride. There was something in the set of his back, though, that disallowed questions and she settled down into the saddle again, letting the motion of the horse lull her into lethargy.

So it was that she came alert with a start at the sight of three huge, barbaric strangers emerging from the fog in front of her. One moment there was nothing but the back of Cian and his horse, then, standing as though in wait for them, leaning on their immense spears and battle-axes, were the wild looking men. Bronwynn gave a gulp of surprise and her heels slammed into her horse's sides even as she yanked at the bridle reins. Her mount fought her and she clung to his mane, trying to stay astride. He settled into a crouch, mud splattered up to his hocks, and Bronwynn soothed him, easing his trembling, even as her own eyes were wide on the men speaking with Cian.

But, involved in earnest conversation, they ignored her, nor was she close enough to hear what they spoke about. Wishing she could ease her mount nearer to eavesdrop, she studied the strangers. They were huge by even Curran's standards. Two were blond, the third had hair the color of a carrot and all three sported mustaches drooping down past their chins. Tattoos of mythical beasts and strange plants and symbols twined and climbed up their massive arms to disappear beneath the sleeves of heavy shirts of mail. Shaggy fur hung from their shoulders and was wrapped about their feet and calves. Heavy helmets protected their heads and wide metal bands were wrapped about thick biceps and forearms. They appeared, she thought, just as she had always envisioned Vikings. Then they were swinging their weapons over their shoulders and bidding Cian farewell.

"Your sire," the red haired one said, "will be pleased to see you, aught more."

His narrowed gaze held to Cian's hard set features before he followed his men as they filed by Bronwynn. Like them, he but glanced at her, then, before he was past, a corner of his mouth twitched in humor and one bright blue eye drooped in a quick wink. She stared after them as they disappeared into the mist, then turned to Cian.

"Who were they?"

Cian nudged his horse on.

"Gallowglass," he told her over his shoulder. "The big one is McClachan Dearg."

"Why," she asked, "did he say your father would be pleased to see you? Why would he not be?"

A humorless laugh issued from Cian.

"Can McClachan Dearg not easily tell you so?" he commented. "He did not allow the deed at Laracorra."

"Nor did you!" Bronwynn insisted, urging her horse next to Cian's, but she spoke to his set profile. "There was aught you could do, held as you were at Carrick. And who would have known de Bermingham would create such slaughter? Not yourself and certainly no Christian man, for what Christian man would do such a deed?"

Cian shook his head at such innocence, his face set even more harshly. But when he spoke there was a denigrating humor to his words.

"I had not thought you to be such a poor judge of human nature or such a delinquent student of history." His tone became harsh, angry. "As for my responsibility for Laracorra, wasn't I the great martyr, so, the magnanimous hero—and myself groveling in selfpity that a woman did so scorn me, so make a jeeringstock of me that I was seeking someone else to jibe and mock me—another foot to truckle beneath? Didn't I find it, too, and more, at Carrick? Hadn't I given myself as hostage to de Bermingham against

my father's wishes, in place of my cousins? And all out of
my own vanity, my hurt pride? Don't the Sassenach regard
the Irish with aught but contempt, even as their women
seek to bed us? Don't they find a dozen ways each day to
ridicule us? Didn't I but accept it so, and de Bermingham
laughing at me, at us, from behind his hand, and all the
while planning the deed at Laracorra?'' He turned to Bronwynn and grinned painfully at her wide eyes, her stunned
features. "Ah, Curran had not told you that, had he? And,
whereas I might not have been able to stop de Bermingham
at Laracorra, I should not have put my name—and my
father's—and my honor—and my father's—at the brunt
of his scorn. Mayhap my father can soon forgive me that,
but 'twill be a long while and more before I'll find such
charity within myself.''

He stared into Bronwynn's eyes, seeing her compassion
and sorrow—and hating it. But there was, he knew, no
word of comfort or denial she could offer—no true word.
Shrugging one shoulder, he turned forward again and
urged his horse to a faster pace. But one corner of his
mouth twitched in a suppressed grin as he remembered
the yolky 'oop' Bronwynn had emitted when she first saw
the mercenaries from the Hebrides. It had sounded, he
thought, not so very different from the gulp of surprise
she had given when passion had claimed her the night
before.

Bronwynn held her horse in for a long moment, her
angry gaze on Cian's retreating figure. Freedom, she told
herself, and the riding of the hills in the mists and milds
hadn't quite the appeal she had thought it would. And
Cian O'Connor was none the less moody for no walls
around him. Then, remembering the gallowglass, she
glanced over her shoulder to see no sign that they had
ever been there nor were they, she knew, a threat to her.
Still, she urged her mount after Cian and stayed just that

little bit closer on his heels, with nervous glances about, until her shoulders slumped and her head drooped with fatigue.

The rain swept through the day, increasing with the hours, until it laved the fog away and turned the landscape the deepest of greens and browns and purples. Then the silver of the rain darkened with the edging in of dusk. It was through rain and nightfall that Bronwynn first glimpsed the rath of the O'Connor. A horn had sounded announcing their approach and she peered out from under her hood to see little but tall, tufted reeds in dark, wind-ruffled water. Their horses's hooves pounded over the wood of a causeway, startling a swan into flight, and her mount, too exhausted to shy, stumbled away from pale wings stabbing upward. Then they were within high walls of log and heavy planking on an earthen rampart. Voices called greetings and shouted news and requests for news. They called names and asked questions in an Irish too swift for Bronwynn to follow. Torchlight was flung into her eyes, then hands reached for her, pulled her down, set her on nerveless legs and numbed feet. Strange faces swarmed at her through the slanting rain, touching her features with curiosity, with animosity, before turning, avid, rejoicing, needful, to Cian. They reached for his horse to take it away and held torches out, the better to see him. They reached to have as much of him as they could in the cold, rain soaked bawn before his father called him from them. A female twin of Booka twisted through the throng to leap on him, spattering mud across his chest. She whined in delight as Cian shuffled her head between his hands, before shoving her away and ordering her to heel. Then other torches came out of the darkness, their flames sizzling in the wet. Other hands reached for Cian, drawing him away, and he reached for Bronwynn, drawing her to him, lifting the edge of his mantle over her against the rain as he was pushed through the people. Then they were at the entrance of a round timber-and-wattle dwelling, its roof oak-shingled, its portal framed in yew and ornamented with beaten bronze, and the torches led them on within.

Halting, Cian resisted the hands, then the hands were gone, leaving him alone, his arm about Bronwynn. For a moment, he held her close, his eyes squeezed shut, his mouth pressed against her hair. Then, sighing, he drew back to cup her face between his palms, his eyes intent. His thumbs lightly smoothed away the rain from her cheeks, her chin. One touched her mouth, brushing across the fullness of her lower lip, and she caught her breath in surprise at the swift sensation the caress evoked. He smiled at her soft gasp and his eyes laughed at her, before becoming suddenly dark, rapt. Then his mouth dropped to hers, taking it, possessing it in a swift, needful kiss.

"Be with me!" he whispered so softly she was not certain she had heard it, then he had straightened away and was drawing her with him into the warmth and the light, following the torches.

(10)

Bronwynn paused in the doorway and stared about at the spacious, whitewashed walls, the rush screened windows lowered against the night, at the blaze of rushlights and the fire burning in the central hearth. Cubicles offering more privacy than any castle great hall were built around the walls. Benches and couches, tables, stools and chests for personal effects were painted with geometric designs and twining mythical beasts and flowers in colors of red, green, blue and yellow, and were scattered about the chamber or placed against a wall. Woven mats were soft under her feet and the faint scent of crushed rushes and grasses wafted up to her nose as Cian, a hand under her elbow, ushered her forward. But it was the man rising from a tall backed chair with arms curved to fit huge hands who commanded her attention.

He rose, quieting his women with a single gesture, while his gaze held to the face of his son. They faced each other, gazing into a mirror of themselves twenty five years older, twenty five years younger, the father a bull of a man on the far edge of his prime, a man still capable of holding against all comers. Here, then, Bronwynn saw, was the man Cian would become, and her throat ached at the thought that she would not be the woman to see him so—a man still more powerful, stronger yet, than the one who had held her from the dew the night before. Only the lines of humor and wisdom etched across the features, the silver shot through the thick crest of hair springing from a wide brow and the mustache drooping its tails below the full lower lip marked the father different from the son.

But Calvach O'Connor was regarding his son with narrowed eyes, nor would Cian, he knew, be the first to speak. A maid servant stood holding a pitcher of water and a bowl to wash the hands and feet of their guests and another carried a stack of towels, but still he remained silent. Then, abruptly, he sat, motioning Cian to do the same. One eyebrow tucked into a scowl, he watched the maids go on about the duty of Irish hospitality, seemingly enthralled. A tray with an ewer of mead and two gem-encrusted goblets was brought and another with bread and fruit, when he at last addressed his son.

"You're alive, then," he stated. "And Curran and Cormac?"

"Themselves, too," Cian answered, as abrupt as his father, "and following fast enough behind us."

"But not the people of Laracorra."

A muscle tightened at the corner of Cian's mouth, but his gaze did not falter from his sire's.

"No," he agreed. "Not them."

Calvach shook his head in an angry gesture and stood to pace about the fire.

"And shouldn't I have known, so?" he acknowledged to no one in particular. "Hadn't you sent word of de Bermingham's interest in Laracorra? I thought to put warriors there, but 'tis a holy place—he knew it a holy place—

and I had not thought even he would violate it so. Wouldn't warriors there, too, have but given him cause to attack?"

"And himself with hostages," Cian stated, his voice full of grief.

His father stopped to stare into the fire, then he sighed, "Ah, and himself with hostages." He turned to study his son. "I had not thought," he admitted at last, "to see you ever alive and with me once more, if only for a day or so."

Cian bit his lip and looked down to study the jeweled goblet he turned about in his hands. When he lifted his gaze, he shrugged.

"Hadn't I a bit of a death wish on me, so?" he conceded, his mouth a wry grin. It was, his father knew, as close as he would ever come to an apology. Still, he could not let it alone.

"And because of a woman," he snorted and Cian could only shrug again, admitting it.

Seemingly lost in thought, Calvach caressed the wide rump of a woman bending over to refill his goblet and Bronwynn wondered if he was even aware he did so. But The O'Connor's scowling eye was on her, as though he had only just seen her where she stood wearily awaiting an invitation to sit or to approach—or to be remembered at all.

"Didn't he even," Calvach informed Bronwynn, "shave off his mustache because that same woman wished him to appear more like the Sassenach? And hasn't he, now, neither Fenella McKenna or the mustache? Instead, he brings me a Sassenach bit of a piece and isn't even a Sassenach piece better than Fenella McKenna? What say you, Girl? Would you have his Irish mustache off him, so, had he one?"

Head up, chin level, Bronwynn took two steps forward, then halted, refusing to step closer without permission. She studied Calvach's own mustache, thick and close

clipped over his long, upper lip and its ends curling down
around his mobile mouth. The women who served him,
too, were staring at her. She did not wish to insult them
or Irish customs. Even the clergy openly held mistresses.
But if there was such a woman waiting for Cian, she wanted
to know of it.

"I would not," she stated, "and certainly not if 'twas as
fine a thing as his father's. Any concubines he might have,
however, would be another matter."

Nonplussed, Calvach stared at her, before throwing back
his head in a roar of laughter.

"At least, she has the sass on her," he told Cian, "and
myself thinking the girl as meek as a mouse, with herself
all big eyes and not a word out of her. Isn't she the first
Norman woman I've met, then, who isn't all sighs and
downcast eyes ever sliding crosswise to weigh the worth of
a man—and what he would like to hear—so she can take
it from him?"

Holding out his hand to Bronwynn, Cian drew her into
the circle of his arm. Pressing their joined fingers to his
mouth, he looked at his father over them, his eyes defiant,
guarded, even as he smiled.

"Had I known you would be disappointed, Da," he
mocked, "had I realized you wanted a woman more Norman, I would have arranged to take Melusine. As it was, I
but grabbed the first at hand in the haste of the moment."

"And wouldn't you have had de Bermingham on your
heels after the coy bitch," Calvach answered, grinning,
"and himself with no mind to the favor you did him in
the taking of her." Then, smile fading, he cocked an eyebrow at their linked hands. "For all that you lived among
them, for all that I lost you to them for so long, I had not
thought you would bring a Sassenach woman back, not as
aught more than a hostage."

A woman giggled at the insulting of a guest, but Cian

merely inclined his head toward Bronwynn, his gaze never leaving his father. A smile touched the corner of his mouth. Whatever problems his father might think could be brought to them by a Norman woman would only be compounded when he found out who the woman was.

"This," he stated gravely, "is Bronwynn, daughter of Robert Fitzhugh and ward of Edward of England."

Calvach stared at him, stunned, then he whistled between his teeth. Turning away, he shook his head, as though not hearing properly, then spun back to face his son once more.

"Did you not consider the ramifications when you took her?" he demanded. "Did you not think you might have Edward—and war—down on all of Ireland—for a woman?"

Cian stepped in front of Bronwynn, jaw clenched.

"There was but time to take the person closest—or would you have myself hostage ever after as a club over your head instead?"

The O'Connor snorted.

"Would you have me believe you took that one only because she was the most opportune? Haven't I eyes in my head to see the way things are between you? And was it, then, but chance that she was the closest to hand, so?"

Cian straightened, mouth open to reply, but his father waved him silent. He was shaking his head once more, pacing all the while, and a grin grew wider with each step. Then he spun back around.

"Ah," he laughed, "the pure balls of it—and de Bermingham with aught to do but kick his dogs and curse his men and twist about like a gaffed eel!" He shook his head once more, his chuckles diminishing as reality sobered him. Then he cocked his eye again at his son, gaze concerned. When he spoke, it was as though he was thinking aloud. "Still, isn't a hostage a two edged sword

and the more valuable the hostage the sharper the edge?
What good is a dead hostage? Won't de Bermingham send
out troops to look for you, for her, if only in the hope that
you do something stupid, that he can take the girl back
with no harm to her? Won't all his ilk be seeking you, if
only to bend *his* nose out of shape by finding her first?
The man is not so well loved, all said. Nor will they give
up, not until all Ireland has been scoured. Won't they
scatter gold and favors and promises of favors to any and
all who will listen to a bribe for word of you—and won't
they find takers enough, so? There will be few enough
places for you to hide without word reaching their ear in
scant time and yourselves on the run again. Won't there
be men enough, too, willing to speculate on your vulnera-
bilities and how best to turn them against you? Isn't it said,
too, of Edward, that he is a master of such craft? Doesn't
every man have one—a soft spot to be exploited, a someone or something with no cost too great that they cannot
be turned against him, a hostage of the heart that can be
used to take all he loves from him?"

He halted in his pacing to stare at his son.

"You are mine," he said at last, his tone almost defiant,
"and perhaps that one will become yours. If so, may God
help you, for they'll not let you keep her, not for long."

"Then I will keep her as long as I can," Cian stated,
features grim. "However long it is, 'twill be more than we
had before."

He felt, Calvach O'Connor suddenly realized, more
weary than he had ever felt in his life, even after the longest
of battles—and more frightened for his son. He wondered
just when it was that men learned that joy and pleasure
were not always worth the pain—and that there was always
pain. When had he, himself, lost that madness, that need
to grasp life in both fists and shake it to his will, that
willingness to cast a hand against fate and—if losing—pay

the piper with no more lament than a shrug? Now, so soon after having him home, he was losing his son to a passion which could make the loss of Fenella seem as nothing. For a moment, anger and hatred for the grey eyed woman surely to bring Cian devastation wracked Calvach, then he shook it away. Perhaps Cian was right, perhaps Bronwynn, daughter of Robert Fitzhugh was worth all the pain and desolation she would bring him. While they had her, too, de Bermingham would not dare lift a hand against the O'Connors. There was a certain advantage in that. And didn't they say, after all, that grey eyed women were good luck? But he did not think so, not in this.

The O'Connor studied her, seeking what it was that had his son's jaw clenching so, that had him as testy and as as twitchy as some callow, lickerish shepherd lad. She was beautiful enough, true, and wouldn't many a fool stumble over their own feet to but catch a glimpse of her? But Fenella had been lovelier. Yet, beneath that guise of perfect blue-black hair and white skin, red mouth and level eyes was laughter and love and steadfast temper. She was such a woman as to stand by her man all their lives. And she was stubborn—that could be seen in the curve of her jaw— and passionate. Did she know how warm her eyes shone when they touched Cian's features, as though she smiled at a private memory of bodies in a tumbling embrace, in a sobbing, needful joining? He did not think so. There was pride there, too, although she was so weary she swayed, yet fought to stand straight.

Meeting his perusal, Bronwynn refused to let it go, her lifted chin and disdainful regard telling him she knew his thoughts. Then someone touched her arm, distracting her.

"Would you like to come with me, Lady?" a warm voice whispered and Bronwynn turned toward the speaker, displaying a line of dark love bites along the length of her white throat. The sight slammed a fist of desire into Calvach's groin and he jerked his sight away, but Cian's smile was one of welcome.

"You know my Curran," he told Bronwynn. "This is Sine, his wife. She'll see that you are bathed and fed, that you have a bed."

Bronwynn looked at him, features soft with fatigue. But there was a question in her eyes, and he nodded.

"My father and I must needs talk, but I will come to you, after."

Still, his eyes held hers before he let her go and his gaze followed her out. The O'Connor, too, watched her go, a scowl between his brows as he thought of the price his son and Bronwynn Fitzhugh would pay for the joy they would snatch from the time allotted them—and he could only pray it would be worth it. Cian, he knew, would never forgive himself if he let her go before he had to, nor would she leave until she must. Suddenly, the two men were in a deep embrace, their features grim set against the tears they both would spill. Then they were laughing, slapping each other on the back and talking at the same time. At last, Calvach gestured his son to sit and handed him a goblet of mead, only to stare at him, shaking his head in disbelief.

"I had not thought," he repeated, "to see you ever alive once more and with me."

"Wasn't I telling you they haven't cloven feet?" a voice hissed. "Didn't I say they would have to have special shoes, if such was true—and yourself saying their shoes were but a ruse to disguise them, so?"

"And wasn't it you," a second voice whispered back, "who insisted the Normans have tails, and yourself citing as evidence the length of their cloaks, and those no longer than ours, so?"

"Whisht!" Sine hissed. "Aren't you both the silly ducks, then, and rude beside? If you haven't aught else to occupy your minds and tongues, haven't I the way of finding you something better to do? Would you have me do so—and the back of my hand to you, beside?"

Sine had fed Bronwynn thick crusted bread and honey and cold mutton, early apples and mead. She had had her hair brushed until it gleamed and, now, Bronwynn, eyes closed, weary and half drunk, floated up to her neck in a tub of warm water. Still, she smiled at the maids' bickering and at the gossip they had believed about the Normans. Wasn't the same sworn upon in England about the Irish? And did she and her sister, she wondered, suddenly missing Cecily, ever bicker in the same way?

Forcing her eyes half open, she gazed about the dwelling of The O'Connor's women. It was more comfortable than his. There were the same sleeping compartments against the walls, the same furnishings, but, instead of swords and spears and shields on the walls, there were hangings of the whitest wools and linens intricately embroidered with threads of red and blue, green and yellow. The rushes on the floor were deeper, more fragrant, the furs and hides tossed over benches and chairs thicker, softer. The fire in its pit seemed, even, to glow with a warmer, softer flame as it sent shadows of blue and lavender up the white washed walls. The women sat gossiping, spinning, tending their children. A young woman, her hair of deep gold veiling her features, leaned over a harp, her long fingers weaving through the taut strings. Squinting against her fatigue, Bronwynn watched Sine shake out a blanket and fold it into a chest. She was, Bronwynn thought, all brown and round, sleek and plump, warm and giving. It was no wonder Curran loved her. Bronwynn thought to tell the woman so, but her eyes grew heavy once more. Then Sine was beside her, shaking her. With her, holding out a thick robe for Bronwynn to step into, was a tall, gently rounded blond woman with self effacing eyes.

"Would you not," Sine asked, her voice tenderly amused, "be more comfortable asleep in a bed? This is Fithir," she added, as though the blond woman should be known to Bronwynn.

Shaking her sleep away, Bronwynn stood and Fithir wrapped the robe around her.

"Curran," Bronwynn mentioned, remembering her earlier thought, "speaks of you and your children all the time. There is little else he talks about."

Sine laughed and shook her head, bundling Bronwynn toward a cubicle. A chest sat next to the door and, inside, there was room only for a bed platform.

"My Curran talks—and all the time, while I would wager, your face going blank, so, when I introduced Fithir, that Cormac did not tell you, even, that he was married. Yet, isn't my Curran all the time telling me I'm his reason for living—when he's not following that wild, young rogue of yours into trouble and out again—which is always, I'm thinking, and myself in a cold, lonely bed? Amn't I thinking, too, 'tis Cian O'Connor who has the honor of being his reason for living?"

There was, Bronwynn thought as Fithir drew aside the linen sheets and wolfskin covers of the bed—wolfskins for the woman who bedded with the son of the chief—deep affection in Sine's gentle complaining of her husband's loquaciousness. Her mention, too, of Curran's loyalty to Cian held too much truth.

"Why," she asked, her voice already sleep slurred, as she slipped into the bed Fithir had readied for her, "do you live in the O'Connor's house and not your own?"

For a moment, something like resentment crossed Sine's

genial features and her gaze touched Fithir's in an understanding that needed no words. Then she shrugged.

"My Curran is gone so often 'tis foolish to have a house of my own and no man to help in its upkeep. Here, too, I've the O'Connor's women for company. Nor have I men acalling my name at my door in the hope of assuaging my loneliness when my Curran's gone." Then her teeth flashed white as she smiled. "And haven't I the privilege of attending visitors such as yourself while the rest of the rath can only speculate and gossip?"

A corner of Bronwynn's mouth tipped up, then she frowned. There was loneliness and hurt in Sine's voice, no matter her light dismissal of Curran's absences.

"He should be here in a day or two," she told Sine, "and to stay for a while. Cian said nothing of him accompanying us."

Sine's eyes lighted, her gaze sliding again to Fithir's, whose mouth held a soft, elsewhere smile. Then she lightly brushed back a wisp of hair from Bronwynn's forehead.

"Ah, won't that make us happy, so," she stated, including Fithir in a way that puzzled Bronwynn, "and aren't we grateful to you if 'tis yourself who brings them back? And more, if 'tis yourself who smooths the grief and anger from our Cian's visage, no matter the dead at Laracorra."

Then she was gone, Fithir with her, the door closed, leaving Bronwynn to snuggle down deeper into the soft bed. Above her, over the top of the wall of the small chamber, she could see the wavering of the fire's glow. There came, too, the faint stains of a harp. Where, she wondered, would Cian sleep that night? And what did *that* matter, she ansered herself, with so much needing to be thought out, to fret herself over, but a faint smile touched her mouth instead. Sine, she remembered, falling into a dreamless sleep, had thought her responsible for easing Cian's grief and anger.

Bone weary, Cian came to Bronwynn late in the night. Wanting only to hold her, to draw something comforting to himself, he slipped into the cubicle he knew to be hers by the mantle tossed over the chest beside the door. There was, too, he knew, the sly, teasing ridicule and the mocking smiles he would have to face if he did not sleep in her bed. Then, unwinding his kilt, he scowled at another thought. She was a hostage first, true, but his solicitude of her, his unthinking display of affection had loudly announced their moment of passion on the hillside above Laracorra. In his people's eyes that act created a responsibility toward her, if only of respect. To not return to her bed for an obvious reason would arouse more questions than those mockingly doubting his manhood. They were questions which could only hurt Bronwynn and she was in too vulnerable a position for him to allow them. Yet, he could not repress a frown of resentment at the thought of how easily his freedom had been taken from him. There was the memory too, of Maire O'Colgan standing on tiptoe to wave to him, welcoming his return to his father's house. She had grown up since he was last home. Her hair was a deeper red, her breasts those of a woman, and certainly fuller than those of this delicate Norman girl in a bed he was not, suddenly, especially eager to enter.

Then a reluctant grin touched Cian's mouth. Was there any man, he wondered, when finding himself paired with a woman, who did not feel a twinge of fear and entrapment and doubt?

Sighing with fatigue, he slipped between the covers and drew Bronwynn to lie spooned next to him, one arm over her. Murmuring, she shifted against him, her bottom wiggling to press into his belly and, twining her arm with his, she drew his hand to cup her breast. His fingers closed over its roundness and, with the beat of her heart in his palm, he felt all doubt and resentment and fear flow away with his fatigue. Grinning again to himself, he wondered both at the perversity of men and why any one of them would even glance at Maire O'Congan's overblown charms if he could have this Sassenach wench in his bed.

Gently, trying not to wake her, not yet, Cian smoothed the sleek falling silk of hair from off Bronwynn's neck, exposing its creamy length to the soft brush of his mouth. He felt the bud of her breast in his palm. His thumb teased it, felt it grow, and Bronwynn turned, sighing herself up from sleep to fit herself more closely to his touch, to more fully expose her throat to his kiss. He took it with his mouth, following the pulse in it up to the lobe of her ear, the line of her jaw. Then he drew back to gaze at her.

Her eyes, her teeth were a faint glimmer in the dim light, and he could feel more than see the lips tilted up in a soft smile. He drew the ball of his thumb over their fullness and traced the arch of her eyebrow, the line of her nose, her cheekbones, as though to commit them ever to his memory. His fingertips were those of a warrior and a harper—rough with torn skin, welted with callouses. His touch was as soft as floating thistledown, as soft as a breath, his breath, as his mouth when he at last lowered it to follow the path his fingertips had traced. He teased the tip of his tongue along the crease of her eyelid, down the length of her nose and around the contours of her lips. Drawing back, her face cradled between his palms, he held her gaze trapped with his before his mouth claimed hers again, deeply, fully, and he moaned as he felt her lips open, as her tongue answered the pleading of his own. A wavering in her throat answered his as his mouth tore away to trace its way down her throat to be snared by the harp of her collarbone. He gnawed at it with his lips, even as his hand caught her breast, lifting it to his descending lips. He heard her mewing sob as he took the swelling bud to draw it in, to suck it into further fullness.

Bronwynn knew she sobbed her need, her throat swelling with it, but nothing was real beyond the aching knot deep within her that Cian's mouth drew into ever harder pulsings of pleasure, of pain. Her fingers wove through his hair, feeling the perfect roundness of his skull beneath her palms, as an errant thought wondered at the marvel of the life, the thoughts, the memories which dwelled within it. Her hands sought one of his to press it about the narrowness of her waist, the flatness of her belly, the flaring of her hips. Then they halted, grasping his wrists, holding them, when he would reach further. Rising to one elbow, Cian looked down at her.

"I would touch you there," he stated.

Bronwyn stared up at him, features unyielding, then she relaxed with a soft sigh to release his wrist, to melt beneath him. Gently, Cian placed his hand over the crispness, the softness at the joining of her thighs and heard the faint intake of her breath.

"Bronwynn," he whispered, and her lips curled up as she touched his mouth lightly, gently, feeling his breath on the tips of her fingers. Then she drew them down the line of his neck to his shoulder and over the smooth muscling of his arm, to the hand cupped over the heat of her. Staring up at him, her eyebrows crooked in a question he had no answer for, she twined her fingers with his, curling them into the heat of her need.

Cian's eyes closed as a desire such as he had never felt before twisted in the very depths of him. He shuddered with it and stared down at Bronwynn.

"What kind of witch are you," he rapped out through clenched teeth, "that you know so well how to arouse a man's lust, how to rend his heart, and yourself a virgin but the night past?"

He saw her flinch at the attack, at the injustice of it. She shook her head, as though doubting her hearing, then turned her face away from him, pressing it into the pillow. But the glow of flames from the fire pit, reflecting on the wall above them, shimmered, too, on the single tear caught in her lashes. And Cian shook his head, casting away his foolishness.

"Ah, a stór," he pleaded, his whisper a sob as he gathered her into his arms, "never turn away from me, so, no matter how unjustly I speak. Don't I need a woman to teach me there is forgiveness, gentleness, and that I need not strike out, hurting first lest I be hurt? Haven't I a fear, then, of anything too sweet, too perfect?"

He caught the tear on the tip of his tongue as he whispered her name and he moaned when Bronwynn turned back to offer her lips, herself. She took his face between her palms, her mouth clinging, giving as he had never been gifted before. Her body seemed to dissolve beneath him, to open to him, and he shuddered with his need, with his struggle for control.

He had taken her roughly, hurriedly the night before in his grief and anger. Tonight, although still weary to the soul of him, he had wanted the taking to be the sweet singing of a long lament and lullaby, a rocking and a weaving, giving and a taking. He chuckled deep in his throat, a harsh laughing, before he delved deep into the warmth and love and oblivion of her, wondering if the passion between them could ever be such a gentle thing as he wished. Laughing softly in response, seeming to understand his perplexity, his desire, and yet soaring with the glory and the power and fury of the moment, of their bodies entwined, Bronwynn tilted her hips to his. Her hands twisted into the muscles of his back, her throat

crooned to him, telling him of her need, her pleasure.
Nor could she stop herself until a shuddering release shook
her, until she heard her own round cry of fulfillment—
and Cian's groaning of her name in response.

(11)

Sighing, stretching, Bronwynn reached for a pillow stuffed with the softest of wool, the most fragrant of dried flowers, to draw it to her, to curl around it. Tucking her hand between her thighs, she winced from the soreness there, then laughed to herself, thinking of how it had come to be. Cian had left her some time before, but she smiled, remembering how she had awakened to his hands moving over her, stroking, teasing with the lightest of touches. His caresses had been slow, artful, as though he had all the time in the world, but the staff of him had nudged into the small of her back, a thing of hard, thrusting urgency.

Eyes closed, her breath soft as though she still slept, she had lain there, savoring the pleasure of his touch as it drew desire into her as skillfully as it drew song from his harp. But the reminder of his own need pressing against her, its promise of fulfillment could not, at last, be ignored. Moving over him, then easing down, she winced from his thrust against tender, abused flesh, only to hear him groan her name in astonished pleasure, and she laughed.

"I had wondered," she whispered, tilting back against him, "if it could be done this way."

He drew her closer. His mouth traced kisses over her shoulder, down her throat, to catch at the lobe of her ear, nibbling on it.

"Ah, and can't it so," he growled into the fall of her hair. He heard her soft, sobbing cry and his in response, felt the rippling shudder of her release and the clenching, spasming of his own, and then nothing but a spiraling fall into oblivion.

Gasping for breath, his heart pounding under her ear, Bronwynn had nestled with her head on Cian's chest. Yet even as his lungs struggled to recover from the exertions of their lovemaking, but she sensed him preparing himself to leave her. At last, he rose up on one elbow above her. Taking up a lock of her hair to twirl, he looked down at her.

"My father will be wondering where I am," he explained and Bronwynn smiled.

"He will," she agreed and his features lightened at such an easy release.

Swinging his feet to the floor, he began to dress. Only after he had secured his bratt with its golden brooch, scowling down at it to do so, did he look at her once more. Sitting on the edge of the bed, he touched a finger to her lips, lips swollen and red from his.

"Can you sleep a while more?" he asked, and smiled at her nod. "Sine will take care of you when you get up, or you can seek me out. She, or anyone else you care to ask, should know where to find me."

Standing, he tucked his knife into its scabbard at his belt and turned to go. Then he bent back over her, his mouth on hers an ardent promise.

"Should you," he whispered, "have any wonder of any

other way it might be done, haven't I the will to put it to
the proof with you?''

Then he was gone, leaving Bronwynn with a satisfied
chortle purling in her throat.

Now, she turned again, stretching, smiling the grin of
a cat at the cream. Then she sobered. It was time to be
up and about, to seek out Cian from people who might
very well resent her, hate her, nor could she blame them.
Her own charity toward those who might well wish her ill,
she told herself, did not make her any less a foreigner.

But Sine greeted her with a smile, a cup of ale, and a
bowl of boiled oats and honey, then sent her out into a
morning denying the rain and fog of the day before.

She slipped by a red haired boy, his face pressed against
the door frame of the women's house as he called out, "tri,
ceathaír, cúig, sé, seacht," while his friends disappeared
around corners and into doorways. Two maids, pails over
their shoulders, nodded at her as they entered the dairy.
In the middle of the bawn, several young men were at
practice with Norse battle axes, swinging them in the Irish
manner, one handed, the thumb controlling the grip, the
aim, while two more wielded knifes, their eyes intent on
each other as they stabbed and feinted in earnest play.
Three women stood by the well, a baby balanced on the
hip of one. A hand shielding her eyes from the sunlight,
Bronwynn's gaze followed the pointing chin of another
woman up to the walk at the top of the earthen and planked
wall containing the rath to Cian and his father. Cian waved
and, her skirts bundled up in one hand, she climbed the
ladder to him. Drawing her under his arm, Cian returned
his his attention to his father, while Bronwynn stared out
at the view she had not seen in the dark and rain of the
night before.

Rushes and reeds crowded the near lake shore, but the
more distant shoreline was wooded. Beyond, to one side,

were low, knobby hills, to the other was the lavender and soft greens of the lowlands where the cattle of the clan O'Connor grazed. On the glass-smooth water of the lake itself, in the blue reflection of the sky above, a pair of swans floated, their blue-grey cygnets with them. Then she turned her attention to The O'Connor and his son. Calvach was smiling at her in a warm welcome and he lifted his chin toward the lake.

" 'Twas here, 'tis said," he told her, "that the four Children of Lir lived for the first three hundred years after their jealous stepmother turned them into swans. And didn't they keep their human wits, so, and their fate the worse for it?"

"Did they always stay swans?" she asked and he shook his head. "When Christianity came they were converted by St. Mochaomhog but, being of such a great age, nine hundred years they lived as swans, all told, they died soon after, yet not before witnessing their stepmother turned into a fearsome flying demon as punishment."

Bronwynn lifted a dubious eyebrow at Cian and he grinned, nodding.

" 'Twas here," he confirmed, "or another lake much like this."

His father laughed, then turned serious.

"I had thought to build a castle there," he said, chin lifting to indicate the far end of the island, "but for what purpose—to live behind cold, stone walls in the dark and damp? And I doubt 'twould be any more secure than this, should the Normans want to take it."

"The causeway," Cian agreed, "is our greatest protection and, if they should want us badly enough, won't they find a way to take us, then? And don't castles hold their inhabitants in as much as they keep the stranger out? Don't we, in truth, hold the Normans inside their castle walls, so, and within the Pale, too, as much as they hold us out?"

Bronwynn drew back to look at Cian, her flared eyebrows tucked into an indignant frown, and he grinned down at her. "Or so went a thought," he conceded, his tawny eyes warm on hers, "I once heard someone else suggest—a Norman it was, so."

"And a woman, was it?" Calvach guessed.

"A woman," Cian agreed, his gaze on Bronwynn.

Looking away, fearing for his son, Calvach noted with relief a small party of riders approaching the causeway and he gestured toward the new arrivals.

"Monks," he stated. "Mostlike but the first of many of those visitors come to greet you or of those all irate or distressed and grieving over the deed at Laracorra. And hadn't we best be presenting ourselves to them, so?"

Not waiting for a reply, Calvach led the way back down the ladder. Nor was he incorrect in the number or the motives of the many people to come to the rath in the next several days.

They came from miles around, from Trim, from Meath and Roscommon, from as far away as Connacht and Kildare. Many owed their allegiance to Calvach O'Connor as their tuath king. Others but honored an alliance. They were warriors and chieftains and gallowglass, priests and monks, harpers and drovers, brehons and bards, many with their wives and concubines. They came to grieve the dead of Laracorra, to discuss means of avenging them and of preventing such another occurrence. And scant little that would be, Cian told Bronwynn bitterly. There would be a troop of Norman soldiers ambushed in one place, another somewhere else, a few killed, more wounded, and the likes of de Bermingham would grow a bit more cautious for a while, would travel outside the Pale a bit better armed and manned. That would be all.

Curran and Cormac and the men Cian had left at Laracorra came at last. Sine pushed though the crowd to her husband, to be picked up and swung about by her laughing, boisterous Curran, while those around ducked away from her flying heels. Fithir, though, Bronwynn noted, held back, standing by the entrance to the women's hall, until Cormac saw her, went to her. But the face she turned up to her husband glowed with her joy, while his, bending down to her, was softened with a gentleness of which Bronwynn had not imagined him capable.

Many who came were O'Connors, whether legitimate or not. They were Cian's cousins and nephews and uncles, stepbrothers and foster brothers and half brothers, spear kin or spindle, and with them came their women. And all his kinsmen bore heads of reddish brown hair, whether a pale sorrel, a warm auburn or the deep russet brown that was Cian's. There were so many that their sheer numbers made Bronwynn's head whirl. Never, she thought, could she remember all of them, even their names were a muddle in her mind. Only a few of the women approached her, although most covertly studied her, a few jealously. It was not, she decided, that they hated or resented her; they did not, although there were those who took affront that a woman of the strangers should so usurp The O'Connor's son, no matter how briefly. It was that they were well aware she was soon to be returned to de Bermingham, to Edward. What purpose was there, then, in getting to know her, even, perhaps, to like her, when she was to be gone soon, and never to return? Their reserve was, she thought with an acrimonious humor, such as they would show a stranger soon to be taken by death, perhaps even a death dealt by themselves.

It was not a reserve shown by all. Bronwynn, so often eclipsed by Cecily, could only revel in the attention paid her by the men.

Secure in Cian's care, leaning back against him, she smiled as Eoin O'Connor took up a harp and settled down on a stool to sing to her. It was obvious he lacked Cian's perfect ear and great talent, as he sought to entertain her with more heart than ability. With each crack of Eion's voice and every time the harp rang in strident discord, Bronwynn felt Cian wince, as though in physical pain. At last, smiling to show he meant no insult, Cian took the harp from his cousin to adjust the wrest pins, to pluck the strings, his head cocked to hear the better. Then, his gaze warm and teasing on Bronwynn, he played, in no more than a splattering of notes, of surf curling onto long beaches and the taste of salt on the mouth, of warm grasses and tall stones—and of a place more secret, more desired yet than any holy well. Then he handed the harp back to his cousin.

"It can take a while," he told Eion, his eyes as he spoke laughing at Bronwynn, drawing her into the glow of his affection for his cousin, for her, "to develop an ear, and to know your harp. Isn't it like a woman, so?"

Still, the words Eion sang praised the gentleness of her manner, the blush of her cheeks, and his amber eyes gazed at her with a flattering adoration only half in play, while Cian sat in pride and a jealous glower feigned for Eion's benefit. But it was for that discord, the falling off key, for the willingness to appear the fool, Bronwynn told herself, that she would remember Eion, never guessing she would see him one more time and remember him for other, more painful reasons—and with grief.

Nor would she forget Lunn Mulvany, the son of the daughter of Calvach's half sister. Gangly, awkward, dangling huge, large knuckled hands graceless unless holding a weapon, he followed her about with a stunned gaze. Refusing to look at her, he offered a bowl of mead as though it was a chalice of holy water. Eyes held sideways, he asked, the question a faint hope born of a desperate infatuation, "Have you a sister, then?"

Bronwynn smothered a laugh of surprise and thanked him for the mead.

"Aye, I've a sister and she's beautiful, with hair of pale gold and eyes the color of the sky," she told him, offering him a fantasy, but he rejected it.

"She's not dark like yourself?" he mumbled, hazel eyes bleak with disappointment, and Bronwynn shook her head. "But is she younger?" he asked hopefully. "Is there time yet that she'll grow dark?"

"She is younger and perhaps a bit darker than she was a few months ago," she told him, giving him back his dream, unable to know he would follow that dream to his death. But he went off, hands dangling, features vague with wistful adoration of a woman he had not yet met.

Nor was Bronwynn given time to grow to know these people. Three days was time enough, Calvach said, for de Bermingham to gather his forces and his wits back about himself. Already, there was word of a reward for news of Bronwynn's whereabouts and a whispering through the narrow valleys and across the bogs, seeking out the secret places where they would abide, seeking out the palm of a greedy man, the will of a vulnerable one. Already, de Bermingham would be wondering if he could not return to Laracorra or take another place, to plant but a few men there—to hold it until the return of Brownynn Fitzhugh, he would say. Some would fault him, knowing well he seldom loosened his grip once his hand clenched about something. There were those, though, who sought the ways of conciliation to hold what little remained to them, who would nod, calling the move reasonable and but a gesture. De Bermingham and his spies, too, would soon be prying about, asking questions, seeking out a weakness, any weakness that could be used to return Bronwynn to the care and comfort of her guardians, her family. And they would find it, Calvach told his son, eyes brooding and filled with concern for Cian. It was but a matter of time. His visage a morose replica of his father's, Cian stared into his tankard.

"Hadn't we then best take all we can of the time we have?" he wondered. His gaze sought Bronwynn out where she sat with Sine, the two of them leaning over an intricate embroidery pattern. Feeling the weight of his dark study, she looked up, a smile transfiguring her face. He did not smile in return and Bronwynn sobered, allowing him to see her need for him and the sorrow that would be hers when they parted—and seeing his. Then Sine touched her hand, drawing her back, although her gaze was still ensnared by Cian's.

"There is a well," Sine told her, "a holy well for lovers. Hasn't it brought my Curran back a time or two, though? I will make an offering there that you and Cian need not be parted. It must be difficult to try always to appear cheerful, as you do for Cian's sake."

Her laugh half a sob, Bronwynn shook her head.

"Ah, no, appearing always happy, that is easy. 'Tis allowing him to see how much I love him, how much of my soul I will leave behind when I go, that is the difficult. 'Tis like being flayed alive, with no skin about me protecting me, yet how can I deny him, no matter how it hurts both of us?"

She turned to meet Sine's gaze with eyes bright with unshed tears and Cian looked back at his father.

"Tomorrow, then—and early—we will leave. The longer it takes de Bermingham to find us, no matter what means he may have found to take her from me, the longer we will have together." His grin was wry with pain. "Think you if I should get her with child, they would let me keep her? Ah," he answered himself with his own bitter laugh, "and didn't, a child bind Fenella McKenna to me, so?"

(12)

Fog veiled the lake in a heavy mist when they slipped away. It muted the thud of their horses's hooves on the planks of the causeway and softened the sliding of a disturbed water rat into the lake to a plop and a sigh. From somewhere came the lonely cry of a curlew. Then they were on land and Cian drew his horse to a halt to study Bronwynn. The mist had turned her pale skin luminous and the wisps of dark hair about her face into a riot of curl beneath her hood. Her eyes, in their hedge of black lashes, were the color of the fog. They gazed back at him, puzzled.

" 'Twill be hard," he stated at last, and Bronwynn knew he meant more than being on the hiding. "I can return you back to Carrick and never but understand why you had to go. And mightn't it be for the best for the both of us, so?"

She held his shuttered gaze, her own confident.

"Would you have me go?" she asked and, a muscle

working in his jaw, he shook his head. "Then, hard or no, I'll stay by you until they take me away."

"Hadn't we best be off, then," he asked, with a small smile. "And it a hard journey we set ourselves on?"

But daily living, the demands of the present have a way of eclipsing fear of the future, the grief of the past. Always, in their wanderings, they had to stay alert to all around them. There could be no wayfarer chance met upon a road seldom traveled or a shepherd come across on some high pasture. Any one could be an informer and all could gossip in their cups of two strangers happened upon where one would expect aught but the wind—and the Old Ones. Wasn't the man an O'Connor, perhaps, judging by his russet hair—and the woman a foreigner? Hadn't the man a harp over his shoulder? Hadn't he heard someone asking after just such a pair and jiggling a purse the while? Even the raths and castles, the huts and houses of clansmen, of allies and alliances could not be trusted. Too many men, no matter their consanguinity, their blood oaths, could bear an unknown grudge, could be a victim of an unsuspected extortion, and Cian and Brownynn kept to the lonely places. But they had each other's company and there was so much Cian wanted to shared with Bronwynn, so much he wanted to see new through her eyes.

Only when they needed food did Cian venture into the company of those he most trusted, leaving Brownynn to wait in some hidden cave or hut or high booley house. Always, fear that she might have been taken, that she might have left him, that she might have been injured or ill or only lonely hastened his return. And always he returned with a jaunty swagger, a soft whistling to toss down the needed supplies. Then he would hold her tight against him, the fragrance of her feeding his mind, his soul, as he reassured himself of the reality of her, and thanked all the saints he could lay mind to that he would have her for that while more and, please God, the night, the next day also.

And that night he would hold her with a fervency that spoke of his fears, of his wishes.

Or Curran would emerge from the night to duck under the low lintel of a hut or booley house or through the entrance of a cave, provisions with him, and the gossip of the weeks before ready to be told. Nor was it, Bronwynn told him, that he found them that astonished her. It was that he always knew when she thought she could not swallow another bite of venison or hare, of duck or quail, trout or salmon—nor did they ever lack for such, Cian being the great provider that he was. Still, she was always grateful to see Curran and the oatmeal and flour with him.

They lost track of the days of the week, the weeks themselves, and all the holy days. Soon, they but proffered a prayer, a small offering at each and all shrines and holy places they came upon, the hidden springs, the sunlit altars of stone, not questioning which deity might reside there.

They wandered west to Lough Ree while violets and cowslips still bloomed in the wet, hidden places, as the hawthorn blossomed, bringing to Cian the memory of Curran comparing Bronwynn to the brier, thorns and all. They followed the Shannon north to Lough Allen and beyond to lonely mountains and the valleys lost between their steep slopes, then beyond Slieve Benbrack through the Bellavally Gap. There, on the lower, rock-strewn slope of the wild Cuilcagh Mountains Cian showed Bronwynn the Shannon Pot. From this pool, he told her, flowed the longest river in Ireland. Roaming farther north and west, they wandered through the green vale of the Glenaniff River, from which great hills ran up either side, to Lough Melvin. West again, they came to a place of mountains of a thousand shades of green and lavender where waterfalls flowed up, not down, so it was said, when the wind blew north from over

the sea. Rivulets and pools were set there amid rushes and
banks of forget-me-nots and moss fringed with tiny flowers
of star-white. Beyond and farther west still, they rode their
horses on the long beaches, the wind in their faces. Born
on a lake, Cian swam like an otter and had long before
enticed Bronwynn to trust him, to trust water and the
spirits who dwelled in it. There, he lured her into the chill
waters of the sea. After, he would taste the salt of the sea
on her mouth, on her nipples, in the cup above the harp
of her collarbone, of her navel.

In the West, too, at the foot of Knocknarea, was a burial
place of the Old People, where wild rose bushes climbed
tall, standing stones, where daisies bent before the wind.
They made love in the shadow of a cromlech, the heat of
summer wafting the scent of roses over their warm skin,
while their horses chomped the grasses near by. After,
curled in Cian's arms, teasing the tender bend of his elbow
with a stalk of grass, Bronwynn idly asked, "If a child should
be conceived here, do you think 'twould be Christian or
pagan?"

Cian scowled; she could feel it. To speak of the future
was something they did not allow themselves—and she
had. Yet, he looked down at her, lifting her chin with his
thumb to gaze more deeply into her eyes.

"Christian or of the Old People," he told her, "the
child would be loved, as is the woman, no matter where
the two of them might be—and haven't I a wonder, still,
if the fey-eyed woman is of this world herself?"

She pressed her mouth into his palm. Lifting a strand
of her hair off her shoulder, he drew his lips down the
long line of her collarbone, then looked at her.

" 'Twill be dark soon and wouldn't I prefer not to test
the Old People's welcome with the rising of the moon?"

But it was not only thought of the Tuatha de Danann
which made Cian apprehensive. They had crossed over

half of Ireland but, if they were far from de Bermingham, they were close to the Norman Richard de Burgh and the castle from which he and his knights patrolled his acres of West Ulster and salaciously eyed those of his neighbors in the hope of gaining more. 'Twas sort of like playing hare and hounds, Cian told her, eyes gleaming with the thrill of the game. Lying on the crest of a hill, they had watched de Burgh and his knights ride by below. And wouldn't the last place de Bermingham looked for them be right under de Burgh's his nose, Cian asked her with a grin that made her brush his back from his brow as she would a little boy's. Would the cramp-minded man credit such an audacity? Cian had grown restive, too, in the West, so far from his home and word of the happenings there. Even Curran would be hard pressed to find them, Cian told her, and Bronwynn lifted a incredulous eyebrow— she had come to believe Curran capable of miracles.

Yet, it had been more than a few weeks since they had last seen Curran, Bronwynn realized, so happy she had been in the West. And it was for the same reasons Cian was unsettled that she did not wish to turn back on their steps. How could she be returned to de Bermingham, to Edward, if she could not be found, whatever the price they might offer for her?

But to live like this—just the two of them and ever alone the rest of their lives—was a flightless fancy, she knew. So, while the last wild iris flaunted its yellow flag in the damp places, while the first autumn aster dipped its head before the wind on the hillside, they turned back through water-splashed mountains. On Lough Oughter, within its maze of islands and channels, inlets and spits of land, they saw the fortress of the O'Reilys on its own small island.

They had eaten nothing but wild game and berries for weeks and Cian left Bronwynn hidden in a copse of birch and alders. Not because he did not trust the O'Reilys; he did, but circumstances could have changed with them in the last few months. Irish politics was like that and he wanted to take no chances, not with her. He returned a few hours later with his saddle bags stuffed with provisions, but she could tell by his face there had been little news of what might be happening at home. Still, he smiled when he greeted her, the relieved hug saying how glad he was that she was where he had put her.

Ever on the alert, they traveled east, following the Blackwater while the leaves of the ash turned their yellow and lavender, the birch a bright gold. Finding the River Boyne, they rode close enough to the castle of Trim, held by the powerful Hugh de Lacy, that Bronwynn could see the sentries high on its massive walls. The hawthorn's fruit had turned bright red when they stood on the Hill of Tara where the high kings of Ireland—the Aud Righ—had once been crowned. He had slipped into Tara—so close to Dublin and within the Irish Pale—once before, Cian admitted, as a young boy. It was dangerous, true, and was what Irish youth did as sort of a rite of passage. He had even sat on the throne—that was part of the dare.

They walked the hill in the moonlight where mounds of ancient earthworks and low walls of rock and soil swelled beneath tall grasses bending before the wind. Once fine palaces and banqueting halls stood there. They could almost feel the presence of those pagan priests and long dead royalty. But Bronwynn would not sit on the stone throne which was said to roar when the rightful king claimed it—not for fear it wouldn't, but that it would. That night, as they sat amid Tara's pagan dead, Cian's arms around her, they saw bonfires flare up, scattered like stars over the black earth across the valley and on the surrounding hills, and knew it was Allhollow's Eve.

But, as much as Cian enjoyed thumbing his nose at the Normans within the Pale, to stay was too dangerous and

he took Bronwynn back across the Boyne. Fallen oak leaves
stirred under their horses' hooves as they rode north and
west, the air seeming to become crisper with each new day.
Once, they heard the crack of the antlers of elk in rut,
fighting for a female. Another time, a bear, sleek with
winter fat, blocked their trail, standing upright to peer
nearsightedly at them, while their horses reared in terror.
Finally, curiosity satisfied, she shambled away. They passed
near Kells, close enough to see the high crosses in the
graveyard and the ninety-foot-tall tower near them, with
its five small windows at the top, one for each road leading
to the monastery. But they were going to a place hallowed
by the Old People, the Tuatha de Danann, to the Lough-
crew Hills, where good Christians seldom came.

There, three peaks formed a long ridge upon whose
tops were pillar stones, scattered earthworks, a ring fort,
and chambered cairns, graves of the ancient dead. It was
not a place where even Cian felt comfortable in the nights,
but on the slope was a long abandoned booley house. It
was, Cian thought, sorrowfully, as good a place as any to
wait for Curran to find them with word to return, to come
in, at last, as they had always known they would have one
day to do. The days grew shorter, still, in that time. They
grew colder and, at night, they could hear the distant
howling of wolves in pursuit of prey. Yet, even as they
waited, they found they could laugh and love, living in the
moment, building memories they would have to feed on
all of their lives.

There was a place Cian knew where a creek swirled about
to form a pool, a pool perfect for luring a woman in to
feel her flesh smooth and warm against the chill of his.
Standing waist deep, they scrubbed each other with sand
until they glowed, until Cian's hands, his mouth could no
longer ignore the rosy tips of her breasts, the falling slant
of her glistening shoulders. Or she would shave him, brow

puckered in concentration, lip caught between her teeth,
as she scraped away the bristle from his cheek with the
razor sharp edge of his dirk. Rinsing off the knife with a
flick of her wrist through the water swirling around them,
she would begin on the other side, until only the soft curl
of his newly grown mustache was left. Rubbing her face
against his, she would pronounce him done, would declare
his cheeks smooth enough to touch even the most tender
parts of herself. Then he would carry her up from the river
to lay her on the grass, his mouth, indeed, seeking out
the most delicate parts of her while she whispered of the
pleasure of it. But the water grew colder with the nearing
of the winter solstice and he found it more difficult to
entice Bronwynn into the water play he so enjoyed.

"It isn't cold," he insisted, kneeling in the creek, the
water swirling up to his shoulders. But it was, even for a
man who went swimming every day, no matter the season.
Still, he stared up at Bronwynn, eyebrows quirked beguilingly, and silently thanked the saints that the winter had
proven to be, so far, exceptionally mild.

She stood above him on the bank, one hand holding
for balance to a twisted branch of an alder tree. Her feet
were white on the deep green of the moss and her toes
curled, protesting the cold damp oozing up between them.
She wore only a linen shift and the chill of early December,
he noted appreciatively, had tightened the tips of her
breasts into buds beneath the thin cloth. And the water
was cold, but he wanted her in it for the feel of her nipples
against him, for the pleasure of warming her later. It also,
he acknowledged to himself, had become a test of her love
for him—and therefore a childish thing—but a proof he
would need in the long, heart-lonely days and nights to
come. It was not a need easily relinquished.

"It was frigid yesterday," Bronwynn protested, "so why
would it not be so today, a day closer yet to winter?"

"Because," Cian told her, wondering if his lips had yet turned blue, "as the air gets colder, the water feels warmer. 'Tis but a matter of comparison."

"If 'tis so warm," she demanded, teeth sinking into her lip to control her laughter, "and warmer than the wind on me, then stand up and prove it! I dare you!"

Cian fought his own grin. Nor could he refuse her challenge. Reluctantly, he stood, exposing himself to Bronwynn's laughter, to her pointing finger.

"I did not know," she mocked, "that it came in different colors. I think, though, that I prefer it pink to the blue it is now, don't you? And it has become such a wee little thing!" She held up her baby finger to compare sizes and arranged her features to a more serious mein as she lifted her laughing gaze to his scowling one. "Do you think 'twill grow again, so?" she asked gravely, biting her lip at the sight of his glowering eyebrows, at the downward tuck of his long upper lip.

She did not see the intention in his eyes until his hand had snaked out, grabbing the finger that pointed and mocked. With a squeal, she jerked back, but the slender branch she clung to snapped and the water came up to engulf her in its frigid embrace. Gasping from shock, she lurched up in the thigh deep water, and grabbed a lungful of air, only to be pulled into Cian's clasp. His body was scarcely warmer than the water, but the mouth he pressed over hers was hot, demanding. Still, furious that he had tricked her, she fought him and the sensations his kiss could so easily arouse. Drawing his mouth from hers, he tossed her over his shoulder, laughing at the blows of her small fists on his broad back. Naked, strolling out of the water with his burden, he carried her to the booley house.

"Damn you," she spat up at him from the bundle of furs he tossed her on. "How could you trick me so? 'Twas not fair!"

"Ah, fair—and is aught fair? And wasn't it easy, so," he grinned at her, "and yourself so gullible."

She swung at him and he caught her fist in one hand. Jerking her wet shift up over her head, he caught the second one, and twisted both her arms behind her back. Then he lowered his mouth to hers.

Bronwynn fought him and the needs his kiss awakened, then felt a soft moan form in her throat and knew she had lost. He, too, heard it and he released her wrists. Her fingers hard in his hair, she pulled his head back to glare up at him, her mouth swollen, her eyes angry.

"Damn you!" she whispered again. "Ah, damn you!"

She twisted over, lifted above him, her mouth once more on his, as his hands trailed up and down her back, caressing her with his fingertips, scratching with his nails, with the rough callouses of his palms. But, seemingly hungry, unsatisfied, her mouth left his, biting, sucking, tasting the clean mossy scent of his skin along the tendon of his neck, the flat nubbin of his nipple, the shallow well of his navel, nipping and tugging the fine line of hair beyond. She paused, one hand gripping his, the other splayed over his thigh. Then her tongue touched him, tasted him, before her mouth engulfed him. She heard his groan of pleasure, of surprise, felt his hips jerk and his hand clench in her hair, as she caressed him in a way she had never done before. At last, she rose to look at him with an impish grin.

"Ah," she chortled, imitating his brogue, "isn't himself but standing all proud and grand, and wasn't I the great idiot, thinking permanent damage had been done to the poor, wee mankin? But isn't such an overweening pride a shameful thing to behold?"

"Then," Cian suggested, voice husky with desire, "mayhap, you had best put it out of sight."

The mocking humor left her and her features grew grave. Her eyes intent on his, she leaned forward to kiss him, her mouth soft, fragrant, as she settled over him, taking him within her. His moan answered hers and his gaze never left her face as she moved over him, finding, time after time, a shuddering release. Finally, unable to bear the sweet torment any longer, he clasped her close, twisting with her, mounting her, taking her, one more time, with him, as she uttered that cry he knew he would recognize her by should he bed a thousand women.

They dozed in each other's arms, how long, Cian could not have said, perhaps moments, perhaps hours. Hadn't she, he would wonder later, roused to ask him if he was hungry and hadn't he grunted that food could wait, that he had more important things to do? Or that could have been another remembered time. He must have risen to feed the fire, for it had been burning well, later. And how long they had slept, he would tell himself after, didn't really matter. What would matter was that it was Curran who woke them.

The faint rasp of a shoe against a stone, perhaps deliberate, the slithering fall of a pebble rolling to a halt against another, brought Cian out of a sound sleep. In one motion, he rolled out of bed to face the low door, kneeling naked, his spear clutched in both hands. Behind him, he knew, Bronwynn had grasped his sword; he had heard the sigh of it being drawn from its scabbard. Then a throat was cleared once, then again, and Cian knew who waited for an invitation to enter. He set aside his spear, his breath winnowing in a mirthless chuckle to himself, as he wondered if he wouldn't have rather faced an enemy, in truth, than the message Curran could be bringing them. Then he grunted an invitation to enter and Curran ducked through the entrance to stand blinking in the light of the fire.

But, this time, there were no provisions with him nor was there that abashed grin of apology for so interrupting their privacy. His quick glance, before he looked away, took in their love sated features, now guarded against whatever blow he was to offer. They sat in their nest of furs and blankets, Cian's arms tight around Bronwynn. He brushed a strand of her hair back from her forehead with a kiss, to tell her he was there, was with her, no matter what. His gaze never left Curran as the other looked everywhere in the small hut but at them. And why, he thought with a wry silent laugh, was the man who never lacked for a word suddenly silent. Then Curran shifted from foot to foot, gathering courage for this necessary stroke to the heart of the man he loved more than even his own brother, and looked at Cian and Bronwynn.

" 'Tis come—the time has," he whispered, then he repeated it louder, his voice gruff with regret. " 'Tis come and you needs must go back."

"Why now and this suddenly?" Cian demanded, as though there was a place for negotiation in this. "And what has come? Who?"

"Fenella McKenna," Curran answered.

Cian's forehead puckered, as though he could not place the name, and Bronwynn stared up at him, features bewildered. Then he shook his head and asked, voice round with false laughter, "And what has she to do in this? Sure, and de Bermingham wouldn't be slackwitted enough to think that bitch worthy of trade for my lady? De Grenville has the dubious pleasure of her now, so she might as well return to Cumberland. Won't de Bermingham—and Edward—have to come up with something far better than that?"

He laughed again at the thought that he would give up Bronwynn for Fenella. But Curran did not return the grin he offered in hope. He stared down at his shoes and muttered, " 'Tis not Fenella he is bargaining with, though she needs must come with the deal."

"What did you say?" Cian asked. But he had heard and Curran knew it. He lifted his reluctant gaze to meet Cian's, for never had he been a man to shrink from looking into the face of a man as he dealt him a fatal blow.

" 'Tis the child," he stated and he saw Cian's face go slack, with stunned disbelief, before his head fell forward, conceding that, yes, for his child he would give up his very soul. Curran heard Bronwynn's grieving sigh as she took Cian in her arms, burrowing into him like a small animal both seeking comfort and offering it. And Cian's arms clenched around Bronwynn as his shoulders shook with his efforts to suppress his rage and grief.

"And your sister, Lady," Curran added, in a vain attempt to offer Bronwynn someone she loved in exchange for what she was losing, "she sends with me her caring, her concern—and her wish to see you soon."

But Curran truly did not think Cecily was any the less the selfish, spoiled child she had been. Still, he stood there, shifting from foot to foot, waiting. At last, whisper harsh, Cian asked, "In the morning, then?" Clearing his throat of the lump blocking it, Curran agreed.

Nodding his farewell, he left, to build himself a bed in the leeward side of the hut. Nor was he to sleep well that night, as he listened to the winds of winter blow around the stone walls, to the wailing of a wild cat, grieving, he thought, for its lost soul, and to his own bitter thoughts.

(13)

Cian held Bronwynn, rocking her, seeking to comfort her and himself when no comfort could ease. His fingers woven through her thick hair, his hand splayed over her skull, he wondered what thoughts chased themselves about inside. If he knew, if there was a way of knowing, then perhaps he could find a means of reaching through the grief of her loss, of his. But there was only one way, he knew, to give themselves forgetfulness, if only for the while, and his mouth sought hers, his breath, his lips soft on her temple, at the corner of her eye, as she lifted a tear-damp face to his, turning, too, to seek his mouth, to seek a momentary oblivion.

"Be with me," he whispered as their mouths met. Their hands touched, softly, gently, as though there was the power to remember the line of a shoulder blade, the curve of a waist, the turn of an ankle within their fingertips. Their lovemaking became a thing of sorrow and joy, of an impotent anger and soaring grace, a needing, a wanting never to let go of something already gone. It became the

sweet singing of a long lament and lullaby, a rocking and
a weaving, a giving and a taking that Cian had once wanted
it to be, had doubted he would ever find. Nor had he, he
realized, his final giving more a melting than a release,
known the price they would pay for it. If he had, he would
never have sought it.

He held her, after, her face in the crook of his shoulder.
His back against the wall, he stared into the final embers
of the fire. Gently, he brushed back Bronwynn's tear damp
hair from her brow, his own features set.

"Ah, a stór, don't weep," he whispered, as much to
himself as to her. "Did we not know 'twould come to this?
Had we not expected it always? Hadn't we, too, more time,
more love than we had thought to have, at the beginning?
Can we not but be thankful for that? Did we not," he
added, voice gruff, angry, "swear we would not weep? Ah,
a stór, did we not know?"

He heard Bronwynn's effort to cease her tears in the
mewing she fought to contain within her shuddering
throat. And his own silent tears flowed down his cheeks
and he thought his heart lay within his chest surely cleaved
in two by a blow more deadly than any yielded by a Norman
lance.

There was little, they found, left to say to each other the
next day—or to Curran. The day was as silent, as dark as
their mood, a heavy fog lying over the world, obscuring
the landscape, muffling the clink of bridles, the creak of
saddles. Silent, they rode through it, each lost in his own
musings. Nor did Curran wonder why they spread their
blankets on opposite sides of the fire to lie down separately,
backs to each other as they stared out into the darkness
that night and the next. Nor did Calvach O'Connor ask why

his son sought a pallet in the men's house and Bronwynn another in the women's.

Cian, his father found when they returned, was silent about most subjects, nor was it any comfort to remember he had always been more introspective than most of his loquacious race. Before, while laconic, there had been a gleam of gentle humor in his eyes at those more talkative, a pointed word when those more garrulous could not think what to say. Now, there was a baffled look there, as though he could not guess how he had come to be so wounded. His soul seemed to hunch within him, as if to ward off another, possibly more deadly blow. Only when discussing the meeting with de Bermingham to exchange Bronwynn for his daughter did he look up from his evening's trencher. His mouth was tilted with a wry, grim humor when he was told it was to occur at Laracorra. Now, they were camped across the rippling waters of the Boyne from the green meadows of the place of the Wier. On the other side, de Bermingham waited for the return of Edward's ward on the morrow, but still the discussion they had held too often continued.

"Ah, sure," Cian laughed, gazing out into the slanting evening showers, "and doesn't the man know how to rub salt into a wound, if only his own?" Dropping the flap over the entrance to the large tent, he turned to grin cynically at his father. "Or are you thinking, mayhap, that he intends to dare for Laracorra again and does but wish to appraise it, to see if 'tis worth the venture? Does he mayhap but use the exchange as an excuse, thus killing two birds with one stone, as it were?"

"I think 'tis no more than that Laracorra is a place central to the both of us," Calvach answered, shrugging.

"And de Bermingham's try for it afore," Cian asked for the sake of argument, "was that but an old habit hard dying and aught more? Or do the English no longer covet their neighbor's property?''

"I do not think he would have tried at all had he not held you hostage. Nor do I think he has any intention toward Laracorra, now,'' his father answered, straightening away from where he sat leaning his elbows on the table, his arms cracking as he stretched them behind him. He glanced upward as the wind blew a complaining ripple over the heavy cloth of the pavilion, then looked at Cian once more. "We, the clans, it seems to me, are holding our own at last. The tide, even, seems to have turned a bit and 'tis more than that the gallowglass can stand toe to toe the equal of any Sassenach pikeman.'' He shook his head at Cian's dubious smile and leaned forward again, features earnest. "Look you at the MacCarthy of Desmond. Hasn't he held his land and taken back more, too, since the Battle of Callan—and the O'Donnells of Donegal. Didn't they halt the Geraldine's at the Battle of Credran and that almost fifty years ago? Can I not name you a dozen other examples of where we've held our own, so, and pushed the Sassenach back, too? Haven't many of them become more like us than we are like ourselves? Why shouldn't they—and their mothers and grandames as much of the clans as ours? Don't they even change their names to fit our tongue the better—and their own, and themselves speaking the Irish?''

"And ourselves, aren't there those of us who build castles?'' Cian asked into his ale. Then he looked up to shrug. "Haven't the Scots and the Welsh helped, too, in keeping Edward's attention on his own backyard and away from us the while?'' He lifted his cup in a ironic toast, one eyebrow cocked. "Here's to the enemy of our enemy. May they always thrive.'' Then he asked, features suddenly earnest, "But we cannot count on it always so, can we?''

His father scowled, disturbed by Cian's bitterness, then

he put his concern away to be examined later. At least he had him talking. And hadn't even Bronwynn lifted her gaze from the fingernails she was tinting a bright crimson. A maid stood behind her stool, twisting her ebony tresses in front into curling spirals and braiding those in back into a multitude of long plaits, then attaching a hollow golden ball to the end of each in the fashion of high born Irish women, although Bronwynn was not one for such female vanities. Perhaps, Calvach thought, she but passes the time, as they all did. Then he shifted farther forward in his chair, bracing his arms against the table. He attempted a chuckle and shrugged.

"Hasn't de Bermingham even invited us to Christmas feasting at Carrick and as many of the clan as I wish to bring with me? Whatever else he is, the man is no fool and can surely see the shifting of the winds here in Ireland."

"It is that 'whatever else the man is' that would worry me," Cian commented. "Hasn't he more turnings than a gaffed eel?"

But Bronwynn was staring at Calvach, her eyes wide with alarm.

"You do not intend to go?" she stated more than asked.

"What do you think the man would do—and himself inviting us into his house and on the holiest of days?" Calvach asked, giving another chuckle. But there was a false tone to his laugh. "Are you thinking, then, that he would violate the laws of hospitality and himself knowing well the punishment? Are not the laws specific there—proscribing any man who would invite another into his house, offer him food, then do him harm or hurt? Even de Bermingham would not seek such condemnation and the shame of such ostracism. There is no worse crime and no worse punishment in Ireland as to be proscribed, to be put outside the law, with every man's face turned from

him, with all forbidden to speak to him, to offer him food
or shelter.''

Bronwynn's chin only lifted higher.

"I think he would not hesitate, no more than did the
Lord of Hay."

Calvach scowled in bewilderment, while Cian strolled
over to lift the flap and stare out at the rain again, no
more than an observer to the conversation. Bronwynn
looked from one to the other, seeing Calvach's purposely
blind resolution and the back Cian turned on his father's
dilemma, so determined he was, now, to wrap himself
away from all pain, all problem, whether in a mantle of
indifference or cynicism. Her smile a sad crimping, she
dropped her gaze to her brightly colored nails and sighed
her own sorrow. Then she sat straighter and her grieving
eyes met Calvach's once more, as Cian wandered back to
pick up his harp and strike a strident discord, glancing
from one to the other with disdainful amusement. His
father would eventually ask the question Bronwynn
needed, such was his curiosity—and he did.

"Who, then," Calvach demanded, "if I needs must play
your game, is the Lord of Hay?"

"Was," she answered, voice round with the sorrow of
an old tale, "the Lord of Hay was William de Broase. He
died almost a hundred years ago in exile in France, put
there by the grace of an ungrateful king, but he had served
the Plantagenets well a quarter of a century before. And
a Christmas day it was then, too, when he invited several
dozen of the Welsh of Gwent to Abergavenny Castle. After
the Welsh had left their weapons outside the door, after
they had washed their hands and had toasted together,
the Lord of Hay drew his dagger and slit the throat of
Prince Seisyll, whereupon his men drew arms secreted
about the hall and slayed them all, including the Prince's
young son. For this deed, he was highly commended by

Henry of England, and the proscription of the Welsh, indeed, their striving for revenge affected him little. His eventual exile had nothing to do with the crime at Abergavenny. If you, my Lord Calvach, had no knowledge of William de Broase, I fear the same cannot be said of Piers de Bermingham. And didn't I hear him say he could not defeat the O'Connors in open battle? Might he then not try treachery?"

The confines of the tent suddenly seemed too small, too stifling for Calvach. Shaking his head as he paced, he snorted his disdain for Bronwynn's female vaporing, while Bronwynn's jaw set harder yet. Her teeth had sunk into her lower lip, and his son watched him with sad, mocking eyes. Calvach seemed almost to be searching for a wall against which to beat his fist, something more substantial than wind fluttered felt. Then he whirled to point a finger at Bronwynn, furious.

"And that," he pointed out, "was, as you said, over a century and a quarter past. Are you thinking, then, that men have not advanced in all that time, that we haven't learned honor, integrity? Times have changed! Men have changed! We live in a gentler world and to even accuse de Bermingham of considering such perfidy is an insult demanding atonement. Nor is Edward his grandfather. He would never sanction such. And you, as my guest, bring dishonor to me and my sept by even suggesting such."

Bronwynn's eyes were pitying and her voice was tender as she leaned forward on her stool to ask, "Was Laracorra an act of honor, of integrity? And am I not your hostage and not your guest?"

Calvach stared at her, jaw set and as aware of the sardonic expectation in his son's gaze as he was of the demand in Bronwynn's. Then, yanking his gaze from hers only long enough to swing two paces to the small table and pick up his cup, he found it empty. Looking back at her as though it was her fault, he shoved it at the maid and she leaped up from braiding Bronwynn's hair to fill it. Grabbing it back, he gave a shake of his leonine head, and sat in his chair once more, rocking back on its hind legs, his brow furrowed into a furious scowl.

"And what would you have me do?" he demanded.

"I would have you not go," she said simply, and he shook his head at her innocence, then glared down into the cup he held low on his crotch. When he looked back up his eyes held a resigned fatalism. His shoulders slumped.

"And if we don't go? If we do not accept the man's invitation?" he inquired. "Is to refuse not an insult and wouldn't the snake of a man announce it to the world as such—and ourselves then owing him a blush fine it would take three generations to pay? Or perhaps he would but ask the judges to award him Laracorra. Is it not saying we do not trust him—whether or not we do? Would doing so not bring down such a mallacht—a curse—on the clan O'Connor that we would be ever damned? Are not the laws a two-edged sword, so? Nor do I trust him—and mayhap he is but hoping I will refuse him. Mayhap 'tis but a gambit to gain Laracorra. But what would you have me do?"

He continued to stare at her until she shook her head and looked down at the hands she held in her lap. There was little, she knew, that an Irish male feared more than being shamed, unless it was bringing shame to his clan— and how wisely de Bermingham had played on it. And, she told herself, her lip caught between her teeth, perhaps it was but an honest invitation, a means of making reparation. But if she truly thought so, why this sense of fear?

As though reading her mind, Calvach leaned forward to place his war-battered hand over the ones she held clenched in her lap. Fighting away tears of frustration, she met his earnest, concerned gaze.

"Don't you know, girl, that I would place my men in as

little jeopardy as possible? Don't you know we will be going with as many men as I can cram into the great hall of Carrick, until we are nose to armpit and halfway up the arse of each other and the hag-ridden, hell-bound Sassenach besides? Won't de Bermingham be fearing there will be aught to feed even that bitch of a wife of his, so many of us there will be—and herself dining, I'm thinking, most-times on nettles and needles and wasps, besides, considering the tongue on the woman. Do you not know I love that great, glowering one there?" He jerked his chin to where his son sat scowling down at the harp he desultorily plucked. Lifting his gaze, Cian held Bronwynn's, a smile about his eyes encouraging her to trust his father, to trust him. "Isn't he the breath of life to me and myself wishing I could protect him from all the harm of living and of ever dying? So, sure, I'd not knowingly place him in danger, would I?"

Leaning forward, he placed his fingertips on either side of her face, tilting it up, forcing her gaze to meet his. His eyes glowed with affectionate laughter as he wiped away her tears with the balls of his thumbs.

"Now, smile for me. Show me you trust me," he ordered.

Blinking back her remaining tears, Bronwynn smiled at Calvach. He would not endanger Cian any more than necessary. But why, she wondered, was foreboding hitching up her spine with the claws of the specter of death? And why, beneath the smile Calvach gave her in return, was there such a grieving? But there was nothing she could do but bend her head again to the maid's grooming, while the rain ran like tears down the walls of the tent.

(14)

As though to mock all grieving, the day dawned bright and warm, a day more of June than December. The rains of the days before had washed clean the earth and sky. Above were high, fleecy clouds whose only purpose, it seemed, was to make the sky but bluer still, and the sun touched every object with irradiance. The River Boyne ran swift and shallow here and it glinted with the brilliance of a hundred thousand diamonds. Across was the brook and the green meadows—and the hillside where Cian had first taken her in his rage and grieving. Little remained of the hospital. The river had swept much of it away and rushes and water reeds grew around and through the rest. Green sod, too, had grown over the new graves in the cemetery in the months that had been Cian's and hers. Yet, there was still, it seemed, a faint odor of slaughter on the light air, a smell of rain falling on charred, smoldering wood.

But in the meadows tents had sprouted. They looked, Bronwynn told herself, aware that anger and sorrow directed the thought, like malignant toadstools growing,

as toadstools do, on the decay and dry rot of old ruins,
of destruction. Above the tents flew the standard of de
Bermingham and before them was the mounted cohort
of himself and his men. Were they, she wondered, as
uncomfortable in their presence there as she was, as were
Calvach and his son, his men? She doubted it. Then the
O'Connor was urging his horse forward and Bronwynn
followed.

De Bermingham rode forward to meet them, Rudulf on
his left side, on his right, Fenella de Grenville. Or correctly,
Fenella O'Connor, Piers told himself, de Grenville having
failed to marry her as he had promised, wise man that he
was. But the O'Connor whelp had divorced her, so he
didn't know the bitch's cursed name—nor did he care to.
He was just glad she would be gone and her whining,
sniveling, mercenary ways with her. Nor was it so much
that she was mercenary—so was Melusine; but at least his
wife had wit enough to conceal the fault in a cloak of
charm, of sweetness—when it suited her purpose. Fenella
what-ever-her-name-was was simply stupid. As much as he
did not care for the Fitzhugh wench's grey eyes that seemed
to know too much, or for that quiet way she had of sweetly
refusing his wishes—and King Edward's—he could only
believe Cian O'Connor was getting the worst of the bar-
gain. Yet it was not for Fenella that O'Connor was releasing
the Fitzhugh woman which might be one of the reasons
the bitch was as foul tempered as a baited badger; Fenella
was scarcely one to play second-in-the-bed. But he was
giving her more credit than due, Piers thought. She was
too enamored of her own charms to imagine she might
not be wanted, and his thin lips twitched with pleasure at
the picture of the wench finding herself spurned—and by
the son of aught but an Irish tuath king.

It was for the child, a girl child, more fool he, that Cian
was giving up Bronwynn, and Piers snorted. Surely, Cian

must realize how strong a bargaining chip he had in his fist—and in his bed, if the gossips could be believed, and therefore damaged goods. That would surely not please Edward, not as valuable a prize to any lord loyal enough to the king to be awarded her. Still, it shouldn't be too difficult for a man to find her attractive—deflowered or not, with bastard or not—when viewing her over the length and breadth of her holdings. But he doubted, now, that she would be of use to his stepson—or to him.

Nor was the child even attractive, with her wide, wary eyes, the scabs about her mouth, and her stringy, filthy hair. But, he thought, in all honesty it would be difficult to guess if the brat was neglected because she was unsightly or if she was unsightly because she was neglected—if one did not know the mother.

He looked at Fenella and marveled at how alike and yet how different she and his wife were. It was only, he decided, the blond hair, the blue eyes, the perfect oval faces that they had in common. Melusine's eyes held avarice, true, but there was also a shred of intelligence, while Fenella's held only banal selfishness and covetousness. Nor would his wife have ever mistreated a child, while Fenella did not even hold her own brat, but had a half grown Irish nursemaid for the task. And a perilous position it was—for the brat. The maid was certainly not comfortable on horseback and burdened, too, with a child. Perhaps, though, that was the thought in Fenella's mind. Nor could he scarcely blame her. The brat, obviously vermin ridden, clutched awkwardly by the maid, was silently sniveling and knuckling with a grimy fist her snot running nose. And whose fault, de Bermingham asked himself, was the child's condition, if not her mother's, and where and why had she learned that trick of weeping without a sound? Then he put all thought of the child aside and looked beyond Fenella to his oldest son, Walter, home from England.

In times such as these and with the deeds such times called for it was best to have blood at your side—and at your back, as was Richard, his youngest, behind him among his knights and men-at-arms. Thomas, the middle one, was still in service with Edward in England. He had, he told himself, reaching down to adjust himself against the hard leather of the saddle, reason enough to be proud of those sons by his first marriage. Yet, there was that need to have a child by Melusine. Why, he did not know, unless it was that feeling that a part of her ever evaded his possession. He did not want to believe she cultivated it deliberately, any more than he wished to have his suspicion that she somehow prevented conceiving a child confirmed. Resenting the ability his wife had of insinuating herself into his mind at the most inopportune times—and the control over him such a power suggested—he squinted at the party of Irish across the Boyne. He sometimes thought, aware even at the times he thought it of how witless the whimsy was, that if he could but bring to heel that recalcitrant tuath king and his unruly subjects, he could control his wife. There were, however, other reasons to destroy the O'Connor and much of his clan with him, political and economic reasons—and all of them concerning Edward, also. If such a deed brought him his wife, all the more good, and it might; she admired deceit only a little less than stalwart feats of arms.

But the O'Connor was riding toward him, now, that perverse tuath king. On one side was his equally stubborn son, on the other Bronwynn Fitzhugh. And a well matched trio they were, Piers told himself. At the very least, the accomplishment of his plans would prevent the union of two such difficult people from creating whelps of their own ilk. Then de Bermingham, too, nudged his mount forward.

Her chin set, Bronwynn blinked against the glare of

sunlight glimmering off the river and the tears threatening
to weaken her. Calvach, beside her, also rode with unyielding visage and beyond him Cian. But she dared not glance
at Cian. To see grief on his features would only make hers
sharper, deeper. She doubted she could bear such and
not fall into a thousand pieces, each piece pleading to stay
with him, each one refusing to return to Carrick, disgracing
him and herself, and possibly plunging all of Offaly—and
Ireland—into war. And if there was no sorrow at their
parting, if his face was merely accepting of their purpose
there? Or worse. What if beneath features set in feigned
heart grief she saw an eagerness to once again lay eyes on
Fenella McKenna? That, she thought, she knew, she could
not endure. A sob swelled in her throat and she swallowed
it back with the faintest of gulps. But the O'Connor had
heard and he reached to take her hand, ordering her
steady, offering her the little comfort he could give. She
thought the gesture would surely break her as the parting
had not, then she drew strength back into her with a breath
that ached her chest and squeezed back, telling him she
would not fail him or Cian. Releasing her at the water's
edge to allow her to go on by herself, as she must, he drew
rein beside his son.

   She felt her horse falter at the bank's rim and she kneed
him on to feel his hooves hesitate, then, with tear blocked
ears, she heard them splash on into the river. An otter,
disturbed by the sudden company, was a glimmer of movement to her blurred vision. Then she turned her horse in
the shallow water to face Calvach O'Connor, to face his
son, and knew both camps leaned forward with expectation, fear, excitement. But she could not, she knew, leave
Cian without seeing on his features what was in his heart.
She could not live the rest of her life in such a lie if he
did not love her.

   He sat straight, proud, fists clenched white about the

bridle reins, his gaze intent on her face, his own expressionless. Then, leaning forward as far as he could, he held out
a hand to her and, stretching toward him, straining over
her mount's neck, she was able to touch his fingertips.

"Be with me!" he whispered and she blinked back her
tears, her chin lifting with pride. "And you with me," she
answered. She thought to tell him of her secret that was,
still, scarcely more than a hope, but knew the gift, if false,
could only hurt him more, and kept silent.

Then her horse shifted, his hoof sliding off a moss slick
rock, and her fingers were drawn from his, their touch
breaking. Gazing at him one moment longer, she memo-
rized his features, then turned her mount, her heels pressing hard into its flanks, and urged him on across the river.

It was with her head high that she passed Fenella in
the middle of the shallow water. Her glance, driven by a
curiosity she could not deny, slid sideways to the woman
Cian had loved before her and she blinked, so much like
Melusine Fenella was, so like Cecily. But the resemblance
was only of coloring, of clothing, for Fenella was dressed
in the height of fashion, her sleeves so long they brushed
the extravagantly extended tips of her shoes. Her skirt was
full and flowed from her hips, her tunic snug about her
waist and breasts, and her mantle was trimmed in fur.
All were in a multitude of colors reminding Bronwynn,
suddenly, of the foppishness of Rudulf de Broc. If Richard
de Grenville had not married his Irish mistress, he had
certainly garbed her—if not in the best of taste—at least
flamboyantly. But Fenella was eyeing her with the same
disdain, her gaze dropping scornfully down from her
plaited hair to her mantle of otter skins, to the wide bands
of embroidery at the hem and sleeves of her surcoat, down
to her knee high, doe-skin boots. Her gaze, though, had
snagged on the gold torc about Bronwynn's neck, on the
heavy, intricately worked earrings, both a parting gift from

Calvach, and Bronwynn caught the rage that they had not been given to her in her eyes. Smiling into the face of the other woman's fury, the woman who had so hurt the man she loved, Bronwynn looked at the child—the one who was truly taking her place in Cian's life.

The brief glimpse of huge eyes peering out from the convulsive grasp of the maid, from over the grimy thumb stuck in a baby-soft mouth surrounded by sores caught Bronwynn's breath in a gasp. There had been a bruise darkening one side of her face and the salty tracks of unwiped tears down infant-round cheeks. And the eyes staring back at her had been so like Cian's that they had taken her heart away. Then they were past and all that was before her was captivity. But she had had the wind on her skin, the mist on her tongue. She had ridden with the foaming white horses of the sea along the wild beaches of the West. There was, too, her sister to see again, Bronwynn reminded herself, and she *had* missed her, had thought of her, worried about her. There were other people, too, at Carrick she would be happy to see, although she could not, at that moment, put a name or a face to any of them.

And, perhaps, she would see Cian at Christmas. It was strange, but the thought held fewer terrors in the bright sunlight of the day than it had in the night, with the wind sobbing against the trembling walls of the tent, with the rains weeping from the heavens.

Bronwynn did not expect a warm welcome from de Bermingham nor was she disappointed. He gave her no more than a glance like a sneer, then he addressed Sir Mortimer, asking him the identity of a man with Calvach O'Connor. Rudulf grinned at his stepfather's disapproval, glad to see another, especially her, in the position so often his. He leaned over to flick a gold ball at the end of a plait with

a disparaging finger, but her chin came up and her eyes
narrowed, warning him off. He flushed and straightened
in the saddle, glancing about to see who had taken in the
scene. Then he looked at her defiantly and snickered,
wiping his hand down his particolored hose, as though
even the attempt to touch her had sullied his fingers.
Bronwynn stared back. He was still her enemy, this callow,
crude youth who, had they been wiser, should have been
her ally, if not her friend, and his eyes shifted away from
hers.

Not waiting for de Bermingham, Bronwynn forced her
mount through the mass of his men and on, away from
Laracorra. The men parted for her, then turned to stare
uneasily from her retreating figure to their lord, then back
again. Caught off guard, angry, de Bermingham, too,
shifted to see her riding away. Nor was there anything he
could do but follow her. Purple with rage, he scowled one
more time at the Irish forces prepared to cross and reclaim
Laracorra at his leaving, then turned to follow the little
Welsh bitch who dared to so humiliate him by matching
his rudeness with her own. Nor did he or any of his men
address her on the long ride to Carrick. If they thought
to punish her, Bronwynn thought, welcoming the silence,
needing it within which to cradle her grief, they had chosen
a poor method for it. It felt as though, with each step of
her horse, a shred of her heart was torn out and left to
lie bleeding on the track behind her, trampled into the
dirt by the horses following after.

De Bermingham would not ignore her for long, she
knew. Too soon, he would be after her with questions,
with demands for information about the O'Connor, his
men, their arms and fortifications. If he had overlooked
his male vanity, she thought wryly, he could have asked
her for the identity of O'Connor's companion.

Nor did Cecily give her such solace as silence. Graceful

as a damselfly, she flew down the steps of the keep of Carrick to meet her sister halfway up in view of all those gawking in the bailey below and staring down from the windows and the wide entrance, the parapets above. Her sky blue surcoat floated about her. The ermine about the sleeves dangling to her knees and about the lowcut, square neckline was scarcely paler than her skin. A white scarf as thin as gossamer and held on her head by a circlet of gold wafted about a face as delicate as itself.

Her eyes were as blue as her dress and glistening with the trace of tears of happiness as she hesitated, looking Bronwynn up and down in a flick of an eyelash black with charcoal and grease. She blinked once in contempt of the embroidery bordering the hem and sleeves of Bronwynn's surcoat, then rushed into her arms. Her breath was fragrant on Bronwynn's neck as she whispered, "Ah, I missed you so! I'm so glad you are back and unharmed!"

Then she drew back to examine her sister more closely.

"We were so worried about you!" she exclaimed, imagining her own hair worked in spirals like Bronwynn's and deciding it flew too much in the face of fashion. Her vision registered the long plaits of dark hair, the gold balls at the end of each, and narrowed in scorn.

"You are unharmed, are you not?"

Not waiting for an answer, she flicked one of the balls with a tinted fingernail, as Rudulf had wanted to do, and scowled, surprised by the weight.

"Those are real, are they not?" she asked, her voice guileless, and Bronwynn laughed, drawing back to gaze into Cecily's lovely face.

"And I missed you," she told her—and found that it was true. She hugged her and Cecily returned the embrace, holding back only enough to study one of the earrings Bronwynn wore. It was a stork, she decided, although she could not pull back so far that she could focus on it easily.

Yes, a stork, its head curving down to rest against one leg with the other drawn to its belly, foot tucked in, yet the lines twisting all as one. The torque about her sister's neck remained a blur no matter how hard she tried to see it. At last, Bronwynn released her and Cecily slipped her hand about her waist, her cheek brushing against the soft fur of Bronwynn's mantle as she turned back up the stairs. Suddenly, the ermine about her sleeves and neckline seemed paltry, thin. And who, she wondered, would not think it rabbit if they did not know she would never wear such? She gave a little chuckle and slid a rueful glance at her sister.

"It could not," she commented, "have been such a horrid captivity if you return dressed in furs and gold." One finger touched the earring, then the torque. "Is that real?" she asked, knowing well enough that it was.

"Of course, 'tis real," Bronwynn smiled. "If you can touch something, 'tis real."

For a swift second, Cecily's soft lips puckered into a pout of annoyance, then she giggled, the sound thin.

"Of course, I know 'tis real, but are they gold?"

Bronwynn pressed the necklace into her flesh, as though to remind herself of its shape, its reality. The grief she concealed so arduously suddenly assaulted her. Her features stiffened with it and she swallowed hard, then smiled, while her eyes seemed to see through her sister's features to another place, another time.

"They are real gold," she assured her and Cecily smiled back.

"May I have them?" she asked lightly, but her gaze was avid. Not certain she had heard correctly, Bronwynn shook her head.

"They were a gift, a parting gift—from the O'Connor."

"And what better luck," Cecily reasoned, "than to receive a gift and gift another with it."

Still, her sister shook her head.

"I cannot. They were given in trust to me."

"In trust," Cecily laughed, pausing to lift her chin and stare at Bronwynn, "and from aught but an Irish tuath king? What would he know of trust or of honor or chivalry—or of the love between sisters? And I thought you loved me. Hadn't you promised our father, too, that you would take care of me? You always tell me so when there is something you want!"

Then she saw that tightening of Bronwynn's jaw which always told her she had gone too far and an unfamiliar blaze of fury in her eyes, and she laughed nervously. "You never know, do you, when I'm but jesting with you. You always take me so seriously!"

Slipping her arm once more under that marvelous cloak of otter skins and around her sister's waist, she swung Bronwynn back on up the steps. She cuddled her face into Bronwynn's neck and whispered so soft that her sister was not certain she had heard the smear of gloating, "But 'twas me Cian wanted, you know. Hadn't he told me so?"

Jerking away, Bronwynn stared at Cecily, blinking in bewilderment, in her hurt and wonder of what she had done that her sister so hated her. But there was only an innocent, questioning smile about Cecily's rose petal mouth. It was Bronwynn, then, who urged her sister on up the tall stairs of the keep of Carrick, not wanting to see anything but that artlessness on her features.

The bailey of Carrick had been swarming with people when Bronwynn entered it from under the heavy portcullis with de Bermingham. Hunters returning with wild boar for the holiday feasting had entered before them and were pushing through the throng to the kitchens. Acrobats practicing somersaults and handstands vied for space with the swinging buckets of dairy maids and lethal lances of men-at-arms. Jugglers and a performing bear rehearsed their acts to the amusement of spit boys and the chagrin of a stable man struggling to control a frightened steed. And all took advantage of the warmth of an unseasonable day in December. In the great hall Bronwynn saw that the yule log was decorated and awaiting its lighting in the huge hearth. Minstrels and strolling players and Irish bards were there, too, and all were underfoot in every nook and space of the castle, practicing their skills and talents wherever a convenient corner could be had and sleeping in the stalls of the stables, under the kitchen tables, on bags of apples in the storerooms. Some would stay through the yule season. More would go, seeking a more lucrative employment, a more discriminating audience—or a less—and all would be driven by the fear Christmas would find them on the road and without a sponsor.

The great hall, too, was festooned with evergreens twined with holly and mistletoe. Bronwynn paused to stare up at the deep green boughs and the bright red berries, remembering violets and cowslips in wet, hidden places and banks of moss and forget-me-nots amid green rushes. It was almost as though she could again see daisies bending before the wind, could breathe the scent of wild roses climbing tall standing stones and of Cian's skin warm from lovemaking. She could feel the first chill of autumn as asters danced in the breeze, as Cian laid her down on a bed of wolf furs on a hillside warm from the afternoon sun. And the hawthorn fruit had turned scarlet, too, she thought, as was the holly now, when Curran had come to them in their hidden place. But Cecily was staring at her, features puckered with puzzlement and Bronwynn blinked away her memories. Obedient to her sister's command, she wiped her cheeks with the back of her hands, not wanting to meet Melusine with a tear streaked face. No one but a fool, she told herself, would give the wife of Piers de Bermingham such power. Then she followed Cecily up the steps to the solar.

Teeth set on the sour flavors of frustration, envy and anger, Melusine eyed her noble ward and waited that extra moment before signaling her up from a deep curtsy. With a circling of her finger, she ordered Bronwynn to turn, to display herself to her. Lips curved into a smile telling Melusine and all the ladies crowded into the solar that she understood her purpose, Bronwynn obeyed. Eyes cool with disdain, smoothing the cloth of her surcoat over her flat belly, she exhibited herself to all who would look and relished Melusine's flush of rage. Still, the older woman eyed her, torn between the fear that her son should wed a woman already with brat by another man, and an Irishman to boot, and worse, that he would lose her and her estates should he object to a pregnant bride. But Bronwynn, she decided, was not pregnant, or not obviously so. Signaling her to approach, Melusine gestured Bronwynn onto a stool at her feet.

"So," she stated in greeting, "you were not caught with brat in your wanderings with your Irish lordling."

There was a hint of desire for assurance in the woman's haughty tone, and Bronwynn only tilted her head, smiling. Her fingers idly plucked at the gold embroidery on the girdle spanning her slim hips, accenting her flat belly and Melusine chose to take, at last, her mild eyes, her lack of response, as assent.

"Do you know how fortunate you were not to quicken in the—how long were you gone—eight months, nine? And the saints know the man must be lusty—all angry, melancholy men are, I've found—and especially the Irish, they say. And all of them seem to be angry and melancholy, so 'twould stand to reason. If you should ever find yourself in such a position again," she told Bronwynn, leaning closer to adopt the role of mother-mentor, "a sponge soaked in vinegar and put up your cunny will prevent a brat—sometimes." She flushed under Bronwynn's mocking smile and looked away, aware she—who seldom revealed anything—had said too much. "Or so I am told. I've no purpose in trying such with my husband so eager for a child." Then her eyes grew sly with prurient curiosity. "How is he," she whispered, "the O'Connor lordling? Is he as lusty as all of my ladies had hoped?"

Bronwynn drew back to gaze into Melusine's lascivious eyes, her own round with confoundment.

"My Lady," she asked with a lack of guile even her sister would have envied, "surely you do not think a maid of my innocence would bed with a man unless wed to him? Surely you do not think a man of Cian O'Connor's honor would so violate a maiden placed into his trust, as I was, no matter the time we spent together?"

Melusine stared back at her, gaze narrowed, angry, nor was she convinced of Bronwynn's innocence. Then one corner of her thin mouth curled up in an admiring smile.

"You are telling me 'tis none of my business, are you not?" she asked, but Bronwynn only gazed back, her features placid and smooth, and she shrugged one round shoulder. "Perhaps 'tis indeed not—and perhaps another of my ladies will try him come the yuletide and be more prone to gossip. And you must be fatigued from your adventures," and a corner of her mouth quirked up to give her statement a salacious insinuation. Then she yawned, as though bored by the conversation and by Bronwynn, herself. "You may go. And, Bronwynn," she called after her, "haven't you gone a bit too native? I hope your garments are less primitive when next I see you."

Bronwynn had paused the better to hear Melusine. Not

bothering to turn around, she listened, head tilted, a faint, derisive smile about her lips. Then she shrugged, whether as an acknowledgement or as a rebuff, Melusine could not have said, before she continued on her way.

(15)

Melusine's question concerning Cian O'Connor's lust-fulness was the only interrogation Bronwynn underwent. She waited, dreading the summons by Piers de Berming-ham and the questions he would ask, the answers he would demand. Nor could she do anything but refuse to answer him. Or she could say, she told herself with a wry little grin, that she had been blindfolded the entire time. He might very well believe her, having as little respect for female intelligence as he did. But the summons did not come and as the days passed, her fear eased. After all, she argued with herself, hadn't he invited the O'Connor to the feasting in celebration of the birth of the Christ child? If peace with the O'Connor was his purpose, why would de Bermingham need or want information on the fortifica-tions of his neighbor, the number of men he could call to arms, the wealth of his lands, the extent of his livestock?

Still, she would have felt more comfortable had de Ber-mingham questioned her. He was not a man easily per-suaded from his goal, his greed, and she wondered why he was so, now. And still that specter of foreboding lingered in the back of her mind and darkened her dreams.

But the apprehension twined with the ache brooding in her soul, blocking her throat, gripping with a fist of need deep within her belly. It wove itself into the grief of missing Cian, of needing him. The foreboding became a part of a ball of rage in the pit of her stomach at de Bermingham, at Melusine, at Edward, at all people who wove schemes that twisted about and tore apart the lives of others. And all to their own gain—until she could not tell what was grief or ache, anger of premonition. Yet the premonition, at least, she could reason away for a few moments of peace, arguing with it with the same logic Calvach O'Connor had used when trying to convince her—and himself—of its foolishness.

And all about her, it seemed, the world prepared for the feasting, for the games and merriments of the yule season. The castle was a welter of comings and goings, of cooking and baking, of the practicing of skits and singing, of hunting for more game to feed the guests, of repairing and sharpening arms, for a mock tourney, too, was part of the entertainment. Yet, Bronwynn felt no part of it— of these people striving so hard to have fun and yet using even this, the celebration of the birth of the Christ child, it seemed to her, to further their own purposes. She knew too well the games behind flattering smiles, the motives behind convivial greetings.

So, behind a wall of indifference, she sat quietly plying her needle, the set line of her mouth disinclining all who might try from approaching her, while laughter and jesting rang off the stonewalls, while her sister huddled in conversations and sidelong glances with Melusine. She sat at the huge table at the head of the hall, sharing a trencher with Rudulf, a half smile of bemusement about her mouth at the thought that anyone might still believe she would one day marry the pitiful creature. She climbed the narrow, steep stairs to the wallwalk, seeking old ghosts, old memories, and often it would be Curran she missed.

One slim hand pressed into her belly, she wondered what she would tell Cian—or if, indeed, she would have anything to tell him. If she did, might it not hurt him all the more to know she walked away from him with his child within her? Or would he see it as the gift she meant it to be—a gift of love—the two of them together in the child, forever, as they could not be, themselves? Did he want, did he need, she wondered, this miracle of a child as much as she did? Sometimes she doubted he would even come to Carrick. The wise thing, after all, the less cruel thing, would be to stay away, sparing them both the agony of gazing into each other's faces across the great hall, of perhaps a hand clasped, and no more, in a silent, anguished communication of love, of sorrow, of need. She even doubted that there would be any place they could be for time enough to tell of the child.

And she counted the days to Christmas. 'Tis less than a fortnight, she told herself, staring into the mists and rains of December from the parapet of Carrck. Then it was but a week and a day. The day passed, and then it was the last Sunday in Advent and six days, then five, four. And with each day passing the certitude grew that she was, indeed, with child.

Christmas day dawned thick, the cold drizzle mingling with a rare sleet and snow clinging damply to all it touched. It curled down out of a grey sky to round the square corners of the parapet, to soften the harsh stone of the walls. It swirled about in its fall to the earth of the empty bailey. Where the people who had crowded into it through the days before had gone, Bronwynn could not guess. Nor would she see Cian, not that day. The great hall was reserved for the guests of de Bermingham and those who would treat with them in negotiation and hospitality and those who would serve them. The entertainment, de Bermingham had explained, would come later, perhaps as late as that evening, perhaps even the next day.

And what better day to make peace, he had asked, than the day of the Lord's birth? Nor were the ladies of the castle to be allowed in the great hall, not while such serious business was being conducted.

He had studied Bronwynn as he stated this and she had returned his stare, features expressionless, while all she wanted to do was weep and wail and kick walls in frustration. All she could think of was that it was to be, perhaps, another twenty four hours before she would see Cian. Nor, too proud to ask, might she even know, until then, if he had come at all, the thick snow fall of the morning thwarting any chances that she might see him as he entered Carrick.

Yet, she had to try and, peering over the edge of the battlement, she heard a voice lifted in greeting and the creak of the rising portcullis. Leaning over farther still, Bronwynn saw figures who had to be de Bermingham and his lords gathered on the steps of the keep to meet the guests. Still, the snow swirled, obscuring then revealing the men and horses clattering over the draw bridge and into the bawn, and Bronwynn lifted herself to perch in the deep crenature of the wall, leaning over farther still. Even on a fair day, it was not easy to see someone clearly those four stories below.

A gust of wind parted the snow for a moment and she saw a guest give up his great sword and war ax. He would, she knew, keep his skean for, no matter that they were there under the laws of hospitality, no one, man or woman, could eat easily without the knife they all carried for the purpose. Another man paused to look up at the parapet, a hand protecting his eyes from the sleet and snow as though he sought sight of someone, and she thought it might be Curran or Cormac. Surely, Calvach would bring them along with his chieftains, his lords, his sons, if only to swell their numbers that bit more. But, peer as she would, Bronwynn could not recognize anyone for certain and she sighed in frustration. Then the men were gone inside, leaving the bawn empty of all life and Bronwynn wondering, still, if Cian was with them.

Shivering despite the warmth of her mantle, she slipped back down to the wallwalk and, chin propped on her fists, studied the falling snow. It would soon cover all evidence that the men of O'Connor had ever been there and she shuddered again, this time more from a renewed foreboding than from the cold. But it was a foolish nagging, she told herself, and most probably nothing more than the qualm of a pregnant woman. Slipping a hand inside her cloak and smiling at the thought, she at last admitted defeat and descended the stairs to join Melusine, to ply her needle, to listen to the minstrels, to laugh at the jesters—and to wait.

But the laughter and gossip could not distract her from her apprehension and de Bermingham's exclamation for barring the women from the great hall seemed too contrived. Never had she heard before of such negotiations occurring before the feasting, the entertainment. After all, wasn't it the purpose of such—to soften up the adversary, to convince him of your sincerity—at least until he sobered? Jamming her needle harder into the linen she embroidered, Bronwynn thought of the look de Bermingham had directed at her along with the news that she would not be allowed to greet the guests—not that day. There had been pleasure and gloating in it at her frustration—that she had expected. But he had studied her almost with a grim determination, as though he would walk through her if she should get in her way. Yet, how

would she do that—and his purpose unknown? Had she
imagined, too, his gaze sidling away when she challenged
it, almost with guilt?

Her own glance slipped sideways, meeting Melusine's—
and Melusine's was the first to fall almost angrily away.
And what did Melusine have to be angry about? Yet, hadn't
it been an expression she had encountered recently too
often on the visages of de Bermingham's men?

Thrusting her needle once more into the cloth, Bronwynn set it aside and stood to walk to a tall, narrow arrow
slit. Drawing aside the tapestry, she stared out into the
night, lower lip caught between her teeth. Not feeling the
cold and damp she let in, she thought of the sweating
blacksmith as he honed sword after sword, battle ax after
broad ax. And the fletchers—had they not been set to
crafting arrow after arrow? And to what purpose? Surely
not to de Bermingham's explanation of a tourney—not
in this weather and not with those weapons.

Entangled in her loneliness and her need for Cian, wal-
lowing in her own misery, she had been willfully blind to
all of the evidence Bronwynn suddenly realized, and had
deliberately dismissed that sense of premonition which
was, now, a fist clenched about her throat, a cold hand
creeping up her spine. Each of the clues alone meant little,
she knew. It was when they were all added up together
that they totaled something monstrous, something too
abominable to be believed. And Melusine's silence, now,
when normally she would have ordered the tapestry
dropped and Bronwynn back to her stool with a caustic
comment about her having lived too long among the Irish,
was but one more clue. Swallowing the taste of bile threatening to explode in a stream of incredulity and vomit,
Bronwynn dropped the hanging and turned to survey the
room.

Cecily's head rested on Melusine's knee while the other

woman gently played with her golden hair. The heads of two ladies were bent over a riot of color as they examined embroidery threads. Two others played a game of draughts. Others gossiped. And all ignored the troubadour singing in praise of Melusine's bright hair, her blue eyes. But Melusine was looking at Bronwynn, her gaze intent. Yet, her voice was loving when she asked why her ward seemed so restless. Its tenderness lifted the hairs on the back of Bronwynn's neck. It walked bony fingers up her arms. Still, Bronwynn only shrugged.

"I but wait to use the garderobe," she answered.

"By peering out the window and freezing the rest of us?" Melusine gently teased.

"Agnes uses it," Bronwynn answered and Melusine made a little moue of sympathy. The length of time Agnes Mowbray could occupy the latrine had long been a source of both humor and impatience among her ladies. Nor did the cold wind blowing through the privy hole hurry her about her business. Still, there was a wary crease around Melusine's eyes and they widened with alarm when Bronwynn added, "I'll but use the one in the north tower."

Melusine half stood, as though to order Bronwynn to stay, then she sat again, scowling her indecision. That grim set to his mouth brooking no argument, her lord had ordered her to keep her ladies, especially Bronwynn, in the solar until told otherwise. But how could she refuse someone the use of a garderobe, especially when she was as needful as Bronwynn Fitzhugh seemed to be, and she nodded. Still, her gaze strayed often to the door through which Bronwynn had left, as she waited for her ward's return.

Skirts in hand, Bronwynn approached the man-at-arms guarding the door to the solar. But he didn't return her smile and the pike he extended across her chest allowed

no passage. Still, she clutched her belly in distress and
nodded toward the north tower.

"I needs must use the garderobe and there is a long
line in there." Her smile this time was more a grimace, as
though from a cramp. "I think the eels were bad. We all
ate the eels."

His dull eyes wavered and Bronwynn drew her breath
in in a hiss of pain. Pushing aside the pike, she flew away,
heading, not for the north tower, but down the steep circle
of narrow stairs to the great hall, ignoring the guard's
shouts to halt. Nor would he come after her, not with the
thought of the other women escaping, all in search of a
privy, to stay him.

But she paused at that final turn of the stairs before the
entrance to the great hall. What if she was wrong? Eyes
clenched shut, her lips moved in a frantic prayer offering
up all she loved to the plea that she was wrong. Then she
listened hard, staring at the stone wall weeping moisture
opposite her. A shouted toast came to her ears, a spurt of
ribald laughter, trampled by another, and she issued a sob
of gratitude, of relief. But she wanted to see, to but catch
sight of Cian, and she stepped around the corner.

Two men-at-arms standing shoulder to broad shoulder,
their backs to her, blocked her view. Rising on tiptoe on
the last step, she peered over the soldiers to the high table
at the back of the long hall. De Bermingham was there, that
she could see, with his arm wrapped about the O'Connor's
shoulder as he spoke into the Irish chieftain's ear. The
others, though, were blocked by the heads and brawny
necks of the men-at-arms and Bronwynn settled back in
disappointment only to see the swords honed to a fine
glimmering the men held behind them, clenched in
mailed fists.

Held behind them, she saw, her thoughts quicker than
a moment, yet far too late, and concealed from the weap-

onsless Irish. And, Oh, God! wouldn't the guards, if placed there to deny someone entrance, be facing her? Yet, they would appear, standing as they did, to Calvach O'Connor as but two observers enjoying the festivities. But it was not supposed to be a time of festivities but of negotiation— or so de Bermingham had told all of those he had not wished to attend.

It was wrong, all wrong! And Bronwynn rose back on tiptoe to tell Calvach so, to shout a warning which caught in her throat, never to be coughed up or swallowed down, at the sight of a knife caught up from its hiding place in the rushes. Wielded by de Bermingham, it glittered in its descent toward the juncture of shoulder and neck of the O'Connor. A sob bursting from her, Bronwynn leaped forward in an attempt to push between the guards. Not even looking at her, one of the men picked her up as easily as a kitten and tossed her back up the stairs. Then he pushed through into the hall to join the butchery, while Bronwynn lay where he had discarded her, listening to the fruitless sobs of a woman and knowing they were hers. She pressed her clenched fists against her mouth but could not stop them. Eyes squeezed shut, all she could see was the glitter still of the descending knife, a sparkle of steel on a veil of blood. Nor could her own elbows pressing against her ears block out the shouts of desperate, unarmed men as they fought with bare, bleeding hands and skeans still slick with the grease of the meat offered them by their hosts. They could not halt the sounds of a broad ax meeting unyielding bone and the table beneath, the suck of a blade drawn from pliant flesh and the thud as it struck again. She felt the brush of feet as archers ran down the stairs behind her, as they stepped over her, around her. She heard the thum of the arrows as they were released—and the twhack as they found their targets.

There was the raging shout of, "O'Connor Abu!" and

no one to rally to it. Someone cursed God in a voice harsh
with rage and another wailed for a priest. Then there was,
for a moment, the appalled silence of children when a
prank has gone hideously wrong—or has worked too well.
It was disturbed only by the sound of dripping blood from
a table, from a lax finger tip.

The taste of tears salty in her mouth, her unbound hair
spread over her shoulders like a raven cloak of mourning,
Bronwynn crouched on the stairs. Her arms were across
her eyes. Her hands were pressed over her ears, but still
she heard someone shudder, whether from disgust or from
a release almost sexual, she could not guess. Another
heaved a sigh, seemingly glad to be done with a deed not
to his liking. There was a creak as someone shrugged his
shoulders, easing the armor he worn concealed beneath
his surcoat. Then someone spoke softly and another
snorted. Someone made a course jest greeted by a snicker,
while yet another laughed and added his own ribald joke.
There was the jingling slap of ringed mail against her
shoulder as a knight brushed past on his way back up the
stairs.

But Cian had once told her that such was the way of
warriors—to be overcome by bloodlust, that somehow, the
more vile the deed, the stronger was the need to vilify the
dead. Yet, she did not want to hear their words—or view
the result of their deed.

But she must and she forced herself to stand, to walk
with fragile knees and mindful steps into the great hall.
She stood there for a long moment, stunned at the sight
of such carnage. A Sassenach priest, she saw, was already
wending his way through the hall, anointing the dead, and,
in that instant, Bronwynn hated God.

Then she put the hate away with all other emotion she
might have felt, burying it so deep she doubted she would
ever feel again. And it might be better so. Someone spoke

to her but she could not answer, her vision snared by a bloody hand print on a white washed wall, even as she refused to see. The man who had made it, she thought, must have been uncommonly tall to reach so high. Someone else took her arm to turn her away, to lead her back up the stairs to the dubious comfort of Melusine. Then she heard the harsh voice of de Bermingham and she was released. Numb to all but her purpose, Bronwynn entered the hall, concentrating on each step she took, and slowly made her way to Calvach O'Connor.

He had sensed the fall of the knife in that last instant, had lifted his arm to ward off the blow, taking the blade in a deep cut baring flesh to the bone from elbow to wrist. But the second try had gone under his armpit and already, she noted, his heavy gold torque was gone from about his neck. Or perhaps, she thought dispassionately, he had had foresight enough to not wear it while treating with the Sassenach.

Fingers gentle, Bronwynn closed his eyes, touched with one fingertip the mustache that had been his pride, and tried to smooth the grimace of rage from his face with her thumbs. It only fell back into his slack features and she at last began her search for someone she could only hope not to find.

They watched her from the corners of their eyes—the men-at-arms, the knights. Yet, their glances skittered elsewhere if she looked their way and she held her eyes cast down to spare them the discomfort, even as she wondered at the many men she knew there, cousins, nephews, sons, brothers and friends of the O'Connor sept. All had been caught by surprise by a perfidious host, by swords and battle axes hidden in the rushes under tables and benches and all easily at hand. Eoin O'Connor, eyebrows crooked in disbelief, stared sightlessly at a tankard just beyond his outstretched fingers. Smiling her sorrow, Bronwynn remembered the flattering adoration in his gaze—and his voice, sliding once or twice off key. Lunn Mulvany sprawled half on a table, half off, and she wondered at Calvach's bringing one so young, so gangly, then remembered the grace with which he wielded a weapon—and the awkwardness with which he had asked if she had a sister. She tried twice then, and with no offer of help, to lift him back to the bench, to the table. But he only slipped away from her to fall again, and she thought how strange it was—the way the dead subsided so into themselves. Then she gave the effort up only to find Cormac McAuley.

She had recognized the massive form as it lay face down in the rushes, felled by a blow to the back of the head and even weaponless, she knew, he had fought well—to be taken only from the rear. Her only wonder, then, was if it was Curran or Cormac. Curran, she knew, would never have allowed Cian to enter the lair of de Bermingham without him. But even as she heaved the lifeless shoulder over, she saw the dark freckle on an earlobe that told her it was Cormac dead at her feet.

Kneeling beside him, she remembered Fithir, her quiet ways, her soft, elsewhere smile when she spoke of her husband. A sob stirred, then rose to a keening wail that paralyzed all who heard it, lifting the hair on the backs of necks, creeping up spines. It rose from Bronwynn's throat, but it was as Fithir she mourned, as Fithir, who would not know yet awhile that she had cause to grieve, for she, herself, dared feel only nothing. Then a hand was slipped over her mouth, her head was drawn back against a fleshy thigh, and Bronwynn stared up at Rudulf. He stared back, shaking his head.

"Don't do that, that banshee wailing," he ordered, and Bronwynn wondered if his mother yet realized that he was mad. "It hurts my head."

He terrified her, suddenly, yet still she unwrapped his

fingers from across her lips and tried to rise. But his yellow
and green shoe, now soaked with blood, was placed on
one of her long, knee-length sleeves.

"I would stand," she stated and he smiled, reveling in
her helplessness.

"Would you?" he asked. "Only if I allow it—and only
if you cease that hideous wailing you no doubt learned
from the natives—not that any of them here will join you
in it."

And he smirked at his own macabre humor.

"How many?" she asked, and he shrugged, disappointed
that she, too, had not smiled.

"Thirty—give or take one or two—enough, all said, to
never again deny us Offaly."

And he giggled. The sound lifted vomit to her throat.
Still, she had to ask.

"And Cian O'Connor?"

His smile became a gloating, but his gaze slid away for
just an instant. When it returned, his eyes were guileless,
and he licked at his lips with a pointed tongue.

"He's here, somewhere," he answered, waving a limp
hand over the slaughter. "I saw him come in with that
huge man of his. You'll find him if you search hard
enough—and you will, won't you, stubborn bitch that you
are? Though he is of no use to you now—not as I could
be."

Rudulf stepped politely back, removing his coxcomb's
shoe from off her sleeve so Bronwynn could rise, but still
she stared up at him, unconvinced he told her the truth.
To send her seeking Cian through still more bodies, many
known to her, while knowing her search was futile was
something which would give him pleasure. But it did not
matter if he lied or told the truth. She had to know if Cian
was there.

Wearily she stood, to note that her skirts were red to

the knee with blood. Her sleeves were crimson to the elbow. She stared at hands stained scarlet. The smell of it hit her—the smell of blood and brain, of fecal matter and fear. Then, through the walls hard held against it, the horror came to her. It came as a fist to her belly, squeezing with a pain she had never felt before around the child scarcely more than a dream. It came as a grief so intense she thought she would surely die of it.

She doubled over with the grief and the pain, even as she fought to hold to her feet, to her consciousness, to the child. Yet, there were so many faces left unseen, unnamed, and Cian could be any one of them. Then meaty arms picked her up and carried her back up the steep stairs to the solar as a gruff voice cursed her as a mettlesome bitch for ever having come down them to stick her nose into something not her business. From somewhere, too, she thought she heard the howling lament of a wolfhound.

(16)

Wanting only to return to her pallet and curl once again around her grief and rage, around her unborn child, nurturing each and all of them, Bronwynn gazed around the great hall. She had expected it, somehow, to appear as it had when she last saw it. There should have been at least some small sign of the carnage which had occurred there so few days before, but even the bloody hand print high on the wall was gone.

Servants were setting up the tables for the evening meal where dead men had lain. A juggler, having stayed while others of his trade fled Carrick, practiced in one corner. After all, he reasoned, employment was employment, no matter de Bermingham's unusual manner of commemorating the birth of the Christ Child. There was, too, Twelfth Night yet to celebrate and surely his lordship would reward someone with such a staunch stomach generously. The walls, Bronwynn saw, were freshly white washed, their brightness unnaturally pristine. Stepping into the hall, she ran a bemused hand over a table top. It had been scrubbed with sand and the grain of the wood slid cleanly beneath a palm unsullied by what once had been there. The benches, too, bore no stain and the rushes were newly cut and scattered ankle deep over the heavy planks.

The Lord de Bermingham himself sat at the high table conferring with Sir Roger Mortimer. With them was a priest laboriously helping the nobles read several parchments scattered beneath their elbows. Lady Melusine stood behind her husband, one jeweled hand on his shoulder, her spindle in the other, scowling down at Bronwynn. But de Bermingham beckoned her forward and the sweet smell of the herbs and flowers strewn among the rushes rose to her nose as she obeyed him, her purpose, her need directing her feet. Nor did he have, she knew, any choice as he gestured for her to speak. Whatever his power in Ireland, it was conferred on him by Edward—and she was Edward's ward. Yet, it was not a shield she dared push too far.

"My Lord," she commented, "you are to be commended on your servants. Do they not reflect well on you?"

De Bermingham glowered down at her from beneath thick brows. He knew she led him and he thought he knew to where, but he could not refuse to rise to her compliment. At least, he thought, she had not chosen meal time, when all the hall was full of witnesses, to address him.

"And why are my servants to be commended?" he asked, curiosity demanding that he play her game.

"In that they rid your household of so much blood in so short a time. I would not have thought it possible to ever remove such a stain."

De Bermingham looked around as though he had not noticed the hall's unsullied appearance before, then back at Bronwynn.

"Aye," he agreed, aware there was no one of those few in the hall who did not listen avidly. "They serve me well nor would I tolerate aught but the best from them. There is little I ask of them that they would not do."

The corners of her mouth crimped into a grim little smile and she tilted her head in acknowledgement of the power behind such a statement.

"Still," she said guilelessly, "the smell is yet there— but through no fault of your servants, I'm sure. Blood, especially in such quantity, will creep into cracks and crevices, will it not? The taint, I'm certain, will always be with you."

She had gone too far. De Bermingham shifted his bulk in his chair and, all humor gone, glared down at Bronwynn. But it was Melusine, defensive of her lord, of her position, who spoke first.

"Should you be up from your pallet so soon, child?" she asked, tone solicitous, even as she added a malicious barb. "After all, you came so close to losing your babe. Pregnancy is difficult at the best of times—and how much more so it must be without the father there to support you."

"My Lady," Bronwynn spat back, her calm features suddenly distorted with rage and grief, "he might well have been here—a victim of your lord's hospitality. How am I to know—now?"

Melusine jerked as though slapped and would have responded, but for the squeeze of her husband's hand and the warning shake of his head.

"I will have no cat fight here, my Lady," he warned her. "Save such for the solar." He looked at Bronwynn once again and his small eyes held the vengeful glare of a baited boar. "Lady Fitzhugh, I would assume you have a purpose in addressing me."

Chin lifted, Bronwynn stared back, hating him as she had never despised anyone before, and not caring to conceal it. Let everyone in the hall, everyone in the world know of his evil and of the heinous deed he had perpetrated—and she would be the first, always, to tell of it!

But the people in the hall already knew of it, she reminded herself, had been witnesses or accomplices, yet served him still. She saw his eyes, then, and knew she had erred. Suddenly, she was frightened to the very pit of herself. She had not cared, before, whether she lived or died. To die, she believed, was to once more ride the wind with Cian, was to see his face again, so sullen, then breaking into that grin that always brought a bubble of joy to her throat. Remembering that smile tilted up the corners of her own mouth and brought a light to her eyes, confusing her observers. Then the fear rushed back for she knew she needed to live. To die would be to leave her sister in Melusine's hands, would have her married to a mad man. For all Cecily's selfishness, her childishness, or perhaps because of them, Bronwynn did not want that.

And if she died, there would be no survivor of de Bermingham's bloody deed, for she was, somehow, exactly that—and but another reason he would want her dead. The man was nothing if not thorough and the saints knew he had much to gain and cause enough to seek her death. He had had thirty three men put to death. Why would one woman give him pause? She needed to live, if only to deny him that satisfaction, that gain. She had to live, too, to bear witness to the deed, to remember the dead. But accidents happened, even to the ward of a king, and who would protect her in a land so benighted that thirty three men could be put to the sword while under the inviolate sanctity of hospitality?

And there was the child.

Dropping her chin a fraction, Bronwynn swallowed against the egg of fear in her throat. To have him sense her terror—and realize the cause of it—would, she knew, guarantee her death. Lowering her lashes, she fluttered them over the shadows of grief beneath her eyes. She wrung her hands, her fingernails digging into her palms to control the shaking of her knees, to steady her voice.

"My Lord," she whispered, "I wish to return to Edward. I see no purpose, anymore, to intrude so on your hospitality—and on that of your fair lady."

She lifted her gaze to meet his and de Bermingham could see no mockery in her eyes, no purpose beyond the one stated. Indeed, he could see no emotion there at all. Still, he had to test, to yet try—if only for the peace of his household; his wife had been so set on the match.

"You have decided, then, that you've no wish to marry my stepson?"

"My Lord," she answered, well aware that an accident to her after she was wed to Rudulf de Broc—by force if necessary—with her inheritance then his, would be most to his liking, "I am no child to believe a marriage should serve aught but political purposes—and to create progeny. Still, I have been blessed in observing the affection between yourself and your lady-wife and would wish for but a pittance of such for myself and the man I marry—should I marry. Or at least a small bit of the respect I see between you. But there is none such between Rudulf and myself, no matter that we've both so earnestly sought it. My Lord, should not a man and his wife be, at least, friendly? Are not we—Rudulf and myself—always, at best, at an armed truce? Yet, I care enough for you, for him, for your lady-wife to wish better for him—and for myself. Won't he have a greater chance of finding it if I am not here? There is, too, as your lady pointed out, the child. Surely, your son deserves a bride without such encumbrances."

De Bermingham studied her, knowing well she played him—and Melusine. Still, there were, after all, other heiresses and those without bastard brats trailing on their skirts. Nor was he concerned with the tales she might tell of his dealings with the O'Connor. He had done no more than many another Norman lord wished to do, had they but balls enough for the work. Hadn't he, himself, even sent a dispatch that very night to Edward, telling him of the deed? Nor did he expect, knowing the king, more than a reprimand, if that, and perhaps another heiress—a more compliant one—sent Rudulf as a reward and, perhaps, with her, peace in his household and a warmer welcome in his wife's bed. It would be, too, several days before a party could be arranged to escort the Lady Fitzhugh to Dublin. Should an accident happen to befall her in the meantime, who was he not to take advantage of it? There were, also, the perils of the journey, itself, to Dublin, with her sister still within his reach. Shifting in his heavy chair, he adjusted himself and shrugged.

"We will sorely miss you, but understand, too, your desire to leave. I will make arrangements as soon as the weather breaks." Nor was there anything but solicitude in his voice as he asked, "But what will you do in England?"

It was her turn to shrug and dangle her inheritance just that much closer to his grasp. If she could be as valuable alive as dead, she might yet see England.

"I had thought to possibly enter a convent. Surely, there are those which would take me and yet allow Cecily to retain the bulk of my estates. There is, after all, more than enough to dower us both—myself to a holy order and my sister to a good marriage—one which will allow her to rear my child."

De Bermingham nodded, small eyes gleaming with greed and satisfaction. For all her stubborn ways and aloof manner, this one was like all women. Hadn't she as much as offered him her sister in return for permission to leave?

"But will your sister be leaving us, also?" he asked and Cecily's fate, she told him with a lift and fall of her shoulder, was out of her hands. "I do not know. I know she loves it here and that, too, she loves your lady-wife. I would want her with me, but should she choose to stay, I cannot force her.''

Cecily, Bronwynn acknowledged to herself, could be counted on to look to her own self-interest. For all of her sister's professed affection for Melusine, she was certain to want the excitement and attention she would find at court more. Yet, she would also conceal her intention to leave Carrick until the last moment, playing her hostess to the end. Or so Bronwynn could only hope.

Nodding, de Bermingham studied her. However she trifled with him, he decided, he would let it go for the moment. But she bore watching and if an opportunity arose, he would take it, for all that she was Edward's ward. Now, though, people were wandering in for the meal and he waved a meaty hand at the space on the bench beside his stepson, inviting her to sit, but she shook her head.

''My Lord, given that Rudulf and myself no longer consider wedlock, I would be more comfortable dining with the Lady Melusine's women until I leave. As I am certain he, too, would feel.''

With that undeniable request, Bronwynn already took one step from under his control, but he could only nod permission. Still, he stared at her from under beetled brows, wondering at her game. Then her chin lifted once more.

''There is one more thing I needs must ask of you.'' For the first time, her voice shook, and her hands were clenched, their knuckles white. He nodded for her to speak, his eyes red and wary on her. Still, she hesitated, wondering just how to phrase her question. She swallowed hard and said, ''I would know, my Lord de Bermingham, if Cian O'Connor was among those here three nights ago.''

The gaze she fixed on him held no more than a plea for the truth, but still he scowled, eyes flinching from the need in hers. Melusine's hand tightened on his shoulder, a reminder he did not need, and he shrugged it irritably away. Then he looked squarely at Bronwynn, jaw clenched.

"He was," he stated, "and I will hear no more of it."

"Thank you, my Lord," Bronwynn whispered. Nor could she know whether or not he lied to her. But it did not, truly, matter, for either way it was better to believe what he told her. How could she ride away from Ireland believing Cian might yet live, yet how could she stay, knowing how very much he must hate her? How could he not? She went to the ladies's table, step firm, head high, while she thought she must surely be bleeding to death within, so full and heavy her heart did feel with pain and hatred.

Bronwynn was seldom away, now, from the company of the women she had eschewed before, there being safety in numbers. She sat mutely by while they primped and gossiped, compared needlework and the latest embroidery stitch, her heart still out the window riding the wind with Cian O'Connor. Yet, she could only wonder, watching her needle appear and vanish through the cloth on her lap, if he would want her, now. Would he not blame her, as a daughter of the invader, for the deaths of his father and the others—for his own? How could he not hate her, if only for the blood running through her veins, that Norman-Saxon blood that could do such a heinous deed? Did she not hate herself for it, wishing herself dead? And it would be so easy to put aside her needlework, excuse herself, climb those stairs to the battlement and throw herself over.

Nor was she as much welcomed as only tolerated by Melusine's women. She had run away to the wild mountains, to the fairie waters with the son of an Irish chieftain, a man with a saffron kilt about his narrow hips, with a harp tossed over his back and a hound as untamed as himself under his hand. A sullen man, true, but they had all seen the amber of laughter in his eyes just waiting to leap alive, the line of passion in his lip begging to be set afire. Nor was there a one of them who had not hoped to be the one to do it. It mattered little that she had been abducted and it was only worse that she would not tell them of it—and of him. Nor could they look at her and not be reminded of Christmas day and the fate of that man with those eyes of smoke and dreams, that mouth waiting to be coaxed into a smile, a kiss.

She placed her pallet between those of Agnes Moreland and Cecily. She ate and drank only that which had been offered others before her. She tried to never be even in the guardrobe alone. Only on the treacherous stairs of the keep did she always make certain no one was too near. A sudden shove of a shoulder or a foot slipped in front of hers, tripping her, sending her down to death at the bottom of the steep flight, would be too easy nor was such an accident uncommon.

Nor did the weather speed her on her way to England; no day was without its share of a heavy downpour that held the roads mired in hock deep mud. That, Bronwynn could not blame de Bermingham for, but still the speculation in his eyes each time he looked at her only frightened her the more. She accompanied the hunt, too, on those few days when the sun did break through long enough for the lords and ladies, the dog handlers and falconers to escape the confines and boredom of the castle. It was safer than being alone in Carrick, no matter that she hated the kill and its attendant blood. From that she could avert her eyes, but the whimpering of the prey and the yells of the hunters haunted her dreams with memories of other whimpers, other shouts.

There had been that day, too, when word had come of

Irish kernes rising out of the mud of the road to Trim to treacherously assault a troop of de Bermingham's men, with but one left alive to tell the tale. The Lord of Carrick had turned purple with rage, had cursed the Gael who, like the hydra sprouted a dozen heads for each lobbed off, who did not obey the laws of progeny like civilized men, but followed, instead, any man who could shout a battle cry. His gaze had turned to Bronwynn Fitzhugh as she sat, head lowered to conceal whatever she might be thinking, and he had scowled, as though disturbed by something he could not speak of.

Twelfth-night came and went with its feasting, its mum-meries, its minstrels and jugglers—so like Christmas should have been. Another fortnight passed and still it rained. Then came three days of fog and mist and, after, three afternoons of a lowered sky and a dry wind. With the change in weather came a dispatch from Edward brought by a troop of soldiers.

Wary, De Bermingham opened it. He laboriously ran a forefinger over its few lines, then broke into a chortle of delight.

"He gifts me an award of a hundred pounds!" he crowed, florid features triumphant. "And he commends me as an example to all his vassals in Ireland!"

Melusine laughed and clapped as the hall broke into shouts of glee, into a wave of cups lifted in toasts of vindica-tion. Backs were slapped in camaraderie, shoulders were pummeled. The ladies gave chirps of delight and fluttering smiles of pleasure and promise to their favorites. The Irish servants stood, platters and pitchers in hand, features impassive, eyes hooded, hiding from their masters what-ever thoughts they might have as they waited to serve again their lords once the tumult died down. Only Bronwynn stared down at the bread she crumbled between nerveless fingers, unaware of the tears streaming down her face.

Yet, why was she surprised, she wondered, remembering the result of Edward's rage when the Scottish town of Berwich had dared defy him ten years before. The town had surrendered quickly enough and on such terms that the garrison was permitted to march out. It was then the king, furious that his nephew, Richard of Cornwall, had died in the attack, had ordered all the males of the town put to the sword. Eight thousand had died before he relented. His heart, it was said, had been softened by the pleas of a procession of priests carrying the Host. Some had cited his grief over the death of his beloved Eleanor as an excuse, saying it had unbalanced his sense of justice. But Eleanor, while always hating the sin and loving the sinner, would not have wanted her gentle and merciful name used to justify such carnage. There had been, too, his vengeful slaying of William Wallace earlier that year.

Still, no matter what praise the dispatch offered, it brought with it troops to escort her back to England. And to Edward, she thought, before her mind flinched away.

(17)

How could he, Curran wondered, with his own rage, his own guilt, know how to ease Cian's? He, too, held the foolish conviction that, had he only been at Carrick, he could have, somehow, made a difference, that, someway, those thirty three men would still be alive. And he knew it was a delusion, but how could he convince his young chieftain of that when he felt, deep inside his own soul, it was yet true? And if it was true, then wasn't he—and Cian—culpable in those deaths, if only by default? If all the keening and the loving logic of the women could not rid him of such a conviction, nor all the grieving and raging of those warriors—each by some strange bent of fate yet alive—how could he, himself, take such culpability from Cian? Certainly, those black gowned clerics, those sackcloth garbed monks, with their offerings of prayers and platitudes, had not done so.

No one had been able to do so, not since word came with a stable boy from Carrick of the perfidy done there that Christmas night. Curran often wondered at the blindness of the Sassenach. Did they not see that the hands that groomed their horses and their women, that prepared their armor and their food held another, stronger allegiance? How long would they be in Ireland before they gained their sight? A stable boy was gone from Carrick and Curran doubted he would even be missed but for the horse he had taken with him. And wouldn't there be a hue and cry of 'thief' and the duplicity of the natives over that one? Others, too, had slipped away from Carrick in the night or while about their chores, a slop bucket, a peat spade, a pike often still in hand, and each with news more harrowing than the man before.

And each bit of news had added to his rage, his grief, his guilt—and to Cian's. Especially to Cian's, with his love of a Sassenach woman.

But the woman was Bronwynn and there was no shame to be put to Cian for loving that one, unlike Fenella MeKenna, who, with her Norman clothes and Norman affections, wisely stayed out of everyone's way. Nor did Cian have the satisfaction as he, himself, had—small as it was—of taking as many men as could be assembled against a troop of the Sassenach lord's men on their way to Trim. Scrapings of the barrel, those warriors had been—a few gallowglass, a couple of beardless youth, an able man or two and several more who should have long before abandoned the pike for a stool by the fire and the gruel served old age. But they, with their grief and rage, had won out somehow and the Irish weather had served them well, for once, with their light horses and still lighter mail. The Normans had been trapped like upended turtles in their armor in the mud. Their heavy war horses had wallowed knee then hock deep in it. They had caught de Bermingham's men by ambush, had lost an ancient gaffer and a beardless youth themselves, but had slain all but one of the invaders. That one they had left alive to take word to the Lord of Carrick that not all the O'Connors were yet dead. Grim work it had been, but it had driven de Bermingham to gritting his teeth once again—and back into his stronghold.

But the relating of the deed had not lifted Cian from his guilt or his grieving. Others, in the days and weeks since, had set aside the keening, the rending of clothing and hair and flesh—as the living must do. While they yet mourned, there were, too, the demands of daily living to get through. Animals had to be tended, children had to eat, needs had to be met, yet not even the child, Siobhan, could draw Cian from his deep desolation. He had seen his daughter but flinch as her mother lifted a hand in casual conversation, yet, remembering Fenella's petty angers, her sudden rages, it had been enough. Citing the bruised cheek, the swollen lip Siobhan had borne when her mother had returned with her to Inishbawn, he had taken her from Fenella. It was Fithir, with no child of her own and so much to give, with a husband dead at Carrick, who had taken her under her wing. Each day she brought the child to her father and he would rouse himself to speak to her, to ask her of her day, of her kitten. Fithir would leave her there until Siobhan, baby fingers tracing the path of her father's tears, would ask him why he cried. Then, with the hope that perhaps with the next day's visit the child might restore Cian's mind, his soul, she would take Siobhan away. Yet, how could she explain to a child so young of the raven that plucked at Cian's heart with its bloody beak of sorrow? So she saw Cian O'Connor's grief, his impotent anger, but iron over the door did not daunt the ouphe-raven from entering nor did a cross over Cian's bed or salt scattered around it deny it Cian's dreams.

Often, Curran wondered if Cian, if he, himself, and those around him would not heal more quickly if they had but been given their dead. The thought of them all together in a mass, unmarked grave haunted all of them.

Surely, their souls would walk the earth howling like banshee until they could be placed in holy ground, until their
deaths could be avenged. Surely, in a just world, wouldn't
the ghost of Calvach O'Connor stand beside the bed of
the Lord of Carrick and give him uneasy dreams?

And didn't the women indulge Cian, so, Curran thought,
even his own Sine—but hadn't she always? Yet, there was
not a man or woman at Inishbawn who had not lost someone beloved at Carrick.

Lifting one derisive eyebrow, he watched Sine try to
tempt Cian with a bowl of oatmeal, honey and dried apples.
Cian accepted it with a faint smile and leaned wearily back
against the wall while she puttered about the bench on
which he reclined, plumping his pillows, shaking out the
bed robes, adjusting the wrappings and checking the splint
on his thigh. After she pronounced it healing well and
had left the warrior's house, Cian set the bowl on the floor,
bending over his propped leg to do so, and slyly exchanged
it for the jug of uisce beatha hidden beneath the hanging
bedclothes. His gaze defiant over the lip, he took a swallow
deep enough for Curran, a seasoned drinker, to shudder,
then picked up his harp. Shaking his head in disgust,
Curran listened to the lament his chieftain played, then
turned his attention back to the huge battle axe he sharp-
ened.

The song it whispered with each soft brush of the whetstone was more fitting a man, a warrior, Curran thought,
than the womanish sobbing of Cian's harp. Cnamhitheadh—Bonetaster—he had named the axe and well had
it earned its name from the Holy Land and on to Wales—
until the defeat of David ab Gruffydd and Edward's subju-
gation of the Welsh. He had swung Cnamhitheadh for
Philip of France at Gascony and with William Wallace at
the Battle of Stirling Bridge. Calvach O'Connor had stood
on one side of him there and Cian, a young whelp scarcely

weaned, had stood on the other and had stood firm. As he would, now, Curran told himself, had he two whole legs beneath him and despite the pout on his mug. Ear tilted to better hear Cnamhitheadh sigh happily of the heads it had split, of the arms it had cleaved, the legs it had taken, Curran circled the whetstone over the edge of the blade and smiled. Always, but for the Crusades, it had been the English he had fought, not out of a great love for the Welsh or the French or the Scots, but from that instinctive enmity for those Sassenach bastards from across the Irish Sea. Or perhaps such hatred was not inborn. Hadn't he, even as a lad, seen them look down their long Norman noses, scorning Calvach O'Connor and the Irish princes as savages because they preferred the company of their clan to that of foreign men of their own class? Hadn't he disliked them ever since? Cnamhitheadh could well attest to that and, now, hadn't his young prince cause enough, the dear saints knew, as well? Pausing in his sharpening, Curran studied Cian from under his shelf of bushy eyebrow.

"Haven't I been asked by several farmers which fields you wish to lie fallow this year," he mentioned casually, "and which given to the oats and the barley? Haven't there been the queries, too, as to which go to the sheep and to the cattle—and which, then, of those to which families?"

The harp sang out impatiently before it spoke of Cian's indifference in a rippling run down the strings. His attention caught by a note not quite perfect, he adjusted a wrest pin then scowled at Curran.

"Isn't it simple enough, then, that a man without wit to come home can figure it out? A field is never sowed two years running, but is let lie fallow the next for the mending of the scars on it, and is grazed the third for the fertilizing, that it may be plowed and planted the fourth. Sure, couldn't you have told them yourself, so?"

"I could have," Curran agreed mildly, "but don't they need to hear it from you? Won't they be looking, so, for someone to be as a father to them, as was your da, and isn't it natural that they would look so to you? And those who are not, will they not seek soon enough to try you, test you—to see how well you wear your father's mantle?"

"And if I haven't the desire in me—and the need—to fit my father's office? And I haven't, I'm thinking."

"Ah, and 'tis no problem, so," Curran answered, testing the edge of his battle axe with a calloused thumb, then applying the whet stone to it once more. "Is there not many another who will soon enough grow into a man's skin and look about to wonder who leads the O'Connors of Offaly?" He jerked his chin toward where three striplings listened with avid eyes as Sionagh, Seanchai to the clan, recounted tales of the clan's valiant deeds. They leaned like untried puppies, arms wrapped about the others' shoulders, heads, one red and two the dark of the O'Connors, tilted toward the ancient bard as he sat in the place of honor beside the central fire pit. "And doesn't that one—Sionagh—feed them meat to build bone and muscle and will enough to stand toe to toe with anyone who calls himself tuath king and himself without, in truth, strength or desire enough to hold it? And if not one of them, are there not landless kerne or neighbors out there with the will to better themselves at another man's expense? Won't they be circling about soon, like vultures about a battle-field? Aren't there those yet among your own men—those few left—who are but still stunned and haven't yet found the strength to challenge you? But they will—and yourself too weak to hold it."

Cian but lifted a dark eyebrow and smiled as a derisive jingle rang out from the harp.

"And you think to shame or mock or frighten me into giving a damn for any or all of it," he stated, setting aside the harp. He looked up at Curran, features indifferent. "Why don't you try for it," he suggested, "and yourself caring so much?"

" 'Twould not be what your father wished."

"My father?" Cian taunted. "And what did he get for his caring but a death through treachery and a mass grave?"

"A son unwilling or too weak to avenge such a death?" Curran asked and was rewarded by Cian trying to rise in a start of rage, fists clenched, jaw knotted white with fury. Then Cian relaxed back on his cot with a shrug and a smile.

"Good try, Curran," he mocked. Then his features grew bitter. "And how would you have me avenge the deed and myself without a good leg beneath me, with my chieftains dead and those who followed them without will or wit enough to choose which fields to sow, which to let lie fallow?"

Setting aside the whet stone and laying the battle axe across his massive thighs, Curran leaned over it to meet Cian's ridiculing glare. Elbows on his knees, chin propped on his fists, he studied his chieftain's shuttered features.

"By living long enough to call upon *their* will and strength," he answered, jerking his chin toward the striplings listening to Sionagh. "By honing your hatred and hoarding your purpose—and theirs—until the time be ripe. Ah, and isn't it a sweet revenge only to be alive and knowing well how much de Bermingham wanted you dead, how carefully he planned for it and how he paces in rage that, however much he succeeded, in you he failed? Don't you know you give him troubled dreams and that you haunt his bedside as surely as does the soul of your father, no matter the skin de Bermingham would put on it when he wakes? And we have those lads, there, and had you, too, been at Carrick, there is not a one of the three of them who could not well pick up the cloak of Calvach O'Connor—and would. Ah, but still, wasn't it a lucky thing, so, that you were not?"

Curran had held Cian's narrow eyed attention, although whether he had fired his interest, he could not have said. But now Cian jerked back as though slapped and swung his legs over the edge of the bench.

"Lucky, is it?" he snarled.

Shrugging Curran away, he grabbed his crutch and struggled to rise, the jug of uisce beatha hooked in one finger. Helpless, cursing his feckless tongue, Curran watched him make his precarious, lurching way through a quagmire of scattered benches and beds, weapons and clothing, the assorted equipment of bachelors, so many of them now dead, and to the doorway. He stood there, the door ajar, staring out into the yard and, at last, Curran found the will to go to him, to be pitiless yet again. He touched Cian's shoulder only to have his hand shrugged away. Still, he would not relent, no matter that Cian's features were wet from more than the slanting rain.

"Ah, Garsún," he sighed, "ah, lad, don't you know I, too, would have gladly died with them there, rather than be forced to live on and their ghosts ever haunting me in my own mind with guilt that I still live, with shame that I was not with them—and with the stupid, stupid conviction that, had I but been there, I could have saved them? And isn't it the easier fate they bear, all said? Don't I even envy them that? But the guilt, the shame is of my own mind, for surely they would not be so foolish, so small of soul as to wish their fate upon us and ourselves innocent of any wrongdoing or cowardly act."

Cian twisted his head further away, but still Curran refused him pity.

"Nor did you fall off your horse and break your leg purposefully—drunk or no—no matter that it saved your life—and mine. And think you I would have gone with them, even if I had known de Bermingham's intention, leaving you behind, no matter the guilt I now feel?"

"And why should you take it on your own heart," Cian asked from between clenched teeth, "when the guilt and shame are mine? Did I not love a woman of the Sassenach—and enough, so, that I broke my leg—I who have ridden a horse since I was but a wee bairn—when drunk I was to ease the missing of her?"

Curran rocked back on his heels, satisfied. This, he had known, was the maggot festering in Cian's soul, but his lord would not speak of her before, would not allow her name to be mentioned. Still, he had to go slow and he scowled. His lord, he thought, would have made a fine monk, a perfect monk—had it not been for that hazel eye so quick to lift at a woman's laugh, so certain to follow the beguiling swing of a skirt. But many men of the cloth were so. It was Cian's need to cleave to one woman, to rest his heart in her, no matter where his eye might roam, that held him from the cloister. And what was it, Curran wondered, in Irish men that they delved so into their souls, questioned so their purposes, their principles—and often looking for the answers in the bottom of a jug—or for oblivion? Surely, if the Sassenach were an example, other races of men did not so flagellate themselves with the lashes of past deeds, of unaccomplished intentions—good or evil, self-serving or all sacrificing.

"Did she not tell the O'Connor not to trust de Bermingham?" Curran mentioned.

"And after, when she was back at Carrick, while the Sassenach were preparing for the 'Christmas feasting', for their 'guests', did she send word of what she must have seen, of the plans being laid for our reception—plans beyond roast swan and boar's head, bards and jugglers?" Cian asked derisively. Not bothering to look at Curran for an answer, he swung the jug up to rest on his forearm as he tilted back his head and drank from it, his adam's apple jerking.

"Was she supposed to? Was she not to be gone forever from all of our lives and it thought to be easier so for both of you? And did any of our people there send word of aught?" Curran argued. "What would there have been to be seen—a few bent heads whispering in corners, a conversation or two hushed at her nearing? Sure, if you have three people, haven't you an intrigue—and isn't Carrick a wasp's nest abuzz with plotting and planning?"

"And after," Cian wondered, voice deepening with his grief, "after de Bermingham's deed, when would she have had time to plot or plan, so busy she was at the hawking, the hunting, and watching the jugglers and tumblers, at listening to the minstrels, the bards? 'Twas said she even attended the bear baiting—she who professed to despise such sport."

Curran studied Cian's broad back, the shoulder he leaned against the carved cedar door frame, the long line of arm as he braced his hand against the lintel. The jug was still hooked about one finger and Cian lifted it once again, then wiped his mouth with the back of his hand. He appeared relaxed, but the knuckles gripping the lintel were white, the balls of the fingertips pressed pale and flat. Peering under the uplifted arm, Curran, too, stared out into the weather, blinking as the drizzle hit his eyes. Then he glanced at Cian's profile, the strong, straight nose, the deepest eyes and firm lips, and thanked God that he had a good woman to curl around in the middle of the night and no suspicions or pain to gnaw like a worm at the core of it.

Nor had his Sine ever given him cause for such. And in all fairness, he reminded himself, neither had Bronwynn done so to Cian. They had both known the cost of their love and of the brief time they had together. Both had willingly accepted it, but de Bermingham's heinous deed had changed the terms of the pact they had made. It had forced Cian to question the love itself, for how could he question his father's decision, his wisdom in going to Carrick after Bronwynn had warned him? He had to take the love he had intended to hold within himself all of his life and, in his need to hit out, deny it, denigrate it. The love had become like an inflamed tooth within Cian's soul, a tooth so painful it had to be removed, no matter the cost. He had had such a tooth, Curran remembered, his tongue seeking a gap in his jaw. He had gratefully, joyously allowed a blacksmith to knock it out with a hammer and chisel, so great the pain had become. But he had never had such a love as Cian's and for that he was ever thankful. But he could not, too, stand by and watch Cian demean the love itself—and Bronwynn—to destroy it.

"Did they tell you—those who have come from Carrick—that she was there, that she saw it?" he mentioned nonchalantly, and saw Cian's shoulders stiffen, as though to deflect a blow. Still, Cian but shrugged and asked as casually, "Why would I want to know?"

"Would you want to know," Curran wondered, regretting the pain he intended to inflict, "that she searched for you among the dead, that she sought you in each face she looked into, in each corpse she turned over? They say her arms were red to the shoulder with the blood of the O'Connors."

"And quick she was to recover, so, and herself ever about the hunting and hawking, the jugglers and bards," Cian shot back. But he had quivered slightly with each of Curran's words and his voice held a plea that his statement be denied.

"She was. Shouldn't she be and herself fighting for her life, for what use was she to de Bermingham once she told him she wanted to return to England, that she would not

marry his stepson? Accidents happen even to the wards of
kings and there was her sister there and that one so sweet,
so biddable—and so wealthy if Bronwynn were to die. What
better way to avoid a fall from the battlements, a trip down
the stairs than to never be alone? And how could she come
here? Sure, wouldn't she know how you would hate her—
if she had not been told that you were among the dead.
Think you of the strength of her, grieving you so, and
herself hunting, hawking, laughing at the jugglers—and
ever fearing and hating the company she has to keep.
'Twould be a cold welcome here, too, that she would
receive from the people and who to blame them? More,
'twould be an excuse for de Bermingham to come after
her, to finish the deed so well begun and ourselves with
scarcely more than a gaffer or two to arm and a couple of
beardless striplings. She's little choice and, mayhap, there
is comfort for her in following the path you would have
expected her to take.''

Cian had given no sign that he heard Curran, but now
the tension in his shoulders eased.

''She thinks I'm dead, then?'' he queried the rain and
the encroaching darkness, as though he had heard nothing
else of what Curran had told him.

''She does that.''

''Ah, and isn't it better, so?'' Cian demanded, his voice
harsh. What strength and will, Curran wondered, had it
had taken to reach that decision, no matter that there
could no other answer, not if he truly loved Bronwynn.
Or did he truly not care? Had he actually come to hate
Bronwynn for the deeds of her countrymen?

When Cian turned away from the slanting rain at last,
the crutch under his arm again, Curran saw that his face
was wet from more than the soft night. But there was an
aura about him, too, of a man who had fought a demon
of his own soul's making and had defeated it. Anguish was

there, but the pustule of rage and hate and guilt had been burst. Still, there was another thing Curran had to say and with it he might break through the apathy biding his young chieftain. He might give him the will to live again, if only to hate, to seek revenge, if only by denying de Bermingham his death.

"Cian," and Cian turned back, his hazel eyes apprehensive, as though fearing one more blow. Yet, Curran had no choice. "She has to fight, to, for the child she carries."

Cian's features were stunned, immobile, but something moved deep within his eyes, bringing them alive.

"She is with child?" he whispered at last and Curran nodded.

"And fight for it, she did. Didn't she almost lose the babe that night and herself so stupefied by all she saw and the searching for you among the dead? They carried her from the hall, so I was told, all doubled up about herself with the pain of it and bleeding, she was, but she'd not allow the Lady Melusine to touch her—nor the midwife. Spit in their faces, she did, and in the face of God, Himself, they said, hissing into His teeth and defying Him to take the babe, vowing to curse Him forever should he do so. Blasphemed, she did, and themselves on their knees and crossing themselves so often and so quickly at the grievous sin of it they looked like windmills." Imagining the scene, Curran chuckled, then scowled. His voice was harsh as he added, "While below them, ignored by them, ah, and even forgotten by them, were their lackies not carrying out the bodies of our dead? But she kept the child—through God's will or her own, who can say?"

Biting his lip, Cian sighed, his eyes reflective as he gazed at Curren, yet seeming to see beyond.

"I woke that night," he said softly, "to the crying of a baby. So clear it was that I went to the door to listen, but it did not come from the women's house nor from the houses of the married men. It seemed to come more from inside my own head, but I could not shake it away. Then it stopped, almost on a gulp, so, like a hungry babe will when offered the pap. I wondered, after, why I had not dreamed of my father and why it was not the sound of battle I heard—or the banshee." Shrugging, he looked away, eyes soft with a grieving joy as he thought of Bronwynn and the child he knew he would never see. Then he turned back to Curran. "You say she is to leave Carrick soon?"

"She is, with Edward's men."

"Then she will be safer, so. And there are those of ours to watch her until she goes. But I would have you go to watch her from afar, to watch for de Bermingham's men until she is on the ship and safe. Will you do so?"

Curran nodded and Cian's mouth quirked up in a grimace of gratitude. Then he turned back once more to stare out into the gloaming.

(18)

The chaos that was Dublin, Bronwynn saw, had changed little since she had last ridden through it less than a year before. It streets were still churned to a morass of mud by passing traffic. Wagons loaded with casks of wine from Italy and barrels of tallow from the slaughterhouses sank axle deep in it, the shouting carters standing to whip their straining oxen as apprentice boys leaned their shoulders into the vehicle's rear. Arrogant Norman knights and nobles, lords of Ireland—or at least of the Irish Pale— rode their destriers through the swarm. They gazed with unfocused eyes on the confusion beneath them. Protected by a company of foot soldiers who pushed and shoved with gloved fists, mailed elbows and lance butts without regard for the lives or sex of the nimble pedestrians. Mud spattered, angered by the casual disregard for their safety and person, those so abused shook fists and shouted insults at the backs of their subjugators that brought a smile of amazement to Bronwynn's grave eyes. Norman ladies attended by foppish admirers and Irish maids stepped cau-

tiously into the street from litters and from the doorways
of merchants, their feet clad in tall wooden pattens to
protect their fragile shoes from the garbage and mud of
the street. Skinny, nimble pigs darted through and around
all of them.

Shops of linens and silks, of ermine, sable and the softest
of leathers, of cosmetics and the finest, most fragrant of
oils lined the narrow, twisting streets rubbing shoulders
with armorers and blacksmiths, butchers, grocers and fish
mongers. Colorful signs hung before densely packed rows
of shops and houses advertising the services of doctors and
lawyers and brehon judges, of midwives and fortunetellers
and scribes. Laughter and shouted curses and conversations in Flemish and Italian, in English and Norman
French, in Gaelic from the Irish, the Scots, the Welsh, and
in Latin from the priests and monks dinned the ears. Red
haired Caledonian, dark completed Cambrian and ruddy
merchants from the Low Countries rubbed shoulders with
native Dubliners, their Norse forebears evident in their
blond hair and great height.

A light mist settled over everything, beading on the fine
hairs of her horse's ears and eyelashes and darkening his
white hide to a pewter gray. It dulled the greens and reds
and blues of the clothes of the passersby, glazed the fur
of her mantle and veiled with a fluid gauze the ships tied
up at the quay on the far side of the River Liffey. It puddled
in the road to be quickly churned in with the mud and
refuse and formed droplets on the steep roofs of the houses
which rolled into each other and trickled down to fall from
low hanging eaves. There rose over all the odor of rotting
garbage and wet wool, of unwashed people and a dank
damp from the river.

Yet, it should have changed, Bronwynn thought. The
whole world should have changed with the deed done at
Carrick, when the man and soul who was Cian O'Connor

was driven from it. His going had left such a hole in her heart that it seemed strange, still, these long days and weeks after, that the whole universe was not torn asunder by his absence. And the death of so many, some so young they had not yet known a woman or fathered a child— how could they have not left a very rending in the sky, the earth? Or are we, she wondered, each of us and our pain, so unimportant to God, no matter what the clergy would say, that one man's death left not even a ripple on the sea of life about her?

She glanced over to see her sister riding with her small nose in the air, her mouth disdainful, while her eyes darted about taking everything in. She had announced her regretful decision to leave Carrick at the very last moment, as Bronwynn knew she would. Cecily was not one to deny herself the best of each world until she had to. Bronwynn's mouth curved in a small, sad smile at her sister's selfishness, yet she had relied on that very character for her own safety. Whatever her host's plans might have been, Cecily had not given him time to implement them.

Then she scowled, remembering an unguarded moment when she had stood at the top of the stairs, called back by Lady Melusine. A red haired, freckled maid had turned with her, bumping her, almost on purpose it seemed after. She had fallen to her hands and knees just as one of de Bermingham's men came spinning around the corner. He had stumbled, catching himself on the corner of the wall, almost tripping over her and on down the steep stairs, where, Bronwynn thought, she was supposed to have gone. Her horse, too, had been brought to her lame, just as everyone was mounted to go hawking. His small eyes glinting, de Bermingham had offered her his regrets for having to leave her alone to entertain herself—she who always, recently, sought the company of others, she who was so frightened to be alone now that she had a need to live.

He had been apologizing for having no other suitable mount, when a stable boy, his features bland with innocent purpose, led a small mare, bridled and saddled, to her. She had thanked him profusely while he stared at her, seemingly bewildered by the extent of her gratitude. She could only wonder if she had imagined the concern and laughter she had seen in his round Irish eyes.

And how, she asked herself, could she not believe in God's personal presence and concern when her own life seemed to be so well guarded? It was almost as though she had guardian angels. But she was not yet safe. De Bermingham could have slipped a coin or two to any one of the men around her; there were fatal incidents aplenty in the streets of Dublin. He had only to send a few men after them to initiate but one more brief scuffle, with a horse hamstrung and one more woman dead in a fall from her mount—and the unidentified assailants fled. Or she could be tipped over the low rail of the bridge over the River Liffey. It would be easy enough. A knife point into a tender spot on her horse's side to make him rear and a hand under her foot to hoist her up and over. There was Sir Henry Franklyn with her, true, sent over by Edward to escort her home. Something in his faded blue eyes invited trust, but he was trapped behind her in the seething mass of humanity.

And the bridge was there ahead of her, spanning lead-grey waters. People funneled into its arching length to form a seething, shoving, cursing maelstrom all along its narrow passage, then were spit out onto the other side. The shouts of, "Give over! Give over to the King's men!," had little effect as the troop pushed on forward, digging through with lances and mailed elbows.

Weapons lifted to batter laggards, the king's pikesmen forced their ways into the packed sea of humanity. Caught in the middle, with only the bobbing shoulders of trapped

pedestrians and men-at-arms between her and the rails of
the bridge low on either side, Bronwynn fought her fear
and wove her fingers through her horse's mane. A huge,
heavy shouldered man, the hood of his plaid bratt low
over his face, took her mount's bridle at the bit and her
panic grew. He held him to the middle of the bridge
despite the mob meeting and shoving and cursing their
way past. She thought she heard him mutter in Irish,
"You'll not be harmed," and her fear only grew, for why
would a stranger have cause to think her frightened?

Glancing frantically back at Cecily, she saw her sister
gazing about nonchalantly, as though the cold, deep waters
of the river did not flow almost under foot. But she had
no reason to fear, Bronwynn reminded herself, wondering
if anyone would hear her scream in such a cataract of noise
should she call out for help. Turning back, she stood in
the stirrups in a vain attempt to see around the bulk of
Sir Henry Franklyn. She met his faded blue eyes, narrowed
with concern, before glancing down at the stranger who
held so tightly to her bridle.

He looked up at her, just a quick, sidling glance, but
Bronwyn felt her heart jerk in her chest. Her breath caught
in her throat and her cry of "Curran!" came out as a
hiccuping gulp. Then they were spit out of the stream of
humanity at the end of the bridge and the man dropped
her bridle to slip away through the crowd.

Stunned into immobility, Bronwynn stared after him,
watching the broad shoulders, the bratt covered head bob
above the sea of smaller mortals. She wondered if her eyes,
her hopes had deceived her, then shook her head to clear
it. But the image of Curran's features remained true. Suddenly desperate, she dug her heels into her horse's flanks
and pressed him through the crowd, her gaze never leaving
the plaid covered head. But it stayed that same frustrating
distance ahead, no matter how Bronwynn pushed her

mount, ignoring the curses of the people she shoved aside. Then he glanced back, a quick look, and, seeing her, increased his pace before turning into an alley.

When Bronwynn finally reached the mouth of the small, squalid street, there was no sign of the man among the low hovels. Yet, she sat there a long moment, wanting to weep and wondering why, if it had been Curran, he had run from her. But Curran was dead. He had died with Cian. Already, she was beginning to doubt her vision, for Curran, she knew, would never have allowed Cian to go to Carrick without him. And never would Cian have allowed his father to go alone. But why would a stranger take her bridle to guide her safely across the bridge?

Unless Cian had survived the slaughter. But surely someone would have been compassionate enough not to allow her to grieve over a man not dead. Surely someone would have told her something, at least given her a hint, a hope. But even alive, she knew, Cian would be lost to her.

But those thoughts, she told herself, led to madness as surely as the fact that the McAuleys always came in sets of twos, were all born twins of each other. It did not have to be Curran who had walked with her for it to have been a McAuley. Nor did it have to be Cian who sent him to her. There were O'Connors enough left to wish her a long life, if only to spite de Bermingham.

Still, she could not yet move. Gazing unseeing down the narrow, dirty alley, she was unaware that thin, scantily dressed women stared back at her. Children with dirty hair had paused in their playing to stand stork-like in the mud of the road, one filthy foot tucked into the knee of the other skinny leg to regard her with adult eyes. The stench of offal and garbage offended her nose. Somehow, all sound of the swarming city was cut off from this place and she could hear the drip of water from the thatched roofs of the hovels, could hear the trickle of it in the gutters. It seeped, she saw, into a huge footprint sunk into the mud of the road.

Then a drop of water plopped on her cheek and, suddenly chilled, she shivered. Sighing, she turned her mount to ride out of the alley and to England and Edward.

(19)

But Edward had changed, Bronwynn found. Once he might have been stern and severe with those he loved and, on occasion, even harsh, but rarely unfair. Now, old age and lack of funds to continue his military and political policies had made him irascible and unpredictable, petty and inconsistant, even, sometimes, maliciously cruel.

He had ordered Edward, his son, out of his sight for six months for insulting a lord of the realm, refusing him funds for the maintenance of his household. Calling him a baseborn whoreson, he had seized his heir's hair in his hands, shaking him, and ripping out pieces of scalp, when the prince requested lands and an allowance for Piers de Gaveston. Then he had ordered the expulsion of Piers, the male object of his son's love and attentions, from England. And Edward's irritability only became worse. Still, but for the pain and humiliation caused others and her own embarrassment for them, Bronwynn found she did not care.

Elizabeth and Joan, the most spirited of the king's many

daughters, were most often able to get their way with their
adoring father, employing coquettishness and cajolery.
Cecily, too, knew well how to flatter, to lower her eyelashes
to cast lavender shadows on alabaster cheeks. Observing
them with an apathetic gaze, Bronwynn considered learn-
ing to flirt, to wheedle, then shrugged the idea away. She
would, she knew, only appear clumsy, false. Nor did
Edward's rantings and threats truly bother her. Dispassion,
she thought, was the perfect armor, for how could you
hurt someone who truly did not care? Only through the
child could she be reached.

Once, she had been able to stand toe to toe with her
monarch, often winning her way and always his admiration.
Now, even had she the desire, she could no longer judge
his temper, so fickle and willful it had become. Remembering how she had thwarted his plans for her marriage to
Rudulf de Broc always made him virulent and spiteful—
and he had only to catch sight of her to remember. That
changed little, too, when Rudulf appeared at court a few
months after Bronwynn.

Edward had stared at him, listening to Rudulf expound
on the warm greetings and effusive gratitudes sent by his
stepfather, on de Bermingham's avowals of love and loyalty,
one eyebrow tilted derisively. As de Broc at last had done
with his multiloquent speech, Edward looked him up and
down, noting the thin shoulders cocked back like a roost-
er's, the skinny chest thrust out, the long, rain soaked
feather drooping from his foppish hat, its tip dripping
green dye on to his red surcoat. Then he had turned
to Bronwynn, his left eyelid—the one which had always
drooped slightly as a gift bequeathed to him and many of
his lineage by some forgotten Plantagenate ancestor—
lowered further in a forgiving wink.

But his greetings of her when she returned from Ireland
had been warm with nothing but rage. He had chosen to

have her attend him in his wife's solar with only Marguarite
and a few of her ladies present. Nor had he allowed her
time to rest after her journey or to wash and change her
clothes. Eyeing her bedraggled gown and mud stained
mantle, he motioned her closer.

"My Lady Bronwynn," he said sarcasticly, as she rose up
from a deep curtsy, "correct me if I be at fault, but I fail
to see your bridegroom with you or, indeed, even as much
as a betrothal ring. And your mantle, however luxurious,
does bear the mark of the savage Gael. Explain yourself."

Bronwynn's chin lifted and she drew a deep breath.
No matter what she said, she knew, she would not please
Edward of England.

"My Lord," she hazarded, refusing to lower her gaze,
"I have not married nor am I betrothed. For all that I
had hoped to honor your wishes, I am aware, also, of the
affection you bear me and did not think you would wish
me wed to a madman. And Rudulf de Broc, my Lord, is
truly insane."

Edward leaned forward in his great chair to regard her
with narrowed blue eyes. Then he sat back, seemingly amiable, and Bronwynn's fingertips grow numb with fear.

"You, Bronwynn Fitzhugh," he said softly, "mistook a
command for a wish. Nor do I care if he howls at the
moon naked. I would have had you married to him and
guaranteeing me the loyalty of Piers de Bermingham."

Her courage returned with her outrage and her chin
lifted higher. Still, her voice was quiet, reasonable, the
memory of thirty-three dead men swelling her throat with
tears. To quail before him would only earn his disrespect,
yet she could not afford to rouse his fury any further and
her voice held no trace of sarcasm as she asked, "My Lord
Edward, does not the man display the utmost loyalty in
slaying thirty-three men under his roof and hospitality?
How could an unhappy marriage for his stepson bind him

any closer to you than that? I saw his gratitude, too, for the reward you gave him, but 'twas for your words of commemoration he was most grateful.''

"And you think the deed was done for my pleasure?" Edward countered, finding himself enjoying again and against his will someone who did not cower before him like a kicked puppy. "I do not think, in truth, that you are so much the innocent as you would feign. Think you mayhap 'twas done more to rid himself of the Clan O'Connor and gain all of Offaly in the doing of it? And a poor job he did, with O'Connors seemingly rising alive out of the very soil he planted them in. So prolific are the Irish and so tangled their laws of progeny, 'tis like trying to destroy one of those creatures which, if one is hacked into a hundred pieces, a hundred of the same will spring up from each.'' Edward paused and, stroking his beard, studied her with dubious eyes. Around them, all was silence, as though Bronwynn was not the only one to dare not breathe. "And all this time," Edward finally continued, "while I am trying to gain some semblance of control over my Irish domain and hold to my Scottish, is my ward, in whom I had placed great faith and trust, following my bidding? Ah, no, she is running about the hills and valleys of Ireland and sharing a bed with a savage enemy of myself, with, verily, a son of those same O'Connors I had set her host to subjegate.''

"My Lord," Bronwynn dared interrupt, "I was taken hostage and many did witness it!"

"Taken hostage!" Edward snorted, leaning forward again to plant his elbows on his knees and glare at her. "You are a woman who could give harpies lessons in cutting the balls from a man with their tongues and amazons the trick of putting a knee to them. And mayhap you bring back another O'Connor in your belly as proof of your gamboling, another cursed Irishman to plague me.''

Bronwynn refused to answer, mouth tightening, eyes narrowing to stare at a point to the left of Edward's head. Still, his baleful gaze fell to the hands she had dropped protectively over a belly as yet as flat as a virgin's. He, who had spawned so many children recognized the gesture and, lips twisted into a grimace of anger, nodded and asked, "When is the brat due?"

Bronwynn moved her gaze from the tapestry she had studied to look squarely at him.

"In six months time, my Lord." Her chin lifted. "My Lord, I beg your permission to go to Cleitcroft, to give birth there."

Edward shook his head and laughed, nor was it a comforting sound. Then, for the first time during the interview, his true rage showed through. He leaped to his feet and in two strides his six foot four inch frame towered over her. Bronwynn held her gaze on the edge of his cloak where it was clasped just below his throat, refusing to quail, no matter the knocking of her knees. A flea, she saw, was crawling across the ermine and she wondered what he would do if she reached out to crack it between her fingernails. The sour odor of an old man came to her and it made her inexplicably sad. He had not smelled so before.

He had never, she had heard, hit a woman and it was this that held her fast to her place. Still, she flinched from the force of each of his words as he rapped down at her, "You have never begged anything of anyone. You would never bend that stiff neck of yours long enough to do so. And, no, you haven't my permission to go to Cleitcroft or any other of your holdings. Whether with misbegotten brat or no, you'll not leave court. You will stay and bear your shame for all to see. You will attend my lady wife until you cannot stand, so strong are your birth pangs. I expect to see you on the hunt and with the hawks and always at table. When we travel, you will travel and you'll not be spared any of the rigors of such journeys. Mayhap you will lose the brat as a result, though I doubt it. You Welsh are a savage, vigorous stock, much to my own displeasure, or I would be well rid of the all of you long afore now. Although why you've not lost it to the Lady Melusine's ministrations and abortives, I do not know. The saints know she must have slipped you a few, considering how her heart was set on this marriage."

Bronwynn blinked in surprise that he would know such gossip. She thought stupidly to tell him she had avoided all food not offered or taken by others, but her king was not finished with his enumerating.

"And when the brat is born, he will be given away as a foundling, where and to whom will not concern you. You will then marry where I tell you."

Bronwynn's head jerked back and her gaze leaped up to Edward's florid features, as she breathed a frantic prayer that he was jesting. But there was no humor in his face and her mouth opened to protest, to beg, to weep. All she could see was a broken trust; Cian's hazel eyes gazing out at her from his daughter's face bruised and filthy with poverty, thin and hopeless from neglect. Never could she let that happen. She realized, then, that she was backing away from Edward, hands pressed over the child tucked deep inside, her head shaking in refusal, until, halted by the wall, she could retreat no further. She stood there, back pressed against the reassuring strength of stone, her eyes, her thoughts leaping about, seeking escape, seeking an answer. Then her gaze lowered and a demure smile formed about her lips.

"My Lord Edward," she whispered humbly, "I will obey you in your decision concerning the child, only begging you to give the choice of fosterage to your lady wife, that I might rest easy knowing him well cared for. But then, my Lord," and her guileless gaze rose to meet his adament one, "I would enter a convent—to make amends for offending you and God—and for denying my child— surely a grievous sin. God's Will and I've no doubt I will find a holy order which will take me for the lands and funds I shall bring them, and forgive me the sins on my soul."

Somewhere beyond the corner of Bronwynn's eye, Cecily gasped and half stood, her mouth agape to protest the prospect of losing her sister and access to her inheritance to a convent. But Edward waved her silent with one imperious jab of his hand. His gaze never left Bronwynn's meek features as his mouth compressed into a tight line. He knew his ward and he knew she was not finished. Arms folded over his wide chest and an ominous scowl on his features, he waited. One eyebrow lifted in dubious encouragement and Bronwynn could not repress a smile, no matter the stakes of the game they played.

"I would, of course," she addressed Cecily, while her meek gaze never dared to lift to face Edward's glower, "and with the holy sisters' assent, grant my sister funds enough to marry well. Or," and she paused. Her eyes, filled with an angry defiance, at last lifted to meet her king's, "should I keep the babe and thus my soul free from such a stain as abandoning my child, I would be free to marry. I have such great trust in you, my Lord, that I would gladly accept whatever match you should make for me once my child is born."

At that, Edward gave a snort of derision; Bronwynn Fitzhugh, he knew, was neither meek nor obedient, but she *was* true, always, to her word. And Edward shook his head in wonder at the love of women for their brats, born or still aught more than a bloody blot in their bellies. He dipped his head to her in acknowledgment of that same awe and Bronwynn knew she had won her child, at least for a while. Yet, it was too soon to allow her elation to show. Her monarch had adopted the capriciousness of an old man, and that made him dangerous.

.   As the king had promised, court was ever on the move. Bronwynn had not expected less, no matter Edward's tirade. His first wife, Eleanor, and now Marguarite had always accompanied their lord whereever his whim took him, and it often took him from one end of his realm to the other and back again as he left little of its rule in the hands of lesser men. With their vast train of retainers and furnishings, of horses, hounds and hawks, very few royal residences or those of his nobles could long sustain him. Soon, often within a day or two, they would be off again. And, wherever they were, Bronwynn attended Margaurite nor was it a burden. The queen became far more a friend and ally than a responsibility.

Yet, no matter where they were or what she was doing, it seemed to Bronwynn as though she lived on a multitude of levels, each independent of the other, even as she was aware always of each. She knew, however, that she dared not allow them to combine, so fraught was each with its own overpowering emotions.

Always, she was aware and frightened of Edward. Always, she tried to avoid his glance, his attention. Still, his gaze seemed ever on her, speculating, planning. Her only escape, it sometimes seemed, was to lose herself in the ever shifting alliances and factions of court, to hide behind the shoulder of the person she spoke with, the tapestry she embroidered. But her promise to him had only opened the door to a myriad of suitors who seemed to have balanced her pregnancy and her properties and found her properties far outweighing any disadvantages of an illegeti-mate child. Indeed, those in need of an heir found her proven fecundity but an added bonus. Their attentions, too, she tried to avoid even as she fought the sense of suffocation, of powerlessness she found in their company.

Bronwynn sometimes thought she had caught the interest of every unmarried man within Edward's realm from baldheaded, dewlapped widowers with a dozen offspring each to unbearded, callow youths and the parents of sons scarcely out of the cradle. And they all watched her with avid, greedy eyes, feeding her panic, her fear.

Nor did traveling lighten Edward's moods any longer and Marguarite did her utmost to protect both the king's son and his wards from his testiness. Sometimes the music she had brought with her from France and taught him to love would distract him from his less violent rages. A soft word from her, too, often had more effect than all the rationalizing his advisors could offer or any excuse attempted by whatever cringing unfortunate who was the subject of his wrath at that moment.

If nothing else worked, she would deliberately divert his fury on to herself, and Bronwynn would watch with helpless rage at Edward's injustice toward a woman she had come to love. Yet she was always selfishly grateful that his fury was so seldom, now, turned on her.

Helplessly, too, she watched and worried as Cecily cast sidelong glances at her many admirers, as she flirted and preened and posed. The slightest compliment from any strutting, posturing popinjay would display her small teeth in a needy simper of pleasure, would tilt her pelvis in unconscious invitation. Each move she made was calculated, her round, innocent eyes lowered and ever shifting about to measure the resulting effect. And admirers were always about her—at the hawking and on the hunt and vying for the honor of sharing her trencher. But they were all second sons or penniless knights or greedy eyed widowers with a need for young, unsullied flesh to devour with age spotted hands and slack-lipped mouths.

And there was Rudulf. Fenella McKenna, Bronwynn remembered telling herself, would not stay long at Inishbawn nor was she truly wanted there. Still, she was surprised to see her with Rudulf, however well matched she thought them. Nor was Siobhan with her mother and Bronwynn could only be happy about that as she remembered how much Cian loved his daughter. But Rudulf seemed always to watch her, mud-yellow eyes slitted with pleasure as he paid court to Cecily, as Fenella became her sister's close friend and confidant. When Bronwynn tried to speak to her, Cecily would only shrug and accuse her of jealousy, would wonder who her sister was to talk, with her belly rounded by the ill-gotten brat of the son of an Irish tuath king. Fenella, too, studied Bronwynn, her smile displaying the pleasure of seeing the woman Cian O'Connor had dared love more than herself brought to heel by the king and a bastard child.

But there was something more to the smile that brought to Bronwynn's tongue questions she would not ask. She knew too well that Fenella would answer her only with disclaimers or lies, while her eyes would mock her with a knowledge she would not reveal. Somehow, in Bronwynn's needful mind, the unshared secret brought to her the memory of a huge footprint in the mud of Dublin.

She wanted to ask her, too, of the people of Inishbawn, then remembered that so few were left alive—only the women. And Sine and Fithir would not ask after her, she knew, so roiling with hate they must be, and she mourned for the loss of their friendship.

But it was only once that she spoke to Fenella and then in defense of Biddie, the tiny Irish maid the woman so often and cruelly abused. She had watched once too many times as Fenella slapped the thin creature for pulling her hair while combing it, for not brushing the fur of her mantle to a proper fullness. Throwing aside her embroidery, Bronwynn leaped to her feet, grabbing the hairbrush with which Fenella had been beating a cowering Biddie and tossed it across the solar.

"You'll not hit her!" Bronwynn hissed into Fenella's startled features. "She's but a child and she does the best she can!"

Mouth twisted into a thin, ugly line, Fenella rose to confront Bronwynn as Biddie scuttled away from the fleeting kick her mistress aimed at her. Her shoulders were hunched and her gaze was resentful on her rescuer. She knew too well and with the hard won wisdom of the underdog that such interference would but bring an even harsher chastening down upon her.

"She's mine," Fenella spat back. "I'll do with her as I wish! Nor will Cian O'Connor's slut tell me elsewise and herself carrying his bastard brat. Or did you learn such coddling of slatterns while in my husband's bed? The O'Connors were always soft with their menials."

Hands clawed, Bronwynn aimed for Fenella's spiteful features. Fingers outstretched, Fenella would have sunk them in Bronwynn's thick hair and they would have been rolling around in the rushes like two battling cats had it not been for Marguarite's admonishment.

"Bronwynn, Fenella, that will be all! I'll not have my ladies fighting like ale wives. 'Tis an insult to me." No matter that the queen's voice was soft, its tone brooked no argument and its effect was immediate. Relucantly, Bronwynn and Fenella backed away from each other, eyes still spitting fire, as Marguarite continued, telling Bronwynn gently, "Fenella is right. The girl is hers to use and train as she will. Even the poor chit's death, should she die by her mistress's hand, would be more a matter between herself and her confessor than of the law. But," and the queen's next words removed the smear of gloating from Fenella's features and, unwittingly, guaranteed Biddie harder pinches, more vicious, if surreptitious, slaps, "it offends me to witness the abuse of any person and especially the meek, nor do I feel such behavior the proper way to train a menial. Are we not commanded to give charity and pity to the weak?"

Lips white with mortification, Fenella dipped a contrite curtsy, but the look she flashed Bronwynn promised revenge. She had made, Bronwynn knew, two enemies that day, not that Fenella had not wished her ill before. There had been nothing Bronwynn could do about that nor did she truly care. It was the enmity she had seen in Biddie's eyes that she deserved and regretted. She should have known better than to interfere. Yet, it had been done and it was too late to make amends.

Still, no matter Fenella's angry glares and her smirking glances at her growing belly or Rudulf's silent snigger, despite Edward's speculative gaze and the attention of her myriad suitors, there was the child within her to be loved, nurtured and wondered at. Always she was aware of him as he grew, as her belly curved. She paused, features astonished, as she felt his first movement, a feeling as faint as the brushing of a butterfly's wing. She found herself laughing aloud as she watched the bouncing bump of an elbow or knee over her abdomen. He would turn within her as she lay in bed, awakening her, and she would cradle him with her hands as she whispered a prayer for his safe delivery, for his health and strength, for a long, happy life. She laughed with Marguarite when the queen told her she would, when the child was born, miss the shelf of belly on which she found herself resting her arms.

There was, too, a constant fear for him. She could not put faith in Edward's promise. Nor could she be certain the man she would accept in marriage would be good to him, would not resent a stepchild and a part of her mind seemed to ever be seeking a way to escape the pact she had made with the king.

It seemed, she sometimes thought, as though she moved though the day, through the doings of the court, within a shell of apathy, the apathy that would allow her to accept another man, one day, in her bed, into her body. Yet, always, too, beneath the apathy, she was filled with a rage, a grief she was forced ever to smile through, whether waiting on Marguarite or watching another miscreant cower before Edward.

And always, with each movement of the child, with each thought of him, came the memory of his father—and grief. With each turn and bump of the baby, she envisioned his warm brown hands on the bulge of her belly and the white flash of his grin of pride and delight which would have surely been on his features. At night, she missed the strength and security of sleeping in the cage of his arms and the joy of taking him within her, of watching his face, sometimes so intent in his pleasure, sometimes laughing with love at the pleasure he gave her. Each day she thought of a thousand things to tell him and the hollow ache of grief would twist in her stomach and swell in her throat when she remembered, a scant moment later, that she would never relate to him the antics of the puppies nesting in a corner of the stables at Dover. Never would she share with him the giggle she had been forced to smother at the sight of Rudulf's latest costume and the foolish terror that had been hers when she had first felt her belly cramping and had thought she was losing the child—or the breath taking relief when Marguarite had told her it was normal.

She wondered, too, if he would have approved of the pact she had made with Edward, if he would have understood the need for it. Would he have understood, too, her man of honor, her intention of breaking the pact should the child die, for break it she would.

And always with her was guilt. If only she had tried harder to keep Clavach from Carrick Castle. If she had searched hard enough, long enough, surely she would have found the words to turn him away from his fate. But she had wanted to see Cian just that one time more, if only a glimpse. For that, she felt the most guilty of all. For that sin, alone, surely she deserved to lose her child.

But the child did not die. Late summer came in long afternoons lazy with the hum of bees. The days smelled of warm earth and of wild roses in the hedgerows, of daisies in the hay fields around Kenilworth Castle. Nights were pungent with the odor of tansy in the dark and sweet with honeysuckle in the moonlight. Mares called to colts gone chasing butterflies and doves cooed from battlements walked by men-at-arms drowsy in the sunlight.

Attended by the queen and three midwives, in an airless chamber crowded by ladies in waiting, Bronwynn went into childbirth. Her naked body slick with sweat, she rode each swell of pain up only to slide down each into a trough of anticipation of the next, while the queen wiped her brow and moistened her parched lips with wine and water. Scarcely aware of the futile fanning of the attendants and the murmurs of encouragement from Marguarite, of the harsh whispers of the midwives, she gripped any hand offered her, teeth set against the need to cry out. Biting her lips to blood, she prayed for the safe delivery of her child, while, behind the lids of eyes squinted in concentration, she saw Cian's warm gaze on her, encouraging her, strengthening her. With each rasping breath drawn from the air of the hot, crowded chamber into starved lungs came the suffocating odor of heavy perfumes and perspiration and the flower strewn rushes crushed beneath the foot. With each she tasted, too, the smell of sweat, of blood and knew it was her own. More than the pain, the smells seemed to build, the air she needed diminishing, consumed by the interminable gossiping of the women as they related horror stories of their own confinements even as they would not cease their fussing over hers.

Then all tossing and fretting over the heat, the smells, the whispers and gossip, the soft encouragement of the queen and the harsh commands of the midwives was swept away in the need to drive her bone weary body to one last effort. Heels scrabbling for purchase on sweat soaked bed linens, hands twisting pain into the cracking knuckles of those which gripped them, her body arched. With three great, grunting efforts, all pain gone and only mindless purpose remaining, her body forced the child onto a sweat, blood and water soaked bed and into silence awe struck with the miracle of birth.

Feeling the baby lifted from between her thighs, Bronwynn heard a sharp slap and an angry, protesting wail. Beneath the laughter of the women, too, she heard "Surely, God will yet take it as evidence of sin," from a lady known for her piousness and Fenella's whispered, "Another O'Connor bastard and isn't Ireland strewn with them? Now, his bratling get has come even to England."

But Bronwynn could only close her eyes, fatigue washing over her. Then she remembered, and fear brought her up to her elbows, her hands frantically reaching for her child. Marguarite grabbed them, clutched them, as she sat on the bed next to Browynn.

"Hush, Child, ah, hush," she whispered. "Aught will happen to your babe. They are but bathing him, then you will have him. Nor will he be taken from you. 'Tis a male child. Did you know that?''

Bronwynn searched Marguarite's eyes and at last smiled and nodded.

"I did," she sighed back. "When he was but a butterfly within me, I knew."

"Rest now, then. You had a hard labor."

Marguarite soothed her brow, murmuring words of assurance, and Bronwynn closed her eyes. But she did not sleep, not even when her son was at last given to her. Cradling his swaddled body, she gazed down at him in wonder as he searched blindly for a nipple and gulped it into a tugging mouth. Still, she studied him, marveling at the tiny hand that gripped her finger so strongly. Her gaze examined each feature of his smooth face, seeking resemblance and found it in the tiny lobeless ear. Unaware of her tears, she traced its form with her fingertip, remembering another such ear. So neat it was, she had teased Cian, that it should have belonged to a woman.

Love for the child swelled within her with an intensity she would have thought impossible—and with it a grief she had never allowed herself to give voice to. It burst from her in a keening wail that struck dead all conversation, all movement within the chamber. It slipped through the high slit of a window as a thin ribbon of sorrow binding motionless the men-at-arms pacing the battlements, before they muttered a prayer and crossed themselves at the pain and fury of it. It was Marguarite who took Bronwynn into her arms, cradling her, sighing to her.

"Aye, little one," she whispered, "cry. You've never grieved for him, have you? You've never let the sorrow go, and you must, for 'twill poison you if you do not—and 'twill poison your son with you."

On the battlements, escaping the raucous entertainment in the great hall, Henry Franklyn paused to listen. The

grizzled warrior-knight bowed his head before the inarticu-
late anguish of it, the rage.

"Ah, God help the poor, small lass," he whispered, "aye,
and her small babe."

(20)

Edward came to visit Bronwynn three days after the birth of her son, accompanied by Sir Henry Franklyn. The king had thickened with age, yet as she lay in her bed he still towered over her from the great height which had earned him the sobriquet Longshanks. He smiled at her from eyes still blue with his lost youth, but the weariness and distrust of lessons well learned shadowed their depths. Nodding at the women who dropped hasty curtsies and backed from the chamber, he inclined his head toward the baby in Bronwynn's arms. Arms crossed over his chest, he rocked on his heels, but it was at Franklyn that Bronwynn glanced warily, wondering at his purpose there, and fearing it.

"They told me you whelped a son," Edward remarked, "and easily for a first birth."

Then his features grew fatuous with the wonder of a man many times a father, yet still in awe of the miracle of birth, the wonder of a newborn. Leaning over, Henry Franklyn at his shoulder, he lightly touched the downy head of the baby, then placed his finger in the tiny, grasping hand.

"Their strength is always an amazement to me," he grinned. "What will you have him christened?"

"Kane," she answered, knowing the Irish name would displease him, and Edward scowled, releasing the baby's fingers. Still, the woman was shortly out of childbirth and he contained his temper.

"You think it wise?" he asked reasonably. " 'Tis hard enough to bear the infamy of being a bastard and you would label him Irish, too?"

"I but honor his father."

Edward clenched his teeth against a rising temper, then noticed the baby's unbound body.

"You've not yet had him swaddled?" he demanded, an expert in the art of fatherhood, and Bronwynn shook her head, jaw set, grey eyes perilously defiant.

"I do not intend to. The Irish do not swaddle their infants and they grow strong and straight of limb. And they walk earlier than do the English. I thought to try it. Have they told you, too, that I will not give him to a wet nurse, but do suckle him, myself?"

Edward again rocked back on his heels, rage rising. Then he frowned at Henry Franklyn.

"And you think to wed this woman?" he snorted. "Well, and good luck to you! I'ld not wish her on any man, no matter her properties and her fair face, much less a loyal friend and liege of mine as you are, but you've had fair warning. The banns will be called today and in three weeks time she'll no longer torment me and mine and fair riddance to her."

He turned, his gaze daring Bronwynn to deny her promise. It was Franklyn who stepped forward, age-faded blue eyes steady on Bronwynn's pleading features, war grizzled face set.

"My Lord," he said, clearing his throat, "the lady has but given birth and the father is not yet a year dead. I would have time to court her with all the courtesy due her, aye, and with that same chivalry you, yourself, espouse. Her name and her position but deserve such." He grinned, then, and his weathered features took on a humor and gentleness belied by his scars. "I vow to you, my Lord, that I will do my utmost to tame her temper and her tongue, to bridle her stubbornness, to keep her from so tormenting you, virago that she is."

Edward's eyes narrowed on Franklyn, hoping to stare him down, but the warrior-knight refused to flinch. This man had proven ever loyal, Edward reminded himself, yet had asked for nothing but to serve—until now. Now, he had come to him, head bowed in deference, features set in an obstinacy only matched by Bronwynn Fitzhugh, herself, wanting a woman the king could only be glad to be rid of—no more than a flea in his small clothes was she compared to his other worries, but still a torment—and he had promised her to him. But he had not known Franklyn would state conditions which would only be lauded by Marguarite and in a way that could almost be construed as blackmail. True, while there were only the three of them there and, for all her faults, Bronwynn was not one to go whining to the queen, Marguarite would hear of it, anyway. At court even the walls had ears and a secret might as well be shouted from the battlements for all the good a whisper might do. He scowled again, but Franklyn did not drop his gaze, and Edward shugged with ill grace.

"My lady wife," he drawled, "will praise your chivalry. The Lady Fitzhugh has ever been one of her favorites— the saints alone know why. So, I will leave you to your courting—and good luck to you. By the Holy Rood, you will need it."

Nodding to Bronwynn, Edward turned on his heel and

left Henry Franklyn alone to stand with war scarred hands
hanging limply at his sides. Clearing his throat, he looked
around the chamber, unable to think of anything to say,
his gaze settling everywhere but on Bronwynn. At last,
finding the silence as torturous as he did and grateful for
the reprieve he had given her, Bronwynn whispered down
to her child's head, "My Lord, I would thank you for your
courtesy." Then she looked up at him and added, "there
are few enough men who would be so, no matter the lip
service they do give the cause of chivalry."

Franklyn shrugged, his gaze meeting hers, honest, forth-
right, all abashment gone in the face of his purpose.

"My Lady, I could do aught else. I know there are other
men, younger men, wealthier, better schooled in the arts
of courting a woman. Given time, I know you would have
chosen one who pleased you better than myself, but
Edward would not give you such time. There are worse
men, too, men who would mistreat you and the babe, men
who but wanted you for your property. I'd not want you
given to one such, not grieving as you still are and not so
soon after childbed."

Then, wondering if he had said too much, Franklyn
looked away again. He bit his lip, then opened his mouth
to speak, only to close it, and Bronwynn took pity on him.
Patting the side of her mattress, she scooted over.

"Would you sit, my Lord?" She found herself smiling
as his doubtful eyes took in the edge of the bed, the door,
and the bed again. "We are betrothed, are we not?" she
assured him. "Nor am I a maiden to be cloistered away
from all harm. Indeed, are there not those who would say
I've no virtue left to need protecting?"

His pale eyes flashed, then, and his jaw clenched.

"Not to me, my Lady! For all my age, I've a strong arm
yet, nor will I brook any slur upon your honor."

Bronwynn could not contain the smile that danced in

her eyes, turning their grey to silver and reminding him, suddenly, of sunlight on water. Still, he stood, ungainly in her presence and uncomfortable without a sword to rest his hand upon, and she patted the bed again. This time, he sat gingerly on the edge, only to bite his lip once more, tongue-tied. But Bronwynn only waited, already aware the gesture meant his mind was working something through and he would speak when it had. At last, his mouth jerked in a grin almost boyish.

"And older, too," he chuckled. "Could Edward not have found you someone older, all drooling and doddering, with a dozen children to fight over his estate when he died, taking it all, and all you had brought him, besides, and leaving you aught for the poor, lad, there?"

"He could have," Bronwynn agreed, and Franklyn shifted on the bed, making himself more comfortable.

"And myself," he said, encouraged, "I may be three times the age of you, but I'm strong still, and mostlike will die with my sword in my hand as a warrior should. Nor have I children to beset you when I'm dead." He paused, mind snagged on something, then said, "I had at first blamed my lady-wife, but I'm thinking, now, 'twas myself at fault. She never denied me, wanting a babe so badly, herself, and I've sired no bastards—or none I've known about."

He flushed, realizing his blunder, and dipped his head in self-reproach. Still, he met her gaze.

"My Lady, you've my apology for that—and my pledge that I will never reprove the babe's birth." He bit his lip once more at Bronwynn's smile of forgiveness and looked down at the child she held. With a large finger battle-scarred, knuckle flattened, he gently touched the baby's downy head, then offered it to the tiny hand as had done his king, and smiled at the grip. When he looked back up at Bronwynn, his gaze was intent. "I would adopt him if

you approve. I would give him my name. It would so pleasure me, Lady, that he would have my estates when I die."

Gratitude flooded Bronwynn—and grief, for by his gen-
erosity he was taking part of her child from her—and
from his father. Her own lip between her teeth, she gently
touched the baby's round head, the small ears so like
Cian's own, as she blinked back the tears threatening to
slide down her cheeks. Then she slipped her slim hand
into Franklyn's gnarled one. Swallowing hard, she looked
back up at him and nodded.

"My Lord," she whispered from a throat aching with
sorrow, "I would be honored."

It seemed, then, that Franklyn was rarely away from her
side. He became a bulwark between her and all insult, all
disparagement. Men narrowed their eyes at his massive,
battle-scarred figure, noted the set of his mobile mouth at
the slightest hint of a smirk and snickered only into the
ears of their most trusted cohorts. Their wives measured
the breadth of his shoulders, remembering the warnings
of their husbands and heeding them. It would not be
themselves who would be called to account for any affront
they offered Bronwynn, but their lords. But it would be
their lords who would call *them* to account, and not gently,
should Henry Franklyn treat them tenderly enough that
they would be capable of lifting a hand to their wives.

With the babe tucked securely into the crook of Franklyn's thick-thewed arm, Bronwynn and Henry rode in the
train as Edward's household followed him in his meander-
ings from estate to estate. With the infant safe on his lap,
Franklyn shared his trencher with his betrothed, offering
her the most tender pieces of swan, the most delicate of
sweetmeats. Even in the hawking and hunting, he was the
doting stepfather and lover, foregoing the bloodiest of the

sport to linger in the shade of oak trees with Bronwynn or ride over flowering meadows, while they could hear in the distance the belling of the hounds.

He bragged of how early Kane lifted his round head, even as it bobbled precariously on the tiny neck. Despite the shaking of the heads of those more experienced, he swore the child smiled at him at two weeks of age and chortled with pride when Kane did at last bare toothless gums at him in a wide grin. And Bronwynn watched, marveling at the man's gentleness, at his lack of concern for gossip, for the men who twitted him for his doting.

Then a shadow of sorrow, noted only by Franklyn, would darken the grey eyes he likened to the moon-touched sea, as she thought of Cian, wanting him, missing him in a way Henry Flanklyn could never fill. But he did not know of the nights she still grieved, or of the longing she had that it was Cian who held the child. She could, she sometimes thought, if she dwelled too much on it, come to hate the gentle knight for so supplanting Cian in his son's life. Knowing it unfair, coming to respect and care for him, she fought to put such thoughts from her. Soon, only in sleep did her mind betray her, waking her from dreams of Cian to find her cheeks damp with tears or her body aching with need. Then she would think of a huge footprint in the mud of Dublin and wonder why it so haunted her.

In autumn, when Kane was two months old, Bronwynn went with Henry to his estate in Gloucestershire to meet the household which would one day be hers. The days were long there, warm with the scent of fresh cut hay, alive with bird song. She rode with him through the afternoons, as he oversaw the harvest, and picnicked with him on roasted chicken and apples kissed with the first frost under trees overlooking the fields. Peace was there, so far from Ireland, and she gave herself to it and to the man who offered it to her.

One night, stirred to need by the promise of winter, she went to him. Wrapping her mantle about herself and lighting her way with a candle, she moved down the long, cold-flagstoned hall to push open the heavy door to his chamber and walk to his bed. Nor was Franklyn asleep. He gazed at her a long moment, then, drawing back the bed clothes, he held out his hand to her.

It was a long, slow loving, as Bronwynn had known it would be. How could it be otherwise with this gentle man? Only after did she weep for the passion of another, the teasing laughter in hazel eyes, the response that leaped like a flame at his slightest touch. And she wept for her betrayal of him. But she went to Henry each night after, needing the comfort of it, the security. And what else, she asked herself, had she to give him for his goodness to her, to her son? Her properties meant nothing to him. And his huge form next to her quieted her dreams. He held her when she woke weeping, shushing her as he did her child's tantrums.

But Edward, concerned by unrest in Scotland, called them too soon back to court. Nor could she go to Henry's bed, there, and Bronwynn found she missed it. It was Marguarite who studied her with a discerning eye and resolved to keep her occupied, to not let idle time undo the good Sir Henry Franklyn had somehow wrought. But the queen had not thought of the memories Christmastide would bring to Bronwynn.

As the flowers of autumn turned sere and the berries of the hawthorn crimson, as the rutting stags bellowed and the forests echoed with the crash of their antlers in combat, Bronwynn became quieter. More and more often, she would blink when addressed, as if awakened from some inner musing. The feast day of St. Ambrose, December seventh, came and went and only when coaxed would she leave her child. Even then, she would excuse herself to rush to the nursery to assure herself he was well. Where grace had been, she grew ungainly, as though distrustful, even, that the heavy planks of the floor would remain solid beneath her feet. She picked at her food, while her high cheekbones became more prominant, her slim wrists thinner.

Marguarite watched, uncertain of what to do and wondering if there was anything to be done as her charge grew even more silent, as her gaze turned inward to the haunted memory of another, more heinous celebration of the Christ Child's birth. She found herself, too, flinching in empathy each time Bronwynn would start at a sudden noise, an abrupt movement. A Norman lord who had spent too much time in Ireland told the queen it was as though she had been touched by the fairies.

Bronwynn studied the festooning of the great hall of Windsor Castle with boughs of evergreens and holly as though incredulous that the anniversary of such a grisly event should be celebrated at all. She cringed away, trembling, when her sister offered her a wreath of mistletoe and silver pine to hang. The gesture was done unwittingly, Marguarite assured herself, for surely no one who had been at the massacre of the O'Connors could have done such intentionally. Yet she could not dismiss the faint curl of Cecily's lip as she shrugged contemptuously and turned away to hold it out to another maid.

As the feast day of St. Thomas the Doubter, December twenty first, approached, then passed, Bronwynn's shuddering gaze avoided the troupes of acrobats and minstrels, bards and mummers, fearful they presaged another such barbarity. But it was Christmas day itself that Marguarite—and Henry Franklyn—dreaded the most.

* * *

The revelry swelled, pounding Bronwynn's head with its raucous noise. Acrobats and minstrels plyed their trade among the crowded tables, adding to the pain in her temples. Countless barrels of wine and tuns of beer, of pitchers of mead were consumed, but, throat quivering in disgust, she could take only the smallest of sips of the sweet red wine Henry offered her. The groaning tables were laden with roasted boar and swan, with pies of eel and pigeon and succulent pastries stuffed with the finest meat, fish and fowl, but she could only shake her head, lips sealed, when Henry held a choice bit of pork to her lips.

"So thin," he thought, feeling the frail bones of her hand as she tried to draw it from his grasp. "She has become so thin."

Worried, he studied the lavender circles under Bronwynn's downcast eyes, the sharp edge of her cheekbones, of her jaw, and knew there was no comfort he could offer her. He could only pray, along with Marguarite, that with the ended of the holidays, when the celebration of Twelfthday was done, that she would find the strength to fight—and perhaps defeat—her nightmares. They threatened to be twelve very long days. Only her obsession with her son seemed to be holding her together and Henry could not help but wonder if such a compulsive love and fear was not, in itself, harmful. It was with this concern that he refused her when Bronwynn whispered, "I would go see Kane for but a moment."

"If you will but take a bite of food or two—and a sip of wine."

Her frantic gaze jerked over the feasting revelers and found no aid. She tried to pull her frail hand from his, but he held fast, his warm smile belying his fear, and at last she looked at him, eyes beseeching.

"I do not trust the nurse," she explained. "Mayhap she has left him unattended."

But Henry only shook his head.

"Take but a bite of two of bread, a sip of wine," he coaxed, "and I will go with you."

Her gaze pleaded with his, searching for a softening and finding none. At last, she opened her mouth—like a baby bird, he thought, and as scrawny—to accept a bite of bread dipped in honey, then another. Shaking hand touching his, she guided the goblet he offered to her lips. She sipped once, twice, and shoved the cup aside, only to turn, her fingernails digging into his palm, to vomit into the rushes.

Helpless, Henry held her heaving shoulders, while his frantic gaze sought Marguarite, silently seeking permission to be excused from the hall. The queen had half risen from her chair, features tucked with concern. It was not unusual for revelers, even at the quietest of meals, to over-indulge and lose their dinner into the rushes, but it was certainly no excuse to leave the king's presence without his nod. She touched Edward's shoulder, drawing him away from his conversation. He scowled at Henry, then, at a whispered word from his queen, nodded his leave.

Swooping Bronwynn up in his arms, Henry carried her from the hall, while curious stares followed him. If they thought that his frown was for the disgrace of his betrothed's behavior, they were wrong. It was a scowl of fear, for she felt as light as a feather, and he knew, should she become much thinner, she would die.

Bronwynn woke with the clash of swords in her ears, the curses and cries of fighting, dying men. She blinked in the dim light of the one torch burning high in its bracket in the wall, listening hard, and the screams and sobs faded away as though from an uneasy dream. Only the gasps and snoring of drink sodden women, their tossing and whimpering, could be heard. Rising to her elbow, she touched her son's head, remembering.

Henry had brought him to her to quell her frantic thoughts. He had stayed with her, sitting beside her pallet, holding her, stroking her hair in an attempt to soothe her fears. Each time she had awakened, whimpering, he had been there to shush her back into a nightmare tossed sleep. Only when the queen's women had come to seek respite from the pain and the queasy stomachs certain to be theirs come morning had he sought his own bed. She was alone now, but for the sleeping women, and there was a nightmare, yet, she had to face. Briefly, she considered seeking Henry out in the chamber he shared with others of Edward's nobles, then dismissed the idea. However great the terror, it was hers, a canker on her soul that only she could lance, if only for her child.

Easing Kane into the center of her pallet, she rose to draw a linen tunic over her head. She propped a pillow between him and the floor, then, whispering a prayer for his safekeeping and her own, kissed his slumbering face. Wrapping her mantle about herself, she tiptoed out of the chamber and closed the heavy door behind her.

A few scattered torches threw futile pools of light down a long passage stretching into a darkness ending, Bronwynn knew, in stone tower stairs spiraling down into a further dimness. But she had to follow it.

Not feeling the cold of the floor on her bare feet, Bronwynn moved from one pool of light to the next, her movements stiff with disuse, taut with fear. Yet, there was a purpose, now, to her motions. She hesitated before the steps curving into a darkness fraught with memories. But these were other stairs, this was another Christmas, she told herself, fighting her terror, fighting the urge to flee back to her son, to curve her body around his and never rise again. She would be safe, there, she knew, from all but her nightmares, from all but the illness that ate at her mind, that tightened her throat against all food, all drink. Drawing her mantle closer about her thin body with fingers numb from the chill, she went on.

Twice her body defeated her. Her head grew light, darkening her vision, threatening to pitch her down the unforgiving stone steps. Her knees shook from lack of food, from fear, and she had to sit, head between her knees, summoning courage and strength from a source she had thought long dead. She was so weak! And each time she rose and went on, pausing only to listen to the sounds of desperate battle, the cries of dying men, which faded always with the calming of her pulse, with the tilting of her head. She could only hear, then, the rustle of a rat in the rushes, the keening of the wind through a window slit, the sigh of her own feet on the steps—and on the wooden planks leading to the great hall.

She stood at its entrance, then, and the clash of swords, the cries seemed to grow louder. She shook her head, once, and they were gone. All she could hear, now, was the snorting of one sleeping man, the rooting snort of another, and the whiffling breath and shuffling jerk of a dreaming hound.

She drew a deep breath, but there was no taint of blood to pause on her tongue. Only the fetid smell of sour wine and mouths slack in drunken slumber came to her—and the scent of pine boughs. Still, snared in memories, in fear, she could not move for a long moment. Then, not yet trusting her hearing, her sense of smell, she stepped forward into her nightmare.

Men-at-arms, nobles, and servants alike lay in awkward

positions on pallets scattered across the floor or on the
rushes themselves, as other men had done before. A young
page slept curled around a sleep-snuffling hound, his
beardless chin sunk into matted fur. Some few men were
sprawled face down across the tables still standing,
unshaven jowls pressed into the wood. One clutched a
wooden goblet tilted at a precarious angle, slack mouth
noisily sucking air. Another lay half splayed over a table,
a hand gripping its far edge. They appeared so like those
other men of another Christmas night, Bronwynn thought,
but that was then and there, this was here and now. And
these men were not dead, but merely sleeping, and it was
only ale and wine that clung stickily to the soles of her
feet, and fouled the air, not blood.

Feet silent, Bronwynn walked among men, pausing to
examine one, then another, all of them oblivious to her
perusal. And the man she sought was not among them,
nor would he be. He had been at another, more heinous
place, no matter that she had not found him there, either.
At last, she paused, her fear, her nightmare expelled in a
soft sigh, and she shuddered, as though awakening from
a dream.

Reaching out, she took a goblet from a man's slack
fingers, intending to but straighten it, then brought it
instead to her own lips. It was malmsey and its pale sweetness cloyed on her tongue, but still she gulped at it. She
picked up a half gnawed swan's leg, her small teeth ripping
at it, her throat jerking as she swallowed. She hesitated,
bracing herself against a table, her knees threatening to
give out beneath her, as her body fought to reject the
unfamiliar sustenance. Then her stomach quieted and,
finding an unclaimed pastry in her hand, she ate it on the
long walk back to her bed.

Kane was there as she had left him, round arms tossed
trustingly out from his body, sweet breath a soft bubble

about his lips. Lying down with him, drawing him into the curve of her body, she stroked his feather fine hair back from his brow, her gaze unseeing on the far wall. Then the tears came with silent sobs as she grieved for men so long dead.

(21)

Henry watched the color wash back into Bronwynn's features, the flesh spring back into her thin face, and he wondered at the miracle that had wrought the change. He saw Browynn's step grow lighter, her throat swell with full, round laughter and knew the miracle's manner did not matter. Even her obsession with her son had disappeared and she no longer clung to him from fear, from an excess of love. Henry could only utter prayers of gratitude, while cursing the six month betrothal he had promised her. He had not considered, then, that the season of Lent would prolong it more, or remember that there was no giving or taking in marriage during those days of fasting both at the table and in the marriage bed. That their wedding day was set for the Monday after Easter was no comfort for the tossing and turning he did now. Nor did it offer ease when he woke from dreams of Bronwynn, her dark hair spread over his pillow, her breasts full and warm to his hands once more.

Edward of England's life style, too, had not eased his

torment. Spring had come early that year and as soon as the roads were halfway dry, the king was off on the rounds of his castles again. Too often, Henry had had to watch Bronwynn's bright face and slim figure as she rode in the procession, her barbaric mantle falling behind her, the hooded falcon that was his gift to her perched on her gloved wrist.

Today, though, was Maundy Thursday—the Thursday before Easter—and he had but four more days to wait. But she was in Caernarvon and he was in Harlech on the king's business. Still, he resolved, he would leave the next day, Good Friday or no, sin or no. Even then, even with good weather and dry roads, the ride was a hard, long one. And, he silently vowed, shifting in his saddle to study the flight of the arrows loosed from the long bows of the king's Welsh, he would arrive in Caernarvon that night or the next morning if he had to ride his horse into the ground to do it. Edward was plotting another invasion of Scotland and the time he would have with Bronwynn would be too short as it was. Surely God would forgive him the violation of a holy day for such cause.

But Caernarvon was so close to Ireland, he told himself irrelevantly. Shuddering, he crossed himself against whatever evil had brought the thought, then glanced around to see if anyone had seen the gesture. But all gazes were on a second flight of arrows and he, too, looked up into a bright blue sky.

It was a beautiful day, he noted and, smiling, hoped the sun shone, too, on Bronwynn. She was, he remembered, to accompany Marguarite to the fair in the town below Caernarvon Castle.

But nothing good, they said, ever came out of Ireland, and cold fingers again crept up his spine. He scowled, pushing the thought away, and urged his horse forward to join his men.

* * *

The queen and her ladies strolled through the fair, alighting at a booth to examine fine linen wimples, pausing to watch a juggler, an acrobat. Like a flock of brightly colored birds, Bronwynn thought, lagging behind, and as chirpy. She stopped at a booth featuring gloves to pick up a leather pair the color of butter and as soft. Then, catching sight of a vendor selling eel pies, she put them back, deciding she should eat something before purchasing them.

Buying her pie, she turned, looking for the queen, to catch sight, instead, of a little girl staring at her. Her thin fingers twisted in her thread worn shift and her face was pitched with hunger. With a sigh of compassion, Bronwynn kneeled and held out her pie. Hesitatingly, not trusting her good fortune or the pretty, warmly clad lady, the child inched forward. At last, she snatched the treat from Bronwynn's hand and darted past a huge dog and into the crowd.

Bronwynn stared after her at the hound, breath caught in her throat. He regarded her in return from under wiry brows, his lolling tongue pink, yellow eyes laughing. Slowly, Bronwynn rose, hand outstretched, her lips forming the name, "Booka?"

But the dog turned, his shaggy tail a flag, to disappear between two tents. Standing on legs gone nerveless, heart pounding a ragged rhythm, Bronwynn followed him. A cart he had slipped under blocked her way and, unable to peer over, she stumbled around it to find herself in a secluded meadow sloping down to a tree-lined creek. The meadow was dotted with grazing horses and the few small tents of those vendors successful enough to afford one. Next to a horse, his back to her, kneeled a man scowling down at the hoof he held on one immense knee. Beside him, resting a plump hand on the man's huge shoulder,

was a child with pale blond hair. The face she turned at
Bronwynn's intrusion was a sweet replica of Fenella's, but
her eyes were hazel—and Cian's own. Skidding to a halt,
Bronwynn stared at her and the man, stunned eyes wide
in disbelief. At last, she backed away, one step, then
another, as though she had seen a ghost. But the hound
was nudging the man's elbow as though it was, indeed,
flesh and blood, the child was whispering into his ear, and
Bronwynn halted. Drawing a deep breath for courage, not
believing the man could be who her eyes told her he was,
uncertain, even, if she wished him to be, Bronwynn forced
herself forward. She halted again, close enough to touch
him, and wondered how he could not sense the intensity
of her gaze, or hear the thudding of her heart.

But he was deep in concentration as he pared at the
hoof, the knife a toy in his huge, freckled fist. The child
whispered a second time, tugging at his sleeve, and he
nodded abstractedly, still bemused by his work. The dog
nudged him again, tail wagging with joy at his news, but
the man elbowed him away. Then Bronwynn touched his
shoulder and her breath came out in a strangled whisper.

"Curran?"

Not hearing her, he hunched a shoulder toward his ear,
as though pestered by an itch, and Bronwynn cleared her
throat to repeat the name louder. He heard her, then, she
knew, for he stiffened and tilted his head toward her, as
though asking her to repeat herself. She silently refused,
and he at last set the hoof down with infinite care and
slowly stood. Reluctance in his every move, he turned to
face her even as he lowered his hand to rest on the child's
shoulder, reassuring her, and Bronwynn stared up into
Curran's freckled visage. Her features were a mask of disbelief, then stunned joy, then incredulous rage. At last, she
found her voice.

"You were not with him there," she accused, her whisper

a croak. She swallowed hard, gaze never leaving his face, and repeated herself. "You were not with him there—at Carrick—and you let him die there—alone."

But Curran was shaking his head. His gaze was directed over her shoulder and the hedge of his eyebrows was wiggling a frantic signal. Someone stood behind her, and Bronwynn was frightened, as she had never been before, of who it might be. If it was not Cian, the disappointment would be more than she could bear. Yet, suddenly, the notion that it might be him terrified her. Lifting her chin in its old, defiant gesture, her body and thoughts feeling so fragile, she turned at last. Cian stood there, features alight with that familiar, cocky grin that had always caught at her heart even while she wanted to slap it away, so insolent, so knowing it was. But there was a wary expression in his hazel eyes and his arms were crossed over his broad chest.

Bronwynn stared at him, shaking her head in disbelief. Palms lifted in front of her, she backed away from him until halted by Curran's massive chest, until supported by his firm hands. Still, she shook her head, and stated stupidly, "You shaved your mustache."

"I had to. Am I not in England?" he laughed, but her mind was snared on another thought.

"How dare you," she whispered at last, "how dare you allow me to think you dead?"

She shrugged off Curran's hands, her jaw set in fury, and advanced toward Cian. He studied her as she came, grin gone, features apprehensive. Of all the greetings he had imagined, rage had not been one of them. He wanted, suddenly, to back away from the fury of it—and the justice. But she was shaking her head again and he stood his ground, assaying another smile.

"How dare you?" she demanded once more, then her fist caught him hard in the belly. He doubled over with the surprise and pain of it, his breath escaping in a whoosh. He fought to bring it back, even as he scowled a warning at Curran's grinning features. But Bronwynn was speaking again, drawing his attention back to her, her voice a furious hiss.

"And how dare you bring the little one with you? 'Twas for her I lost you—and gladly—yet now you deliberately expose her to such danger. Now, you dare bring her here so close to her mother's clutches, when I paid such a price to free her? And wouldn't Fenella rejoice in having her back, if only to have another soul to torment? How dare you!"

Fury raged again on Bronwynn's features. Her fist was clenched and aimed once more toward Cian's belly. Prepared this time, he caught it easily and twisted her arm behind her. Refusing to let her go, he held her struggling body against his own until he could speak. Then, catching her second fist, he held her away from him, the better to address her furious features and to judge the effect of his words.

"Siobhan still has nightmares if I am gone from her too long and only I seem able to soothe them," he attempted to explain, the reasoning that had convinced him to bring his daughter with him and into such danger sounding weak, now, even to his own ears. But de Bermingham had taught him well, with the deed done at Carrick Castle, that life was fragile. It was his own hobgoblin that now caused him to believe that to have someone he loved out of his sight was to have him imperiled. To even think of leaving his daughter alone for more than a day or two, even with Fithir, was to turn his mind wild with panic, his thoughts dark with fear. But he had no words to tell Bronwynn— or anyone—of such a weakness. Yet, angry as she was that he might have put Siobhan in jeopardy, it was the other, he knew, that truly enraged her, that had caused her such grieving—and he had to find words and charm enough to make her forgive the unpardonable.

"Ah, a stór, he crooned into her set features, "didn't we think it better, then, that you believe me dead, and ourselves not knowing if de Bermingham would think to finish a job not yet done? What better excuse could he have had than to come after you, had you come to me, and ourselves with scarcely enough men to ward off the flies from the midden?"

"And how could I have come to you," she spat back, "with your father and his men dead—and the deed done by Norman hands? Would not those who survived stone me dead in the bawn? Cause enough they had to hate me and hate me they still must do. And we had made a pact, had we not? Aught had happened to change that! Nor have you told me what you do here—or has the O'Connor taken to the roads with the peddlers?" She nodded toward the harp slung over his shoulder, then her gaze dropped the rough, peasant clothing he wore. "Or do you sing for your supper, now?"

Cian ignored her question, his thumbs gently circling the knuckles of the fists clenched in his. The mockery had gone from his smile and his warm eyes held her furious ones.

"Ah, sure, something happened to change our pact, a stór, did it not? Did you not bear me a son?"

It was, for a moment, as though she had not heard him, then the rage in her features collapsed into terror. Her head shook even as she wondered at his great hate for her. Yet what a mighty revenge it would be for whatever part he thought she had played in the murder of his clan—to take her child from her—and how so very Irish. She could see that, just as she could understand the hatred, knew, even, that it was justified. Did not the shanachie relate such tales of vengeance with glee? And didn't the sons, under Irish law, go with their fathers and the daughters with their mothers? But she would not allow it, never, and she wished, suddenly, that Henry was there to protect her, to protect them both. But there was Edward! Once told, he would keep Kane safe, and a wave of relief rushed over her, before she realized she could not tell him. No matter his threat or his hate, this was Cian. Edward would certainly see him dead, finishing the job de Bermingham had so bungled. Just being in Wales put Cian in danger. Still, she straightened to hiss into Cian's astonished face, "You'll not take my son from me!"

He stared down into her defiant features, his head shaking. Releasing her fists, he cupped her face in his hands and tilted it up to his, his gaze drinking in the beauty of it—and the terror in her eyes.

"I did not come for our son only. I came for the both of you. I had not realized, before, how much bone of my bone you had become—and blood of my blood. I've a great need of you in my bed, in my life. 'Tis like a hole in my soul no other woman can fill—and haven't I tried, so, with any one of them who will lie down long enough for the attempt?" He grinned, then, and cocked an eyebrow at Curran. "Won't that great man, there, testify 'tis so, and himself following me ever about like a third leg, myself wanting his company or no?"

But there would be no help from Curran. The massive man stood with hands spread in wistful impotence—quarrels were much simpler between himself and his Sine. Nor did Bronwynn follow Cian's glance or answer his grin, and he sobered. Gnawing his lip, he studied each features, wondering how to reach her, convince her. Surely, she could feel the aching need he had for her—the hard shaft of him pressing against her belly.

"Nor do the people hate you, no more than I do," he insisted. "Haven't they wit enough to know you had aught

to do with the deed at Carrick? Haven't they seen me, all
this last year, moping about with my face as long as the
lying tongue of the Sassenach for want of you. Won't they
welcome you back, so, and themselves loving you almost
as much as I do? Wasn't it with the blessing of Fithir,
herself, that I came—and Cormac dead at Carrick?"

"I am to be married," Bronwynn asserted, features obdu-
rate no matter the coaxing of his fingertips along her jaw
line, on the soft feathers of her eyebrows.

"And isn't it said that Henry Franklyn be a good man,
a kind man, but he is not the father of your son. Nor has
he so many years in front of him to miss you as I have—
and isn't the missing of you a hollow within the gut of me
aught else can fill? I want you, a stór. I want you and our
son—and the other children of our love sure to follow."

"You would have me leave all I have, aye, and my sister
and a good man who loves me to follow you, to live with
you in a mud and wattle hut in the wilds of Ireland?"

"I would," he smiled. He had her at least thinking of
it and that with Bronwynn, he remembered, was half the
battle. Given time, he could wheedle any cat from a tree.
But he had scant time. "Franklyn, should you marry him,
would be given all you have, leaving you aught but his
good will. And isn't your sister aught but a child so grasping
she does not even know what she wants unless another
finds it first? She'd not even know you were gone until
there was something new she coveted and needed you to
get it for her. You know 'tis so. And didn't we find great
pleasure in that mud and wattle hut, so?"

His mouth lowered to hers, as soft as a falling leaf, and
Bronwynn stood spellbound by the familiarity of it. Sinking
his hands into her hair, he turned her head to take her
mouth more fully, his lips, the tip of his tongue pleading
with hers, asking for more. The hard length of him pressed
against her, stirring an answering need she had thought

long since dead. She heard the purring response in her throat, felt her mouth open under his, seeking the feel of him, the sweet taste. The hands she had pressed against his chest, holding him at bay, curled into the cloth of his tunic, clutching at him as her knees threatened to give way, as an imperious ache gripped the most secret part of her, demanding to be filled. It shook her with its present strength, with her memories, and she clung closer, pressing up against him, as an urgent need she had known for too long only in dreams stirred hard within her.

But she always woke from those dreams to grieving, to sorrow, to a guilt she could never propitiate.

Gathering her strength in a burst of anger, fear and anguish, she shoved herself away from Cian. Confident in the yielding of her mouth, her body, and taken by surprise, he let her go, then grabbed for her, but she was backing away, hands outstretched to ward him off, her head shaking in denial.

"You lie!" she accused, "If I cannot forgive myself for no more than being of the same race as de Bermingham, how can you or any O'Connor dare to absolve me? How can you not remember, as I do every day, every hour, that I was there and, surely, there must have been something I could have done to prevent the deed, if only to make my warning to your father the stronger? Yet you dare tell me you forgive me—and you lie! You lie to gain your son."

Cian was shaking his head, but with each step he took toward her, she retreated another, refusing his protests.

"No, I'll not listen! You think I don't remember your sorrow and rage at Fenella's taking Siobhan from you? How much more you must want your son—even to the taking of a woman your people have such cause to hate with him. Nor would your people come to love him, not as Henry does. How could they—a child of the Sassenach? No, you'll not have him. I fought for him that night, when

I wanted so to repudiate all I had seen, even to my own soul and that of my child. I fought for him because something good had to come from such evil—and from the love we had then. But we can have it no more, not with the deed at Carrick between us, no matter your denials and your lies."

"Bronwynn, I do not lie. I swear on the soul of my father. If you will but listen to me."

His own jaw square, his mobile mouth tight with intent, he held his gaze steady on her features, but behind her he saw the wheel of a cart. One quick step and he had caught her wrist. When she tried to jerk away, she found herself trapped by the tall wheel. She turned back to face him, eyes holding the hurt of a deceived child, and he wanted only to hold her, then, to allow his mouth, his body to convince her of what words could not. His eyes tried to tell her so, but a voice calling Bronwynn's name broke the tenuous bond between them. Not looking away from his eyes, she lifted her voice in answer, "Cecily, I'm here."

Her sister slipped from between two carts to come to an abrupt halt, eyes wide at the sight of Cian. Then they narrowed, avidly taking in the scene. For a second, her old jealousy flared, but Cian and Bronwynn seemed more combatants than lovers now, and Cian was eyeing her with an apprehension she could only view as a challenge. Skirts swaying, she approached Cian and her sister, preening even as she walked and only halting when the tinkling bells in the hem of her surcoat brushed against Cian's rough leggings and she lightly touched his sleeve. The faint ringing of the bells, the touch on his forearm, brought Cian's blinking gaze to her hand with its gleaming oval nails, then up to blue eyes round with delight, to red-tinted lips parted to display perfect teeth gleaming in greedy pleasure. He stared at her, controlling the impulse to jerk his arm away

from her touch. She was too much a danger for him to
offend her.

"Ah, Cian," she smiled. " 'Tis good to see you again—
and in England."

Frowning, Cian glanced at Bronwynn, wondering if she,
too, heard none of the astonishment at seeing him alive
that should have been Cecily's. But Bronwynn, tears washing her cheeks, was drawing her wrist free of his grasp and
backing away from him. He would have stepped after her,
but her head was shaking, telling him, "no". Cecily, too,
had tightened her touch on his arm, forcing his attention
back to her, the slight dig of her nails a warning that she
would not be ignored.

"I regret," she smiled at him, "that I have to take Bronwynn away. I'm certain you've so much to discuss. Seeing
you alive must have been quite a shock for her. But the
queen is returning to the castle and wishes Bronwynn with
her." She shrugged and added, her voice mocking the
possibility, "Mayhap you can see her another time, perhaps
at supper with our lord Edward."

Cian smiled back, his muscles stretched with the false-
ness of the expression and the desire to slap her.

"Mayhap," he agreed, then he looked at Bronwynn.

She waited for her sister, head held up and tilted warily.
Her gaze was on his in mute appeal, pleading that he go,
that he not try to see her again. Still, he stepped toward
her. Moving slowly, not wanting to send her to flight, he
reached into his tunic to draw out a pair of soft, butter-
yellow gloves.

"A stór," he said softly, "would you take these? It seems,"
and his smile was bitter with pain, "I shall have no use for
them."

She held his gaze, throat convulsing on a sob, as she
took but one glove, leaving the other in his outstretched
hand. Then she turned and was gone. Shrugging at such

perverse behavior, Cecily smiled one more time at Cian and followed her sister, the tiny bells in her hem singing with each provocative sway of her hips. Cian stared after them, gaze blank on the space between two tents into which they had disappeared, until he felt Curran's hand on his shoulder.

"Hadn't we best, then, be getting back to Ireland," Curran asked, "and your purpose here to no avail?"

"And are you thinking," Cian countered, voice rough with anger and disappointment, "that she will tell of our presence here?"

Curran scowled, then shook his head.

"Not that one. For all her denials, she loves you too much to wish to see you dead. And won't she," he chuckled, knowing Bronwynn, "find a way to lame her sister's vicious tongue? Still, we have no more purpose here, unless you think to sell the last of those wolf skins or to earn a coin or two as bard."

"I do not," Cian answered. His daughter slipped next to him to hug one leg and his long fingers caressed her bright hair, as he scowled, gaze still on the gap between the two tents. "Nor do I, in truth, like Siobhan so close to her mother's grasp—and Edward's. Myself, sure, don't I ever seek trouble and didn't that one once say she thought I had a death wish on me?" His chin lifted, indicating the spot through which Bronwynn had disappeared, and he grinned, slapping Curran on his broad shoulder in sudden camaraderie. "And you, have I ever denied you your fair share of danger and yourself ever lathering after it, so, like a hound eager to slip the leash at the first scent of a fight?" Then he sobered as quickly as his mood had lightened. "But I've not won what I came for, have I?" Then he shrugged, eyes narrowed in thought. "And we've agreed, haven't we, that she'll not speak of our presence here— not for a while yet—and she'll keep her sister silent, too.

Am I not thinking, then, that there might be other ways to skin a cat and means enough to use Cecily's hatred and jealousy? And are there not means other than persuasion to win what we came after and Bronwynn perhaps more amiable to them in Ireland?''

He turned, then, one hand clutching a yellow glove, and grinned at Curran in a way that only roused the other's concern and fear. And the apprehension was for Bronwynn, Curran realized, for didn't he know his lordling and the lengths he would go to when he set his mind to something he wanted? Nor had he ever seen him want something as much as he did Bronwynn and their child.

(22)

Nor did Cecily speak of Cian, not to Edward. The threat of a nunnery was enough to hold her tongue. If Bronwynn did not have the power to send her there, Henry Franklyn did, with his sword at Edward's command and his voice in Edward's ear. Yet the warning was not enough to curb the furious hatred and resentment in Cecily's eyes each time she looked at Bronwynn. There was a gloating satisfaction, too, that night, as she watched her sister struggle to appear as though all was normal, forcing a smile on stiff features, feigning an interest in conversations she did not hear. Marguarite, too, Cecily saw, watched Bronwynn in concern. But Cecily had not been able to withhold the secret from Fenella; it was too good. Bronwynn could see that in Fenella's avid, feeding eyes, in the display of her small, pointed teeth.

Still, Bronwynn could only ignore them. The shock of seeing Cian alive had been too great for her to brood on either her sister's or Fenella's acrimony. His laughing eyes, his mouth on hers had summoned forth too many emotions, too many needs so long unfulfilled—and with them, too much grief and guilt. Suddenly and more than anything, she wanted Henry there and the bulwark of his arms around her to hold at bay all the feelings roiling within her. She craved his strength, his presence, for there was, too, that urgent need to gather Kane up in her arms and run to Cian, offering up herself, her child, no matter that she knew he did not truly want her, could only hate her. But Henry would not be back until the day after next, late on the day after Good Friday.

Caught up in her conflicting emotions, struggling to appear as though nothing was wrong, Bronwynn did not notice when Cecily's resentment and Fenella's spiteful voraciousness became something more ominous. Only after supper, after accompanying Marguarite to her chamber did she catch Cecily's gaze on her, filled with a sly gloating, and Fenella's with a rapacious expectation. She stared at them, mind and vision snared by the virulence of their expressions. But their eyes had quickly dropped away, leaving her with a vague apprehension. Later, as she suckled her son and after she had carried him back to the nursery, each time she glanced at her sister and Fenella, while she forced her attention on the minstrel singing to the queen's ladies, they had their heads together, lips whispering and features smug.

The plotting worried her as she at last was allowed to curl into her pallet's cold comfort to stare sightlessly into the dark. But whatever they planned, she assured herself, Henry would return in two days. In the meantime, the concern was something to hold against the memory of Cians laughing eyes, his demanding mouth. There had been, too, a new harshness and grim strength to Cian that frightened her with its purpose. Haunted by nightmares of his broad shoulders, of the russet curls at the back of his neck retreating just beyond her fingertips, only to have him turn, at last, his face a mask of death, she would wake.

Yet, somehow in her restless sleep, she seemed to have found a certain peace and resolution. Waking, refusing yet to open her eyes, she listened for the sounds of the women around her rising and preparing for the day. It was a sound, she decided, she would miss when she was married, when she had gone with Henry to his estates. At the thought, she knew, with Cian's resurrection, she could at last bury him and find another life. It would not be as fulfilling, as exciting as one with Cian, but it offered peace. Had she not always yearned for that, no matter her love of the wind on her face and her hatred of walls? Eyes still closed, she listened again, but there was only silence. It was later than she had thought. All the other women had long since gone to communion and possibly were even at breakfast or finishing it.

For a moment, she frowned, wondering why Kane's nurse had not brought him to her. But he was, like her and like his father, a late riser. Didn't they all like to lie abed, listening to the sounds of morning and savoring the warmth, the laziness of it?

Angry at allowing herself such a thought of Cian, she rose and dressed. Kane was probably screaming his rage and hunger, his small face red and skewed over Erda's thick shoulder. Tossing her mantle around her against the late March chill, she went to him.

But his nurse was not in the nursery nor was Kane in his cradle. Only a dull-faced wet nurse was there, suckling her swaddled charge. Nor had she noticed when Erda had left or if she had taken Kane with her. Frustrated at the woman's lack of wit, Bronwynn whispered, "stupid cow," beneath her breath and sought out the kitchens. It would not be, she told herself, the first time Erda had taken her charge there to sit in the warmth and gossip, Kane cuddled against her shoulder.

But Erda sat on a stool near the huge hearth, a mug of ale nestled in her broad red hands, no child with her. She looked at Bronwynn in surprise and welcome, then scowled and stood, the stool falling with a crash behind when she looked twice at Bronwynn's feature.

"My Lady," she whispered, "where is the babe?"

"You do not know?" Bronwynn demanded, and Erda shook her head, pale eyes round.

"He was not in his cradle when I woke this morning. I but thought you had come and taken him to the solar." She stood a bit straighter, gathering her courage. "Haven't you done such afore, my Lady?"

So she had, Bronwynn told herself, gaze blind with terror as she stared at Erda's fearful features. Her breasts, she realized, were heavy with milk. Then she knew, and she whirled on her heel and was gone. Her mind spun frantically as she ran, trying to make sense of her suspicions, wondering how best to gain the answer. But Marguarite and her women, finished with their repast, were not in the great hall. Desperate now, Bronwynn flew into the solar and halted, clinging to the door frame.

At the interruption, Marguarite looked up from the breviary she was reading aloud. Her ladies, too, turned. Their mouths, piously crimped as befitted the holy day, fell open at the sight of Bronwynn's distraught features, but Marguarite stood, the breviary almost slipping from her fingers, to whisper, "What is it?" but Bronwynn ignored her.

It was her sister's attention Browynn sought, but Cecily held her gaze downcast as she drew a comb through Fenella's long hair, then picked at an nonexistent tangle. Fenella, though, was staring at Bronwynn, eyes sly with pleasure, then she drew Cecily down to whisper in her ear. At last, her sister lifted her gaze to meet Bronwynn's. Her features were bland with innocence, but her eyes gleamed. A corner of her soft, pink mouth twitched with satisfaction—and Bronwynn knew her suspicions were correct.

In three strides she was on her. Knocking the comb away, Bronwynn twisted her fist in her hair and jerked her to her feet. Sobbing, Cecily would have protested, but Bronwynn dragged her to the door and, not releasing her grip, flung her around the corner and out of view. Furious, Fenella stood to go after them, but Marguarite's voice cut across the babble of her ladies.

"Stay!"

Fenella halted and turned in disbelief.

"But my Lady, you saw Bronwynn. Surely, she will do Cecily harm."

Smiling, Marguarite nodded.

"She might, but scarcely without provocation. I only regret she'll mostlike not so chastise you after."

She dipped her head toward a stool and Fenella sat. Then, after a brief glance in the direction of the door, the queen returned to her reading.

Fist still clenched in Cecily's hair, Bronwynn flung her against the wall.

"Where is he?" she hissed into her sister's stupefied features.

"Who?" Cecily managed to stutter and Brownynn slapped her twice, bouncing her head off the granite wall.

"Don't play with me! I haven't the patience or the time. Kane is gone and so is Fenella's surly wench, or you would not be combing the slut's hair, would you? Do you think me blind, stupid, or both? I want the truth."

"I don't know what you are talking about," Cecily whimpered, "and you hit me." Her tongue flicked at the corner of her mouth, tasting blood. "You hurt me."

Not hesitating, Bronwynn slapped her.

"The truth!" she stated between clenched teeth, face

inches from Cecily's. "Now!" Her sister's bravado collapsed and she began to babble.

"They be with Cian, Biddie and Kane, both. Biddie took him from the nursery after you and Erda were asleep. Fenella arranged it, all of it! She sent Biddie to Cian, offering him Kane, if he but promised to take her with them to Ireland on last night's tide." She smiled tremulously into Bronwynn's appalled features in a vain attempt to placate. "He will be fine! Cian will love him, you know that. Look you on how he doted on that brat of Fenella's."

"You stupid little bitch," Bronwynn said almost pityingly, "if you say aught of this to anyone, if you tell anyone of where I may go, I will see you hang for a witch—and that conniving, spiteful, slut in there with you. If I cannot, Henry Franklyn will. That you can believe. Taking a child from his parents is not a crime dealt with lightly—and Henry Franklyn, if you will recall, has intentions of adopting Kane. If you say aught," she repeated, bouncing her sister's head off the wall for emphasis, "I will see you hang. Remember that."

Bronwynn released her then, and turned away only to pause, her mind already plotting. Nor did she notice that her sister had slid limply to the floor. Only Cecily's vengeful hiss brought her attention back and Bronwynn suddenly indifferent, watched her try to stand, to speak.

"No, I'll not say aught, you can depend on that," Cecily spat out, wiping a trickle of blood from her mouth, even as she edged for the safety of the solar—and it seemed so far away. "I know how you are when you want something— or someone. You'll let no one and nothing stand in your way—including me, your sister! You've always put yourself before me. You were given everything! Papa left you everything and never once thought of me. And see what you do with it, dressing as somberly as a nun and never having fun. 'Tis no wonder the men don't want you, dull, ugly

stick that you are. Melusine was right about you and so is
Fenella. Yet you always look down your nose at my friends,
even when they want but to help you, to show you how to
dress and flirt, just like you scorn the men who like me.
You are just jealous, like Fenella says. Nor do you ever
think of what I might want or need. You even prefer that
puling bastard brat of yours over me!"

Bronwynn studied her dispassionately, wondering how
she had been so blind to such jealousy, but she found she
no longer cared that her sister might hate her. She could
only marvel that Cecily did, indeed, seem to believe the
pap she spewed. Nor was she done spouting her vitupera-
tion, even as she inched ever closer to the solar.

"And you're such a fool, thinking that Cian loved you!
He but used you, just as he's using you now. And you're
such a dupe. 'Twas easy as taking a honey pap from an
infant to send word to him of Biddie's wish to return to
Ireland and her willingness to take that brat of yours with
her as her price. Didn't he leap at the chance, though,
and it done right under your nose!"

But Bronwynn had merely given Cecily a look of
immense pity and was turning. She was daring to walk away
and Cecily straightened away from the wall and took a step
toward her, features contorted with malevolence.

"And didn't Fenella and I laugh so at your grieving your
heart out," she hissed, "and all for a man as alive as you
and me."

At that, as though not certain of her hearing, Bronwynn
turned back.

"You knew he was alive," she wondered, "and you did
not tell me?"

Cecily smiled then, her lips curling over her teeth, and
dipped her head in acknowledgement and satisfaction.

"I did. I heard de Bermingham whisper of it to Melusine
in their bed—that he had killed the O'Connor but failed

with the whelp. And Fenella, hadn't she seen him in Ireland?''

"And you let me think him dead?" Bronwynn asked, voice as cold as the bottom of a well. "You let me eat my own heart over a man still living? Why?"

" 'Twas amusing," Cecily shrugged. "Melusine thought so and so did Fenella."

Then she saw she had gone too far and turned to dash to the solar. But her sister was faster. Grabbing Cecily by her hair, she flung her to the floor. Her foot caught Cecily in her belly, knocking the breath from her. Bronwynn stood there a moment longer, staring down at her sister as she gasped for air.

"I wish," she said at last, uttering the most virulent curse she could think of, "that you never want for anything, that all should come to you before you ever know what it is to desire, to need, to love."

Then she turned on her heel and was gone, her sister put behind her, only her purpose, and a desperate planning remaining in her mind.

(23)

Sheltered from the wind by a ledge of rock, Bronwynn stared out at the strand where a small boat was being prepared. Worried, she glanced up at a lowering sky and tried to twist a ring no longer on her finger. It had been enough and more to purchase passage on the boat across to Ireland, her motley crew of Welsh and Irish with it, and the ring was now on a thong about the dirt encrusted neck of their leader. It had not been enough, though, to coerce them into sailing on a holy day. She had been forced to hide until the next morning in the loft of a waterfront ale house. And flea ridden it was, too, she thought, scratching.

The torque, the earrings given to her by the O'Connor, the gold balls to dangle at the ends of long plaits would buy her men to take her to the edge of the Irish Pale. How she would make her way from there to Inishbawn, she did not yet know. But she would.

Still, she regretted parting with the betrothal ring, just as she regretted with all her soul leaving the man who had given it to her. He was too kind, too good to be hurt so—

and with no word, no justification from her. He would return that evening to find her gone, God willing, she thought, blinking back tears. She glanced once more at the sky, then jumped at the touch of a hand on her shoulder. Jerking around, she looked up into Henry Franklyn's battle-grizzled features.

"Your sister," he said, his attempted grin a painful grimace, "told me where you had gone—and why. Whatever fear your threats inspired, mine inspired worse."

Biting his lip, he took her hand and gently drew off her glove. There was a tremor in his hands she had never noticed before as he slipped the betrothal ring back on her finger and curled her fist around it.

" 'Twas my gift to you," he explained, "to do with as you would, but I would rather you gift it to Kane than buy the service of that ilk." He nodded toward the boat crew, then looked back at Bronwynn. The wind, he noted, had drawn long strands of dark hair from her plaits and he tenderly tucked them back. "I gave them money enough to buy you safe passage."

"Henry," Bronwynn whispered, but he shook his head.

"I know you must go and I would God I could go with you, if but to keep you safe. And I would God I could bring you and Kane back with me. But I would have to beg leave of Edward and he would insist on sending men with us, and wouldn't we, then, have a war on our hands? All for the taking of a babe by his father, and that father wishing but to draw the woman he loves after them."

Bronwynn would have denied it, but he touched her lips with a quieting finger.

"I put it out to Edward that you were having second thoughts about our marriage, that you had gone to your Welsh relatives to think it through," Henry continued. "He cursed you as a stubborn, foolish female, but his eyes gleamed at the thought of your estates. You will forfeit them to him, you know.''

"But I'll be back," Bronwynn insisted and Henry gave a smile of pain.

"Mayhap," he agreed, blinking against the wind and the moisture it had drawn to his eyes, "and I would gladly take you back. But I think you'll not. I think you'll stay where your heart is, your soul, and they are with him. So it should be. You've need of a young man, a strong man who will ever draw your passion to him. Nor have you forgotten him, no matter your affection for me." His finger touched her lips again at her protest. "And, no matter your denials, I think he wants you. 'Twas a far, dangerous way to come to claim a child, when a man can father many another, as your Cian O'Connor has proven. Aye, I think you'll stay and you've my blessings on it."

"But I love you," Bronwynn whispered, and Henry gently wiped the tears from her cold cheeks with broad, rough thumbs.

"I know," he murmured, smile sorrowing, "and I was blessed with it. You gave me a joy I thought no longer possible. I will love you for it ever, just as I will hold you in my heart until I die." Then his smile turned bitter. "And, if God should curse me so, even after."

He looked away, then, blinking hard. When his gaze dropped back to hers, he nodded toward the boat.

" 'Tis time to go for both of us," he said, "for I haven't the heart in me to watch you leave and you must sail afore the weather worsens. Nor have I the courage to do this again tomorrow."

He drew her into his arms then, to inhale for the last time the fragrance of her, to touch her lips with his. Then he turned her around to set her walking down the long strand toward the boat before swiveling on his heel to climb the rocks back to the land. He fought the urge to turn, to watch her leave, and knew he would never again draw in the smell of the sea and not feel his heart crack with pain.

She had come this way with Cian, Bronwynn thought, two years before. There was the same dolman rising high on its hill, the same curve to the earth, felt more than seen through a heavy, damp fog. But she had ridden, then, with a wild excitement in her heart. Now, there was but a grim purpose in her mind—and the fear that she might fail. And, even if she should find Kane, if she could claim him, would she have milk for him? Somehow, it seemed so important. Slipping her hand under her mantle, she touched breasts which produced less each day, no matter that she expressed it every night and morning. But the worry was, she knew, but a tool to hold at bay other, more terrifying fears.

And, those two years before, she had ridden with the prideful men of the O'Connors. Now, her companions were three battle-scared, villainous gallowglass she had hired in Dublin. But she had been fortunate to find men willing to see her so far into O'Connor lands and, now, wasn't she but a day and a half from Inishbawn, itself? But there was little comfort in the thought, for she did not know if Kane would even be there. Nor did she, she reminded herself, have any plan on how to confront Cian.

Drawing her hood closer about her face against the heavy misting, Bronwynn glanced around at her dubious escort. But other men, men with familiar faces, were riding out of the fog from either side of the track and, when she turned back, thinking to flee, Cian sat his horse in front of her. His glance took her in in one swift appraisal, then he ignored her to nod at her companions.

"Skelly, Caley," he said, then he looked at the third. "Tavis. You've my thanks."

He held out his hand and Tavis dropped the gold torque into it. Hearing Bronwynn's hiss of outrage, Cian turned to lift a derisive eyebrow at her.

"Were you thinking, then," he mocked, "that I would allow you to ride halfway across Ireland unprotected—and yourself the mother of my son?"

"Where is he?" she demanded, swallowing the fury he could rear in her even in the best of times.

"At Inishbawn," he answered lightly. "Where else?"

Not waiting for an answer, he urged his horse forward and Bronwynn, forcing her tongue silent on her protests, her questions, was forced to follow. Only Curran had favored her with a small grin and a wink that seemed to mock. One more night, she calmed herself, just one more night and the next half day's riding, and she would see her son. Cian, at least, had not given any sign he would not allow it. How she would pass that night, with so many questions and with Cian so close, she did not dare to wonder. But he did not want her, that she knew, no matter his declarations, his attempted seduction in Wales. He had already taken what he wanted.

And the night came too soon. Drawing up before an abandoned booley house, Cian and his men set about making camp, nor did he glance at Bronwynn as she sat on a rock watching them. With no more than an abrupt, "There's a bed made for you inside," Cian handed her a bowl of mutton stew.

"Thank you," Bronwynn muttered angrily into her bowl and Cian cast a mocking smile her way.

"My pleasure," he grinned, and his voice held an intonation she refused to hear. She stared after him and abruptly all the doubts she had held at bay for the long journey rushed over her. There was nothing she had to offer him, nothing he valued that he would trade for her son. All she could give him were her pleas, her tears, and those, she knew, meant nothing to him. Whether she had come to Ireland or not meant little to him. It but offered him the opportunity to be cruel, to taunt her with the loss of Kane, to punish her for the death of his father. Lowering her face to deny him the pleasure of viewing her despair, her grieving, she stood and sought her bed. She sank into the nest of soft furs over a mattress of ferns, not noticing the warmth, the fragrance. Stifling her sobs, she at last let desolation and hopelessness guide her into a nightmare tossed sleep.

She clung to its poor comfort, still, as she felt the furs being lifted, as she felt a naked body slide down against her own. Gentle hands touched her face, brushing back the strands of hair clinging to her cheeks with the damp of her tears. A voice murmured endearments as lips grazed her forehead, the line of one feathered eyebrow, then moved to suckle the lobe of one ear. Hands held her, caressing her shoulders, her back, the length of her arms, twining their fingers with hers and bringing them up to have each knuckle nibbled, before cupping her breasts, then the mouth claimed hers. Half asleep, she sighed, her body moving closer to his, her hands finding their way around his waist, the core of her growing warm with an ancient, consuming need.

But the murmured endearments had been in Irish and the mouth on hers, the hands cupping her, their fingers all too wise, were Cian's. Abruptly, she jerked her mouth from his and shoved him away. But he took her with him in his roll to the cold earth of the floor. Pushing against him, Bronwynn fought to escape, to stand, even as he laughed, body heaving with it, into the hollow of her neck. She fought harder, then, under the goad of his cruel mirth. Twisting, she tried to escape the grip about her waist, but he held her easily, still shaking with laughter. Her hands found his thick hair and she jerked at it. He only caught them with his own and twisted them behind her, rendering her more helpless still. She brought one knee up, then, her aim sure, but he turned, catching the blow on his thigh, then held her down with his body's weight.

"Ah, a stór," he grinned down at her, features lighted by the flickering of the campfires outside, "isn't that a blow for a miscreant—or a whore? I would not have thought yourself capable of such—if I had not been blessed so by you afore. Are you telling me, then," and his features grew heartless, "that my advances are not welcome—and myself thinking you might prove warm to me, yourself having so much to lose."

"You bastard!" she hissed up at him, but Cian only lifted one derisive eyebrow.

"Surely," he said, "you're not believing me to be a Norman lord, one who spouts respect of women and the laws of chivalry, then rapes the daughters of peasants in their own huts and murders unarmed guests at the high table. Haven't I scruples of a different sort—and the will to use another coercion when words of reason and protestation fall on stubborn, deaf ears? Haven't I something you must value over your own honor and isn't such honor worth relinquishing for such a prize? Or is it that you fear me?" He grinned at the apprehension suddenly in Bronwynn's eyes, then all levity fled. "Then hadn't we best, my Lady, continue where we left off but a few moments past—yourself proving warm to me?"

"You would use my son, our son, to rape me?" she demanded, incredulous.

"I would," he answered and there was no humor in his smile. He rose and held out his hand. She stared at it with loathing, but he lifted an eyebrow in warning. Eyes hot with anger, she took it and he lifted her to her feet. Holding back the tumbled bedding of furs, he gestured her to lie down and, after one glare at his set features, she obeyed. Body rigid, hands clenched at her sides, she felt Cian slide down once more against her, intruding between her angry vision and the thatched ceiling above her. Then she turned her eyes to the side, to stare at the door of the hut and the reflection of the campfires outside. Pulling the bed-clothes up over his shoulders, Cian looked down at her and a small, reluctant smile, quickly gone, tugged at his mouth.

He drew one finger down the line of her jaw from beneath her earlobe to her small, square chin. Then he lowered his mouth to hers to trace its unyielding shape with the tip of his tongue, to draw in her lower lip, sucking at it, pleading with it. But she did not answer and, fingers hard on the hinges of her jaw, he forced her teeth apart to taste the honey of her tongue, to beg it to twine with his to no avail. Rising to his elbow, he gazed down at her shuttered features and, if she had looked, she would have seen an infinite sadness in his face. But a small, wry smile still played about his mouth as he drew his hand down to trace the shape of her collarbone, to circle the roundness of her breast and splay his fingers over her ribcage.

"I had often wondered," he whispered, "if the carrying of our child would have taken this from you, this sweet inward curving of your waist. 'Twas always one of my favorite parts of you to hold between my hands in our lovemaking and yourself over me, riding me, your face laughing at the pleasure you gave me, then turning, so suddenly, with your own rapture."

His hand moved to her belly, his palm pressing into it, as he studied her features for any sign of surrender.

"But this, I'm thinking, is a wee bit softer, as I would have it in the mother of my child. I would not have you carry our son and with no sign after. And these," he whispered, hands cupping her breasts, "aren't they heavier, so, and with the milk of motherhood? I had not thought, once, that I would ever see you suckle our child and it grieved me."

With one finger, he lightly stroked a coral hued nipple and a corner of his mouth tilted up as a drop of milk beaded its tip. He lifted it to his lips to taste it, before lowering his mouth to trace his tongue around the circle of her areola, feeling more milk rise to his lips. Then, groaning, he drew in the engorged tip of her to feel a rush of sweet, warm liquid fill his mouth. With the gushing of her milk, Bronwynn felt an unwanted yielding, a reluctant softening of her flesh beneath the weight of Cian's. A throbbing fist gripped the inner core of her, painful in its demand, even as it loosened the hard-held rigidity of her limbs, as it parted her thighs to allow his touch, to allow his sigh of exaltation as he felt the dampness of her, the swelling.

Rising over her, then, once more, he placed his hand on the curve of her face even as her eyes defied him, even as she smelled the fragrance on herself on his fingers. Nor had her resistance disappeared with her desire, Cian discovered, as he began to lower his mouth to hers.

"No!" she spat up at him. "Damn you, no!"

She jerked her face away, fists clenching in his hair, yanking him back, as her body flipped beneath his, denying him. Catching her hands, he twined his fingers with hers, cupping her face between them, thumbs hard on her cheekbones. Then his mouth took hers as she tasted her own milk on his tongue. A sob broke through her throat with the yielding of her mouth, her tongue to answer his demand, to issue her own. His body took hers and she felt herself part for him, to him, taking him with the need so long remembered with grief, so new, now, with a desire she dared not trust, could only accept with the knowledge that it would not last beyond that moment.

Cian held her, then, taking her with the sad, slow pleasure of a passion long denied. He watched the play of anger across her features as her body betrayed her. He saw the anger turned to a hunger that thrust up against him, demanding satiation. And twice he watched the hunger become a yielding, a taking, a consummation that puckered her eyebrows in concentration, that brought a yolky sob to her throat. Then he lowered his mouth to the line of her shoulder, as he breathed in the memory of her passion's fragrance, as he took her once again, his own need now driving him, to a place where, for one brief moment, they were one, with no memory, no tomorrow. He went with her, then, that third time, with a giving, a taking he had come to tell himself could only be a flowering in his memory, so much had he missed her, needed her, so agonizingly sweet, so achingly a celebration of life, of love it was.

Lifting his head at last, afraid once more of what he would see on Bronwynn's features, Cian turned her face toward his. She stared back, features again closed, her eyes once more shuttered against him. Then she turned away, curling into a ball, closing him out. He drew her against himself, feeling the familiar curve of her spooned against him and studied for a long time the reflection of the campfires as they danced over the stone walls of the booley house.

(24)

Inishbawn appeared to be a magic place from the lake shore where the reeds grew dark, where the waters lapped. It seemed a place of the fairies, of the Sidhe. Shreds of fog veiled it and the thatched roofs rose above the mist, touched to gold by the late morning sun. Blue smoke rose to twine with the fog, hiding, then revealing the light gilded walls.

But it held no magic for her, Bronwynn knew. Only Kane was there for her, and perhaps sorrow, for Cian had given her no word, no hint that she could take him. She would find only hatred for herself and the perfidious race she had been born into from the others, from those she had once loved. It was a hatred well deserved, yet she would be there under the laws of hospitality, and her mouth quirked with bitterness at the thought, so little had such laws protected the men of the clan O'Connor. Still, she had been unable to sense such rancor in the men riding about her. They showed her only courtesy and, if they were aware of their chieftain's taking of her the night before, there was no lifted eyebrow, no smirk quickly hidden by a war-scarred hand.

Nor had there been a sign from Cian that he regretted it—or that he even remembered it. He had been gone when she awoke. He had offered her breakfast, had shown her only deference as he helped her mount her horse. He had ridden next to her, body swaying easily in the stirrup-less Irish saddle, yet somehow he held himself away, remote. He had proven himself an able pupil, Bronwynn admitted to herself, for just so did she hold herself from him. It was safer so, and gave lie to the passions they had shared the night before and to whatever words of love and need he might have uttered. Then the causeway was swaying beneath the horses' hooves and they rode through the gates of Inishbawn.

It was the same, Bronwynn thought. Surely, the same old men sat by the wall, the same old women by the well. Youths armed with hurleys played in the center of the bawn while others practiced with bows and arrows, with sword and lance under the eye of a grizzled warrior. Young girls strolled arm and arm near them, speaking in giggling whispers, tossing their hair and their glances at the young men, while their mothers stood in doorways, spindles in hand or a baby on their hips.

Yet they all had paused as the band rode. They studied Bronwynn, prepared to avert their eyes to another, less interesting object should her gaze meet theirs. Those acknowledged by Cian's nod or spoken greeting answered with a tilted head or a murmured response, while their glances cut toward Bronwynn. But she held her gaze on the women's house. It was where Kane would be, she knew, nor could she bear to meet the hate-filled stares she could feel crawling over her skin. And Cian rode beside her to her goal. Dismounting, he held his hands up to catch her as she slid from her horse.

But she did not meet the gaze he dropped to her averted features, for Fithir was emerging from between the carved posts of the doorway, Kane in her arms. Haltingly, afraid it might yet prove a cruel hoax, that Cian might yet hold her back from her son, Bronwynn went to him.

He chortled when he saw her, jumping in the other woman's arms, and Fithir uttered her soft, familiar laugh. Kissing his dimpled fingers, she relinquished him to his mother. Still, she held his hand, refusing to let it go until Bronwynn looked at her. Then, with a gentle finger, she wiped away the tears streaming down Bronwynn's face.

" 'Tis glad I am to see you here, Bronwynn, daughter of the Fitzhughs, though 'twas a sinful deed that brought you here, one surely only a man could conceive of. I've missed you, as many of us have, once the shroud of our grieving was lifted from our eyes. Though not so much, I'm thinking, as the O'Connor, there, and himself ever aglooming about when not seeking solace between another woman's thighs—and failing, always, to find it. And may-hap," she laughed, " 'twas his glooming and his rutting that made us yearn for you so. But the wee one is hungry. We did not feed him though he has gnawed his knuckles this past while, Cian telling me you suckled him yourself and myself thinking you might have as great a need of him as the child of you."

Bronwynn had blinked when Fithir spoke of the O'Connor, almost expecting to hear Calvach's booming laugh, before realizing it was Cian she referred to. And Fithir was studying her, the joy of welcome in her eyes turning to sorrow.

"But you'll not be wanting to stay, will you," she asked, "no matter that we want you here, that the O'Connor wants you here? You've but come for the wee one, no matter that you'll take a bit of my heart with him when you leave, and all of Cian's. Still, whatever cause you're thinking we might have to hate you, sure, you should not have turned it so on yourself."

Her face pitying, she studied Bronwynn's averted features a moment longer, before stepping aside. Brushing past her, Bronwynn entered the women's house with her son. Her face tear streaked, Bronwynn sat and opened her surcoat to Kane's nuzzling mouth. He gulped the proffered nipple in and she smiled down at him, throat tight with love, with grief.

It seemed she sat so for hours, her gaze never leaving the features of her son, tears flowing unheeded down her face. Only when Cian entered, only when he touched her face, brushing away her tears, did she know she wept, and looked up.

There was no derision, now, in Cian's eyes as he drew up a stool before her and sat down. His features were grave and there were lines, she saw, etched in his face that had not been there the night before, lines of sorrow, of loss. She wanted, then, to touch them, to smooth them away and bring back the dance of laughter, of mockery at all life's twistings and turnings to his tawny eyes. Unable to bear the hurt of it, she dropped her gaze, and felt, instead, the weight of his own on her, on their son. At last, he touched her breast with a gentle fingertip, then traced the cheek of his child.

"I had not dared hope, once, to ever see you so," he whispered, "nor had I reckoned the grieving in me to see you go."

Unable to trust her ears, Bronwynn jerked her gaze up to him, but he was studying his nursing son as though to etch the sight forever in his mind.

"You intend to let us go?" she wondered, disbelieving.

He stood abruptly, the stool falling unheeded behind him.

"I will provide an escort for you to Dublin and themselves with instructions to see you've a safe craft to Wales. But I'll not go with you." He paused, his gaze on her averted profile. "I'm thinking 'twould be too painful a thing. I'm thinking I should never have brought the small one here—and yourself after him. Aren't I thinking, too, a stór, when you carry him away from me in your round arms, you will take from me a small part of my heart? And with your own going, won't you take the rest of it, so, leaving me bleeding, empty, leaving my ribs no more than a harp for the wind to blow through? Can you tell me, a stór, how a man lives with so great a hollow within himself?"

He saw her throat jerk with a sob, saw the renewing flow of her tears. Gently, grieving with her, for her, he touched them with one finger.

"Ah, a stór," he consoled, "don't be sorrowing so, not for us. Hadn't we known long ago that 'twould be so and yourself telling me too many times?"

His throat caught on an attempted chuckle and he would have drawn back his touch, would have left her then, never to see her again. But she had grasped his hand, turning her face into it, and he felt her lips on his palm. Kneeling, feeling the trembling of his heart, swallowing down a sudden hope, he lifted her face to his, forcing her to look at him. Her face was streaked with tears, her eyes dark with them. Damp wisps of hair clung to her cheeks. Her mouth was swollen and red from her weeping. But her gaze held his, defiant still, even as her lips moved in a silent plea, as her eyes tried to tell him what her pride, her doubt could not yet allow.

Still disbelieving, he smoothed a strand of hair back from her face and lifted her chin higher yet with his forefinger. Never, he knew, had he thought her so beautiful. Hesitantly, not yet trusting the joy leaping through his veins, he brought his mouth to hers to feel her hand on his cheek, to hear the sigh of her surrender, to taste the salt of her tears on her lips—and to know that he, too, wept. Then he picked them both up in his arms, his love and his child, and carried them across the bawn to his own chamber, his face drowned in the dark fall of her hair.

A few months later, when Bronwynn had grown placid with her second child, a minstrel came to Inishbawn. Along with his song, he brought word of the world. Edward of England, he told them, had set out that spring to assay once again the subjection of Scotland. Becoming ill, however, he was forced to turn back to Burgh-by-Sands. There, from his bed, he had composed messages of farewell to his family—and had issued his final instructions.

Piers Gaveston, his sons' lover—and the minstrel shook his head at the strange ways of the Sassenach—was not to be allowed to return to England but by order of Parliament. One hundred knights, vowing to remain for a full year, were to go to the Crusades. His heart, placed in a casket, was to accompany them in death as he had so wished to do in life. But his flesh was to be boiled from his frame and his bones placed in a hammock to be carried before the army back into Scotland that he might lead the way to victory.

But Edward II could not have hied himself faster back to England on his sire's death—for, indeed, Edward Longshanks had truly died—had he grown wings like the faeries, the minstrel informed his enthralled audience. An unnatural thing, isn't it, he wondered, a son who denies his father's death bed wish—and his own oath on it, too, and his lips pressed, so 'twas said, on a bit of the Holy Rood? Bad cess to one such as was this latest Plantagenent. Good luck, too, wasn't it, to the Scots, with themselves so close to England and such a weak king on its throne? And the minstrel's listeners nodded. And, too, gossip had it, Piers

Gaveston was already back in England, no matter the old king's dying order or the protests of Parliament.

But that wasn't the whole affair, the minstrel continued—and wouldn't he soon be at the nut of the matter—for some few of Edward Longshanks' men had continued in the effort to contain the Scots before finally giving up and retiring back to England. They had had light losses, mostly men-at-arms, as was so often the case with the Sassenach—didn't they ever sacrifice the little fish to save the bigger? But one lord of the realm was slain, the minstrel related with the Irish love of the perversities of fate, in a small, obscure scrimmage, a Sir Henry Franklyn. 'Twas said by those who knew the man that his heart had gone out of him, stolen by a woman, leaving him with no will to live. And wasn't it passing strange then, that, when mosttimes a man seeking death so seldom finds it?

But not so strange, the minstrel thought, as that the O'Connor's wife was Norman and that she had turned her face aside at word of Henry Franklyn's death. Or that she wept, however silently, while twisting a heavy ring of Norman design about her finger. Even stranger, he told himself—and all those who would listen later and at other hearths—was the comforting of her lord and husband in her sorrow.

AUTHOR'S NOTE

Sir Piers de Bermingham, Baron of Tethmoy, did indeed invite Clavech O'Connor, Lord of Offaly, and his chieftains to a celebration of Christmas and have them massacred. Sources vary as to the date, citing both 1295 and 1305. For the purpose of my story, I chose the latter. Edward of England did reward and offer him words of commemoration. Edward died as written on July seventh, 1307, at Lanacourt, Scotland at the age of sixty-eight. Marguarite, referred to more often as Margaret, lived well after him, dying on February 14, 1318. Her effigy is preserved in Westminster Abbey. Piers survived to an old age and Berminghams still live in Ireland. The O'Connors, however, far outnumber them.